Hottento

ALSO BY BARBARA CHASE-RIBOUD

Poetry

From Memphis & Peking
Portrait of a Nude Woman as Cleopatra
Untitled: Collected Poems (forthcoming)

Fiction

Sally Hemings: A Novel
Valide: A Novel of the Harem
Echo of Lions: A Novel of the Amistad
Roman Egyptien (in French)
The President's Daughter

DOUBLEDAY

New York London Toronto

Sydney Auckland

Hottentot Venus

A Novel

Barbara Chase-Riboud

PUBLISHED BY DOUBLEDAY
a division of Random House, Inc.

DOUBLEDAY and the portrayal of an anchor with a dolphin are registered
trademarks of Random House, Inc.

Book design by Dana Leigh Treglia

Library of Congress Cataloging-in-Publication Data

Chase-Riboud, Barbara.
Hottentot Venus : a novel / by Barbara Chase-Riboud.—1st ed.
p. cm.
1. Baartman, Sarah—Fiction. 2. Women—South Africa—Fiction. 3. South
Africans—Europe—Fiction. 4. South Africa—Fiction. 5. Exploitation—Fiction.
6. Women, Black—Fiction. 7. Racism—Fiction. 8. Europe—Fiction. I. Title.

PS3553.H336H68 2003
811'.54—dc21
2003048907

ISBN 0-385-50856-5

PRINTED IN THE UNITED STATES OF AMERICA

November 2003
First Edition

1   3   5   7   9   10   8   6   4   2

To Nelson Mandela

Contents

Part III
PARIS, FRANCE, 1814

Part IV
CAPE TOWN, SOUTH AFRICA, 2002

The Heroine's Note

*O*nce upon a time, there was a Khoekhoe nation called the People of the People, who inhabited the eastern coast of South Africa. In 1619, we were discovered by the Portuguese, who, besides civilization, brought us syphilis, smallpox and slavery. They were followed by the Dutch, who gave us our name, Hottentot, which means "stutterer" in Dutch, because of the way our language sounded to them, and who introduced us to private property, land theft and fences. They were succeeded by the English, who organized us all into castes and categories and who called themselves and others like them white, and us, Hottentots, Bushmen and Negroes, black, although, to my knowledge, none of us ever chose that name. And so to tell this, my true story, I was stuck with a name we didn't choose but must use so that those who gave us these names may listen. And, although Hottentot is an insult equivalent to nigger, I used it in this, my story, just as Negroes use that word they do not recognize themselves by with whites, who gave them that name to begin with. I am sure that God doesn't call me Hottentot any more than He calls them white.

S.B.

Hottentot Venus

Part I

Men can do nothing without the make-believe of a beginning. Even science, the strict measurer, is obliged to start with a make-believe unit, and must fix on a point in the stars' unceasing journey when his sidereal clock shall pretend that time is Nought. No retrospect will take us to the true beginning; and whether our prologue be in heaven or on earth, it is but a fraction of that all-presupposing fact with which our story sets out.

—GEORGE ELIOT,
Daniel Deronda

1

SIRE,

The natural history of living beings poses, above all, complications the mind has no conjectures on which to base a previous state. Nothing explains the origin and the genesis, which is ever a mystery by which all human efforts have not achieved anything plausible.

—BARON GEORGES LÉOPOLD CUVIER,
Letter to the Emperor Napoleon
on the progress of science since 1789

*G*reat Eland, the English month of January, 1816. There was no freak show today because it was New Year's Day, and it was my birthday. It was the coldest Paris winter anyone could remember and the city was blanketed in snow, ice creaked on the Seine and hundreds of skaters glided over its surface. The bells of the Cathedral of Notre-Dame tolled to celebrate King Louis's gift of three hundred and twenty francs to feed the freezing and starving poor of the city. I imagined my friends, other freaks of nature, other things-that-should-never-have-been-born, gathering on the cobblestone courtyard of 188 rue St. Honoré getting ready to make their way to Warren's Nest Tavern to celebrate the day. Miss Ridsdal, thirty inches tall and thirty-five years old, Miss Harvey with her perfectly white knee-length silken hair and pink eyes, Mr. Lambert, a twelve-foot giant, Count Boruweaski, a two-foot midget, and Miss Duclos, the lovely bearded lady.

As for myself, I was much too sick to join them. My master, Sieur Réaux, had left early to celebrate with the other circus managers at a large dinner, but I was too ill and too ill used even to care. I burned with fever and my chest seemed clogged with a mysterious mass that all the coughing in the world could not relieve. I had felt this way for months. The spasms would seize me and choke me like a murderer. My chest would burst with pain so that I held on to whatever I could find to cling to, a table, an armchair, the doorframe, to keep from falling. The large white handkerchief I always carried clutched in my hand these past weeks would come away spotted with blood. The Khoekhoe had no word for what was wrong with me, but the English did. Alice Unicorn, my servant whom I had found in a Manchester mill two years ago, explained it to me. After five years, I was used to the snow, I knew how it felt against my skin, could taste its cold wetness when it fell against my lips, knew its special chill in my bones. I needed to return to a warm, dry climate she said, or I would die. In other words, I needed to return home to the Cape of Good Hope where I had been born and where my brothers and sisters were. I wondered if I could ever do that.

If it hadn't been this day, I would have been on display in the animal circus of my master, exhibited in an eight-by-twelve-foot bamboo cage just high enough for me to stand and almost naked, shivering in my apron of pearls and feathers, my leggings of dried entrails, my painted face, my leather mask, my dyed and braided hair, my doeskin red gloves, my sheepskin *lappa* slung over one shoulder, my necklace of shimmering glass and shells, my crown of feathers, my cowrie seed earrings, able to stagger only a few paces, or crouch over my brick kiln for warmth, or obey the shouts of my keeper, who amused and harangued the crowd with his barking soliloquy. Surrounding me would be scores, sometimes hundreds, of white faces, all peering up at me, a sheen of horror, pity or terror occupying their faces, or perhaps a smirk of amusement, contempt or nervous excitement; eyes gleamed, lips pursed, skin transpired. Cries, insults, shouts and laughter would at times overwhelm me as if the waves of the ocean engulfed me except it was not salt they deposited but liquid hatred, which

4

beat upon my naked skin, my bare feet, my burning face and scorched brain. I had learned over the years to divorce myself from the crowd, to hover just above it like a purple heron in flight. I learned to feel not, to listen not, to think not. I decided to understand no language, not even that of pity or compassion, for this too was part of their game; to pity the monster, the animal, the dis-human, the ugly, the heathen, the Hottentot.

I was the black Moor, evil encased in black skin, a warning and a symbol to all those upturned faces and jammed-together bodies that God could punish them as he had punished me with expulsion not only from Eden but from the human race. I was a thing-that-should-never-have-been-born, a creature made in Eve's image yet, unlike her, not part of mankind. I was a female who was the missing link between beast and man, a wonder of nature created only for the delectation of discovery by hordes of paying Parisian customers, who for three francs could, from a distance, contemplate the form and color of monstrosity.

Sometimes, I would growl or spit, scream or hiss insanely. Sometimes, I could laugh and dance, sing and play my guitar. Sometimes, I would play the clown by rolling my eyes, sticking out my lips, shaking my backside, but sometimes my feet won't move, my hands won't pluck at my guitar, my knees won't bend. Sometimes, I am too cold or too sick or too full of morphine to move. Then, there are loud protests from the stinking, hawking, spitting, tobacco-chewing, foul-breathed audience that they are not getting their money's worth. They did not want a statue of Venus, but a heaving, stomping, undulating, living Venus, with beastly breasts, beastly hips, beastly eyes and above all a beastly face that held no beauty for them. I was the glue of common contempt and rejection that held them all together.

At times, I would recognize a familiar face in the crowd. It would emerge from the haze of dusty white faces for the second or third or umpteenth time. Someone who had returned to make sure what he had seen the first time was truly real, that he had not dreamed the apparition before him. Assured, he could once again gaze upon the impossible and contemplate the unimaginable. I hated them most for they reminded me that there were humans amongst them—something I didn't care to believe. Others returned so that they could tell their wives or children or neighbors and friends. Others must have returned for other reasons, for amongst the strangers there was always a repeater. And sometimes our eyes would meet and I could see fear at war with compassion and I would laugh inside and recall the rainmaker's warning: There is no medicine for those who are not human.

No one understood my need to remain here if only to prove the fact of my existence. I refused to be a figment of their imagination. I would be real in all my Hottentot monstrousness. I was real, I existed, I ate and slept and pissed and shat and loved and fucked and cried and dreamed and bled. My humanness was the only thing I possessed. My right to exist was the reason I stayed. The hew-haws and ha-has wanted to erase me, damn me to extinction, but I wouldn't go. I remained stubbornly here. I refused to move my ass. I was famous, a household name, Frenchwomen dressed Hottentot style, all kinds of things were given that name, everything that was ugly, savage, uncivilized, brutal, deformed, reprehensible was called Hottentot, my name.

The rooms I lived in were filthy despite all of Alice's efforts at cleaning them, which, to tell the truth, were not always the best. But Alice and I understood each other. Alice was more a keeper than a housemaid, more nurse than cook. She was the only person I had to talk to now: the only human between insanity and me. Alice had begun to teach me to read and write in England. Just because you don't know how to read and write doesn't mean you are stupid, she would say. The word "illiterate," that's different from stupid. You ca' be illiterate and smart and you ca' know to read and write and be stupid . . . If she hadn't followed me to France, she probably would be dead by now. You sav'd me life, Sarah, she would say, I'll ne'r forgo' that. Alice would stay until two o'clock to prepare my daily bath in the huge French copper bathtub that sat in the corner of the bedroom. She would then return to her own room until supper. Alice Unicorn was the only white woman I had ever had as a friend who was not thirty inches tall, a prostitute or did not have a beard.

The great blue and white cast-iron coal stove whose fumes blackened everything stood guard in the corner. I counted the number of tiles on it as I always did each day. The fumes had yellowed and cracked the wallpaper that had once been a matching bright and beautiful floral design in blue and white, like the tiles under my bare feet. Despite the filth around me, I was determined to remain clean, my skin soft and smooth, unblemished as when I polished it with whale fat. I spent my waking hours, out of the cage, trying out new grease and pomades, oiling my face and neck, my hands and feet, my breasts and thighs. I dipped my hands into the softness of kid, satin and velvet gloves, which I collected by the dozens. According to Alice, my body was, in fact, insured by Lloyd's of London for more than five hundred pounds. This must have been my new owner's idea. I could not imagine my former master, or my former husband, thinking of it. All that was so long ago. I no longer thought nor cared about it anymore. I couldn't. I would go crazy if I did. All I wanted now was the hot peacefulness of my bath: to sink down into oblivion with my opium pipe and my gin. To live only in dreams. Dreams of a time when I was not a thing-that-should-never-have-been-born.

The copper tub gleamed in the oil lamp's glow, lit early in the seal gray of a winter's afternoon. Steam lifted from its sweating sides and rose like the Cape mists. Alice poured buckets of hot water into it, filling it almost to the top. The fogginess made the sparse furnishings disappear: the bed, the ottoman, the round table, the piles of pamphlets, the circus posters, my flesh-colored silk sheath and glass beads hanging from a hook on the wall. Alice had carefully laid out my face paint and oils, but the rest of the room was a disorderly, unkempt cell of despair. Leftover food had not been cleared away from the table, on which my medicines stood amongst bottles of gin, eau-de-vie, a few Christmas oranges and old receipts for the rent. Newspapers, broadsheets and theater bills were scattered every-where. Everything was stained and dirty. Even the air I breathed seemed unclean, even the fire in the fireplace and the fire in the stove, which burned constantly in my battle against the cold. I pulled my robe closer around me and watched as Alice prepared my pipe of *dagga,* which she placed on the little stool beside the bathtub.

—There's nothing to eat, she said, shaking her head.

—No matter, I replied, imitating her Manchester accent. I don' wan' n' food.

—There're Christmas oranges, she replied. I'll peel on' for you.

Alice sat two more oranges on the stool beside the tub and laid out the orange sections on a dirty napkin. The odor of the orange was the last smell I remember. And it was not the pleasant, sweet smell of the yellow flesh and orange peel, but the stench of sulfur and the aftertaste of blood. I rolled a section around on my tongue. I swallowed, tasting it. A thin sheen of sweat had broken through my skin. I shook as Alice helped me into the bath. She averted her eyes from my apron as always, but I no longer bothered to hide it from her. I sank into my refuge gratefully, the bitter acid taste still on my lips, my eyes closed, my arms at my sides. My hips caused some of the bathwater to spill over onto the floor and the new towels. It made my lit pipe hiss. I held my breath and sank under the surface of the water completely, my eyes open. Underwater, I couldn't see the ugly ceiling, the ugly furniture, the ugly floor, the ugly boots of my master, the ugly lamp illuminating the ugly blackness.

—Goodbye, Sarah, called Alice as she left. I listened to her turning the key in the lock, locking me in. Then, after a moment of hesitation, as if she had changed her mind, I heard the key turn again, unlocking the door. Alice had left the door open. Alice was freeing me. I could, at this moment, walk out of this room and this life, a free woman. I could leave Réaux and the circus forever. If only I had the will, I could get out of this tub, get dressed and leave before he returned. I could hobble in my wooden platform shoes across the courtyard, past the fountains, through the iron gates, past the concierge's lodge, the lone bare linden tree, the frosted lit windows. I could step across the open rushing gutter, bloated with sewage, rain and snow, hail a cab and be gone.

I had been sick for a long time before Alice noticed. Longer than I could remember. It probably started in the spring, around the time I had been examined for three days in the King's Botanical Gardens. The Cour des Fontaines was not a place to be in bad health. Les Fontaines were the water reservoirs for the waterworks and gardens of the King's Palais Royal. The entire quarter extended from the Palais Royal's vaulted archways, with their galleries and shops, and food stands and cafés, bars, pastry shops and promenades, to Les Halles, the meat district, the stomach of Paris, not only its stomach but all its internal organs—its heart, liver, intestines, its shit. The slickest, fastest, largest, most brazen rats ruled our quarter. They were the best fed of the city, scurrying here and there, fornicating with the lesser rats of Les Halles. The district was a maze of alleys and narrow streets and culs-de-sac lined with dozens of theaters, music halls, circuses, bars, coffeehouses, restaurants, exhibition halls, casinos, taverns and whorehouses. All kinds of animals, human and otherwise, lived here, on exhibit: elephants, giraffes and camels, tigers, snakes and parrots, and all the parasites they brought: fleas, ticks, lice, mice. This was where I lived.

They exhibited me at number 188 rue St. Honoré, which had once been the Catholic College of St. Honoré, a convent up until the Revolution destroyed it. Now, part of it was a brothel, and the old wine cellar was used as latrines for the whores. The furnished hotels nearby housed cheap prostitutes who plied their trade amongst the slaughterhouses that filled the district. There were also the gaming houses like the Good Children Gallery, a favorite haunt of my master, which housed all the games of chance: roulette, *biribi, passe-deux, trente-et-quarante.* Nearby were famous, luxurious cafés such as the Thousand Columns, where my friend Madame Romain presided over the cashbox as "la Belle Limonadière," empress of the Palais Royal gardens.

Belle had a lot of competition: Madame Tussaud's waxworks, Italian marionettes, Chinese shadow plays, live rhinoceros, amazing cutout portraits from black paper made by Monsieur Silhouette, snake charmers, fortune-tellers and double-jointed Siamese twins. Belle also had me, Sarah Baartman, as competition on view six days a week, from eleven to nine, for the sum of three francs per person. I hung in a suspended cage above a wooden stage as if I were a wild animal. An army of paying spectators came to see me as each day, on command, I played my guitar and sang, jumped and danced, felt their breath on me, their eyes, filled with contempt, curiosity, repulsion and amusement. I smelled it. I drank it. I endured it for money, or so I believed. Money which equaled freedom and independence, or so I believed. But why I really endured it, I do not know. Just as I didn't know why I still remained inert and lifeless in my bath when the door to escape was open. Hung across the façade of the largest exhibition hall in Paris was a life-size banner with the words in block letters:

THE HOTTENTOT VENUS

On exhibition here. Direct from the Dark Continent. The HOTTENTOT VENUS, just arrived from the banks of the Chamtoo River, the Cape of Good Hope, South Africa, the most authentic and perfect specimen of the race of people called Houswaana. This extraordinary phenomenon of nature is unique in Europe up until now. As extraordinary as she is astonishing, in this Venus, the public has the most perfect human specimen of the race, which inhabits the regions of southernmost Africa. The HOTTENTOT Venus's name is Saartjie Baartman.

She speaks Dutch, English, and her maternal language, in which she sings original songs. Her color is closer to that of Peruvians than that of Africans, whose hair and features she has. Venus wears the dress of her country, with all the rude ornaments worn by those people. Venus plays the Jew's harp, an instrument that, according to the great explorer Levaillant, is well loved amongst her race.

Like the inmate of an asylum, I lived that advertisement every day, rain or shine, wet or dry, summer and winter. Except today.

I studied the dirty, faded walls, scarred with a thousand outrages, age, rain, graffiti, humidity, ticks and roaches that nested underneath the wallpaper and dropped to the floor as soon as the candles were snuffed out. Just like fat ladies, giants, dwarfs, four-legged Siamese twins and one-testicled midgets crept out of the circus as soon as night fell. If I hadn't been ill and it hadn't been New Year's Day and if it hadn't been my birthday, I too would have crawled out of my bamboo cage in the white stone exhibition hall along with all the other freaks in Paris in the year 1816. I would be playing my guitar or pacing up and down my eight-by-twelve-foot cage for ten hours a day. I would be naked under a tight sheath of flesh-colored silk transparent enough to reveal my tattoos and my apron. High society would wine and dine and gawk until midnight. Men and, more and more regularly, women would poke me with their canes and parasols, make faces, shout gibberish and curses, rattle the cage to make me fall, spit and hurl insults they thought I didn't understand. Sometimes I noticed a look of pity, even a tear on a spectator's face. When that happened, my day was unbearable, for only then would I admit that I was still human.

There were always aristocrats in the crowd, *le beau monde,* and the clergy came not only to see me but also to have the thrill of mixing with the lower classes and riffraff of St. Honoré, braving the possibility of being robbed, beaten or kidnapped. Elegant carriages parked far away. Bodies were packed so tight that no one could breathe. Fine perfume covered the stench. Fashionable ladies in their transparent, clinging, flimsy dresses fainted. Men drooled. Gentlemen fought their way out of the crowds with walking canes, kicks and swords. Sailors and soldiers swaggered amongst the citizens returned from Waterloo and Tsaritsyn. They all came. Like addicts to opium, they could not stay away nor hide their fascination. And

I stood there. Sometimes shaking with cold. Sometimes shaking with rage, and sometimes not shaking at all but still as a mountain lion stalking its prey, listening to the sound of francs falling into Sieur Réaux's cashbox.

The bells of five o'clock mass chimed. It had begun to snow again, lightly. Snow no longer fascinated me as it once had. This winter had been the coldest in memory, or so French people claimed. So cold, the new King Louis had had to feed the starving, freezing and homeless of Paris out of his own pocket. The city's firemen never slept because fires broke out all over the city from exploding stoves, clogged smokestacks, out-of-control bonfires that spread to surrounding houses. The outlines of the Tuileries Gardens, the Louvre Palace, the Concorde bridge, the paths of the King's Botanical Gardens, called Le Jardin des Plantes where I had come face-to-face with the Emperor Bonaparte, who was now rotting on St. Helena, softened under a blanket of snow. When the bells ceased, all sound disappeared. There was only stillness.

I closed my eyes and reached for my pipe. I was not leaving for anywhere. Not even to St. Helena, that harsh and barren island I had passed through when my bones had been supple and young. The *dagga* my tribe had smoked for centuries had a different name in Paris: cannabis. I lifted my pipe to my lips, preparing to float away on a cloud of forgetfulness. I wanted to forget the walls and the stove and the rats and the humiliation and the crowds and the freaks and the men I serviced for Réaux, and the hunger and the dreams that were now out of my reach even if I had had the courage to flee. Before I could take a single puff, a spasm of coughing seized me, the pain growing like a plant inside me until it burst into a terrible wracking, gurgling sound and a warm liquid rose in my throat. It took me a moment to realize that it was not bathwater but blood. Not the tiny drops that had often spilled from me these past weeks, but a full pumping gush of the proportions of the fountains outside.

As I reached for a towel to stanch the blood, I overturned the oranges on the table and they rolled across the dirty floor away from me. I tried to call out, and in my panic slipped under the surface of the water, choking and waving my arms. My huge hips and buttocks were held fast, wedged against the sides of the tub. My shape held me prisoner. I couldn't move. I screamed. But there was no one to hear me. The scream turned to a gurgle as I struggled to rise, twice almost drowning in water and my own blood. Suddenly my flanks pulled free, and with my last strength I rose from the rose-colored water like the Venus of my name, a torrent of blood from my hollow, exhausted lungs clothing my nakedness. Tears of it streamed across my breasts and down my body like Miss Harvey's hair. In the irregular gray reflection of the windowpanes, which held in them the flickering points of lit candles, I appeared in a way I had never seen myself in the mirrors I so avoided. The horizontal slit eyes with their swollen lids, the high cheekbones, full bottom lip, small neck, heavy breasts, delicate hands, golden color graceful arms, huge haunches and overwhelming buttocks floated towards me.

Sideways, I was a quivering, trembling, hideous mass of flesh; a peninsula, a continent of ridges and dimples and valleys and craters split by the great divide of my backside, from which extended a foot of bulbous curls and rolls of fat. The small of my back curved up like the neck of a crane. This was why they called me a freak. The same reason they called me Venus. And like the Venus I was, I rose from my bath, standing up without leaving the tub, concealing my apron with my right hand, surprised that I was leaving this world and surprised that I had no thoughts about leaving except to think, Sarah Baartman, you are too young to die. How could I imagine that death would not end my life? That I, a monster of imagination, not nature, was to begin a posthumous life of such drama and complexity that it would last for centuries? A life even more monstrous than the one I had just quit?

—How come I here? I asked myself. How come I here?

Outside, the Seine slid open, snow drifted against the houses along the narrow streets like the foam of ocean waves, a carriage passed, its wheels muffled by the shards of ice that lay everywhere and on my soul. The hooves of the snorting, smoking horses pocked the virgin snow that lay before number 7 Cour des Fontaines, their heads stretched downwards against their harnesses.

I heard my mother singing my birthday song in her soft clicks and coos. My name song. Ssehura. I fell forward towards the flash of light. Reaching out blindly, I cried for help in Khoekhoe. I knew only that I was twenty-seven years old this day and I wanted to live.

2

SIRE,

The examination of the organization of a living being and the particular consequences that result in his way of life, the phenomena that he manifests, his relationship with the rest of nature, is what can be called the natural history of that being.

—BARON GEORGES LÉOPOLD CUVIER,
Letter to the Emperor Napoleon
on the progress of science since 1789

*S*hit moon, the English month of September, 1792. If my story could begin the way the penny posters that advertised my person as Venus began, there would be a watercolor backdrop of sea and sand and coconut trees along a wide, mile-long, white, white beach that stretches beyond sight into invisible whiteness. It would be my third birthday and on the wild empty beach two naked babes, myself and my cousin, would be playing in the sun while two black and white penguins waded in the surf nearby. Watching not far away would be my mother, Aya Ma, a girl not more than twenty-six who had seven children, four males and three females, of which I was the youngest. This is my oldest recollection.

I am speaking now in Khoe, my maternal language, a language white men have never mastered, a language complex and subtle enough to express anything I have to say in English or Dutch, any line of poetry, any rhyme or proverb or quotation from the New Testament. So you will not hear from me any pidgin Dutch or coy Negro dialect. What is English is rendered in English and what is Dutch in Dutch, and what is Khoe is rendered in Khoe. As I have said, this is my oldest recollection.

Mother's soft voice with its clicks and coos would be singing my birthday song, explaining the meaning of my name to me and that I was Khoekhoe, the People of the People who had ruled the lush forests and grasslands of the Cape as hunters and herders from the days of the Great Flood. Perhaps speaking to herself, she would have explained that this long desolate beach was now a war zone. The Khoekhoe were at war with the Dutch, who had arrived years ago and who were themselves at war with the English, who fought us, the Dutch and the Trekboers for possession of what no one really owned: the land.

The Dutch had set foot on our beaches a hundred and forty years ago and had built a fortress, which was now the Dutch East India Trading Company. Over the years, my mother's tribe had been pushed back further and further into the interior away from our ancestral grazing lands. My mother's nation now consisted of small encampments along the beach, and our great herds of cattle were reduced to the few hundred head we drove to the Xhoa market in treks lasting more than twenty days.

Even after they had taken everything of value—the land, the cattle, the gold—the English still raided our settlements for sport, hunting trophies to hang on their walls or send back to England. Or to punish Khoekhoe men who refused to work for them as miners and slaves. Severed heads were very much prized and bands of riders would raid our camps of mostly women and children while the men were gone and decapitate anyone who stood in their path. They would scatter the herds, whooping and yelling, then pick off the fleeing people with their rifles.

When I was almost four, my mother was killed in one of these raids. With the eyes of a child, I remember her severed head rolling along the beach and stopping at the water's edge, then being scooped up by a yellow-haired horseman riding hard as if it were a plaything that he had to retrieve. As Aya Ma tried to outrun him she had taken wing like a heron, her elbows flapping in a futile effort to fly away, her lips jutting out like a beak, her neck outstretched in a bird's landing position.

My father had been away at the market in Xhoa and didn't learn of my mother's death for almost a month. So it was very hard for him to believe she was dead at all. In fact, he never really believed it. For him, she had only run away and left him alone with seven children. He never took another wife. He divided us up amongst his relatives and left with his herd on long treks north that would last for many moons. But he would always return for his children's birthdays, and though from then on he was never a real father to me, I always accorded him the honor and respect I owed him.

Five years after my mother died, he too was killed by the same English landlords for trespassing onto a cattleman's land while driving his bullocks to market. That year, I was nine. It was my birthday and Daddy had just sung my song. I was with him, helping him herd, when I heard the sound: the noise of a thousand sticks tapping gently upon a tree. Then it grew and grew and I knew it to be the beating hooves of galloping animals. I scrambled under a rock as the sound, which at first was very faint and thin, became louder and wilder with what might have been shouts of warning or screams.

Then I heard gunshots in the distance. Cattle were moving. Guns were firing. There was nothing to do except hide. My excitement was fierce although fear ate into my brain. The sound of tapping on trees grew louder and louder until it became a rumble mixed with an echo that was like distant thunder. As a herdswoman, I knew this was not thunder but the bellowing of desperate animals, mixed with the screams and shouts of the shepherds as they approached. I saw a lone koodoo buck that had somehow gotten mixed up with the herd. It flew past me like a flash of lightning, foam on its lips, its tongue hanging out, followed by a raging bull so large he blocked out the light.

Then, the stampede arrived—a countless heaving mass, it seemed to my small person crouching trembling beneath a boulder. They flew at me, plunging down a steep incline nearby: cows, bulls, calves, heifers, bullocks, oxen, even a zebra all mixed together, all snorting, bellowing, crying and running. They were all different colors, their long horns flashing. The thunder was fearful, the sight bewildering as they rushed by me, a mighty moving mass so tight I could have walked on their backs. Calves got swept off their feet and were carried forward by the moving bodies of their mothers or other heifers. At the very last moment, the herd swerved and passed, avoiding the rock under which I hid, for no wall, no fence could have saved me. Trees snapped in their wake and were stamped into a ravine as they turned as one. The shouts and curses of the shepherds mixed with the cries of the animals.

Then I heard a new sound, of horses' hooves and the snap of pistols, rifles and whips. The Khoekhoe herders were being shot with rifles, cut down with cowhide whips or decapitated with broadswords. They had only their crooks, which they flung down as they ran for their lives. An English voice shouted,

—We've got them all! Not a Hottentot left!

The riders began to beat the bush now that the herd was scattered, looking for dead or hiding Hottentots, trampling the high grass under their horses. A band of horsemen were still chasing my father. He and a handful of survivors were running as fast as they could towards the ravine. But they could not outrun the horses. Their heads rolled as one by one they were seized by the hair and beheaded or caught in the lash of a bull-whip which lifted them from the ground, twisting their heads off their shoulders as they ran, leaving their legs still pumping. I heard another white voice, breathless and choking with dust.

—Halt at the ridge and round up the herd, forget the niggers!

A red-haired rider waved his gun wildly above his head, then turned his mount in a circle before plunging into the ravine at full gallop. Below perhaps thirty Englishmen were firing upon the whole village. Some villagers had spears, some, arches and arrows, some were completely naked, having run their leggings and *lappas* off their bodies. As they stumbled and were cut down, a great cry, which was a mighty curse, rose from them, to which I added my voice. The herders who had not been killed made a last stand, turning back and charging the mounted horsemen. It was the beginning of a massacre. The whole tribe, women and children, fell as one, packed as close together as the stampeding cattle had been, snarling like beasts, howling and yelling while the white men shouted.

—Kill the niggers.

And they shot into them at point-blank range, moving them around with their mounts like sheep to the slaughter until the Englishmen's arms were so tired that they couldn't hold their guns up to aim. The tribe's first

16

rush had taken the whites by surprise and had driven them back at first. The spears and knives of the armed villagers slashed the flesh of their horses, causing them to buckle and throw off the riders, who, once on the ground, found themselves fighting hand to hand with no room to use their guns. But a second band of whites rode to the rescue, wielding ropes, whips and rifles, driving off the remnants of the defending cowboys, leaving in their wake the dead and the wounded and taking with them all the heads they could find as trophies. Amongst those dead was my father.

The massacre is all I remember of my father. Yet from time to time, other recollections rise to the surface. I recall he was a small man, perhaps five feet with a pale yellow complexion and braided hair to his waist. He had killed a mountain lion once and wore the skin as a *dappa* until the day he died. When they found him, his *dappa* had disappeared along with his head. I often wonder if he wasn't just as happy to die. After the murder of my mother, he lost the taste for life and left our welfare to his brothers and sisters, escaping her memory on long cattle drives to the interior as if fleeing the reality that he had lost her. Only our birthdays were sacred and I wept because despite all, he had sung to me for my ninth birthday.

The massacre was never punished. The Hottentots, or "stutterers" as we were called by whites because of the sound of our language, were fair game for both the English and the Dutch. We were no good as slaves. We refused to work in the mines. We would not work the land. We would not live in stone houses. Then there was our incomprehensible language, which resembled no other and was so filled with clicks and clacks it was impossible to speak. The Boers called it "Hottentot," and not a language at all but the gobbling of a turkey. We, in turn, hated the Dutch language of grunts and gurgles, but at least we could speak it. It was their language which should have been called "Hottentot." But as always, the white man won. I often wondered about that.

We had names for everything, every thought, every state of mind, every month and season, every object, the sun, the stars, the planets, yet we had not named anything for them. They used not one word, not one adjective of ours, even to describe things they had no words for themselves. I wondered how was it that they got to name everything, and we nothing. In their frenzy to do this, they would take all the children of six or seven and round them up into groups and send them to schools where the teachers were white men who doubled as priests and medicine men. We the Khoekhoe had never had much use for priests or medicine men. We didn't believe in religion and worshiped nothing except existence itself. That seemed to upset the white men at the school more than anything. We considered Jesus just another shepherd. Like us. Like our ancestor Tsuni//Goam, whom we called "Wounded Knee." Nevertheless they prevailed.

I was now a complete orphan. My aunt sold me to a Wesleyan missionary, the Reverend Cecil Freehouseland. The reverend was a tall, drawn, dark man full of passages from the Bible, which he could quote for days on end without ever repeating himself. He was neither young (for that wouldn't have been dignified) nor old (for that would have implied that he was mortal). No, he was of that indeterminate age the Dutch called the full force of his faculties and the English called the prime of life. He had a short black beard, bushy black eyebrows and piercing blue eyes that were to me the same color as heaven itself. He was strong, barrel-chested and wide-shouldered, and he often worked in the fields of the mission, his torso bare, wearing only cotton leggings. His breast and arms sprouted a mysterious black pelt like an ape and there were tufts in his ears and nostrils. He was a man of few words and many parables and I fell in love with him with all my nine-year-old heart. I loved him exceedingly. I watched every movement, every glance, every gesture and tried to anticipate his every desire. I was always ready when he wanted me and endeavored to convince him by every action, every glance that my only goal was to serve him as a daughter and a slave. I have since thought that he must have been a serious, wonderful man. His actions, his smile, his projects, his generosity corresponded very well with such a character.

Every day, at the mission, the reverend would read from the Bible to us children. He changed our Khoekhoe names to English or Dutch; Ssehura became Saartjie, which was "little Sarah" in Dutch. When I first saw him read, I was never so surprised in my life as when I saw the book talk back to him, for I believed it did as I watched his eyes scan the book and then his lips move in answer. I wished it would do the same with me. As soon as the Reverend Freehouseland had finished reading, I followed him to the place where he put the book, and when nobody was looking, I opened it and put my ear down close upon it, in the hope that it would say something to me. But I was heartbrokenly disappointed when I found it would not speak to me, and the thought immediately came to me that the book wouldn't speak to me because I was black.

Stubbornly I listened and listened, day after day, finally convinced was I that books in general and the Bible in particular wouldn't talk to black folks.

The Reverend Freehouseland would often talk about his "contract" with God and how sacred it was. How as a young man he had dedicated his life to saving heathens and spreading the word of God. At first, he had chosen China and had begun to study the language, which, he claimed, resembled Hottentot a little, but was a lot more simple. Then, in a sudden illumination, his contract with God had come to him. It was to be black Africa, austral Africa, the Cape of Good Hope, the most diminutive of God's provinces where the most destitute and wretched of God's children lived in sin . . . The Hottentots. This contract was sacred. The most sacred act of his life. All contracts were sacred, a sworn vow to be kept under all circumstances. They represented one's given word, which was the very essence of Englishness and English faith. The word of a gentleman. And the word of Christ. A renegade was a traitor not only to himself but also to everything his soul stood for if he broke his word. Debt was the same. A debt was to be honored. If it was impossible to pay it, you might even have to sacrifice your life to save your honor. He asked if I understood. I told him that I did. It was like a warrior's honor. Death was preferable to want of courage.

—I deem you to be an honorable girl, one on whom I can depend. One who knows the meaning of dignity. One day I'll take you to Manchester in England where I was born, but you'll have to stop thinking the Bible doesn't talk to colored people.

About a quarter of a mile from the mission stood a very fine *kowkow* tree, in the midst of a small wood. I never failed to go there once a day, sometimes twice a day, if I could get away. It was my greatest pleasure to sit under the shade of this *kowkow* tree and pour out my heart to it when I was unhappy. I would go and sit there and talk to the tree. I'd tell it my sorrows, as if it were a friend. I couldn't understand why, if you could talk to a cross made of dead wood, you couldn't talk to a tree of wood which was alive. In those days, I was a quiet, sulky girl who repented at five o'clock each morning my vanity, my selfishness, my stubbornness, my pride, my vindictiveness, my envy of others, all sins. The Khoekhoe had a very strict code of behavior and a code of honor that was relentless. To this I added the admonishments of the Wesleyan mission with all its Thou Shalt Nots. When this burden seemed to be unbearable, I would go and talk to my tree. I found more comfort there than in the mission's chapel because, as I saw it, the tree *was* a cross. I don't know even now if I truly believe that the tree was Christ. All I know is that whenever I was treated with ridicule and contempt, found myself unbearably ugly or alone, I would go to the tree and the tree would not only listen to me, it would talk back to me.

The Reverend Freehouseland died suddenly of the cholera. On his deathbed he told me that he hoped one day I would consent to talk to a book, especially the Bible, and that I was hereby free, and no longer a slave, that he always prayed for me, his favorite, and that in his will he had left me ten pounds. My only friend, my love, my protector, had abandoned me, just as my mother and father had. Every place in the world was the same to me from then on. For a long time, I dreamed only of going to England, where I believed all men were like him. And above all places in England, I wanted to see Manchester, where he had been born and where his body was now buried.

The Reverend Freehouseland's family never awarded me my ten pounds. And for good measure they sent me back to my clan. I returned to find that two of my brothers had died, one from smallpox, the other in one of the never-ending raids of white settlers. Our clan had almost disappeared from the earth like the others. I began to believe the Hottentots were the most wretched beings on the earth.

When I was freed by the Reverend Freehouseland, I was almost thirteen years old and approaching the age of marriage. My father's sister, Auni, who, except for selling me to the reverend, had always treated me kindly, like one of her own children, changed completely towards me now that I had been sent back home. She turned harsh and rigid and inflexible, not to say cruel. She suddenly had all kinds of rules and restrictions, mysterious rituals and secret manipulations. She was determined to produce a bride. I was shocked at the malevolence and discontent this project evoked in her. Was it because the task was impossible? Was I as ugly as all that?

Even so, the village judged me a marriageable and desirable virgin. I had beautiful small hands and feet and a tight cap of black curls that glistened with cocoa butter. On my head I wore a headband of long, thick braids of elephant grass, coiffed in elaborate designs. I had wide horizontal eyes without a fold at the lid and a high round forehead which took up half my face and gave it its heart shape. My cheekbones were high and fierce, my eyebrows plucked into a black line. My broad, full mouth with its jutting bottom lip was almost round, like a split papaya, and made an O. My eyes were light brown with almost no white, which had a bluish tint. My nose was short, my neck slim and long. I had small narrow shoulders and pear-shaped breasts tattooed in indigo with dark areolae. My waist was the smallest of all the virgins of the village and its size accentuated my wide jutting buttocks and sumptuous, mountainous hips. My clan carefully cultivated my shape according to our traditions. Like my peers, my bottom parts were massaged with butter and secret swelling ointments until they sprang a foot from the curve of my spine. I was fed the peanut oils and corn porridge and honey that would add even more flesh to them and more pounds to my thighs above the knees. My shape became my reason for being and that of my guardian. My shape became me and I became my shape. From time immemorial, it had been so for Khoekhoe women.

Some marriageable females could hardly stand or hold up their own weight. There was one maiden, Fulikiki, who had to be carried from place to place on a stool, her hind parts were so heavy. If she stood up, she toppled over backwards like a doll. Her brother would set her in place, her earlobes pierced with gold, a plate of honeycomb in front of her into which she sank her perfect white teeth, making the gold glitter. But the crowning glory of our beauty was our sex, now hidden under the elaborate beaded apron all maidens had to wear. My aunt began to cultivate its size and shape for it was the ultimate symbol of my femininity, my sexuality, my worth as a bride, much more so than my virginity. My aunt was charged with this treatment and she applied herself diligently. She knew it was my only chance in life: a husband.

She herself carried me to the compound for young girls when my menses came, lugging me piggyback so that my feet would not touch the ground. She cooked the porridge and flower bulbs and honey to fatten my hind parts. She taught me the medicine I needed to know. She performed the numerous rituals that had to be performed daily. She heated the water for my daily bath because washing with cold water was taboo. She groomed my skin, my feet and hands, rubbing them with coconut butter and beef fat. She showed me how to weave aprons out of multicolored feathers, to make necklaces from crushed ostrich eggs. To tan the thongs of skins I wore around my ankles. I was an orphan, after all, with no mother to guide my steps forward towards marriage.

She also occupied herself with the ways of Khoekhoe women who made their sex more attractive by artifice.

Aunt Auni made two incisions on each side so that the flesh curved downwards and placed a small pebble within. As the stones stretched the delicate membranes, she would insert a larger, heavier pebble until the flesh had descended to the length she desired and found beautiful. She explained, but I already knew from my sisters, that for my future husband, the act of love was not only the penetration of my vagina but also the enfolding of his gland within those fleshy lips. This would augment the ultimate moments of his pleasure. For my husband, I could procure rapturous levels with this apron of pulsing flesh filled with racing blood, fluttering like the burning wings of a butterfly or the fiery folds of a medusa. Each month the pebble got heavier and my bride-price increased. My aunt beamed with satisfaction.

It had been so through generations of Khoekhoe women, though no one knew how or why the apron had begun, not even the midwives, not even the rainmakers. Auni believed that there had been an ancient goddess so endowed and that my mother and her mother and her mother's mother's mother, nearly all the women in our clan, followed this custom. It went back to the beginning of time before the Flood when we lived in Namibia, the land of the People of the People. Then, we had lived along the coastline formed by soft warm currents which blew the waters of the sea northwards, creating a garden of rich underwater plants, providing food for the penguins, seals and sea lions that bred in the rocks and caves. Ever since the Flood we had lived here in ten clans of hunters and herders of cattle. Our chiefs were not born but elected, mostly for their ability to make rain. There was no central authority over the clans. There was no dictator, no hereditary prince, no king, no nobles. There was no word in Khoe for property or slave. The territory between the Orange River, which we called the Chamtoo, and the coastline from Namaqualand to the Umzimvubu River where it empties into the eastern Cape was ours until the Dutch came along and took it. We lost our grazing lands, our stock, our trade routes with the Bantu. We lost three wars, endured ten famines and four smallpox epidemics. We the hunters became the hunted, first as slaves, then for sport. We lost all idea of the past, even the names of our own rivers. And we clung to a few old customs so lost in time they couldn't even be explained, like the apron.

None of the Khoekhoe ever cultivated the soil. We wandered about from place to place with our herds of long-horned cattle and flocks of fat-tailed sheep. Our principal food was the milk of our cattle, drunk as a rule after being allowed to thicken. The milking was done by the women, while the general herding and pasturing of the cattle were in the hands of the men. In addition to milk, we ate wild fruits, berries and flower bulbs of various kinds, gathered by the women from trees and bushes or dug up out of the ground. We ate them either raw or baked or roasted. Meat was a luxury we obtained by hunting, never by killing cattle. In addition to game, all sorts of small animals and even insects were eaten in case of necessity. The domestic animals were never slaughtered, save on festive or ceremonial occasions, but any that died of disease or other natural causes were eaten with great joy. When hard pressed by hunger, we would eat almost anything that could be swallowed. For us, the ever-present need for grass and water for our herds and flocks compelled us to live and move in small, separated communities.

Our land was exploited on equal terms by all the members of the tribe. It could under no circumstances become the property of one person, nor was it held to belong to the chief; and it was generally regarded as inalienable. The vendetta system was in force amongst us, and the chief of the tribe did not possess the power to prevent the members of two clans from carrying out blood vengeance on one another. The heads of the clans were often jealous of one another; there were constant rivalries and disputes, which sometimes flared up into open warfare. Time and again a powerful clan would go off on its own, asserting its independence of the others; and clan loyalty was always stronger than the tribe.

Within the clan was the family, consisting of a man with his wife or wives and dependent children. All the tribes permitted second and third wives, although as a rule only the most powerful and wealthy men had more than one wife. In any case, the number of wives seldom exceeded two or three. The first wife was the chief wife, and she took precedence over the others.

The camp was built in a vast circle, enclosed with a great fence of thorn. Within the fence and round the circumference were the huts of the people, each hut facing inwards to the center. Members of the same clan had their huts close together, and the tribal rank of a clan could be seen in its distance from the huts of the chief and clansmen. A great open space in the center served as a corral for the stock at night. Special enclosures were made for the calves and the lambs, but the cattle and sheep just lay in the open before their owner's hut until they were driven out to graze in the morning.

After my return to the clan, they called me wild because I roamed restlessly amongst the dunes and short grass which linked the land to the continent, dreaming of Manchester and the fortune that had been stolen from me. I would wade in the hollows between the flooded dunes in winter and spot the hippopotamus that roamed the lakes the floods made. We the Khoekhoe were nothing, I thought. Our ten clans were dispossessed, or enslaved; the young men no longer owned herds. My father was dead and my mother murdered, what would my life be here? Where could I go? I wasn't wild. I was desperate.

It was a Khoesan custom that young people could choose to live with one another without a contract of marriage. The couple could at any time dissolve the union or sanctify it with the banns of matrimony. However, once the banns had been posted and approved by the elders, no other man could intrude on a husband's rights by contract. This was a sacred obligation. The punishment for adultery was death. The guilty parties would be buried in the sand up to their neck with only the head visible. Both man and woman would be stoned to death. An adventure outside the trial marriage, however, carried no sanction or penalty. It simply meant the end of that couple's union. I chose a drummer, Kx'au, a first cousin from my own clan, as a trial husband and for more than two years we lived together in his family's village.

Kx'au's village was a long way from my clan's encampments, nearer to the brick and wood town of Cape that had been built as a fort by the Afrikaners. His village was more dangerous than my village because white raiders from the Cape made yearly attacks on it. Moreover, there were rumors of a new war between the Boers and the English, who had taken the land the Boers had stolen from us. We heard of new inventions for warfare that the English had brought to bear: repeating rifles that spat lead like a fountain, the wide canoes with giant cannons that could bombard towns and villages from the sea, safe beyond the firepower of the attacked. Men spoke of fire bombs that could destroy a whole cultivated field, and finally of the Dutch Boers, who were being driven out of Orange into the hinterlands and towards what was left of our lands. But I never believed any of this had anything to do with us. The yellow-haired white men fought amongst themselves over lands which didn't belong to them. So what? At least they left us in peace for a change, too busy to raid and murder and spread disease.

And so Kx'au and I raised our hut and moved in together. We were both virgins and the mysteries of our bodies became new shared knowledge and a rapturous passion. Our youth and stamina substituted for our lack of experience. I can still see Kx'au standing backlit in the fiery shade of the sunset, his wide shoulders hung with antelope, a rhinoceros-horn-handled ax strapped to his left wrist. His tight deer leggings and moccasins beaded and stamped, his hair braided long with a headband of fine ivory teeth. His herding stick held in his right hand, his bow and arrows slung over his left shoulder. His gold bracelets shone, his nostrils widened with the scent of evening. We would make our fire for the night, prepare our meal, read the stars and close the door of our woven mat house.

To my great happiness, I conceived a child. Kx'au never lived to see it. He died mysteriously in the bush of gunshot wounds. He may have gotten caught in the crossfire of a skirmish between English and Dutch troops, for it was the English year of 1805. My shock at hearing of the death of Kx'au caused the baby, a boy named !Kung, after his grandfather, to be born too soon. I remembered nothing except my bloodcurdling scream when they laid Kx'au's body at my feet. !Kung, my sweet infant, survived only a few months, just long enough for me never to forget him. He was so small and so brave, fighting to live, to breathe with a ferocious will. The same will that pulled at my breast emptied it of milk, a will to survive that matched mine. I watched him fight and lose. He finally stopped sucking, although I held him to my breast for another day. I decided to leave Kx'au's village. I didn't want another husband, neither temporarily nor by marriage contract. I could not survive another murder.

Before I left, I consulted the rainmaker whose name was Magahâs. She was an ancient, hideous dwarf with deep-set black eyes, a great toadlike-shaped head with long braided hair. She resembled an antique, dilapidated baboon and her name !Naeheta Magahâs meant the thing-that-should-not-have-been-born. Magahâs lived in a cave that was a million moons old. The inside was covered with ochre, yellow and black paintings of sheep and bullocks and long-horned cattle that sped across the walls and over the ceiling in movements of terrible verisimilitude. The dwarf stank. She was covered with whale blubber and red clay paint and hung with dozens of rosaries made of smashed ostrich eggshells. As payment for her advice, I had brought her five woven grass mats, a straw hat and two gourds of sheep's milk. A handsome fee.

—No, was the answer. You must not go to Cape Town. If you do, your soul is lost for a million moons. If you go, you will never return to the Khoekhoe. A hundred winters will pass and still your spirit will wander, and the spirit of your spirit. And their spirits, those of Kx'au and !Kung, will never be still.

—But I will die in this village. I am young. I must work to survive. My life is still ahead of me.

—Your life will be behind you if you leave. You are a female, find another husband, make another contract, have another child.

But I knew if I did that I would die here.

—The Khoekhoe are dying out. We are starving. They are killing us with rifles and with the pox. If we don't die of gunpowder, we die of melancholy. There is no meat, no herds. We cannot hunt. Our spears and arrows have no power against cannonballs. My clan has disappeared. They hunt us like animals. A husband cannot protect his own family anymore.

—You think you will be safe in Cape Town? As slave to a white family?

—I am free. I was freed by my master, the Reverend Freehouseland . . .

—I tell you I see a great lake of water, storms and tempests, white rain and white cliffs as high as the sky, canoes with wings and cities of dust and stone. I see monsters of all shapes and sizes, dragons and reptiles, animals we have no names for, sicknesses that are foreign to us, corruption and death.

—I will die if I stay here.

—You will die if you go. Within ten winters.

—Can you give me some medicine?

—There is no medicine against a world not made up of human beings. Yet they are not beasts either. I have no name for them just as I have no remedy. They call themselves another race of men because they are white. But they are just like the People of the People . . . In the beginning we called the white men who came Ipurun, or tadpoles, because of their gray color and the way they swarm all over everything. Or Khoeku !gaesasiba ose, "men without stillness." She shrugged. Now we just call them Hur-inîn, sea people—which means the same thing . . .

—But have you no medicine . . . ?

—I *said* I have no medicine. No medicine except the earth beneath your feet—the earth of the People of the People. Fill this bone box with it and you are invincible—not your flesh, of course, but your spirit. Hang this around your neck and never lose it. Part with your liver before you part with this . . .

—There is one weapon, she said. It is a curse so powerful and so terrible you must use it *only* if it is a question of life or death. Repeat it after me . . .

She whispered the words, which seemed to have been forged in fire . . . I shrank from the ugly sound of them.

I took the box filled with sand and put it around my neck.

—Remember how separate and how variable are the fraternities that sway us in this life from birth to death. At one time we are all spiritual, at another all physical. At one time, we are sure that life is a dream and that real life is elsewhere. Or that this life on earth is all we have and we must make the best of it. But there are lives you live through others. You, Sse-hura, live through your dead child, your dead husband, your dead parents. You love them? You live through them. Like a clan of chattering baboons, we talk about love and our loves being immortal like the stars. But who knows but that the stars are only shadows cast by our own eyes? Desire is as fleeting as water and as shallow as a rhinoceros's mud bath. Passion flows from nowhere to nowhere. We are full of faith yet one single event can blot out all hope and life becomes as black as a panther's back, as fleeting as an owl's sleep.

—Only very stupid people never change, Ssehura. Only the simple-minded believe in eternity and permanence. The English do. The white man does. "Constant" is an English word. We have no word in Khoekhoe for "constant." Is the sun constant, or only constant to each floating sun-beam?

—If you want to say you have eaten, you must guard your thoughts as well as your tongue. Listen to the rats stirring in the thatch and look for snakes in the grass. Trust no one, especially those who sleep on your bosom.

3

SIRE,

The first thing that strikes us in our study of existence are those powers of physical force by which foreign sub- stances are attracted into their orbit, and retained for a certain period long enough for them to be assimilated and finally, these substances having become their prop- erty, distribute them according to the functions they are to exercise.

—BARON GEORGES LÉOPOLD CUVIER,
Letter to the Emperor Napoleon
on the progress of science since 1789

$\mathcal{P}$ale moon, the English month of July, 1805. The next day I left the village at dawn and set out on foot for Cape Town. Since I had no place else to go, I decided to return to the orphanage at the Reverend Free- houseland's mission. It was a twenty-three-day journey. I wrapped my be- longings in a mat and carried the bundle on my head. They consisted of some cooking pots, my eating bowl, my headrest, a small spindle and a guitar. As I set out, it seemed to me I was leaving what the Reverend Freehouseland called Eden: a garden richer and more beautiful than the painted illuminations of his Bible, filled with birds of paradise, flamingos and white cranes, rhinoceros and Cape lions, tree monkeys and orang-utans, river buffalo, carp and bullfrogs. I was thrilled to travel alone.

At dawn, I would rise just as the mist lifted and the level horizontal sun illuminated the earth as if for the first time. A few nuts, a bowl of hot water with milk and flour, and I set my bundle on my head and began my trek. I kept the Table Top Mountains to my right and the Umzimvubu River to my left. I headed southwest, and as I moved, the land moved with me. Sometimes I was only a speck in the monumental sand dunes that spread to the edge of the sea. Sometimes I was a ferret burrowing deep into the woods and forests of the mountain's valleys. Above me, thousands of birds in a thousand colors cruised in flight, swooping and diving, contesting the pollen of orchids the butterflies sipped. Elephants and buffalo washed themselves in great stagnant pools and twice I saw a great antelope herd in the distance heading towards the plains. I passed a troop of giraffes; their awkward gallop flinging their necks into arcs. They were beautiful to watch, these gentle creatures that caused harm to no living thing, not even the trees they nibbled on. I had stepped from the noisy village into silence. It was all around me yet everything was alive with the murmurings of life. The air at the beginning of the Pale moon month was like river water, cool and pure. The great vault of the sky, the deep blue of blue violets, was so huge and hung so low, it seemed the top of my head scraped against it.

There was silence and yet no silence, for the animal world continued swarming, bleating, chanting, crying, chirping, roaring and buzzing around me. I was alone with myself. I decided which foot to place in front of the other, which path to take, when to stop, when to continue, where and when to sleep, what and when to eat. It was a strange sensation, god-like and serene. I had never ventured beyond the frontiers of my village as a mother and a married woman. But now I gathered strength from placing one foot in front of the other, of bearing only my own burdens. I gathered strength from the soil. I carried sacred sand around my neck. I took destiny in my arms and vowed not to let it go until I existed. Time went by slowly. My movements flowed one into the other with a strange purity. Except for the laugh of a hyena or the coughing of a distant lion, nothing stirred between the earth and the sky, in which small clouds floated like lamb's wool in a hollow of iris blue.

I trekked through forests and woods full of wildlife: lions and ele-phants, wolves, elks and jackals, lynxes, rabbits, badgers; on the beaches, otters and penguins and seals; on the plains, zebras with red legs, ash-colored ibexes, goats, wildcats, elks, hippopotamus, wild horses, buffalo, boars. In truth, there was so much life between the mountains, plains and sea that it was an effort of memory even to name them all; the ostriches, for example, and the peacocks, cranes, black storks, geese, pelicans. The sea yielded its own wild creatures: sea lions, whales, sharks, tuna, salmon, rays, mullet, eels and carp. I skirted the edge of a gently curving shore to pick sea urchins, which the Dutch called "rock-roses," from the sand. If my own people called me wild, it was true. I myself felt most alive amongst wild things.

I was afraid of nothing, neither the wilderness nor the sea nor the mountains. Nights in the forest, even the sounds of wild beasts never really disturbed me. I slept when I was tired, put one foot before the other when I was not, my ankles bound in yards of cowhide, my belongings bal-anced on my head or slung over my shoulder. I was sixteen and I had my whole life before me.

I stopped along the river's edge. The water looked black and cold, the light was growing thin and the shade of the mountains loomed, making it even darker. In the bluish light, a great purple heron stood, as tall as I, although the long shadow made the beautiful bird look even taller as it edged out over the surface of the water. The heron's legs and the tips of its wings were blacker than the shadows. Its beak was black on top and yellow underneath. I squatted down and watched silently, suddenly seized by the sense that this was someone I knew, not merely a bird.

The heron stared first at me, then at the river. Daintily it took slow del-icate steps towards me, lifting one foot, then the other out of the water, pausing as if for the beat of a drum before again replacing it on the bed of the river, each movement a ritual, a dance, a message. The heron turned its head from side to side, waving, its sharp beak like a weapon as it made slight movements of its narrow head. I was sure now it was a spirit. Had it come to send me back to the encampment? It was completely alone, wading in the dark waters. Like all of its kind, it was solitary, always in exile, governed by no laws of flocking birds. No one ever saw these birds mate, nor sighted them with their families. This one seemed even more lonely than usual. An exiled bird like me, without a home anywhere.

It stopped on a welt of mud next to me. It lifted one foot, leaving its footprint in the sand, and kicked its long, scaly legs back as it slowly opened its wings and, with a sound like a wave hitting rock, glided towards me. Its neck was bent forward in a double curve as if someone had broken it. I looked into its sad eyes as it lifted its body over me, its breast almost touching the top of my head. I felt the bird's passage like a blow, the sweep of cold air, the blue shadow of its wings, the prickling of my skin. It was my mother. I knew. I remembered my aunt telling me over and over the story of the massacre, how the women, my mother included, had broken into flight just like this exiled bird, flapping their arms as if they might fly to flee the hail of bullets, their *lappas* billowing out behind them as they leapt over the dead and wounded running to the sea. But they seemed to move without speed as if time itself had stopped. My mother kept turning around to look behind her, stopping to stand stock-still like a small animal fascinated by the cobra bewitching him, losing precious time and finally taking the sabers that mowed them down like wheat. All along the beach, the slaying went on and on under the sounds of the double-barreled rifles, the whips and the swords.

Was this my mother's spirit? Had that bird been a real heron or a ghost in the form of a heron?

I remembered the old Khoekhoe tale about how the heron had gotten the bend in its neck.

—There was a jackal, my aunt had begun, hunting among some rocks when he spied a dove up above him beyond his reach. "Little dove," called the jackal, "I'm hungry. Throw me down one of your children." "No," said the dove. "Well then, I'll fly up there myself and eat you too." The poor frightened dove, thinking everyone could fly, including the jackal, threw down one of her children and the jackal ate it. The next day he returned and another baby bird went down his throat. The poor mother was weeping bitterly when a heron passed by and asked why she wept so bitterly. "I weep for my poor babies. If I do not give them to the jackal, he will fly up here and devour me too." "You foolish mother," replied the heron. "How can he fly up to get you when he has no wings! Jackals can't fly! Don't give in to his silly threats!"

—So the next day, when the jackal returned, the dove refused to hand over another chick. "The heron told me you can't fly after all," she said. "That nosy heron, I will pay her back for her wagging tongue." The jackal found the heron in a cool pond looking for frogs. The heron lifted his left leg with scales as big as fingernails, tipped his head a little to the right and looked down his beak at the jackal. "What a long neck you have," said the jackal. "What happens when the wind blows? It must break in half!" "No, I lower it," said the heron, bending his neck a bit lower. "And when the wind blows harder?" "Well, I bend it a little more," replied the heron. "And when there's really a gale?" asked the jackal. "I bend it down to here," said the heron, lowering his head down to the ground. The jackal jumped on the heron's lowered neck and cracked it right in the middle so that it snapped. And from that day, the heron had a bend in his neck . . .

I imagined my mother's neck stretched into a curve like the heron's, her arms flapping, fleeing for her life. The Khoekhoe had once flown; now they all had bent necks from jackals stomping on them. I sat for a long time beside the river and let the scene before me escape into night.

I had gathered a good supply of wild berries and bulbs to tide me over: wild strawberries, wild geraniums, narcissi, sweet white violets, sorrel, bloodroot, blueberries, milkweed and gladioli. I wondered how far my exiled bird had flown. If it knew how it had gotten its bent neck. The days between me and the Cape Fort dwindled as the barren sandy beaches with bronze ore thrusting through their surface gave way to pasture land, then grasslands surrounded by mountains, the highest of which was Table Mountain. At the foot of the mountain, I passed through marshy groves. In them, I met troops of screaming baboons that danced and yelled in the trees above me. In the evenings, fireflies and night animals kept me company and I looked out for the lions, which had given the mountains their name. I crossed countless streams and rivers, tree-shaded and sweet with sun-warmed springs. Finally I came into sight of the Dutch East India Company's gardens just outside of Cape Town, with its plantations of lemons, oranges, its close hedges of rosemary and laurel, all fragrant in the sun. At this time of year, winter, the mountains surrounding Cape Town were covered by a deep bank of cloud that gradually crept down their sides as evening approached. Gusts of wind gave motion to the air, and blew in several different directions at once, sometimes vomiting forth a true gale from Devil's Peak.

I walked through the rich edible salt flats, which used to belong to the Khoekhoe. Large white crystals of salt floated on the marshes or dried on the sandbanks, making a strange, forlorn landscape. While it was white in its natural deposit, when dog days scorched it with ferocious heat, the crystals split of their own accord into gleaming blue surfaces. I began to pass men on the road. Not hunters or warriors, but slaves and servants and old men on some errand. Men whose lives were over. I could have taken any of them in a fight for I was strong and fast and fearless. Kx'au had taught me how to use a bow and arrow, to defend myself with my walking stick, how to run, how to scale a tree, swim a river or camouflage myself with leaves and river silt when I wanted to hide.

I began to smell humans. The road began to fill with people going to or coming from the Cape Fort. I was happy to see faces and hear voices on the dusty road, sending up a cloud of languages and dialects. I had been lonely, I thought, without realizing it. There were dogs and pigs, chickens, goats, squawking cocks and fat-tailed baby lambs. Women carried jars of fired clay on their heads. Men carried cages filled with everything from serpents to parrots. Anything that could walk was on a leash and everything walking was edible. There was nothing that was not merchandise. It ebbed and flowed up to the very walls of the town. Mobs swarmed around the gates that were manned by police and customs officers.

I remembered from my orphanage days that today, Thursday, was market day. A long caravan, which must have come from the east, passed through the gates. Unending, the trail of heavily laden camels circled the walls, edged on by blue men in saffron and white kaftans, their heads and faces hidden under wide turbans, the unwound ends that fell to their shoulders, pulled across their mouths against the sand, dust and heat, leaving only their eyes to be seen. I slipped into the city with the caravan, keeping to the shadows of the moving animals. Once inside, I tried to get my bearings. I put down my bundle. The main street was brimming with people of all colors and shapes. Some were familiar, Dutch and Afrikaners, English, Xhosas and Bantus, but there were also Indians, Chinamen, Arabs and Semites, yellow, white, red, brown, dark-skinned Africans. They all moved in a different manner, on foot, in carriages, on horseback, and camelback, in litters, sedan chairs, and covered wagons, carts, palankeens and rickshaws. Dogs ran unleashed everywhere. There were white women who carried small tents to shade them from the sun, like those used by certain Africans to denote a prince or person of importance. There were white men in wide straw hats, linen dustcoats and gun belts.

The odor that rose from the street was a combination of vegetables and spices, the raw pine of new buildings, rotting garbage, cooking oil, garlic, musk, perfume, camel urine, dog shit and smoke from iron forges. In the years I had been gone, everything had changed. I stood in the middle of the road, covered with the red dirt of the street and my journey, dumb-founded. I was barefoot and wore only a short *lappa*. I picked up my belongings and sat them back on my head. I was like a dog that couldn't scratch. The horse-drawn carriages, sedan chairs and carts made a detour around me every which way and in both directions. Someone yelled,

—Get out of the way, you stupid Kaffir!

I couldn't tell who had called out, because so many people swirled around me, my head turned: soldiers in bright red uniforms, cowboys, slaves, railroad men. There were sailors from the port, miners from the mountains, caravan men and cattlemen. There were priests and pastors, farmers and gentlemen. All manner of animals roamed or were tethered in front of the pastel brick and wood houses: horses, camels and drome-daries, donkeys, mules, buffalo, longhorns, shorthorns, even a reindeer. Stray dogs, cats and pigs strolled along the wooden planks that served as passageways for those on foot. On each side were shops and stalls of every description in the open air or under the wood and mat arcades: baskets and bread, herbs, salt, grain, sweets, jewelry, cloth. I was overwhelmed.

I made my way past a white-and-black-painted church with towers like spears piercing the azure sky, the governor's house of yellow stone, the penitentiary, the police headquarters that I recognized from when I was a little girl. I was more and more apprehensive. Did I have the right to be in Cape Town? Was I a free woman? Did I need a pass? There were also terrible sights: beggars and lepers with no hands or feet, a public gallows with a corpse still hanging, a chain gang of convicts wearing striped pants and shirts, their feet shackled to fifty-pound cannonballs.

Lost now, not remembering the way to the mission, I felt the hatred all around me, like a thick fog. For the first time, I noticed there was no Khoekhoe on the street. I felt hostile eyes and coarse laughter following me. I stopped in my tracks, thinking, What is it? Am I naked? No. I have covered myself from head to knees. Is it my size? I am the size of a twelve-year-old child. Is it the way I walk? Have I dropped something? Violated some unspoken taboo? Insulted a passerby? Then the words floating around me, rough and contemptuous, became comprehensible.

—Kaffir.

—Bushwoman.

—Really? I thought there was a town ordinance prohibiting these people.

—Look, Mommy, a Hottentot!

—Pygmy!

—Savage!

—Cannibal!

—We hunt them in the north.

—My uncle has a stuffed trophy head . . .

—Can't you read the sign that says no dogs or Bushmen allowed?

—Get off the sidewalk!

Someone shoved me onto the road. I stumbled on in a trance, the hurtful insults hurled at me from all sides. Some were shouted, some spoken plainly. My stomach curled into a ball of fear. My heart accelerated. I walked faster, steadying the bundle on my head, wishing that the red clay dust beneath my feet would swallow me up. Passersby avoided my eyes. They moved away from me as I passed. Children stared and moved closer to the skirts of their mothers. I remembered what the rainmaker had said about not going to Cape Town, that I would lose my soul, my *n/um*. But now it was too late. Had I been blind to all this at the orphanage or simply too young to understand? Or had things changed in the past years? It was still, I thought, not too late to turn back. To run. But where would I go? How would I live if I didn't work? Another husband? I couldn't survive another murder.

I tried to figure out my way. I finally asked a passerby in Dutch. He looked at me as if I were a talking dog.

—The St. Luke Orphanage, he repeated slowly in Afrikaans as if he were speaking to an idiot, is on Blacker Street, about a ten-minute walk. Take the next street to the left, all the way to the end, and then turn onto Merriberry Road . . . You'll see the bell tower . . .

—Thank you, sir, I said.

He just kept staring at me. He hadn't expected me to understand a word he had spoken. Finally, he shrugged, shook his head sadly and went on his way in the opposite direction.

The familiar sound of the school bell brought me to the gate of the compound. I put down my bundle and rang the gate bell. I knew the guardian who opened the gate, a Bantu.

—Ssehura, he cried out.

At least someone was happy to see me.

—Saartjie, he said, using my Dutch name, how did you get here? What are you doing here?

—I walked.

—From home?

—Yes.

—And you walked through town?

—Why, yes.

We were speaking in Khoe.

—It's a wonder you didn't get arrested! The Khoekhoe are prohibited from entering Cape Town. There are thousands of them camped outside the walls to the north of town. The English, who have defeated the Dutch and taken their colony, have decreed that Hottentots must be in the service of a white person, live in a fixed place and carry a pass in order to enter the town.

—But this place is built on the People of the People's land! How can they prohibit us from walking on it?

—You are prohibited from owning it as well. I heard you got married.

—My husband is dead. My just-born lived only a few months.

—Oh, Ssehura. I'm so sorry to hear that. So you are alone in the world once again.

—Yes. Mambu?

—Yes?

—Someone shoved me off the sidewalk coming here.

He gazed at me strangely.

—Didn't you know there's a war going on? The Hottentots have been attacking white settlers in Namibia. There have been massacres of whites . . . It's a miracle you got through town without getting killed yourself. All Hottentots are banned from the city.

—That's why people stared! Why a man spat on my moccasins!

—You were lucky, Saartjie. You could be in jail now. Come in, come in before somebody else sees you!

—I had to come. I need work. My husband died. My baby died. I

36

couldn't stay there. I would have died too! There's no food, nothing. I couldn't stay there; my life would have been over!

—What can you do?

I looked at him blankly. I could "do" nothing that would interest anybody. I could milk goats. I could gather wood and food. I could make a fire. I could have babies and wear *lappas*. I could build a house with bent twigs and cover it with reed mats. I could walk for many miles without tiring. I owned a slingshot. I could sing and play the guitar. I could herd cattle. I was a shepherdess. I knew a little medicine. I knew a little rainmaking. I was a very good archer. I could hit a target at ninety paces. What could I do? I could swim. I could search and find iris bulbs to cook in flour batter. I could . . .

—I can't do anything, I said.

—If you stay here, the headmistress can fit you out for housework. You remember your lessons from the time you were here? You speak a little Dutch and English from those days? You can learn to sew, to cook, to clean, to be a nursery maid or a laundress. The Reverend Freehouseland taught you some English, didn't he?

—Dutch and English.

—Yes, well, that's all to the good.

—He left me an inheritance.

—I know the story. But he's dead now. His family has returned to England. Nobody remembers about it anymore, and it's just as well. What would you have done with the money he left you anyway?

The porter Mambu opened the double doors onto a large high-ceilinged room where thirty or more colored women all dressed the same in white smocks stood behind rows of white-draped tables with coal irons on them. Each had a shirt in her hand. Each had a bonnet on her head. At the front of the room stood the teacher on a raised dais. She spoke in Khoe, then in Dutch. She shouted as if raising her voice would force them to learn faster. The rows of black faces were intent, perspiring with the heat of the irons. The windows were wide open and the white curtains stirred. The teacher's voice resounded against the vaulted ceiling.

—First, take the collar of the washed shirt with two fingers, this one and this one, turn it towards you . . .

—They are learning to be laundresses. You could start here with ironing, then washing, bleaching, mending . . .

All eyes were lowered onto the white shirts, held with thumb and forefinger. Each pair of hands clutched the cloth, clutched and smoothed it carefully, bringing down the hot weighted irons with a dull thud, forcing out every wrinkle, every ridge, every imperfection.

They resembled a troop of penguins with their white starched bosoms and their white starched caps, black arms flapping, heads bobbing in rhythm with the teacher's lips, not able to make any sound themselves. Perhaps, like penguins, they had no vocal cords.

—I'm glad you've returned, Saartjie, poor orphan . . . poor widow now—We'll find you a home . . . a good family of Boers.

That night, I pulled the thin cotton sheet up under my chin as I lay on the narrow plank bed in the women's dormitory where thirty other inmates slept. The scent of warm female flesh, like baked bread, rose all around me as they snored softly. The day for them had begun at half past four. Tomorrow it would for me as well.

I stared up at the dirty brown wooden ceiling as I would have stared at the night sky only a day ago, and thought of the wooden boxes called coffins the English and the Dutch used to bury their dead. I was as dead as the dead in those coffins. These sleeping colored women were dead. For twenty-three nights I had slept on the fragrant earth with only the stars above me. How long before I would sleep again under the moon, wrapped in my husband's antelope skin, my headrest caressing the nape of my neck, the amulet given me by the thing-that-should-never-have-been-born dropped onto my heart, which beats and beats and beats? Not the sickening pounding of a long-distance runner, but the steady, steady rhythm of an unborn child in his mother's womb, muted, fragile and determined to live.

The days following that first night blended into one. I learned cooking, cleaning, flower arranging, silver polishing, washing, ironing, napkin folding, gardening, preserve making, even a bit of hairdressing and wig making. I tried to think only of the task at hand. I was found to be not apt for housework and it was decided I would become a children's nurse. My breasts sometimes ached for my own little one and it didn't displease me to hold one of the mission orphans in my arms.

Sometime later, at the approach of Star Death moon, Mistress Van Loott, who had taken the Reverend Freehouseland's place, called me into her office. It was a Sunday.

—Saartjie, I think I have a family for you. They will tend to your pass and your registration. This is Colonel Caesar, a planter from the Flat Mountain Valley. He's looking for a nurse for his children.

A tall cherry-faced white man stepped from the shadows.

—Colonel Caesar, this is Ssehura. We call her Saartjie, little Sarah.

—How do you do? I said in English.

He didn't hold out his hand, but placed his wide straw planter's hat on Mistress Van Loott's desk.

—How do you do? I said in Afrikaans.

—You understand Afrikaans? he asked.

Mistress Van Loott answered for me.

—Yes, she was at the mission as a child. She went back to her tribe but she hasn't forgotten your language.

—Indeed. Fine. She can't read or write, can she?

—No.

—Don't want any Kaffirs that can read or write around the farm. Too much damn trouble—too dangerous. They teach it to the Kaffir children . . . Learning spoils the best niggers in the world.

—No, I assure you, she can't read and she can't write.

—How old is she? She looks no more than ten or twelve . . .

—I'm sixteen, sir.

—Oh, she's a grown woman, Colonel Caesar, a mother and a widow.

—Oh, I see, not a maiden at all . . .

Mistress Van Loott looked confused.

—Oh, no, she's a widow, and I assure you she can't read and she cannot write, she repeated.

I thought of the mute book that wouldn't answer black people but I said nothing.

—We've got three small children under six. Clare, Karl and Erasmus.

I was content. I loved children. I would take care of the three as if they were my own.

—I love children, sir, I said, still speaking Afrikaans.

—Is that so, Saartjie. Well, that's fine. My wife'll be real pleased. She likes Hottentot servants even if they do have a reputation for running away.

—She won't run. Will you, Sarah?

—No, ma'am.

Run where? To the Khoekhoe garbage heap outside of town? To the famine in Namibia? Into the sea? Run where? I was a prisoner in my own country.

—Well, Saartjie, get your things together. You'll be leaving with Colonel Caesar at sunset. His wagon train's traveling by night.

I was overjoyed to leave this coffin of a house. The idea of returning to the outdoors, of sleeping once again under the stars, of being close to a herd of cattle, pleased me greatly. The image of my father flashed before me.

—I herd cattle, sir. I was brought up to do it.

—As small as you are?

—Yes, sir.

Miss Van Loott laughed.

—You'd think she would have trouble even standing up. Some of them look as though they are going to fall over backwards. But Saartjie is amazing. She runs like a man. Long distance.

—Well, fancy that! A shepherdess. Well we have lots of fat-tailed sheep too. Maybe you can mind the sheep when you're not minding Clare, Karl and Erasmus!

A moment of awkward silence fell.

—I'd like to speak to Saartjie alone, Miss Van Loott.

—Of course, I'll go and sign her release.

Mistress Van Loott left the room and Colonel Caesar ordered me over to the window.

—Come here, Saartjie, I want to see you in the light.

—Colonel Caesar . . .

—Call me Master.

—Master . . .

—Walk over here by the window.

I approached him, my heart in my mouth.

—Just want to feel you up a bit, Saartjie. I'm a good Christian, faithful to my wife . . .

He opened his breeches, took out his organ wild with red hairs like an orangutan's posterior. I stared at it with horror. His organ had two testicles . . . I wondered if all white men were so deformed.

—What you staring at, Saartjie? Can't tell me you ain't never seen a man's penis before—you a married woman. Now kiss it.

I knelt down before this horribly deformed man, not knowing what he expected from me. But before I could act, his free hand groped under my smock, clutching my backside, and it was over.

—Ahhh, he gurgled. You'll do nicely, Saartjie, he said when he had come to himself.

I got up off my knees, wondering if I should tell Mistress Van Loott what had happened.

—Now, no need for you to tell Miss Van Loott. It won't happen again. Not like you're a virgin or anything. Correct?

My silence was taken for consent. I had three choices, I thought. I could stay here in this coffin and hope for another employer or I could run away to the Khoekhoe camp outside of town and starve or I could take my chances with Mrs. Caesar's children and Mrs. Caesar's vigilance over her husband. Surely a white Christian woman would protect me?

When Mistress Van Loott entered, she couldn't meet my eyes.

—Here are the papers, Colonel, all in order, was all she said, despite my ashen face and his red one. She didn't care. She didn't want to know. After all, masters had certain rights over their servants and I was, after all, of that race. It was strange to feel that in the judgment of those above you, you were scarcely human: I even wondered if their belief was more than half right—that I really mattered less than a camel, less than a dog, without a *n/um*, that even my shape was not human according to civilized people.

—That's all, Saartjie. You're dismissed, get your things.

I turned to leave, glancing over my shoulder at the man who was now my master. He was dressed like all the planters of the region, in a white felt three-cornered hat and a long dustcoat split up the back for riding. His sleeves were turned back to reveal hairy forearms. He had on breeches which covered his legs to the knees and soft short camel-skin boots tied crisscross halfway up his calf, the rest being bare. His shirt was open at the neck and little hairs peeked out. His long waistcoat almost swept his knees and was of white linen with bone buttons. His curly red hair was tied back with a green ribbon and he carried a long rifle and a hunting knife. There was nothing extraordinary about him except his height and the color of his eyes, which were a pale gray, like a winter sky, under those red eyebrows and red lashes. He smelled too. But then, all white people smelled. Only white babies smelled good.

I lingered one moment more, thinking I should remember something about my new patron—some little tic, some special attribute, so I could give him a name in Khoekhoe and not think of him only as master. I decided his gray eyes were like a winter sky. *Sao/homaib* . . . Then I thought, No, *Sao/homaib/ao-mûs/gam,* winter-sky-snake-eyes. That's what he would be from now on. Then I smiled. He was in fact *Sao/homaib/ao-mûs/gam-kharara,* winter-sky-snake-eyes-two-testicles . . .

The colonel glanced at me in what he took to be a friendly way—as if I were actually a human and not an animal, who could talk and feel and now had charge of his three precious babes. Then his gaze closed, as did all white people's on second glance. His winter-sky-snake-eyes returned to the same blank stare I always saw in whites' eyes when they looked at me. Or rather through me. As if, after twenty years of daily observance, they couldn't for the life of them remember my name.

As I left, Mistress Van Loott whispered,

—He won't bother you . . .

I bit my lip to keep from laughing. She really believed that. I wondered how she explained all the colored orphans at her mission.

That evening, the wheels of the long wagon train groaned as the lead wagon turned on itself out of the corral. It stretched a half mile across the plain like a huge pink seashell: longhorn cattle, bulls, bullocks, mares, calves, fanned out from the spine of wagons loaded and ready to move. The blue light struck the dark shiny coats and white jutting horns of the herd and their odor rose from their own dust. I could barely make out the herders and cowboys or the black silhouettes of the San and Xhosa shepherds gliding silently amongst them. Like a lazy animal stretching, the train began to creep forward slowly, moonlight outlining the braying, snorting, crying, creaking mass. We passed an encampment of Khoekhoe, miserable blank-eyed, filthy, weaponless people huddled around campfires, for the night was cold. Wolves and coyotes howled in the valley. The blurred, dark shadows of the herders moved amongst the animals. The torches of Cape Town burned bright in the distance until they disappeared behind the hills, leaving only the oil lamps swinging on the wagon posts like fireflies as guiding lights. They and shooting stars lit the way, for it was now Star Death moon.

4

I am a monogenist, all humans come from a single creation divided into three races: Caucasians, Ethiopians or Negroes, and Mongolians. It is not a coincidence that the Caucasian race has gained dominion over the world while Negroes are still sunken in slavery and the pleasures of the senses and the Chinese lost in the obscurities of a hieroglyphic language . . .

—BARON GEORGES LÉOPOLD CUVIER,
Thirty Lessons in Comparative Anatomy

Star Death, the English month of February, 1806. The Caesar farm stood low on the slopes of Table Mountain Ridge, part of a valley that sang with wild animals, savage birds, wolves, jackals and Cape lions. The wide square house stood surrounded by great shade trees, groves of fruit trees, mango arbors and vineyards. For me, the house was another coffin. White with square black pillars and a veranda on all sides, it seemed to have descended from on high, pushing aside the tall pale grass to settle its backside into the landscape like a brood hen. There was no courtyard; instead the henhouse looked outwards in all directions so that I saw only horizon, filled with grasslands and wheat fields that led softly to the next ridge. There was always a fresh wind blowing and the wood and brick house, built in the Dutch manner, was situated to catch the slightest breeze. The polished plank floors were always cool under my bare feet and thick walls kept the African heat out.

There were no other Hottentot servants. All the others were Xhosa or Bantu and they looked down on me. Several were Muslim, two were Christian and the others, like me, believed that no one god or gods had the answer to the mysteries of life and so stuck to believing in rocks and rivers, the sun and wind, trees and earth, and listening to them and speaking to them, following the old ways.

The Caesar family was a typical Boer family, consisting of father, mother and three children. Added to this core were four dogs, a cat, a parrot and sixteen servants. Peter Caesar, for that was my master's given name, was a Dutch Afrikaner, although it was rumored that he had some Khoekhoe blood in him as well as Irish. This was servants' gossip. I never found out any more about him except that his grandfather had come to the Cape from the town of Dokkum in the Netherlands some sixty years previously and had worked as a shipping clerk for the Dutch East India Company. He had made war on the Hottentots, searched for gold and homesteaded, that is, stole, a tract of Hottentot land that had been almost thirteen square miles, and began to raise cattle and wheat. Caesar's father lost much of this land in the panic of 1742, when he had invested all he had in the Dutch East India Company and the English had won the war. So Peter Caesar was not a rich man. He had a brother, Hendrick, who lived about a week's trek away in another valley nearer Cape Town, who also raised cattle and who also was not a rich man.

My master was well known as a good, strict, Calvinist white African, fair and God-fearing. So, despite what had happened, Master Peter became the voice of authority in my new life. He never again touched me once I was under his roof, and for that I was grateful. I was grateful, quick, docile, affectionate and trusting. Just like the other animals that belonged to the family: four dogs, one cat and a parrot. The four dogs, all basset hounds, were named after cities in Holland: Amsterdam, Rotterdam, Haarlem and Monnikendam, which had been long ago shortened to Amst, Rott, Haar and Monni. The cat's name was Simplicity and the parrot was named The Hague. Master Peter was so tall, almost six feet two, that my head hardly reached his diaphragm and my neck hurt when I had to look up at him. For that and another reason, I kept my distance. I usually stood a good ten feet away from him whenever I had to speak. He seemed to like this: "Little People," he called me, and I learned from him the reason the Khoekhoe were called Hottentot. It was because of our strange way of speaking with click sounds and expulsions, which white people were incapable of mastering and which sounded to their ears like stuttering. The Dutch word for stutterer was Hottentot. It was not a pretty word, he said, and it's an insult too. Which, I asked, is worse?

—Oh, about the same, he said, there's little difference at all . . .

His wife, Alya, also had her ideas about how far away from her I should stand. All her servants were ordered to keep their distance of ten feet. She didn't want to smell them or touch them and she didn't want them breathing on her person. This was one of the many ways she fought Dirt.

—What is life, she would say, but stink and shit? Dirt, Dirt, Dirt.

Her only reason for living was to rid the earth of it and protect her family from it. So we would stand ten feet away from her, raising our voices as if we were about to decapitate her to inform her that dinner was ready, or the cat had disappeared, or that the rain had stopped. I would hold the youngest of her children, Clare, in my arms, with little Karl clunging to my skirts and Erasmus, the oldest, hung on my neck, while avoiding breathing upon her. I was paid a salary of one Dutch shilling a month, and meals. I slept in a little lean-to cabin at the back of the kitchen. Sometimes I accompanied the family to Cape Town to buy supplies, pick up shipments from Holland, visit the bank and call on their friends who had children of the same age, so that they could play with Clare, Erasmus and Karl. I would sit with the other mammies, nannies, obeahs, ayahs, wet nurses, dry nurses and governesses and gossip about the masters. My mistress was known by all as Frau Von Shit and she would die with that same epithet.

The trips to Cape Town gave me a chance to explore the city. I now remembered where the governor's house was, the penitentiary, the cathedral, the High Court. I learned what a bank was, a market, a blacksmith and a stable. I admired the beautiful horses, equipages and riding saddles. I began to recognize what the various painted signs and advertisements said but I still refused to talk to books. I quickly learned the names for everything beautiful and luxurious in Cape Town: dresses, hats, shoes, gloves, necklaces, earrings, rings, petticoats, corsets, lace, ostrich feathers, handkerchiefs. I gazed at boots, swords, pistols, top hats, bonnets, eau-de-vie, silver mirrors and dreamed of far-off places. Manchester, for example, where the Reverend Freehouseland had been born and was now buried. I decided England must be the heaven he had told me about, where everything was milk and honey. And so that faraway island became the motherland that I had lost. I dreamed of it as I stood listening to the cries of seagulls and hawks in my very favorite place: the wharves, watching the tall ships leave and enter the harbor, admiring these great canoes with their branchless trees furled in sails of scarlet, blue or white. These were my happiest moments.

The day that I speak of, a great ship had come in. The dockers were unloading her and the sailors were running here and there furling sails, hauling in ropes, fixing the ship tight to its moorings. From the hold of the ship emerged a single line of chained black men, blinking in the sharp reflection of the sun. They limped down the runway naked, their heads shaved, silence in their very limbs, while other black workers looked the other way.

On the top deck stood a lone figure, perhaps the captain, in a splendid uniform of scarlet and blue, his tunic draped with gold cord and braids, his buttons flashing in the sun. He was very dark and his blue-black hair escaped in the wind and made a collar of fur around his head like a great noose. A long polished instrument the thickness of a bamboo rod was strapped to his left wrist and hung at his thigh. The sun burned his silhouette against the indigo sails. A great nostalgia came over me, a sense of loneliness. Even though he was white, he reminded me so much of Kx'au I almost cried out; he had the same wide shoulders, was the same height, the same weight, had the same stance, even the collar of fur.

Just then, a band of roving white boys, Boers from their looks, turned the corner of First Street, yelling and playing catch, searching for mischief. They had spied me, a Hottentot, and were heading my way. I pulled my *chapur* around me and over my head. The fact that I had a pass, a patron and a fixed address would make no difference to them. They were out for fun and adventure. They could beat me, rape me, torment me or murder me for amusement. I hurried away, down the next alley, leaving the beautiful ship and its mysterious master, stubbing my toe on the cobblestones as I hobbled away.

The loneliness remained with me as we traveled back to the farm days later. The lead wagon, followed by the supply wagon and Master Peter riding point on his favorite horse, Sphere, followed the seacoast for almost a day as it meandered through the marshes and savannas and salt lands surrounding Cape Town. Finally we turned eastwards into the silence of the vineyards and wheat fields that marched up the ridge. The African light died on our eyelids and our lips, it painted the hides of the horses and oxen indigo, it swept across the cliffs, painting them scarlet and purple with its fingers. The night sounds closed in and the fireflies awoke. One even had the illusion of real peace, although in this wilderness, with the eyes of roving wolves upon us, with the wars of nature all around us, there was no peace.

That night, my master stood at the head of his table and bowed his head.

—O God, merciful and full of grace, our heavenly Father, it is only by thy majesty and divine love that we are called on to conduct the affairs of this colony so that justice be maintained amongst these savage and brutal men and that your true and reformed doctrine shall be propagated and spread for the honor and the glory of your sacred name, we pray and implore you to enlighten our hearts with your heavenly wisdom and grace so that this colony, this family, this factory will serve to magnify and honor your name, and in your name we bless this food. Amen.

Mistress Alya's head bobbed up and down in unison and grave agreement with her husband's prayer. Her hands twisted under the perfection of her white apron (she always wore a fresh clean one for dinner). The table, laden with food, sparkling with silver, brilliant with dazzlingly laundered linen, dressed with starched and embroidered napkins shaped like boats anchored with tiny silver clips, decorated with flowers and candles, was always a beautiful sight to see. I stood with my tray of food, barefoot in blue and white starched smock and apron, a white starched turban hiding my braids. A barefoot footman in Indian tunic, pantaloons and fez stood at attention behind the chair of Master Caesar. A tall Bantu butler who took every occasion to slap me for my errors and inexperience served the meal.

It had taken me a while to get used to Mistress Alya.

—Souls should shine with cleanliness, repeated Mistess Alya. The impure heart can never be freed from dirt . . . The polluters, she continued, come in two guises, internal and external: evil thoughts and alien cultures.

Mistress Alya had a cleaning regimen that illustrated this commandment and she followed it with military precision: the steps, porch and path leading to the house and the front hall were to be washed every day early in the morning. On Wednesdays, the entire house was cleaned, on Monday and Tuesday afternoons the reception rooms were dusted and the furniture polished. Thursdays were scrubbing and scouring days, and on Fridays the kitchen and cellar were cleaned. Dishes had to be perfectly washed after every meal. Laundry was done every day. When sheets were folded, the end used for the feet could never accidentally be turned so that it could be used for the head. Pillows were plumped up each day so feathers could breathe, as were the down-filled coverlets. Chairs and tables were cleaned, cobwebs removed, anti-insect measures taken, using lye on the floor and chalk and turpentine on the walls. Moths were repelled by camphor, flies and wasps caught in strips covered with honey. Shoes were removed on entering the house and slippers provided. The feet of the whole family were to be washed every evening.

The cows and their stalls were washed every day. The tails of the oxen and cows were tied to pillars so that their urine and dung would not soil them. And in the kitchen hung a flat-ironed starched towel embroidered with the motto:

My brush is my sword; my broom, my weapon
Sleep I know not, nor any repose
No labor is too heavy; no care too great
To make everything shine and spotlessly neat
I scrape and scour, I polish and I scrub
And suffer no one to take away my tub.

Mistress Alya suffered from insomnia. She could be seen in the early hours of the morning like a haunt or what we called a "fawn foot" flitting from room to room with a dust rag.

—Cleanliness is godliness, she would whisper over and over, wringing her just-washed hands.

As I understood it, to be clean was an affirmation of independence. What was cleansed was the dirt of the world: pollution and injustice. Dirt disguised violence and torture. It prevented self-knowledge. Cleaning made everything distinct and clear like the African dawn. To keep oneself clean was to set oneself apart in a world of confusion and foreigners. Dirt was vagabond. Dirt was the appetite of the flesh. Dirt was folly, disorder and sex.

The Hottentots, she would say, were not only dirty, they were filthy. They smeared their bodies with butter and dung. They wore entrails around their necks. They painted their faces. They spat and urinated on brides and grooms. And when there was nothing to eat, they ate dirt rather than starve. I began to bathe myself twice a day, rising at dawn to wade in the river that ran through the farm or filling a wooden trough with hot water from the kitchen and letting the waters close over my head.

One of the things it fell to my lot to do was to wash the feet of the family gathered in the large sitting room or the screened veranda every night. I would bring in a steaming basin of water, kneel before each family member or guest, remove their shoes and stockings and carefully wash their feet. I would repeat this ritual as many times as there were white people present. Sometimes it was only Master Caesar and his wife. Sometimes the master's father-in-law, Donald Van Wagenaar, a retired army colonel, would be present. Sometimes a maiden aunt, Mistress Agnes. And sometimes there would be the master's brother, Master Hendrick, or other guests. My washing of their feet seemed to be a ritual that soothed and reassured them in their superiority. They would smoke their pipes, drink their gin, discuss Afrikaner affairs as freely as if I were a piece of furniture. For indeed, I did not exist as a person any more than Rott or Amst or Haar. And so, in this way, I learned a lot about the world as they saw it, as it really was and how it would be in the future. I learned of events far away from Cape Town, in places like London, Amsterdam, New Delhi and Malay. I listened as I cut toenails, massaged the feet of Mistress Alya, whose only vice that I could see was the voluptuous wiggling of her toes. Her feet were long and narrow with little balls of flesh at the tip of each toe. As I washed the feet of more and more people, I realized each foot told a story. Each foot had a private life, a temperament, an occupation, a sex, which might or might not be the sex of the person to whom the foot belonged. There were farmer's feet and hunter's feet, soldier's feet and gentleman's feet. There were cowboy's feet, and herder's feet, cook's feet and aristocrat's feet. There were honest feet, sick feet, noble feet and vulgar feet, beautiful feet and feet that lied.

The latter was the case of Master Hendrick, who had long handsome feet that lied. Sometimes his visits would last for months, although he had a wife and several small children. But his wife, Mistress Lilly, never came. The two Caesar women didn't get along. When Master Hendrick came, he hunted mostly wild boars and lions. He left his family for months at a time. Perhaps he saw them thirty days out of the year: at Christmas, Easter, All Saints' and what the Dutch called the *wijn oogst*.

As well as being beautiful and lying, Master Hendrick's feet were restless and strong, with no corns or calluses or other deformity. They were very long and slightly wider at the toes than at the heel and his second toe extended further than his big toe and they all had nails with big moons like polished ivory. They were not feet that looked as if they had tramped through bush and savanna, mountains and desert, rivers and jungle, wilderness and the wild forests of the Cape. His feet seemed to have eyes, which stared at my shape under my loose-fitting smock. They joined the eyes in his head, which never took themselves off me. I heard them blinking, blinking as they contemplated the starched white span of cotton that covered my hips.

Master Hendrick was seven years younger than his brother, but the spitting image of him. He was above average height like him, with broad shoulders, hands that looked exactly like his feet, and a complexion so darkened by the sun and the outdoors it was almost my color. He had a big nose and thin lips and the same fiery wild hair as his brother with tufts of it all over his forearms and chest. His eyes were the same winter-sky gray as his brother's. When he emerged from the bush, he dressed like a gentleman in a soft kid duster to the ground and linen shirts, silk vests and silk stockings. But in the bush he wore cutoff sailor pantaloons stuck into heavy riding boots, rough slave-cloth shirts and a wide felt hat with a cock feather. He was so strong—I had seen him strangle a wildcat with one hand. He wrestled cattle, broke wild horses, hunted lions and rhinoceros. He was never without a pistol, a hunting knife or a cowhide whip. He was famous for using all three exceedingly well. He boasted that he and his brother had Khoekhoe ancestors and I believed him. This made me feel safe with him. And it made him seem almost human to me, for a *Khoekxa !gaesasiba ose* . . . a white man.

Master Hendrick roamed the Khoekhoe lands like one of us, his restless feet never still, his caravans and wagons, his hunting parties and bearers crisscrossing the landscape searching for that one stroke of luck, that one chance that would bring him the fame and fortune he believed he so fully deserved. He thought, like me, that the world owed him more than the life he had, and he often, unlike me, complained about it. His brother would only laugh and rebuke him for not being grateful to God for what he did have. Mistress Alya would simply shake her head in disgust.

I was now twenty. I had been in service at the Caesar farm for almost four years. One day, Mistress Alya surprised me in my bath.

—What are you doing bathing in the middle of the day? she said.

—It's my rest hour, I replied, rising . . . I . . .

—What's that? she cried. She was staring at my sex in horror. I had forgotten to hide myself.

—My apron, ma'am.

—Your *what?*

—My *apron* . . .

—It's . . . obscene . . . horrible. Cover yourself!

I pulled up my smock from the floor and held it against me.

—Don't you ever let anyone see you again or that filthy appendix . . .

—But, I protested, a Khoekhoe girl must submit to this . . . arrangement. Otherwise I would find no husband!

—I have heard of the Abyssinians and the Egyptians cutting girls, but never the contrary . . . said the mistress.

—I wouldn't know, ma'am. But I knew the Yousha tribe and the Fula and the Sarahuli excised part of their womenfolk's sex, then sewed them up so that it took ten minutes to urinate and ten days to complete their menses, "the sewn women," they were called. But I would never repeat these secrets to Mistress Alya, even though female circumcision was considered clean . . . I remained silent.

—You know what I'm talking about, you filthy girl. You get your clothes back on and get back to work. The sight of you is so repugnant, I cannot fathom how you can live . . . *Vuile bruiden . . . Ribaude!*

She cast one more horrified look at me, but I had hidden behind my discarded frock. Unbidden tears rolled down my cheeks, glistening like the rest of my wet body. My mouth trembled with pain and my heart pounded with agony. I was weeping openly now, in huge deep sobs I could no longer control. I crossed my legs to hide my femaleness even from myself, my arms hanging limply at my sides, my mouth opening in the grief of an O. I sank down hoping the water would not only cover my nakedness but swallow up my life as well.

A few days later, Master Hendrick arrived from Cape Town driving a newly purchased herd of shorthorns. That night, he performed his magic tricks for the family, making everyone laugh. He was famous among Cape society for his magic, some of which he claimed to have learned from the rainmakers. To me, he was a rainmaker, full of omens and power. His sleights of hand were clever and the company laughed and clapped. Even the children were allowed to stay up to watch, and little Clare sat on my lap, her legs pumping, screaming with delight. I pressed her closer to me.

After I had put the children to bed, I brought out the basins for the footbaths. As I knelt before Master Hendrick's, I could feel his eyes on me, as always, and hear his pale eyelashes blinking. I said nothing, bending low over the restless feet.

—I hope you will be happy with my brother, Saartjie, we shall miss you. Certainly the children who love you so will miss you, but Hendrick has made us a handsome offer for your services.

I looked up breathless and confused. An offer? But I was not a slave to be bought and sold! I won't go, I decided stubbornly, my head down.

—I will pay you two shillings instead of one . . .

I couldn't hide my surprise. I turned to Mistress Alya. She knew how much I loved the children. She knew if she sold me, she was also selling me to Master Hendrick as a concubine. She had done it as casually as she would call a dogcatcher to round up a stray dog. She, the great clean Calvinist Christian! I had served her faithfully. I was her favorite servant, she had said. Surely she wasn't going to send me away, the orphan she had sworn to shelter. Surely she wasn't giving me body and soul to Master Hendrick! I was her daughter, she had said.

—Once you're finished with my feet, Saartjie, Master Hendrick said lazily, you're to go to your room and pack up your things. We're leaving early tomorrow; I'll come and fetch your bundle.

I was still folding my clothes when the door to my cabin in back of the kitchen opened and Master Hendrick entered.

—I love you, Saartjie. Been eyeing you, I have. Seems you've got something under your skirts that's a wonder to see . . . a phenomenon . . .

In my mind I heard the rainmaker's words: *There is no medicine against a world not made up of human beings.*

Before I could reach the door, he was upon me. He caught both my wrists and held them with one iron fist. He took a cord from his pocket and bound them together while I kicked and screamed. Then he threw me on the bed and attached me to the bedposts. The children must have heard my screams. Everyone must have heard them. He took out a linen handkerchief I had ironed for him that morning and gagged me. Then he sighed deeply and sat down on the one chair in the cabin. He watched me squirm and plead with my eyes.

—Surprised you, didn't I? But you're really not surprised, are you? I saw the way you looked at me, nigger slut. You asked for this. You've been asking for this ever since I saw you. Ever since the first day you washed my feet . . . I love you, Saartjie. I swear I do. I'll be good to you. I've been told you Hottentot women have a jewel between your legs that can drive a man insane. Now, let's see . . .

Fear coiled inside me. What was he going to do? This man who had two testicles instead of one—What kind of man was this?

—Good God! What's this?

I tried to answer but I was gagged. Roughly, he pulled the handkerchief out of my mouth.

—My apron, I gasped.

—The Hottentot apron—I thought it was a legend, a myth like mermaids, he whispered. But you're real . . .

When he had finished, he straightened up, contrite, and untied my hands.

—Saartjie, I'll never do this again. Never, you have got to believe me. Forgive me. I didn't realize . . .

The sheet had wound around me. I gnawed at the edge of it. Yes, that's what all white men said: Forgive me because I didn't realize . . .

At breakfast, no one would meet my gaze. They had all heard my screams. Master Peter announced my departure to the children, who immediately began to cry and wail and cling to me. Mistress Alya stared stonily ahead, fingering the lace at her neck. My eyes met hers and they spoke volumes. They said, You are a woman like me, with a womb like me, and a child like my dead one. I was your daughter. I trusted you and you betrayed me. But Mistress Alya's eyes held only indifference, if not a mean satisfaction. She had done her best to keep me pure and clean and scrubbed. But I was polluted. I was filth now. Better to sweep it away, under the rug, out the door. What had I done to deserve this, I thought, except exist?

There was still another surprise.

—I've changed my mind, said Master Hendrick. You'll stay here, Saartjie, with Peter. I'll come and go. Life in the bush is no place for a woman. You'll be here when I return.

It was an order, not a statement.

The children quieted down when they realized I was staying. Clare was sucking her thumb again. Clean linen flapped on the clothesline. Karl and Erasmus played amongst the new washing waiting in the baskets to be hung out. I had already washed the sheet I had been raped in. It now was as white as snow. The rainmaker had been right. I felt it. I would never return to the banks of the Chamtoo River again.

I now lived in the same house with a new master, but the farm remained. Sometimes the light would dawn so thick that to spit into it was to have your saliva fly back into your face. I walked down to the river every morning to bathe a little before dawn and again at twilight, before the world awoke or after it was asleep. I realized why the Khoekhoe believed themselves the original rulers of the Cape. They had inherited Africa's light, so pure, so high, so clean, I thought, it must be the original light of creation the Dutch and English Christians worshiped.

I would wade out into the river, the indigo blue framing me, delineating my form and defining it in harmony with every other color and every other shape. Each day, I was reinvented according to the law of Africa. I rose at dawn and by nine, when I awakened the children, the house and everything in it that I was responsible for was scrubbed, cleaned and perfect.

Sometimes in the evening, before I bathed, I would walk amongst the cattle, corralled for slaughter or sale, and count horns, Khoekhoe style. Sometimes, I would trot a mile or two, softly pacing my steps, breathing in the thick liquid air by mouthfuls, my nose open and upturned. My hips and backside would not allow me to run, their size and weight acted like a piece of wood against a turning wheel. Yet I traveled lightly and quickly to the same spot in the river, where it widened until you could not see the other shore. There, thousands of pelicans nested, so close together their

54

bodies hid the earth and the earth seemed to undulate of its own accord. There, I would take out my gourd, fill it with river water, spill a little on the ground for the earth spirits and drink, taking little sips of indigo at the same time.

Sometimes on my way home, I would meet the purple heron, standing in the middle of my path, blocking my passage, demanding her right-of-way. It always frightened me no matter how many times it happened. And I would always dream of the meeting that night in bed. I would lie rigid on my narrow cot, thinking that it was almost four years since I had been expelled from the orphanage and condemned to the Caesar farm. It wouldn't kill me, I said to myself. But I knew in my heart I had exchanged one coffin for another and that I would never leave the prison of Cape Town. I would never leave the prison of the Caesar farm. I would never escape the slavery which was worse than prison and never ending against which I had no defense. Solitude stole over me like the deep blue of twilight, spreading its sadness.

5

Every organized individual forms an entire system of its own, all the parts of which mutually correspond and concur to produce a certain definite purpose by reciprocal reaction, or by combining towards the same end. Hence none of these separate parts can change their forms without a corresponding change in the other parts of the same animal, and consequently, each of those parts taken separately indicates all the other parts to which it has belonged.

—BARON GEORGES LÉOPOLD CUVIER,
*Discourse on the Revolutionary Upheavals
on the Surface of the Globe*

April 1809. I first heard of the Hottentot from her master, whom I met in a tavern in Cape Town the night I disembarked from the HMS *Mercury*. His name was Hendrick Caesar, a fact I didn't learn until the next morning.

I had ended up as his drinking partner at the Elephant Horn Tavern and I had told him that while I was ship's surgeon on the SS *Mayfair,* Lord Farington, painter to the Court of St. James, had painted three Hottentots that had been imported from the Cape. This enterprise, I explained, had been fascinating to the general public as well as the aristocracy. During the sittings, the cream of high society filed by—Lord

Darmouth, Lord Blagam, Lady Banks—not to mention the townfolk; they all came to see a Hottentot!

—Think what a sensation your servant would make in London, I exclaimed, she would be the first Hottentot to set foot there, I told him.

—And as, if you say, her shape is so extraordinary as to be absolutely *freakish*, well my friend, you would make a fortune . . .

Hendrick Caesar had only smiled into his glass of beer. I knew what he was thinking: that I was one of those new breeds of British gentlemen, white men, who roamed the British Empire searching for fortune and adventure. That I recognized neither moral nor physical limits. Blasé and cruel men like myself were basically bored and found England as small as a prison. We were aristocrats, second or third sons with no inheritance, with funny names, funny uniforms, bred to resist pain, hardship and alcohol. And he was right. Moreover he had no illusions about his own limitations. He was a provincial who had never traveled outside of the Transvaal. He had not been sent back home to school in Holland, but like his brother had been educated by clerics in South Africa. The idea of taking his Hottentot to London and exhibiting her was so outrageous he had burst out laughing.

—No, I repeated, you can make a fortune with this girl—Saartjie, your little Sarah, as you call her, enough to recoup your cattle and investment losses and send your two sons to Oxford . . .

—Well, I must say, this is the most amazing conversation . . .

—Look, I am a ship's surgeon; I've traveled all over Africa and India. I supplement my income by exporting museum specimens from South Africa. I've just prepared a shipment which includes a giant elephant tusk, a white rhinoceros, several great ape skulls, a dozen severed trophy heads and a giraffe hide that's sixteen feet long. Scientific exploration has exploded in the wake of colonial expansion. Scientists must conduct rigorous studies of everything that is new, rare, unusual, exotic, even monstrous in nature. Monsters, according to the great scientist Bacon, are more than a portent or a curiosity. Rather, they are one of the major divisions of nature: one, nature in course, two, nature wrought, and three, nature erring. That is, what is normal, what is artificial and what is monstrous. This last category, monsters, is the bridge between what is natural and what is artificial . . .

The Boer shook his head. He was having trouble following my discourse, but he was having a good time anyway.

57

—Have you ever heard of the Hottentot apron?

—Why yes, I replied, Levaillant described it in his *Travels*, but General Jensen claims it isn't true. Isn't it a legend?

—No, he said. It's no legend. I've seen one. Saartjie has one. But how could you exhibit that . . . he asked, shaking his head.

I sat up straighter. This was really getting interesting . . . Cannibals, Amazons, mermaids, freaks were my métier. It was what I searched for, wandered the globe for, bought and sold and bartered, dying of thirst for that one moment when I possessed the unique, the precious, the scientific. It was what I lived for.

—Well, why don't you come back to the farm with me and see for yourself?

And as morning broke, we started off for his brother's farm. The Boer was a taciturn man without much conversation and no imagination and he had not been able to get in a word edgewise since last night. I had not shut my mouth for the past sixteen hours, and he had hung on to every word. The voyages, the miraculous escapes, the explorations, the surgical operations, the wars, the women, the wonders of Scotland. What, I wondered, hadn't I talked about? I had certainly told him my life's story: I had been born Alexander William Dunlop of Saint James, Middlesex, Scotland, into an upper-class family of three sons. I had been educated at home, then sent to the University of Edinburgh to study medicine. I had joined the army as a surgeon, then resigned to enter the Royal Navy. I had served as a ship's surgeon, but as I had found the work both brutal and monotonous, I had set out to make the fortune I would never inherit from my father, since everything went to my elder brother, as an adventurer and explorer. From royal and mercantile vessels, my naval assignments darkened into pirate, slaving and smuggling expeditions. My scientific training had given me a taste for exploration and my travels had expanded to China, India, America and Africa. I spoke Dutch and English, Spanish and French, German, Chinese, Xhoe and several other African dialects. I knew I seemed to the Boer not only reckless but totally lacking in moral and physical restraint. Certainly I was courageous, but to what end? It was not that I was an evil or bad man, but rather that I placed no limits on what was acceptable as a means to an end. And my purpose was fame and fortune despite the fact that I seemed to do everything to prevent this happy state of affairs. Certainly I could have married well, with my genteel upbringing and title of doctor. Or I could have become a priest, rising in social standing through Jesus Christ, or I could have become a true hero: a scientific explorer, a privateer in His Majesty's navy, a functionary in the Home Office, even a foreign office spy in His Majesty's service. I seemed capable of just about anything; my charm, my smile, my dark good looks would have gotten me far had it not been for some fatal flaw that even I recognized. I was rotten to the core. I am sure the Boer decided to watch his purse strings around me and not to be influenced by my charm. Then, he forgot. In the end, the conversation returned to his Hottentot. I said nothing about a cage, but it was already in my mind . . . the setting, the cruelty, the drama . . .

—Well, the Boer had reasoned, I certainly don't think Saartjie would agree to go to London under any circumstances. She's a shepherdess. A simple, even simple-minded, nursemaid. How could she conceive the advantage of a trip to Europe or London? Or be shown to princes and kings? Besides, I don't think my sister-in-law would agree to part with her. She sets quite a store by her. She made me leave her at the farm instead of my taking her back with me to the reserve.

—Your sister-in-law? You, a Dutchman, not master of your own sister-in-law?

—No, he said. And we both burst into laughter.

We were still laughing when we arrived at the frontier of the Caesar farm the next day, as if we were the oldest and best of friends, although we had been perfect strangers twenty-four hours before.

—Maybe I ought to introduce myself, said Hendrick Caesar, repeating his name.

—Glad to meet you, Hendrick, my name is Dunlop, Alexander William Dunlop.

It was early evening of the same day before we actually reached the farm. I whistled at the size, breadth and beauty of it with its serene landscape of cattle grazing and wheat fields swaying.

—No reason to leave all this, I said.

—All mortgaged to the hilt, replied Caesar. They've already foreclosed on part of the land, beyond the ridge there.

As he spoke, I saw for the first time, his Hottentot servant come over the rise, barefoot, her gourd hanging at her waist, a bunch of wild poppies in her arms.

—Saartjie! Hey, Saartjie, come over here, I want you to meet my friend here, Mr. Dunlop.

The Boer had frowned. The Hottentot just stood there as if she were rooted to the ground, staring at me as if she had seen a ghost.

—Saartjie! I'm calling you!

—Yes, Master.

But she didn't move. Instead she crossed her feet and offered up her flowers to me.

—Welcome, Master Dunlop.

I edged my mount closer to where she was standing, and bending down, I accepted the homage as if it were the most natural thing in the world.

—Extraordinary, I murmured, my eyes sweeping over Saartjie's shape. Extraordinary . . .

That night after supper, which was elaborate and copious, the family retired to the salon and the Hottentot brought out the basin to wash the feet of the family. Since I was a guest, she uncovered, washed and dried my feet first. As she went on to attend to her mistress, I reached out and placed my hand on her backside.

—You have a gold mine here, Hendrick. You should profit from it. Steatopygia is a fascinating topic to Europeans. It is perfumed by sex, deformity, monstrosity and prostitution. Whatever is forbidden. And like yellow journalism, whatever is forbidden is big news. The exhibition of *lusus naturae* draws a healthy interest in London. Unusual and unnatural beings are in great vogue. The stranger the creature, the stronger the draw. After such a voluptuous end to such a fine supper, I can only compliment the lady of the house . . .

I rose then and in my bare feet padded over to Alya Caesar, kissed her hand and clicked my heels together. Since my feet were bare, this had the most hilarious effect. Everyone laughed. I endeared myself to Alya Caesar and Saartjie forgave me for touching her posterior.

Hendrick and I stayed smoking on the veranda after Alya, the children and her mother, who was visiting, retired for the night. The steward stayed to tend to our needs but I noticed Saartjie lingering in the salon to eavesdrop on our conversation. I obliged her.

—As I was saying, from 1800 to 1804 I took part in my first expedition of discovery, which was sponsored by the Paris Academy of Sciences. That's what started me collecting specimens during my travels. The new-style anatomists and doctors wanted real cadavers, skulls, body parts. They were tired of stealing them from cemeteries. One of my first assignments on our arrival at the Cape was to look for exact information on the so-called Hottentot apron. The singularity of this organ of generation was too piquant not to have excited the curiosity of most of the individuals attached to the *état-major* of my ship. I was assistant ship's surgeon and my friend L'Haridon, the ship's doctor, performed some very particular observations on the kind of orgasm that part could be susceptible to. The head of the expedition was Dr. Péron. In 1805, after making a sensation in London, he lectured on the subject at the Institute of France. Many drawings were made during that expedition, by Lesueur, Petit, Lebrun, Thibault, many of which have since disappeared. Imagine setting up another sitting for other observers to draw the fabulous Hottentot. The Academy would pay a pretty penny for that privilege. As I've said again and again, no female of that race has ever set foot on English soil . . .

—There has always been a rumor, I continued, that the Hottentots were hermaphrodites, but it was founded only on conjecture. Several gentlemen I know took it upon themselves to resolve the problem. They discovered that the women have a supergenital membrane that falls down beyond the lips of the vulva, nothing more. I shrugged.

—But one can see how this rumor started if the female Hottentot has an appendix outside the organs of generation and the men have eliminated one testicle . . . Between the two deformities, a mythological creature was bound to be born . . .

—Then they have this strange language that sounds terrible and no nation on earth can imitate. Thank goodness they are capable of learning Dutch and English. They have no laws and no religion—they worship the moon. They don't build or plant, and have no fixed place to live, transporting their tents and fixing them wherever they find grazing land for their cattle. They eat anything—roots, berries, entrails, raw meat, whether beast or human. If a woman has twins, one is eliminated so that the other profits from the breast, and when male children reach the age of twelve, one testicle is removed so that they can run better.

—Saartjie does have a strange language, which seems impossible to speak, said Hendrick.

—It *is* comprehensible, I said. It is one of the most complex languages in the world. Strange that it should be spoken by simpletons . . .

—Of course, I continued, Voltaire claimed they have no language at all, but this is not true. The language we speak of, Khoe, contains a set of implosive consonants, called clicks or clucks, which do not exist in the English phonological system. To further complicate things, not only do most of the words begin with a click consonant, but also the number and variety of these clicks are modified still further by vowel colorings and variations of tone and pronunciation that make it ten times more complicated than Chinese, which is possibly the world's most difficult language . . .

—Three of these consonants consist of these sounds—the noise made by the lips in lightly kissing, as when you kiss your hand; that made by smacking the tip of the tongue against the palate, as you do when tasting a flavor, or as some women do when they express petty vexation; and the clucking noise made with the back part of the tongue against the palate to urge a horse forward or to gather chickens; these are all very common. A vowel sound often repeated resembles the French *eu*, but uttered from the chest with the singsong drawl of a boy driving away birds . . . In fact, it seems that the Hottentots have two vowels more than European languages; one is expressed by the famous click of the tongue, and the other by a suction of air between the tongue and the palate. Yet, with a few of these clicks, a Khoekhoe chief can command two hundred warriors in battle, a rainmaker can cure an illness, two warring tribes can lay out a treaty . . .

—Tomorrow, ask Saartjie to repeat a phrase in her own language or give her a sentence to translate and you'll see exactly what I mean.

—How will we know if she's really saying what we ask her to if we can't understand her language?

—She looks honest. I trust her to tell the truth. She'd never lie— besides, I bet the children speak Khoe—just ask them . . .

Through all this, the Hottentot was standing behind the curtains, spying on us. I was sure she did speak Khoe to the children and that they answered her. But it was only a guess.

—I've been taught since I was a boy, interjected Caesar's voice as it wafted out onto the night, that the Hottentot is ruled by prostitution. Adultery has no meaning for them, nor does virginity. The poverty of their mental universe can be seen in the poverty of their language. For example, they have but one word for maiden, woman and wife. They are at the nadir of primitive lasciviousness. There is no difference between the Hottentot and the prostitute, so there is no moral deterrent to using one as the other . . .

—Even as a Christian gentleman?

—Even as a Christian gentleman.

—Should we not be saving these females instead of taking advantage of them?

—They are to all intents and purposes, unlike the prostitute, beyond redemption.

—Even your little Hottentot, Saartjie.

—Oh, no, no. Never, croaked Hendrick. I've never touched Saartjie. Nor would I allow anyone else to—she's family! My boys' nurse.

—You've never even peeked at this . . . apron of hers?

—No, he lied.

—Then how do you know it really exists?

—I don't know really . . . my wife says it does.

—Come now, Hendrick. There's no one out here but me, surely you were curious enough to . . . look . . .

—No.

—Well, would you allow me to examine her, as a medical doctor?

—No, Dunlop. I'm afraid not. Besides, she would never agree. She's extremely shy and has the modesty of a white woman.

—Actually it doesn't matter if it exists or not, as long as people believe it does. Do mermaids have tails? Does Cyclops have one eye? Is Isis a baboon? It's what people believe that counts.

I noticed a shift in one of the shadows projected onto the floor of the veranda. I smiled. Saartjie was not above spying on her masters or eavesdropping on their conversation like all good servants . . .

—After all, friend, I concluded, determined to shock the Hottentot, a cannibal is not necessarily ferocious. He eats his fellow creatures not because he hates them, but because he *likes* them . . .

The next day, at breakfast, Alya Caesar invited me to spend a few weeks at the farm with them while my ship was made ready. She had already opened and prepared the guesthouse for me and assigned me a servant. I would be so much more comfortable here than in a dirty noisy hotel in town, she insisted. To Hendrick Caesar's surprise, I accepted eagerly. It was like agreeing to live like a monk. There were no pretty tavern waitresses nor spectacular red-haired whores on the Caesar farm that I knew of. But I knew what I would do for entertainment.

For entertainment, I spied on Saartjie when she bathed. Eventually, she caught me at it. And forgave me. I proceeded to seduce her.

Listening to me, Saartjie would drop her head as if her ears had been opened to the voices of the world. She heard beyond the ramparts of Cape Town to the swell of waves breaking on the beach with monotonous and solemn vibrations, as if all the earth had been a tolling bell.

—And then, a ship's a ship and a voyage isn't marriage, I whispered.

—It is not a marriage contract, she whispered in return.

—I've never taken a false name and I've never told a lie to a woman (which was a lie).

The Hottentot's teeth chattered.

—You're cold.

I put my arms around her, wrapping her closely in her cotton *lappa*.

—Hold the ends together in front, I commanded.

—What did you come here for?

—To be . . . to be surprised, I replied, truthfully. I have been everywhere and done everything . . . Yet I remain alone, unattached to anything . . .

—Oh, but I am sorry for you—don't you have a home?

—Some such place as this? I'd kick it down around my ears!

—And where do you hope to die?

—In the bush somewhere; at sea, on a bloody mountaintop, at home? Yes! The world's my home. Anyplace is good enough as long as I've lived there. I've been everything you can think of, ship's surgeon, army doctor, soldier, anatomist, dentist, slave trader; I've sheared sheep, harpooned whales, rigged ships, prospected for gold, hunted wild game, collected fossil specimens, gambled in St. Petersburg, robbed tombs in Cairo, turned my back on more money than your master will ever see or you can imagine!

I overwhelmed Saartjie. She tried to pull herself together. I straightened up, away from the wall, and said:

—Time to go.

But I did not move. I leaned back and hummed a bar or two of the song I had been singing at dinner.

In the bay of St. Helena
Stands the island of St. Helena
Where surrounded by my comrades
I behold a strange lass with skin so black
Who fled in fright to see men so white . . .

I stopped, embarrassed, I had completely forgotten Saartjie's origins.

—It's a cruel song, about Hottentots, I ended, censoring the rest of the lyrics.

—It's the song of the gold prospectors, of the restless men who mine the riverbeds of the Hottentot country and the kingdom of Monomotapa for gold. During the dry season, they can find gold nuggets in the cracks of the dried riverbeds, like pearls . . . It's all desert: cracks in the earth making canyons that you can't see the bottom of; and mountains—sheer rocks standing up high like walls and church spires like the white cliffs at Dover, only a hundred times taller. The valleys are full of boulders and black stones and pyramids made by Ethiopians. There's not one blade of grass, one tree, one cactus to be seen. And the sunsets are redder there than anywhere else in the world, I said.

—Red?

—Blood red and mad as hell.

—You would rather stay there on land?

—Not in that country. It gives me the shivers sometimes. I look for specimens there, that's all—I have a gift for it and a fever . . . The animals, the desert stones, the skulls, the artifacts, sometimes even gold. But it is not for the gold or even the artifacts . . . it's the wandering about *looking* for things.

—The Khoekhoe have a word for men like you; they call you *Khoeku !gaesasiba ose*—men with no stillness . . . I bet no mistress can hold you.

—No longer than a week, yet I am fond of women—so many different ones: Chinese, African, European, Arab, so many different shapes and colors, skins and hips and bottoms, legs and feet and hair . . . Anything for a woman, a new woman or a woman of the right sort or a woman like I've never seen before—the scrapes they have gotten me into. I love them all. I love them at first sight. I've fallen in love with you already . . .

—Saartjie, little Sarah . . . I sighed. Yes, Saartjie, come here.

—I don't have a very pretty face.

—No matter. I don't take to faces very much . . . It's your . . . aura . . . your mystery. You are a rare specimen, unique. Worth a lot of money brought back to England . . .

I reached out, mesmerized despite myself.

—How about showing me your apron . . .

—I couldn't do that, Master. No, Master.

She was suddenly terrified. After all my words. She thought I only wanted to fuck her. I laughed angrily.

—I can simply take a look if I have a mind. Hendrick doesn't mind.

—No, she groaned, backing away. I'm a married woman.

—Married, are you?

—A widow.

—That's not the same as being married and you know it. You are a lone female and you're not a virgin. You need protection. What if I took you with me to England . . . You could make your fortune and stop being a slave.

—I'm not a slave.

—Well, what is this, I said, looking around the decrepit bare wooden cabin, Versailles?

—What?

—The governor's palace? I laughed, but this time good-naturedly.

She made a movement as if to escape, but stopped and raised her hands to her temples.

—You are making me crazy! Sometimes you treat me like a princess, then next like a slave, then like a whore! What am I? A woman or a thing-that-should-never-have-been-born?

—You are nothing but a vagabond, she added angrily.

—I'm a surgeon! And a damn good one. Nigger bitch. Come with me to England, where you're free to be anything you like. We'll make a fortune. Money. Gold. Understand? Freedom! Slavery was abolished in England three years ago!

I held up my hand mockingly.

—I swear if you are not famous in a month in London, I'll send you back home to the Cape.

—You will have to. I shall make you . . .

—Look who's talking . . .

—Yes, look who's talking . . .

Instinctively Saartjie drew in a deep breath and took a step towards me—then a step backwards, having crossed the line between master and servant.

—How long does it take to sail to London?

—About eight weeks.

She had not moved, but remained half turned away from me, with her head in her hands.

—My word, I continued with a wry smile on my lips.

—I have a great mind to . . .

Her elbows trembled as I clutched them in my fists.

—Escape, I concluded without a pause. You'd be a free woman . . .

Saartjie still hid her face in her hands. I drew her closer to me and took hold of her wrists gently. I breathed into her ear.

—Saartjie, do this for me . . .

I tried to uncover her face. She resisted. I let her go then, stepping back a little.

—I've already spoken to Hendrick. He'll sell you to me.

—I'm not his slave.

—He can sell you as an indentured servant. Think on it.

She nodded quickly, shamefaced, trembling with emotion. She bowed her head.

—Oh, go away, she murmured. Please, please, go away. There will be only trouble. You bring only trouble.

—Riches and perhaps trouble, I said, you females always give me trouble, I whispered softly. Never fear. I've never forgotten any of you.

I held out my hand and in the dim light Saartjie stared at the coin lying in my palm. It was a gold napoleon, more money than she had ever seen.

—You can't buy me. I'm not a slave.

—Who said anything about slavery? I'm talking about bride-price—that's a lot of cattle. I laughed. Since you say you are an orphan, to whom do I pay the bride-price?

—My father's sister.

—And where is she?

—In Namagua, I think.

—And how would I get this gold napoleon to her?

—I don't know, Master.

—Well then, I'll just have to keep it in the bank until we return, won't I? I smiled and winked at her as I dropped the coin back into my purse. Or shall I give it to you?

Saartjie shook her head dejectedly.

—I cannot sell myself . . . You can't buy me. I'm not for sale.

The next moment, I swept the Hottentot up in a powerful embrace. I kissed her face with an overmastering ardor as if to bury the very soul I claimed she didn't have. The kisses broke into the citadel of her loneliness. Her eyes were closed. She was mine. I turned and left her, abandoning my conquest. She gathered up her skirts and ran after me.

—Stop, she shouted. I'll go. I'll go.

I continued walking away from her, my fateful tread echoed malevolently upon the stones. Presently her voice grew fainter as though she, too, were turning into stone. I could feel the desperation that took hold of her at that moment. I was going, never to return! I would leave without her, forever. Leaving her to die in this godforsaken place. As if she were struggling in a dream, Saartjie called out my name in a final appeal.

—Master Dunlop! I'll go. I'll go . . . I promise, I follow.

The echo of my footsteps joined the faint sound of my triumphant laughter, mixed with the night sounds and the voices of restless crickets and wolves. There was no hint of human life in the desolate landscape. The Hottentot and I were totally alone in the world, solitary, lost in this fiendish, hopeless country where she possessed not even a footprint. And she was totally mine.

Inside the main house, Hendrick must have heard my laughter or her frightened cry. A window opened and into the silence her master spoke to her, over my head, high up in the black air.

—Saartjie, Saartjie, you come on in here and wash our feet. Tonight, be a good girl, we're taking you to London!

Hendrick couldn't believe how perfectly everything was turning out. I had solved all his problems. He would lease his preserve out for two years. His wife and children would come to live with his brother. He and I would take Saartjie to London, present her to the scientific world as the first female Hottentot ever to set foot in Great Britain. We would make a fortune off Saartjie's monstrous shape, which would be immortalized for all time . . .

Hendrick hated to admit the feeling of pleasure and excitement I had aroused in him. He had never been abroad—out of Africa. He was suddenly a different man. He was a man who was ten years younger. Visions of visiting Amsterdam and Rotterdam as well as London and Paris danced in his head. Heady meetings with famous doctors, newspaper interviews, introductions to society, all this I told him would be a natural consequence of our future voyage and our stupendous discovery. Hendrick wondered out loud why he hadn't thought of it himself long ago.

I took the Hottentot to Cape Town to petition the governor of the colony for her passport to England. Whenever she ventured into Cape Town, she wore a *chapur* so that her Hottentot origins would not be recognized. We rode into town together on two of Hendrick's best saddle horses. Saartjie rode silently beside me, looking like a child mounted on a huge black stallion. Yet she was calm. Grave. She controlled the animal, I noticed, surprisingly well.

The governor's house was in the center of town, a massive yellow and black brick building with a classical porch of white columns. To one side of the building were the Government House and the Central Bank. To the other side was the long, hard, sinister expanse of the colony's penitentiary, which looked like any other government building except that there were armed soldiers stationed every few yards, and a public whipping post.

A chain gang of slaves passed us as we dismounted. The men were dressed in striped cropped pantaloons. They were bare-chested and some carried the marks of terrible lashings on their backs, raised welts and crisscross scars that were sometimes white, sometimes dark brown or pomegranate red. Their heads were shaved and their gaunt, brutal faces were blank. Almost all were Hottentots. The chains sang, but the men didn't. They all seemed drowned in a kind of interior silence, deeper than mere absence of sound, the silence of death, as they stood dejected in the shadow of the penitentiary walls. I glanced at Saartjie, who had hurried away from them towards the entrance to the building. Even in her disguise Saartjie walked swiftly as if she had a destination. A Hottentot loitering in Cape Town was liable to be arrested. A Hottentot had better run to wherever the hell she was going.

I was received by Lord Calledon himself. Since the Cape was once again an English colony, he had very little to do on any given day. Reading dispatches, receiving important foreign visitors and issuing passports were major activities. These coupled with building a new opera house, giving lavish dinner parties and suppressing all Hottentot resistance was what the governorship of the newest British conquest consisted of. For this he had paid the Crown the lordly sum of fifty thousand pounds. As the British government's representative, he was not only responsible for suppressing the Hottentots, but was also appointed their official guardian, as they were considered too imbecilic to be allowed to look after themselves.

Lord Calledon and I held a fascinating conversation and spent an agreeable hour discussing everything from Verdi to James Madison before talk turned to the question of obtaining a passport for my partner, Hendrick Caesar, an Afrikaner, and the servant who would travel with us.

—And the name of his servant?

—Saartjie, that is, Sarah . . .

—Last name?

—Baartman. Sarah Baartman.

—She is appearing in person?

—Yes, she's just outside in the anteroom . . . If you'd like . . .

—No, no, that's not necessary. I need only to ascertain that she appeared in person to request her passport.

—Thank you.

—My pleasure, Dr. Dunlop. And have a safe passage home.

As we walked down the wide red-carpeted hall to the exit, I showed Saartjie her passport. She recognized the Crown's seal and reveled in the incredible beauty of the document with its black letters running across the page like, as she put it, !Naeheta Magahâs's painted bulls.

—It means you have free passage out of Africa.

—It means, said Saartjie, who was now Sarah, that I am free . . .

I felt a qualm but said only:

—Free as a bird.

—Can I keep it?

—Of course. A passport is personal property. Just don't lose it.

We left the horses tethered and wandered down to the wharf to look at our ship in harbor. It was the *Exeter* and in a few weeks it would take us to England's shores.

—I will call you Sarah from now on, I said, since that's the name on your passport.

—I never liked Saartjie. My real name is Ssehura.

—Ssehura, very pretty.

—Sarah Baartman is pretty too. You know, I have a secret. One day, last year, I came down to the wharves to look at the boats and saw you for the first time. You were standing at the hull of a tall dark green schooner with indigo sails. You had on a red and blue uniform. Your hair was longer than it is now, and you had some kind of brass instrument attached to your wrist.

—That's why I was so surprised to see you at the farm. It is as if all this is the rainmaker's prediction . . . she continued excitedly.

—Who's the rainmaker? I said. I knew what a rainmaker was.

—Why, !Naeheta Magahâs, the thing-that-should-never-have-been-born . . . It is like meeting the purple heron on the road, who looks after me . . . It's fate.

—You *saw* me? A year ago? My God. I remember that day. The ship was the *Asia* out of Madagascar. The instrument I held was a new telescope I was trying out. Fate, I said, it must be.

—Yes, *wigchelvooden,* said Sarah in Dutch.

6

In one word, it is necessary that we not be blinded by a single species of living matter, but compare them all to each other and pursue the life and the phenomenon of which all beings that have been endowed with a portion are composed. It is only at that price that we can hope to lift the veil of mystery that conceals the essence.

—Baron Georges Léopold Cuvier,
Thirty Lessons in Comparative Anatomy

*B*lack moon, the English month of May, 1810. I found myself standing on the deck of the HMS *Exeter* with a new name and a new passport. Sarah Baartman. I whispered it to myself as I leaned against the rails and watched the fortress of Cape Town become smaller and smaller. The ocean beckoned and I succumbed to dream of discovering what a world that had abolished slavery would be like. I had no one to say good-bye to. Everyone was dead. I had no one to explain to why I was making this voyage. If I explained it to another Khoekhoe, I would have had to say that I was traveling to Bakuba, a faraway land in the sky from which no Khoekhoe had ever returned.

According to Master Dunlop, this ship was a schooner of three masts and six hundred tons. It carried merchandise from Ceylon, Java, Sumatra and Zanzibar. The passengers were lodged on the main deck, which was portioned off into cabins and common rooms. We were more than twenty.

The white passengers on the HMS *Exeter* were not happy that there was a Hottentot amongst them. They complained bitterly to the captain that I should be in steerage with the other servants and Africans. As usual, Master Dunlop had an answer. I was desperately ill, under his care, on my way to London to seek aid from a renowned specialist. When the passengers then complained of a "diseased Negro" on board who could contaminate everyone, Master Dunlop invented still another story: I was a princess worth my weight in gold, certainly not suffering from a contagious disease. As royalty, I could not mingle with common folk, and so a special dining room was set up in my stateroom and I took my meals alone. It was still not clear to me how I had come to be upon this sailing ship moving swiftly across the waters of the Atlantic to London. I hadn't planned it this way. And Master Dunlop, had he paid my bride-price or had he not? Was I his wife or simply a kidnapped Khoekhoe, to be used to beget riches for two foolish white men? Whatever it was, I thought, it was *wigchelvooden*.

The passengers continued to snub me and we kept to ourselves. From time to time, Master Dunlop descended into the belly of the ship to check on his animals, his giraffe skin, his skulls and fossils. There were, I realized, people down there as well: servants and slaves and captured Africans belonging to the white passengers on deck.

In the evening, when everyone else had retired for the night, I emerged from my cabin to roam the upper deck, my *chapur* hiding my race and my figure just as it had in Cape Town. But nothing would replace those nights under a canopy of blinking stars, surrounding a crescent moon. It was the Black moon month, or May, and the constellations would fix themselves once again in the heavens, and milk and honey would flow back at the Chamboos. I spent my lonely watch counting the flying fish and the shooting stars and opening my nose to the sea winds. The Cape moved further and further away until I could no longer smell land. The stars became brighter and brighter as the haze that land produced lifted and I could see them clearly in a sky that met only the perfect mirror of the ocean. Imagine my surprise when I learned that Master Hendrick would accompany Master Dunlop and me to London as partner to Dunlop and manager of my person. I began to wonder who was paying our passage and underwriting the bills, but I didn't dare question either of them. I felt safe with Master Dunlop. He had promised. The gold coin in his palm was the guarantee.

The herd of white people who flocked on deck every morning dressed as if they were attending the governor's new opera house in Cape Town, those who refused my presence amongst them were of all sorts: English immigrants and Dutch refugees, students returning to school, merchants transporting goods, army officers, soldiers of fortune, women heading towards marriages, or sons to attend funerals, a good crowd of twenty whites who strolled the deck, played whist, fished, read books or engaged in long conversations that sometimes included dark looks in my direction if I ventured on deck. Sometimes, I ignored them, needing the walk and fresh air. Sometimes I appeared with Master Dunlop and Master Hendrick, following slightly behind them in a servant's mode. There were several black sailors on board with whom I passed the time, listening to their stories even though they were forbidden to mix with the passengers. Black servants didn't count, however, and they assumed I was a maidservant traveling with my masters. They taught me much about the ship and took me down into its entrails, with its cranks and screws and chains and gears, its ropes and sailcloths, cannons and kitchens. They also taught me a lot about white people I didn't know.

I took happily to the sea, found it thrilling and never experienced seasickness. I kept to my room, venturing into company only with my masters and once entertaining the passengers with a song on my guitar.

The days passed one after the other. We were more than ten days out of Cape Town when one evening, having slipped away from my cabin after my lonely supper, I met Master Dunlop.

—You like ships, I see, he said, catching me unawares.

—Yes, I like the closeness of the sky, I said. I like the speed, like riding on the back of a whale, slicing the waters that open up before it like grass. It's those, I pointed upwards, indigo sails, that I have never seen spread like that, like the wings of a bird, like clouds . . . The Khoekhoe don't have sails . . . We have only canoes for fishing.

—I know how you feel, I too love the sea, where everything is possible, where every path lies open before your very eyes, there . . . Just over the horizon, whatever your heart desires. The sea was made for dreamers. Or perhaps dreamers were made for the sea . . .

—Why doesn't this ship get lost in all this? How does it know where it's going? It follows the sun?

—It follows the stars and constellations.

—Which are always changing.

—No, *you* change, Sarah, the stars remain fixed.

—I would like to change.

—So would I.

Master Dunlop turned his back against the railings and leaned back, peering down at me. Stars, like the eyes of a staring crowd, surrounded him like a glittering curtain blinking as if alive, as mysterious as Master Dunlop's soul.

—You look like a spirit, all covered up in that white *chapur.*

—Perhaps I should go scare some of the other passengers . . . Booooooo, and I lifted my arms in the air.

—Do you know what an odyssey is?

—No.

—Well, an odyssey is a long voyage by sea in which you search for something, a person, a treasure, redemption, revenge . . . And along the way you suffer many trials and tribulations and dangers and you almost die and you fall ill, and you are rescued, and you fall in love and you do battle with monsters . . . And in the end . . .

—And in the end?

—In the end you return home, to the point of departure, and nothing is changed and no one even knows you've been gone because no one is waiting for you.

—No one waits for me. Does someone wait for you?

—No.

—That's sad.

—It's just a story a poet made up . . . The world's first hero—or the world's first fool, he said.

—The hero, what was his name?

—Ulysses.

—The Khoekhoe worship a hero like that, his name is Wounded Knee.

—Wounded Knee, he repeated.

After that, he left Master Hendrick and me to our own devices. He seemed more silent, thinner, more fragile than when he was on land, as if the sea brought out some inner anguish.

—Head winds day after day, he murmured. Won't we ever get a decent slant on this passage?

As the days passed, an atmosphere of oppressive quietude settled upon the ship. Every passenger suddenly seemed to close himself up in a sullen cocoon. Very little was said. As if by common consent, human speech was abandoned to the greatness of the sea and each passenger was prisoner of his own private thoughts. For me, those thoughts were of a mysterious and unimagined future that lay just beyond the line of the horizon. The ship seemed to carry the burden of a million lives, it groaned, it creaked, it heaved, it rolled, it rumbled and breathed with the souls of past passengers. And shouldn't it be so? The black sailors had told me that more than once in her long life, the HMS *Exeter* had been a ship fitted out for slaving along the Guinean coast. I had looked up at her masts towering towards the sky, immense and indestructible, her sails wrapped, sheltering splendid trangressions, skimming proudly over a graveyard of sins. We were approaching the Cape of Storms, famous for testing the greatest ships with its horror, and its bravest sailors with its terribleness. I turned and lifted my face. I smelled rain. Low and distant thunder carried itself on the air too, and we seemed to be traveling towards it.

A strong wind swept by and I felt the uneasiness of the ship beneath my feet. A single burst of lightning quivered in the sky as if it flashed into the vault of Magahâs's cave, illuminating it. Then wind and rain came stampeding across the dark mass of the sea, chasing the ship like the thousand cattle of Magahâs's secret chamber. Lightning now struck at will, as if it had especially chosen us for its target. The wind howled. Furious gales attacked the ship like personal enemies. Rain descended, beating like drums on the deck and rails, and the storm took us over one by one as if it wanted to rout out the screaming terrified infant in every one of us. Drenched on deck, I listened to the storm's voice.

—Want to leave the Cape of Storms? it seemed to say.

—We'll see about that. You would like your life back? You will have to get past me. For I rule here, not white men. The sea is mine and no man, white or black, can outrun me or outstare me . . . just try it . . .

The HMS *Exeter* seemed to stand at attention, magnificent and immobile on the waves, contemplating what the storm had just told her, then she dipped sickeningly deep into a tree-high wave that struck it like a palm striking a drum and made the old ship groan and cry out. There were faint cries also from the frightened passengers. We were alone in the immensity of the ocean. In the middle of nowhere. Ten days or more from the Cape. The birds had left. The swaying masts infested with squirming men riding up and down them, bent like reeds before the wind. The ship's wake, long and white and straight, trailed to the west as if we were going backwards. The sun was gone like the birds, disappeared beneath the heavy rain clouds. The squall, coming from behind, finally caught the ship and dissolved itself in a deluge of hissing, drumming, stupendous rain. The heavens opened up its entrails and rained down all the piss of God. It left the deck glistening clean and the sails darkened. I shivered in delight. Was this happiness I asked myself? The ship began to race before the storm, trying to outrun the white-capped waves, urged on by the shouts and worried whispers of the sailors as they ran back and forth moving things and tying down ropes and affixing everything on deck. Then came the horror.

Master Dunlop came out on deck, calling me by name.

—Sarah, Sarah, for God's sake! I've been looking everywhere for you. Get into the common room with the others! This is a real hurricane!

The pale green eyes held fear. But I was happy. I was indifferent to the storm as if a great burden had been lifted from my shoulders. I had steeled myself against the worst and found my fate so fascinating that I felt an overwhelming dislike for Master Dunlop, who wanted to take me away.

I heard Master Dunlop crying into my ear, but the wind got between us, suddenly I was hanging on to him like the weight of a stone and the sides of our heads knocked together.

—Sarah, Sarah, you're going to drown! Get in there!

But my heart had been corrupted by the storm and I rebelled against leaving it. I would not obey any order except the mysterious craving for its fury I had found in my soul.

Master Dunlop pulled and half dragged me below, bellowing orders to sailors at the same time that he shoved me into the crowded room. The white passengers looked up, cowering in various corners, some had slight wounds where they had bumped against the furniture or hit their head against a beam. There was not a greeting amongst them. They spoke not a word to me and moved away from my person. Many turned their backs, trying to look unconcerned; others, with averted eyes, sent half-reluctant glances out of the corners of their eyes. One or two stared at me frankly, but stupidly with their mouths open in indignation. They resembled thieves caught in the act. They didn't want a Hottentot to share even their own destruction. They'd rather I be anywhere else, safe and dry, than amongst them partaking their fate. I, for one, was convinced we were all going to our watery graves together.

Outside, the full force of the storm struck the ship. The decks had become too dangerous. Dazed and dismayed, sailors as well as passengers, except for Master Dunlop and the captain, had now taken shelter under the bridge, which was pitch dark and flooded. At each rise of the ship, we would all groan together in the blackness, and outside, tons of water smashed against the belly of the whale. The passengers were as safe as they could be, but they did nothing except grumble, complain peevishly or scream in terror like sick children. They pleaded for light, for air, because all the hatches were battened down. They cried for their mothers and vomited. The odor of urine and shit pervaded the air. No one could see his neighbor, so that we were all equal, all black, all smelling the same, all speaking the same common language of terror; we cried and screamed, shouted and prayed, or were silent. Since we were all part of the same blackness, I thought, did this mean that I no longer had a color? In this miserable hull, in this black hole, was I at last a person? Or was there something even in blindness that exiled me from humanity? I could hear the storm plainly. Its howls and shrieks seemed to take on a human sound of rage and pain. I felt like crying, not out of fright, although I was frightened, but out of sympathy for the storm's pain. The whistles, clicks, howls of the wind mixed with terrible bumps and shattering thumps that rattled my ear as if sea monsters beneath us had risen from the depths and were demanding entrance. The monsters knocked and knocked on the hull, either begging to be let in or commanding the sniveling, whining, screaming passengers to shut up. The ship rolled on its side and a great collective groan pierced the darkness as we thrashed from side to side, sliding against the wet, slippery walls of our coffin. Suddenly, our cries ceased as if we had obeyed the monsters of the deep. The wind died down. There was the sound of water seeping through the portholes and hatches. There was water up to our knees. My skirts pulled me down. We were sinking.

A trance fell over everyone like a numbness of the spirit. The bodily fatigue of holding on to existence had pierced the hearts of all of us within the tumult of the struggle. It was a cold, penetrating fatigue brought on by the suspense of expectations of catastrophe, and it struck deep in that space where the soul was supposed to reside. In a second the waters would wash over us and it would all be over. I felt Master Hendrick's heavy arm across my shoulder. I was wet and cold and stiff in every limb, swift visions of my former life passed before my eyes: my father corralling cattle, my mother's laugh, the pull of !Kung nursing at my breast, a sword or was it a rifle reflecting the sun . . . and then, nothing.

The darkness was suddenly pierced by a radiant beam of light. The hatch was unlocked and the head of Master Dunlop appeared in its halo.

—It's over! he shouted into the darkness. We're taking on water, so you must come up before you drown. But we can make it to St. Helena for repair!

There was only stunned silence from below as we raised our faces to the light. We were saved.

A blank rocky wall blocked the horizon, which in the distance appeared totally without trees, shrubs or even grass. I could not detect the smallest dot of a bird in the vastness of the sky overhead and the rocky islet lay on the sea like a loaf of bread floating on the naked line of the horizon. The black formation resembled a huge castle, its height towering to the low clouds, the cliffs leaning over the ocean. Their sides rose higher than Table Mountain, above the level of the sea. They looked like the ridge of a saddle with the pommel to the north, and as we approached nearer, the dark, somber mass of rock lifted like a forbidding hand. It was impossible to imagine anything more menacing or uninviting; as if the underworld monster who had so chastised us at sea had risen up out of the depths to frighten us once again.

This was St. Helena, Master Dunlop told me, the last piece of Africa, the only thing that stood between us and England. The wounded ship, half adrift, two masts broken, sails tattered from the winds, a hole in the keel, made for the dark reefs, sending out a tender to announce our arrival and a God Save Our Souls because we would have to be towed into the harbor. The sailors told me that notice had to be given to the governor of the island before we could pass the battery of cannons and reach safety. Nevertheless we managed to salute the fort with the one cannon that had not been jettisoned overboard, and when the fort returned our salute, the terrible echo was truly grand. On a distant height stood the citadel high above the sea. Just under the summit was a cave and a small beach where the passengers of the HMS *Exeter* finally reached dry land.

The frightened, exhausted white people limped onto the beach of the fortress. They were saved, they all cried as they set their feet on solid earth. Was this, I thought, part of Master Dunlop's odyssey? This detour back to Khoekhoe land? This island had always been ours, and the small group of whites who inhabited the island were far outnumbered by the Khoekhoe. I imagined this was how the first group of white men had arrived at the Cape of Good Hope: cold, forlorn, starving and afraid. We had lost all of our supplies and reserve of water in the storm. But the captain had saved the cargo. Master Dunlop's giraffe skin was safe. So was I. Master Dunlop had taken charge of the weary passengers while the captain and the ship's doctor had gone to the governor's mansion escorted by soldiers. Soon there would be more soldiers and food and clothing, but for the moment, we all stood huddled together on a white beach, surrounded by mountains, ravines and forest that seemed to have been created yesterday. To the west, I could see the square stone tower of the lookout, but on the other three sides, there was only ocean, thick jungle, dark volcanoes and swept sky.

Even in catastrophe, I was still ostracized by the white passengers. I stood apart from them and contemplated the mystery of this island. This was the last soil that could be called Africa. This was the last Khoekhoe territory in the world. Why, I thought, were the English occupying a fortress and a harbor when the People of the People outnumbered the garrison by hundreds. Why, I wondered, hadn't the Khoekhoe driven the English and the Dutch into the sea? The island was owned by the Dutch East India Company and everyone on the island either worked for or was a slave to the company. A few Hottentots still herded, but most were captives alongside those from Goa, Malaya and Madagascar. In the beginning, the Khoekhoe had inhabited all the land, but with the arrival of the Portuguese, the French and the English, any land which was worth preserving had been snatched from their hands.

From the only landing place, the road ran along the foot of a perpendicular cliff from the pier to the Government House and over a draw-bridge past a battery of heavy guns. There, through an alley of trees, was the reinforced gateway, which led to St. James Valley. Near the opening, between the two mountains, was the valley, which divided the island. The left side of the island was clothed in woodlands and greenery to the very summit of the rise. By contrast, on the right side was the wild nakedness of harsh rock, desert and boulder. The beauty of one half and the horror of the other astonished everyone that took this road. The history of the island was clear from where we stood, it had erupted from the depths of the sea, forced up by the underworld fires of volcanoes. It was as if the Reverend Freehouseland's Garden of Eden existed side by side with the reverend's vision of hell. The soldiers came to escort the passengers by mule and horseback through the rift of the valley, where we passed the barren, treeless rise of volcanic rock on one side and a paradise of flower-ing trees, shrubs, waterfalls, green pastures, woodlands and flora on the other. This great divide, like many things in nature, had no explanation, said Master Dunlop, just as night and day or black and white didn't.

All this time, Master Dunlop had been a changed man, never com-plaining once. Treating injured passengers and sailors, laying up medi-cines, organizing and comforting as if he were the ship's surgeon. In fact, there existed a ship's doctor for the HMS *Exeter,* a Mr. Harley with whom he played *trente-et-un.* But the passengers had faith only in Master Dun-lop. After the storm, I had once again become a maid of all work to the sickened and weak women passengers. Suddenly, reinstated as a servant, I was again greeted with friendly smiles, polite demands, easy first-name intimacy, as if now that the world had been turned upside down by the storm, and then right side up, everything had fallen back into place.

The ship was towed into the harbor under the direction of the captain and put in repairs, which would last, if all went well, ten days. The cap-tain was anxious to get under way. He had saved most of his precious cargo, although all the exotic wood was waterlogged. There were several fleets anchored at the fort, and a multitude of small vessels. All the pas-sengers from the HMS *Exeter* were housed in the town and Masters Dunlop and Caesar took lodgings in a rented house near the town square. Just as the captain fretted about his expensive cargo, so Master Dunlop fretted about his giraffe skin and his Hottentot while he spent most of his time with the governor. St. Helena, however, was deemed safe enough and secure enough to allow me to ramble around the island escorted by the sailors from the HMS *Exeter*. It was in this way I discovered the paradise of Fairyland and amused myself by picking watercress in the early morning in a place called Lemon Valley. The midshipmen of different ships met and fraternized together there, sometimes having long arguments about some point of politics or history, sometimes ending in a boxing match. Fairyland on the south side of the island consisted of softly rolling green pastures and woodlands out of which rose columns of smooth grayish rock that appeared to be sculpted by an invisible hand. From the top, the view descended in splendid ridges of wildflowers, waterfalls, ravines and eminences to the sea. The beauty and grandeur of Fairyland amazed and astonished me. One day I took Master Dunlop to see this wonder of nature. He rewarded me by singing the same strange ballad he had once begun to sing to me on the farm. He sang it in an astonishing deep and beautiful voice that gave me chills:

> *In the bay of St. Helena*
> *Stands the island of St. Helena*
> *Where surrounded by my comrades*
> *I behold a strange lass with skin so black*
> *Who fled in fright to see men so white*
> *She couldn't speak our tongue*
> *Nor we that of her tribe*
> *She was more ferocious than*
> *The horrible Polyphème*
> *As naked and black as twilight—*
> *Unavowed by God, soulless it's true*
> *A death sentence justified*
> *A Cyclops for Ulysses—*
> *We returned to our fleet*
> *Informed of the abject perfidy*
> *Of the obnoxious designs*
> *Of this bestial, cruel and perverse people—*
> *Hottentots.*

He spit out the last terrible word, "Hottentots," with a kind of glee as if he were happy to wound me.

—But that's what I am, a Hottentot, I protested.

—Yes, that is indeed what you are, and soon all London will know it—you'll be famous and so will I for discovering you.

One night we went to the sandy beach of the island to spy on the spawning giant turtles who crawled ashore during the night to lay their eggs on the beach. We watched them come out of the sea, many at a time, to deposit two, three thousand eggs in the sand and then return once more into the ocean. At dawn the sun hatched the eggs and small gray newborn creatures pitifully and desperately made their way out of them, crawling on their bellies towards the sea while flocks of seagulls and eagle hawks swooped down on them, breaking their shells, tearing at their flesh, as orphans they struggled to return to the deep. The beach was strewn with carcasses and the broken shells of baby turtles eaten by birds of prey.

—Look how majestic! The mystery of evolution! he said. This is nature in action, the survival of those who are most fit to survive.

—It's horrible. Mother turtles who abandon their young on the beach to die.

—Don't humans do the same, after all? Don't mothers bring their children into a world to become cannon fodder in wars, fought over beaches like this one? Do they have a choice really? he sighed.

—The question is do the turtles *know* they are acting in this cruel manner by leaving their young to die? Have they *chosen* this despicable act or do they really believe their progeny will make it back into the sea and live? Or is it some instinct, some great hand that pushes them to do what they do despite themselves? Even knowing it is wrong? And *is* it wrong? What is murder exactly? The strong will make it to the sea, or at least some of the strongest; those that crawl faster; that break their shells first; some that even crawl over their fellow turtles—just like men do. A few of the thousands will survive to mate and produce more turtles, who will in turn abandon their young on this same beach. Why do you think the mothers lay so many eggs? Because she knows most of them are doomed. Would it be, for example, more human to make her *choose* which ones? To force her to *decide* between this egg and that egg, who would live and who would die? Do the larva of this earth, our own species, mankind, have this power of decision? No? Then, why should a turtle have it? So our turtle leaves all of them on the beach to let the laws of nature decide . . . And once in the sea, do they know where to go? Or do they go blindly in search of their progenitors? Or do they accept their fate—that they are completely alone in the world, that they have been spawned not by mothers, but by monsters.

—Why do you show me such a fearful thing?

—It isn't so horrible—there are a lot of things more horrible. There's a terrible beauty in this struggle for life.

—Is this law of nature you speak of your so-called God? Jehovah?

—I don't know that nature and God are the same thing.

—I don't believe in God, I said, I believe in the turtle.

—I don't believe in either God *or* the turtle, replied my master.

—In what do you believe?

—I am a man of science. I believe in objective truth. I believe in dispassionate reason.

—What does dispassionate mean?

—Hard. Cruel. Without mercy. And without recourse.

—Are you like that?

—Yes.

We sat side by side in silence, the terrible scene before us. We remained for many hours like that, without exchanging a word. That night was a night of felicity. I made love to Master Dunlop, my future husband, Khoekhoe style, in the manner of the goddess after whom I was shaped. I reached down into my entrails and brought forth ecstasy. My master was astounded, amazed, happy and humbled.

In this funky world of contrasts, of paradise and hell, it seems that no one had ever left this island without permission, according to the ship's Negro cook, Fletcher. It was a gigantic penitentiary, set in the middle of the Atlantic Ocean. According to legend, only two escapes had ever been successful: one in 1693 by a band of mutineers, and another in 1799 by an American artillery sergeant and five foot soldiers, who had been sentenced to hang. St. Helena, added Fletcher, was the only spot in the British Empire from which, or to which, an expedition could sail with the certainty of keeping its destination secret. We were four hundred leagues from the coast of Africa, he said, and a thousand from England. It would take us another eight weeks to arrive at our destination.

Whatever the island enjoyed beyond air, water and watercresses, had to be brought from elsewhere said Cook Fletcher. But the garrison had everything we needed to replace our supplies: mutton and beef from the Cape, water, figs, oranges, lemons, pumpkins, pomegranates, apples and pears from the island, teas, sugar candy, nankeens, Indian silks, pepper, spices, muslin handkerchiefs, longcloths, ginghams from the warehouses of the Company, as well as flour, pease, oatmeal and pork. The rich provisions brought by North Americans, who exchanged them for stores from the East without having to make the long perilous journey to India and China, were all in the hands of the merchants, who in turn sold them to the South Americans. Water was really the only thing the island offered for free. And turtle was the only fresh meat.

And so, in several weeks, we were repaired, dry and provisioned. We set sail once again, leaving the garrison, the fort, the pasturelands, the majestic mountains and a population of two thousand souls, not counting the soldiers, behind us, other fleets arriving to take our place as we set sail. We left behind both the part of St. Helena which was paradise and the part of St. Helena that was hell.

After our shipwreck, everyone on board the HMS *Exeter* seemed more human, more generous, more kindly with one another. Our feelings of a common humanity, and the fragility of life we had so recently been reminded of, made us better people and better passengers. The whites no longer snubbed me, but spoke to me civilly for the rest of the voyage. Master Dunlop was more excited than ever, having survived many storms at sea. Master Hendrick took to saying his prayers even more fervently and to drinking even more whiskey but with more joy. The captain, who had navigated us through our ordeal, was deemed a hero. So was Master Dunlop, who had played such a heroic role in the face of danger and disaster. Even Fletcher and the sailors were less rough one with the other, grateful that no man had been crushed or swept overboard in the wake of the storm.

For nearly eight weeks, we sailed into the northern Atlantic winds with calm seas and good weather, reaching Dover on Shit moon, the English month of September 10. Dover's tall cliffs were the same as those of St. Helena, except that St. Helena's were black and Dover's were white. And the white salt canyons divided my life in two as surely as St. Helena was divided into desert and green pastures. Everything changed, as if the story of my life was just beginning. I never spoke another word of Khoekhoe. What was a person without her mother tongue? Only my *lores* talisman's fine grains of sand spoke in Khoekhoe. The cliffs, as we sailed by, closed behind us like a lid and a bottom clasping. I could not bear to look back. Hidden behind those great white walls were my dead baby, my dead husband, my dead mother, my dead father, the dead Hottentots who had starved in Namaqualand. The colors of home disappeared and everything became the color of African dust.

I put my hopes in Master Dunlop. Hadn't he saved us all in the storm? Wasn't he a doctor, a hero, a rainmaker? What did I have to fear? I was a free woman in a free country with a bride-price of one gold napoleon.

On the day we docked, I took my English clothes from the trunk: a white dress with a scarlet sash with long mutton sleeves and a high neck, a straw bonnet with a scarlet veil that matched my sash, red kid gloves, red leather boots and a red parasol. I dressed carefully in my white women's clothes. I went up on deck and stood amongst the other excited passengers. The giant schooner was towed through the locks of the great river by miniature canoes far below us. According to Master Dunlop, this was the Thames River which flowed directly through London Town. When I stepped off the ship, I was surrounded by more white people than I had ever imagined existed in the world: as many as there was elephant grass on an endless plain; bodies and faces, not one of them like mine.

Part II

London, England, 1810

Slave, I before reasoned with you but you have proved yourself unworthy of my condescension. Remember that I have power; you believe yourself miserable, but I can make you so wretched that the light of day will be hateful to you. You are my creator, but I am your master.

—MARY SHELLEY,
Frankenstein

7

SIRE,

The brain is at the same time the last station of sensible impression and the receptacle of images that memory and imagination bestow upon the spirit. Acknowledging that relation is the material manifestation of the soul . . .

—BARON GEORGES LÉOPOLD CUVIER,
Letter to the Emperor Napoleon
on the progress of science since 1789

Shit moon, the English month of September, 1810. I created a sensation on the wharf, in the customs house, in the open horse-drawn carriage we took to London piled with luggage covered with Master Dunlop's giraffe skin. In the lobby of the hotel on Duke Street off St. James's Square, ladies' and gentlemen's mouths dropped open as I excitedly exclaimed in Dutch and my few words of English over the beauty of London and the Londoners themselves.

Dazed, I marveled at the flocks of pigeons, the noise and rumble of hundreds of carriages, the porte-chaises, the horse-drawn carts, the wagons pulled by bullocks and the new horse-drawn omnibuses. I clapped my hands over the wide magnificent boulevards that led directly to important public buildings and sumptuous palaces. My master told me that one single noble, the Duke of York, owned almost half the real estate in London. The income from the duke's properties, he said, was greater than the King's. Squares and circles, parks, fountains, mews, crescents abounded along with streets lined with shops and boutiques selling every possible item of luxury or necessity: hats, wigs, shirts, frocks, pictures and furniture. Around every corner were tailors, dressmakers, shoemakers, apothecaries, restaurants, pubs and coffee shops, arcades, open markets. London Town was full of trees, parks, gardens, zoos and flowering lanes. Yet it was still dust-colored compared to the Cape. I would suddenly come face-to-face with the magnificent cathedral of St. Paul's, the houses of Parliament, Westminster Bridge or the Bank of England. My heart would beat wildly as I gazed upwards at the famous Tower of London dungeon on the Thames river.

There were plenty of amusements in the city: opera houses, theaters, circuses, gaming houses and casinos, puppet shows and dance halls, Chinese shadow plays, opium dens, and fairs of every kind. More importantly for us, there were dozens and dozens of public exhibition halls, none more prestigious or beautiful than that of the Liverpool Museum at 22 Piccadilly, known as Egyptian Hall, owned by the illustrous William Bullock.

Egyptian Hall was the most fashionable place of amusement in London. Since the first month of its existence less than a year ago, twenty-two thousand spectators had walked through its doors, explained my master. More than eighty thousand Englishmen had set eyes on Master Bullock's thirty-five-foot-long boa constrictor, his seven-foot-tall North American brown bear, the albino alligator from the Congo and fifteen thousand birds. The official name for the great collector's brand-new building was the Liverpool or London Museum, but everybody in London called it Egyptian Hall because of the building which housed it. Ever since Napoleon's invasion of Egypt and his scientific expedition, he said, the English had been obsessed with everything Egyptian. Bullock had surpassed himself by having his builder create a perfect replica of the great temple of Hathor at Dendera.

Master Dunlop, who had had previous dealings with Master Bullock, was elated. This time, he boasted, he had two curiosities in hand, a rare and beautiful giraffe skin of more than eighteen feet in length and a genuine female Hottentot.

A few days after our arrival, we drove up to the imposing museum facing Piccadilly, which outshown all the buildings on the square. The front was covered with blue granite stone into which Egyptian pictures and writings had been carved which covered its entire surface, out of which stepped two sphinxes and two giant nude statues. Master Bullock was no ordinary member of the London amusement trade, I was told. He was a traveler and a naturalist and a member of several learned societies. He had started out by buying rare specimens from the captains and crews of sailing ships for his own amusement, which is how Master Dunlop met him and how Master Bullock had begun his own cabinet of curiosities. Many of his specimens had come from Master Cook's voyages to the South Pacific and Master Barrow's expeditions to Africa, he said.

The masters passed through the ornate doors into the interior while I waited outside in a closed, shiny maroon carriage parked at the curb.

I sat rigid and straight against the dark blue velvet plush of the vehicle in my white women's clothes, the veil of my hat pulled down over my face. Suddenly I saw three men emerge from the doorway hurriedly. They approached, Master Dunlop leading the trio, his arms waving as he carried on a heated conversation with the third man. I half listened to them arguing as they entered the carriage. For over an hour, I had studied the stone front of Egyptian Hall, marveling at its size and richness—my eyes taking in everything, darting from the building to the street, to the crowds of quick-stepping passersby. I remained silent as the three large men jammed themselves into the carriage. I guessed that the man I didn't know was the famous William Bullock, come to look me over. I didn't smile. I couldn't, I was too petrified. I merely threw him a sullen glance and remained speechless.

—She speaks only her own language, my master insisted. Saartjie, this is Mr. Bullock.

—Happy to meet you. I said finally.

Master Bullock was as startled as if he had heard one of his stuffed specimens speak.

—I thought you said she spoke only her own language. She speaks the King's English.

—Only a few words, said Master Dunlop, cursing his own stupidity under his breath.

—Mr. Bullock, may I present Sarah Baartman.

The men soon got down to business. They told Master Bullock that I was a South African prize straight from England's newly conquered colony that would go down a storm in London, much more astounding than the most exotic of his animals. Master Bullock listened carefully, his high forehead with its sparse chestnut hair carefully combed over his baldness caught the sharp light that filtered through the venetian blinds of the carriage. Master Dunlop was leaning forward intently, waiting for Master Bullock's reaction.

Master Bullock's eyes undressed me as he spoke, his lips pursed into what might have been a smile. He bounced up and down, shaking the carriage.

—Well, since she has this monstrous arse which is an attribute of Venus—Kalipygos, meaning *belle fesse,* beautiful behind, lovely arse, splendid rump, whatever—wouldn't it be fitting to call your specimen Venus? The Hottentot Venus? How's that?

—It's brilliant! It's perfect: Kalipygos, beamed Dunlop. I like it. The Hottentot Venus!

He gesticulated with his hands, making an imaginary frame with his long narrow hands.

—Yes, added Master Hendrick. It has a ring to it . . .

—And it is certainly perversely descriptive, added Master Bullock dryly.

But even as he enjoyed his birthday-song naming, I knew he wasn't convinced. He kept asking if I was a slave. Besides, he continued, he exhibited stuffed animals, not humans. Where did I belong in the chain of evolution? Was I truly a *lusus naturae,* a freak of nature, or just an ordinary lower rung of humanity? Certainly he had heard of the legendary Hottentot apron. It had been described by Levaillant and Barrow, he said. Yet Master Bullock was tempted. He knew his audience, he said.

—The English are a nation of starers, he stated. The Cape Colony we have just wrested from the Dutch represents the unknown, the darkest, the most exotic reaches of Africa. The public would want to domesticate anything that emerged from such a savage place to ensure that the wilderness, and the savages within were now *theirs, their* territory, *their* savages. Decidedly, he added, the people of London would adore her . . .

But Master Bullock looked uncomfortable, even ill. He looked like he was going to throw up.

—This carriage is the jungle, he said suddenly. I need some air, he complained. He opened the door of the carriage, and jumped out insisting that the rest of the conversation take place on the sidewalk not in front of me. But I peeked out at the men and heard them arguing on the pavement from behind the curtained window, pulling the lace back with my gloved hand, my feathered hat bobbing up and down as I tried to get a better look.

I could see that Master Bullock was shaking and his paleness had turned scarlet.

—I cannot in good conscience exhibit a live human being in an animal museum no matter how . . . extraordinary. But I will purchase the giraffe skin. I'll give you one hundred guineas for it . . . but not Miss Baartman . . .

—The Hottentot Venus, interrupted Master Hendrick. That's her name now.

—Yes, well, the Hottentot Venus then, sighed Master Bullock, wishing to escape.

I realized Master Dunlop had failed. He was never going to get Master Bullock to exhibit me. After all his promises.

—That's your final word, sir?

—That's my final word, gentlemen. I don't think it's correct or proper. I can buy the hide of your giraffe, sir, but not the hide of your Venus. I don't think the English will react positively to such a show, after all. If you'll come back inside, we can complete the transaction for the giraffe. I know, however, several men in the London amusement trade who may be able to accommodate you.

—In two years, you would have made a fortune exhibiting her to the public, whined Master Hendrick to no avail. It only annoyed Master Bullock.

—If you'll excuse me, Mr. Caesar . . . Good day.

Master Bullock turned and walked back inside the museum with Dunlop trailing after him, leaving Master Hendrick standing on the sidewalk, blocking the quick flow of London pedestrians as well as my view.

Having followed the heated sidewalk discussion, I realized something had gone wrong. Master Hendrick was standing with his hands on his hips, looking like he did when he had failed to break a bull. When Master Dunlop finally returned, he was too red-faced and furious. Both got back into the carriage.

—I don't see why we should share the profits of our discovery with a showman when we can rent a hall and do it ourselves. There's space, according to an acquaintance of mine, at 225 Piccadilly Circus. We have a name, we have a slogan. To hell with Mr. Bullock, said Master Dunlop.

—What name? I asked softly in Dutch.

—I'll tell you, said Master Hendrick, when we get back to Duke Street.

—Why the Hottentot Venus, of course, laughed Master Dunlop. The name Mr. Bullock gave you in the carriage. You are the one, the only, African Venus! You like that?

—What's a Venus?

—A beautiful arse, according to Mr. Bullock, a beautiful arse.

—Venus is a Greek goddess. She is worshiped as a symbol of love and beauty . . . by white people.

I adjusted my veil without speaking. I was not happy. We had been in London only a few days. But my masters were already at odds with each other on how to present me to London society. Master Dunlop wanted to advertise me first to the scientific community as the first genuine Hottentot ever to be seen on English soil.

—We ought to go to the Explorers Club and to the Academy of Natural Science and get testimonials, he said. We need proof that she is the first Hottentot female ever to set foot here.

—And have the surprise of her appearance usurped by a bunch of scientists and lords who will take her over and leave us at the back door of their private clubs? asked Master Hendrick.

—At least one letter from an anatomist at the College of Medicine as a bona fides for the public. Lovejoy, for example.

—I thought you were our bona fides, Alex, with your diploma from the College of Surgeons and all your connections to London's scientific world. Saartjie, I mean the Venus, must be sold on her surprise value— Africa on Bond Street, not some academic description by Lord Paterson or anyone else. Have you seen how ordinary people stare at her? She's a phenomenon . . . Most Londoners have never even seen a black before— why, she can't even ride out in a carriage or cross the street without stopping traffic!

Just then, something frightened the horses and the carriage lurched forward, throwing us all against each other, as if we were back on the ship. We continued towards home in silence, each one lost in his own thoughts.

8

SIRE,

In a living body, each part has its individual and distinct composition: none of its molecules remain stable: everything comes and goes successively; life is a continual whirlwind of which the direction, as complicated as it is, remains constant as much as the type of molecule that is engendered remains constant, but not the individual molecules themselves; on the contrary, the actual living matter will soon be no more, yet it is the driving force that will constrain future matter to function in the same manner over and over again . . .

—BARON GEORGES LÉOPOLD CUVIER,
Letter to the Emperor Napoleon
on the progress of science since 1789

Shit moon, the English month of September, 1810. It was Master Hendrick who found the exhibition space for me at 225 Piccadilly, right across the street from Master Bullock's Museum. It was a cavernous skylit hall that accommodated dozens of exhibits, each competing for the shillings of the public. These were the showcases for the English and Irish freaks who worked the London amusement circuit. As in a village square, open or closed boxes were available to any impresario or self-managed attraction on the way up or down that could pay the deposit on the rent. The exhibitions ranged from pictures to the morbid thrilling of freaks, and monsters.

—I was counting on being able to get more backing in London from other showmen . . . I've invested all I had getting her here. I'm broke.

—You have the one hundred guineas you got from the sale of the giraffe skin, replied Master Hendrick, annoyed.

—I need that money. I'm not going to let you squander it on rent and publicity when we have no guaranteed box office receipts.

—Well, we won't get any receipts if we don't advertise. All the letters I sent off to the Royal Academy of Science, the British Medical Society, the anatomists . . . got no reply! As for guarantees, you're the one who guaranteed me a fortune in return for my investing in half of her with you—what's made you change your mind?

—I haven't changed my mind.

—The hell you haven't. We wouldn't be here except for you and your promises. You should have known the Slavery Ordinance of 1803 would get us in trouble with the law.

—Sarah's not a slave. She's a free colored.

—Nevertheless, it does change the situation.

—I've got to send the giraffe money to my wife.

—Your what?

—My wife. I'm married and she's found me.

—You bugger! Saartjie thinks you're going to marry her! She says you two made a marriage contract—a contract in which you promised to wed her when we got to England!

—Well, I had to promise her that to get her on the boat!

—She says the money she earns is her dowry to you, you son of a bitch!

—You think I'd really marry that monster! Go native with that freak? You can have her, Hendrick—I'll sell you my share in her.

—She'll never agree to exhibit herself without you. She loves you.

—Yes she will. I'll convince her. Besides, if I do a disappearing act, she'll have no choice if she ever wants to go home . . .

—You fucking pig, you bloody bastard! Why didn't you at least tell me this before! I'm your bloody fucking partner!

—Because I don't trust you, bloody fucking partner! I don't trust anyone. If you've been before the mast as long as I was—seen and done the things I've seen and done, been a ship's surgeon on a goddamned slaver . . . you wouldn't trust anyone either. Been at sea as a privateer too—in His Majesty's fucking navy—There is *nothing* in this world that could get me to trust you or anyone else, especially a woman . . . Go find her another husband—it's all the same to her anyway. She doesn't love me—a Hottentot is ruled by prostitution. Morality has no meaning for them, nor does virginity or marriage. The poverty of their mental universe is so great they have only *one* word for virgin, woman and wife!

—It's true, continued Master Dunlop, they make marriage contracts and I made one with her. But there's no difference between a Hottentot wife and a Hottentot prostitute that a white man is bound to respect.

—You've seduced her, you shit!

—I've never touched Sarah until St. Helena! That's more than you can say . . .

—Liar!—

—I *never* forced Sarah! She seduced me on that island! She's a monster of sex and provocation, an insatiable siren! A heartless, shameless savage . . . a superstitious man-eating, dirt-eating heathen . . .

—Is there no moral deterrent at all in your character, Dunlop?

—None at all. There is no difference between a Hottentot and a prostitute, so there is no moral deterrent to using one as the other.

—We are not prostituting her, we're exhibiting her.

—For money.

—For money? Isn't she doing it for money too?

—To recuperate her rightful inheritance, she says.

—Shouldn't we be saving this female instead of exploiting her?

—Saving her? Come on, Hendrick, to all intents and purposes, she is, unlike the prostitute, beyond redemption.

—You, a Christian?

—You can talk of being a Christian after what we've done? Saartjie Baartman got me back to London . . . where I belong and where I intend to stay—here or somewhere in The Midlands. Never to return to the sea or the Cape again. Or anywhere near that wretched bloody heathen continent called Africa . . .

—How much?

—How much what?

—How much for her?

—I'll sell you my share of her for two hundred guineas. Since we are Christian gentlemen who honor their obligations in business dealings.

—What should I tell Saartjie?

—Tell her I'm dead. Tell her I got in a brawl in Covent Garden last night and got myself stabbed and my family claimed the body—Tell her I've gone back to sea—Tell her anything you want. Tell her I loved her to the end. That her name was on my lips when I expired. Good Lord, man. Use the imagination God gave you!

This was all happening behind the closed front door of the flat we occupied on Duke Street in St. James Square.

I had just come home from shopping and was about to turn my key in the lock. I heard everything from behind the closed door, then I turned the key, pretending I had just arrived home.

Master Dunlop was pacing up and down the room, limping, holding his knee as if he were wounded.

—You know what? You know that Hottentot men have only one stone? The other, the left testicle, is removed from baby boys by their mothers. You know that? It's barbaric. It's as bad as eating flesh!

—I'll give you five hundred guineas for her, not a penny more.

—Then I'll bloody sell her to somebody else!

—Sell who? I said, sick to my stomach.

Startled, both men turned towards me.

I had taken to riding out in a closed carriage in the late afternoon to explore the streets and shops of London. Sometimes I would stop the carriage and walk amongst the pedestrians, trying to memorize the English name of every possible acquisition in London. As in Cape Town, I went out heavily veiled or with a deep wide bonnet that hid my features. I was fascinated by the splendid shops, which had become my only pastime. Veiled and gloved, hatted and dressed in white women's clothes, as I had been that first day, I spent hours strolling down Oxford Street. I would step into a watchmaker's cabinet, then a shop selling fans and silk, then one of china and glass. There were spirit booths with their crystal flasks of every shape and form, each one lighted from behind, which made the different-colored spirits sparkle. Behind the new plate-glass windows were the confectioners, bakers, fruiterers, chocolatiers and their pyramids of pineapples, figs, grapes and oranges. Most of all I loved the Argand lamps made of crystal, lacquer, silver, brass. Behind the great pane glass of windows lay slippers and shoes, dolls, boots, guns, glasses, beautiful dress material hung in folds to imitate real dresses. I would turn down Charles

Street to Soho Square to look at Wedgwood displayed in cabinets along the walls and on large tables as if a dinner party was about to begin. Salesmen moved around between sculpted columns that rose from polished floors. There were over a hundred and fifty shops in Oxford Street alone. The English, it was said, were a nation of shopkeepers. I had heard Master Dunlop himself quoting the Emperor Napoleon. I loved to ride past prisons that looked like castles, banks that looked like temples, exhibition halls that looked like pyramids . . .

There was a shop that I had fallen in love with at the corner of Bond and Jermyn Streets called the Charming Hand. It was a French glover, whose stock of gloves and fans was the best in London. I laughed as my hands slid into the soft contours of kid or silk as if I had plunged my hands into a crock of paint. These sheaths fascinated and enthralled me. My hands could not only be a hundred different colors, but a dozen different textures; the softest scented kid, gossamer black lace, wool, silk, smooth satin, cotton, crochet. My fingers could be decorated with seed, pearls, embroidery, fur, beads, flowers or bows. There were wrist length and elbow length, arm length and fingerless. The shop smelled of scented, tanned leather and watered silk, and not even the astounded glances of clients or salesladies could keep me away. I spent hours trying on pair after pair. I came so often that both the owner and the clients got used to my extraordinary appearance and treated me just like any other customer. In less than six months, I had bought a hundred pairs of gloves. My favorite color was scarlet chamois, then indigo blue, deep and magnificent, then saffron yellow kid, then embroidered silver, gold, or pale pink roses, or hand-painted with delicate scenes of forests and woods. I possessed gloves decorated with feathers or pearls, or knitted in bright colored wool or cotton. When the shop ran out of samples, I invented my own made-to-order designs. The shop owner's curiosity was satisfied only when he learned that Miss Baartman was the famous Hottentot Venus.

Sometimes a black gentlemen or black beggar or turbaned servant would pass me on the street. Several times I tried to follow them for a few steps, hoping I could speak to them in a language they could understand, but they usually ignored me or walked faster than I could, or disappeared into a waiting vehicle or behind an iron gate. I had learned the words for everything from kid gloves to chocolate, Beefeater gin to cashmere. It had taken me only one day to learn to count in shillings and pounds and to recognize the different coins and banknotes.

The unhappy subject of my masters' recent conversation put down her packages and looked from one to the other.

—What's wrong, I said in Afrikaans.

—Nothing. Huh, well, Alex here must return to the Cape, said Master Hendrick.

—It's nothing, Sarah. I'll be back in a few months. I promise . . .

I sat down slowly, because my knees would not hold me up.

—But the . . . show.

—. . . Will open without me, said Master Dunlop. It's you they want— Hendrick has found a hall; we are printing up the advertisements and tickets. Everything will go on as planned. I'll return as soon as I can, but this is a matter of life and death . . .

—Life and death, who . . . ?

—It has nothing to do with you or even the Cape. It is an old affair come home to roost.

Master Hendrick looked at him in disgust.

—But I . . . we need you. You must stay, I insisted, terrified.

—You are in very good hands. Everything has turned out as I promised, hasn't it? We will all make a fortune, and when I return we'll all spend it!

I was confounded. Master Dunlop was my rock, my anchor, my safety. Without him, I believed, nothing would be accomplished in London, yet he had been talking about selling me back to Master Hendrick.

—Sarah, we'll talk about it later, after I've packed and sent my trunks to the ship. I'm sorry, truly sorry, but it can't be helped . . . it's only temporary.

He looked helplessly at me, then at Master Hendrick, who glared back at him with contempt.

—I'm going out. I have several appointments. You two discuss your business and leave me to make the final arrangements for the hall . . . Somebody has to . . .

Master Caesar left Master Dunlop and me in the crowded disorderly room. I had refused to do any housework upon setting foot on English soil and discovering that there were white maids to clean up after me. I had also stopped washing Master Hendrick's and Master Dunlop's feet.

—I won't let you go.

—You can't stop me, Sarah. I've . . . I've got to get away . . .

—But your promise!

—Promises can wait . . . I'll be back . . .

—When?

—I don't know.

—At least explain . . .

—I don't explain to niggers—

When Master Hendrick returned, Master Dunlop and his trunks were gone. I was sobbing quietly in a corner. The room was dark, as no candles had been lit. My new clothes and purchases were scattered everywhere. I was quite naked except for the *lappa* draped around my waist.

—I'm lost, I said in Afrikaans.

—No. All's not lost. We will manage without him . . . Until he comes back, of course.

I pretended to believe him. I knew only that I loved Master Dunlop as I had loved the Reverend Freehouseland—with the passionate single-minded trust of a nine-year-old.

But I wondered if it wouldn't have been better for everyone if I had never overheard their conversation and he had just told me Master Dunlop was dead . . .

Every class of people from dukes to sweepers mingled in a stampede of movement and noise at 225 Piccadilly, which proudly advertised a show for every taste and every class. People dressed in their Sunday best came to gawk at a living male child with four hands, four arms, four legs, four feet and one torso born in Manchester, a pair of Bohemian sisters joined at the pelvis, a Welsh female dwarf, forty-four years old and thirty-six inches high, a bearded woman, German Lilliputians and of course a fat lady. There were piano players, singers, a strong man and the "Wonderful Fistic-Stone-Breaker" who could lift five hundred pounds with his teeth. There were clairvoyants, tarot readers, fortune-tellers and an exhibit of the royal Ashanti golden stool, captured by the British during their African campaign of 1809.

I was sure I had passed the frontier of the real world into the thing-that-should-never-have-been-born land as Master Hendrick escorted me through the maze of stands, platforms, tents, pagodas and stalls, each with a pitchman hawking his wares to the jeers, cheers, whistles and simple exclamation of the crowd. Any day would find a certain measure of princesses, dukes and earls, actors, servants and clerks, merchants, tailors and bankers. Each exhibition had its price, from a penny to several shillings. The fat lady was seven feet tall and weighed six hundred pounds. At the other end of the scale was Mademoiselle Camancini, the Sicilian fairy who weighed twelve pounds, was thirty inches in height with feet hardly three inches long and a waist of eleven and a quarter inches around.

The tiny mortal, whispered Master Hendrick, had received more than two hundred visitors at three shillings apiece last Thursday and the editor of the *Literary Gazette* had fallen abjectly in love with her. But all I saw was another thing-that-should-never-have-been-born with a wracking cough, a voice like the whine of a baby lamb and haunted eyes.

—There is a rumor, he continued, that Mam'selle is not French at all, but Irish, but even so, such a minute form sustaining the function of life, is sufficiently astonishing . . .

I turned my head to look at a beautiful tall Englishwoman with pale eyelashes and red blond hair wearing the latest gossamer clinging high-waisted dress with a heavy fringed cashmere stole thrown over her shoulder. Instead of a bonnet, she had on a high turban held by a rhinestone clasp holding an ostrich feather. She stared back at me curiously, immobile, tapping her parasol.

—Her manager, Dr. Gilligan, continued Master Hendrick, is a doctor who lives in our same hotel with his wife and mother-in-law. He takes care of the fairy on her travels and pays attention to her health. He's taking . . . Are you listening, Saartjie? He's taking her on tour to Liverpool, Birmingham, Oxford and Manchester—with her family's consent, of course. They live in Dublin.

At the mention of Manchester, I grew pensive. Would I ever see Manchester and the grave of the Reverend Freehouseland? Would I ever recover the ten pounds I had been robbed of? My inheritance?

—The Royal College of Surgeons have offered, if any misfortune should occur to cause the child's death, to give him or the family five hundred pounds for her remains for the purpose of dissection and the use of her remains for science—but wait until we open! We'll charge more. She costs two shillings and an extra shilling if you want to pick her up or fondle her. Look, here it is, we've arrived.

At the very end of the hall stood a wide alcove festooned with red curtains just under a high square window. Inside, there was a platform about three feet off the ground. The floor was wooden and sprinkled with sawdust. Directly behind the back curtain was a small windowless dressing room and a door leading to the communal courtyard outside. It was called the courtyard of miracles because all the circus attractions gathered there to eat, smoke and talk.

—This is our stand, Sarah, bought and paid for. The handbills are being printed now and the posters painted. I have ordered exotic plants and palms and a map of Africa in relief. Over the alcove will be written in bold letters, "The Venus Hottentot, the first of her race ever to set foot on English soil!"

Master Hendrick went on excitedly but I myself was strangely subdued and silent.

—Couldn't we wait until Master Dunlop is returned? I asked.

—Goodness no! And waste all that rent! No, no. I'm doing everything the way Alex had planned it down to the merest detail—You shall wear, for the sake of decency, a silk mousseline sheath so formfitting and so exactly matched to your own color it will be like a second skin. Your leggings and moccasins, your jewelry and pearls, your apron and the leather mask to hide part of your face as you requested, are all ready. We open this Monday without fail.

—Why do you think he hasn't written all this time or sent word that he is safely arrived?

—Why, Saartjie, didn't I tell you? I got a letter from him yesterday. I'll read it to you when we get home.

I was elated. He had not abandoned me. Back on Duke Street, Master Hendrick took out a piece of paper, began to read the letter from Master Alexander to me:

My dear Sarah,
Please, don't worry. Everything is going exactly as I have planned and I have had some success although I may have to stay away longer than I had planned. I regret not to be there for your triumph, but I am sure Hendrick has everything under control.
When I return, we will plan a traveling show to see England, which

is much more than just London. Country folk have never seen such a spectacle and several businessmen have made inquiries for bringing you to their factories in the north of England.

Don't eat too much chocolate nor imbibe too much gin. Be home soon.

My precious one, lovingly.

Alexander Dunlop.

I listened quietly to the words of Master Alexander. For the first time in my life, I wished that I could read them for myself. But I was decided. I would obey him and I would wait for him. My dream of freedom, fortune, a new way of life was not in vain. I determined not to be a dog-in-the-wind, but to stick to my goal. All this I silently promised myself. I would be somebody one day and the haughty English who despised me and had conquered my country, would pay gold to see the original landlords of the Cape in the flesh. The insignificance of my former life, my former slavery, my poverty would be washed away. I would invent a new existence that mattered, become a real person, able to exhibit my true nature. I would be recognized as a human being with dignity and power over my destiny. I began to believe this growing sensation of strength, of purpose, of having the last laugh—anxiety had disappeared with Master Alexander's reassuring words and the fact that he would be coming back soon.

Master Hendrick drew a satisfied breath of relief, as if to say there was so much to do and so little time, he didn't need a revolt from me just now. There were the two-shilling admission tickets, the letters to the Academy of Science and the Royal College of Physicians . . . He cursed Master Alexander for leaving him in the lurch and with all the risk! He would regret it someday, he swore. He changed his shirt and cravat before leaving to deliver the throwaways and check the text of the advertisements he had placed in every London newspaper. When he left, I nervously braided feathers for my apron. It was Shit moon, I thought, the month the Khoekhoe gorged themselves on fresh goat's milk—four months since I had left the Cape.

Morning Post,
THURSDAY, SEPTEMBER 20, 1810

The Hottentot Venus has just arrived. She can be viewed between one o'clock and five o'clock in the afternoon at number 225 Piccadilly. She comes directly from the banks of the Chamtoo River, at the frontier of the Cape Colony. She is one of the most PERFECT specimens of this race. Thanks to this extraordinary phenomenon of nature, the PUBLIC will have the occasion to judge to what extent she surpasses all the descriptives of historians concerning this tribe. She is dressed in the costume of her country with the ornaments usually worn by her people.

She has been examined by the outstanding intelligentsia of this city. Every one of them has been astonished by the sight of such a marvelous specimen of the human race. She has been brought to this country by Hendrick Caesar and their appearance will be brief, beginning Monday next, September 24, the tariff being two shillings per person.

When the curtain drew back for the first time and I walked onto the wooden stage and became the silent, unmoving, unblinking object of the audience's gaze, the silence was like a cannibal's mouth. My skin burned as if I were standing in a circle of fire or the glare of the morning sun on Table Mountain. I was more than Africa for them, I was a thing-that-should-never-have-been-born. I was everything they, thank God, were not. I wore a leather mask which hid half my face, as if the entire vision of me was too monstrous to contemplate. It was my idea. I thought to hide my shame. The mask stopped the audience's gaze cold, leaving them floundering naked like hooked fish on the edge of a great mystery while it cloaked me, who was truly naked, within a veil of even greater mystery. I was a sold-out, sensational success from the start. In a few days, I was famous all over London. Crowds flocked to see me. So many visitors crowded into the small stall that the police had to be called to control the flow. In the first week, Master Hendrick took in five hundred pounds. Songs, poems, penny posters, cartoons and newspaper articles soon abounded. My master couldn't believe his eyes or his good fortune.

—Step right up, ladies and gentlemen, gentlemen and ladies, he would cry, for the thrill of a lifetime. Just arrived from darkest Africa, the true, the only, missing link of evolution, ladies and gentlemen, the Hottentot Venus, never before seen in fair England, a most perfect specimen of that race of humankind. Discovered in the newest English colony of the Cape of Good Hope, at the tip of southern Africa. Nubile, twenty-one years old, female, a true phenomenon of nature, the virgin Eve risen from the Garden of Creation to the first, primitive level of humanity.

Step right up, ladies and gentlemen, examine the legendary Hottentot apron, her amazing hinder parts that are truly unique. Absolutely no fakery, only freakery here! *(Laughter)* Guaranteed authentic by the Royal Academy of Science! This shepherdess has lived amongst the most savage animals of the forests as one of them. She is real. She is unique. Her race is protected by His Majesty King George's government as a scientific wonder as well as for its imbecility. Step right up, please, and behold the African Eve—the wonder of the Cape of Good Hope. She can be viewed for only two shillings per person. Two shillings only for a look at the female wonder of this century and the Hottentot apron. Limited engagement. Step up now!

From the first, I was astonished by the viciousness and the voracity of my audience. On the very first night, hundreds of people dressed to the nines pushed and elbowed the crowd, craning their already long necks, winking and chewing tobacco, shouting and waving, stomping and clapping, cheering and hurling epithets. My head swam, understanding nothing of the English cries and shouts the audience hurled at me. I appeared on the stage raised about three feet from the floor at one end. Then, at a cue from Master Hendrick, I walked forward, my body covered in a tight sheath of flesh-colored silk mousseline, and paced the length of the runway, my sighs and anxious glances at Master Hendrick turning into real sullenness if I was ordered to smile, or to play my guitar, or to sing or to jump or run or look this way . . . or that. Master Hendrick would invite the spectators to examine me to assure themselves nothing was fake. Some of them accepted the invitation by touching my backside or searching for evidence of padding. One pinched me, another walked around me, a gentleman poked me with his cane, a lady used her parasol to ascertain that all was "natural." Master Hendrick sometimes used a long piece of bamboo to prod me around or move me forward or backwards. But worst of all, the laughter—raucous, lewd, predatory, and hate-filled—never stopped. It erupted at the slightest excuse, a stumbling foot, a tear, an epithet from a spectator, the shrill whistles and catcalls of the gallery.

I spied the same white woman I had seen on my first visit to 53. She was very tall and very narrow and dressed all in black as if she hated the frivolous colors of the current fashions, all those greens, pinks and lavenders . . . Black, at any rate, suited her. It went with her long pale face and beautiful gray eyes that were cool, and I imagined her hand on my brow would have been like the touch of ostrich feathers. Her gaze would have quieted a reckless fever. She was with another woman and I despised her because beholding me, her eyes had filled with tears, reminding me I was still human . . .

The "Hottentot Venus" soon eclipsed the other exhibits. Master Hendrick took in more than five hundred pounds the month of Speckled Ear, October. That, he exclaimed, was more than six thousand pounds a year. Crowds began to arrive clutching the penny posters that had begun to circulate or the newspaper caricatures asking for autographs, which Master Hendrick would sign "Venus" with the date or on which I would make my mark. I thought of the taunting boys of Cape Town, white farmers running amok with their horses and whips, the English soldiers with their rifles and bayonets. These people gaping at me were the same—the same race that had murdered my mother and beheaded my father with the same mindless cruelty, the same unyielding desire to devour and destroy. Yet they loved me. Sometimes I would whisper the ancient Khoekhoe incantation for the dead, "I am here for the pain. I am here for the desperation my pain brings me . . ."

Then Master Hendrick added the bamboo cage. It was eight feet by twelve feet and five feet high so that I could hardly stand up in it.

—It's only show business, he said.

I accepted my fate.

From my cage, the crowds gazing up at me seemed to bay and bray like my father's herds of longhorn cattle. They milled around, pushing and shoving, barking with laughter and ridicule. The top hats of the men and the pointed plumed turbans of the women bobbed and weaved like points of ivory elephant tusks. Why had I not expected all this laughter and ridicule? I needed no understanding of English to feel the hatred of the crowd, their derision and contempt. My heart pounded, my chest contracted with rage and hot flashes of humiliation flushed my face and stomach. Yet I bore it all, for hadn't I myself chosen it? How could I have imagined that white people could be any different in their own country than they were in mine? But I had promised Master Alexander to wait. Now that the money was flowing into our coffers, my dowry was assured. The pain, the humiliation was a small price to pay. After all, no Khoekhoe would ever see me or know I had disgraced the ancestors in this revolting way, with this revolting mob.

Often I would fall into a trance and hear neither the crowd nor my master's voice. Sometimes I used my *dagga* pipe to produce the same effect. The French had another word for the *dagga* I smoked: they called it cannabis . . . On those wild days when I dreamed, I dreamed of Africa, not as I know it to be now, but as it had been in the ancient time of the Khoekhoe, almost as if I had lived another life back then, almost as if I belonged back there then, not here now. I didn't mind the cage then. It became my home. I had gambled and lost and this was the price I paid: the eternal hyena laugh of the world.

Master Hendrick was overwhelmed by London's acceptance of his "Hottentot Venus." He had been searching his whole life to make a killing, he told me, and now he was famous as the impresario of "Venus." The other showmen fraternized with him; he received invitations either with or without me to prestigious salons and galleries.

Famous people began to seek me out. The Duke of York paid a visit. He was addicted to freak shows and attended dozens during the year. The whole of London society and English aristocracy followed in his wake . . . including several royal princes and princesses. One evening, the famous actor John Kemble visited me backstage after witnessing the inhuman baiting I had endured with sullen indifference. I was hardened now to all provocation. My eyes were blank. My lips fixed. My hands clutched. Master Kemble paused at the door of my tiny dressing room, his eyes fixed upon me, advancing slowly towards me without speaking. As he gazed at me, his underlip dropped for a moment, his famously handsome face suddenly underwent a sea change and softened almost to tears, rendering his masculine beauty even more apparent.

—Poor, poor creature, he uttered at length in his baritone actor's voice. Very, very extraordinary indeed. He then took my hand in his, keeping his eyes on me. Almost without thinking, I spoke a few lines of Khoekhoe softly.

—*Sats ke !gâi Khoeba îsa Khoeba!*

—What does she say, sir? asked Kemble, turning to my master at the sound of this incantation. Does she call me papa?

—No, answered Master Caesar. She says you are a fine and beautiful man.

—Upon my word, replied Master Kemble in surprise, taking a pinch of snuff from his silver snuffbox, suspending it between his finger and thumb. Upon my word, the lady does me infinite honor.

I whispered something to Master Caesar, who nodded and left the room to return with a small pouch covered with beads.

—Venus would like to present you with some of her African *dagga* . . . as a gift and souvenir.

—Upon my word, Madame, thank you . . . I shall cherish this moment.

—Sir, if you would care to touch her . . .

—No, no, poor creature, no! I daresay she is ill used enough, this poor female, without that. She's not an inanimate thing to touch and paw. No, this is one of the most melancholy sights I have ever beheld, yes, melancholy.

Master Kemble stalked out of the enclosure; as he turned to his companion, another actor, named Henry Taylor, I heard him say:

—Good God, how very shocking. What brutes and thieves are the public . . . the same that pay to see me . . . recite Shakespeare . . .

9

There are a multitude of intermediary movements of
which we have no notion. How many combinations, dis-
sections, have taken place in that interval? How many
affinities have been brought to bear? And who would be
the physiologist who would dare to venture any conjectures about the innumerable operations that take place in
that impenetrable laboratory? Being that human chem-
istry, despite the happy efforts of our contemporaries is
still in its infancy when we compare it to that of nature.

—BARON GEORGES LÉOPOLD CUVIER,
Thirty Lessons in Comparative Anatomy

*O*ctober 1810. I looked up at the sign hanging over the entrance of 225
Piccadilly. In large elaborate gold letters, it read "Hottentot Venus." I
made my way into the darkened interior, striding almost a head above the
milling, agitated crowd, my walking stick opening up a passageway
through the spectators at the competing stands. Barkers and animal trainers pleaded for my two or three shillings, proposing every deformity, accident of birth, human degradation, eccentric skill and degenerative
disease on earth for the delectation of the English public. I passed by the
stands of Caroline, the Sicilian princess, Anna, the albino, and a dwarf
named Captain Lambert. Onstage, a giant struck a pose and John Ran-

dian, the torso man, lit himself a cigar. Irritated and not a little apprehensive, with my walking stick I struck off a filthy gypsy child who was trying to pick my pocket. The deeper I penetrated into the dense, shadowy labyrinth of stalls and stages, stands and tents, the more wretched the specimens on display became and the more disturbed I became. I was sinking into a cesspool of dwarfs, midgets and bearded fat ladies, spineless contortionists, a foul-smelling rhinoceros and twin babies joined at the head. It was not only the ocean of forms and faces, it was also the babble of the hawkers, the showmen, the trainers that swelled around me like the muck of an inferno.

A bare-breasted snake charmer wiggled her tongue at me. All around me, the well-dressed middle-class crowds hummed and stirred, seeking thrills, vicarious experiences and exotica. To my amazement, there were many well-dressed women in the mob, which seemed in a festive, congenial mood. I finally reached my destination, a pavilion built like an African hut, over which hung the painted banner proclaiming:

The Hottentot Venus in London! The first time the world has ever seen this extraordinary and perfect specimen of this race of mankind!

Under this proclamation, in much smaller letters was the notice:

Parties of twelve and upward may be accommodated with a private exhibition of the Venus Hottentot between seven and eight o'clock in the evening by giving notice to the showman the previous day. (A woman will attend if required.)

The showman was a certain Hendrick Caesar, who pulled back the curtain as a hush spread through the audience. I saw that there was something in the shadows of the barred bamboo cage huddled over a kind of brick oven heated by a Bunsen burner with which it tried to warm itself. It wore only a thin flesh-colored silk sheath which clung to its body, sculpting every line of it. It was a figure of such loneliness and despair, crouched there, that my eyes filled with tears when I realized it was actually a woman. An African woman, sitting on her haunches like a beast.

The showman spoke to her as if to a dog, commanding her harshly:

—Stand up! Sit down! Come forward!

According to the command, the creature moved lethargically back and forth, up and down, pacing like a wildcat. She even did a little jig and picked up a small guitar, on which she plucked a tune and sang something in a strange, bewildering language at which the audience began to laugh. I saw that the woman was almost in tears. Several times, she lashed out at her tormentors, her face flushed with embarrassment. She shook her head in disbelief as the spectators booed and cheered. She shouted at the presenter. He raised his hand against her. Then, he turned, all smiles, to the crowd,

—Step right up, ladies and gentlemen, and verify that there is no makeup, no fakery, only freakery . . . ha ha ha!

The audience surged forward as if they were going to devour the woman alive. She cringed although she must have gone through the same thing scores of times.

Yet even I was frightened. My heart accelerated and my breathing became shallow. The crowd was like hounds at bay, snickering and howling insults, chewing tobacco, spitting and coughing. Even without looking around, I knew I would see that particular lurid stare of pure folly with which people contemplated black skin. It was a kind of dumbness, beyond hatred, which at least had to be rationalized. No, this was pure homicide. I had seen such glares in prison guards' eyes, in policemen's stares, in judges' surveillances. In faces looking at *me* . . . I was inured to being looked at as if I were a criminal. But never, I thought indignantly, had I met with such an inhuman, degrading spectacle as this, or such a perverted presentation of a human being as I saw in this lone pathetic figure before me.

I was a theologian, the son of an aristocratic Scottish planter and a slave woman. I had dedicated my life to the radical cause of abolition and had founded the African Association, which was famous for defending the rights of slaves and freeing and repatriating as many as it could. The association fought and campaigned against racism in England and the horrors of slavery in the West Indies.

I was too outraged to remain. I turned on my heel and pushed my way out of the enclosure amid the hoots and jeers and laughter, which rang in my ears and burned my brown-skinned face with indignation.

—A slave woman is being exhibited and exploited as a freak, caged like a wild animal in a circus right here in London!

—How do you know she's a slave? asked Zachary Macauley, the president of the African Institution, looking up from his desk in their opulent offices, not far from Piccadilly.

—Well, she's black and she's African. How could she *not* be? No free black woman in her right mind would endure such degradation of her own free will! This . . . this show is an affront to female modesty for the amusement of a bunch of voyeurs . . .

—Is this the so-called Hottentot Venus?

—Yes.

—First of all, she can't be a Hottentot. She would never have been allowed to leave the Cape Colony. My friend Lord Calledon, who is governor there, would never have knowingly allowed the expatriation of a Hottentot.

—Well, if she isn't a Hottentot, she's certainly an African!

—She could be an Englishwoman faking exotic origins. It's been done before.

—Well, the least we should do is check. It's terrible. Her keeper is a Boer, a man named Hendrick Caesar. He's written a letter to the *Morning Chronicle* defending his right to exploit his "servant," but I'm sure she's his slave. I'm sure of it! We must free her.

Macauley looked up at me, leaning or rather pounding on his elaborate Georgian desk. I was making this one-ton block of English oak shake. Just like I had made conservative Britain shake, I thought.

The Wedderburn name was one of my burdens. I was Robert Wedderburn, one of several illegitimate children fathered by James Wedderburn of Inveresk, a rich Jamaican plantation owner. I was the grandson of Sir John Wedderburn of Blackness, whose family had fled to the West Indies after the defeat at Culloden of the Scottish army of independence in 1746. My grandfather, Sir John, had been captured, tried for treason, then hung, drawn and quartered by the English. I always believed I had a lot of old Sir John's blood flowing in my veins, because as his grandson, I had provoked and endured the repressive wrath of the British government ever since I had arrived in England. I was a licensed, self-taught Unitarian preacher who believed there should be an affinity between black West Indians and the British working class, between London's artisan class and the ultraradical party. This, in turn, had spurred my crusade to rid Britain of chattel slavery and colonial slave trading. Together with the tacit help of the member of Parliament William Wilberforce, I had founded the African Association, which along with the Missionary Society and the African Institution had worked to bring about the abolition of slavery on English soil, which had occurred three years ago.

—But isn't it a circus? asked Macauley. Isn't she part of some freak show?

—Freak show? Because she's an African? A freak?

I could have snatched him from his comfortable seat and throttled him. But Zachary Macauley was simply stating a fact. He too had passed by number 225 and read the circus posters outside.

—Peter and I will investigate the actual situation of the Hottentot Venus tomorrow, he said. On one condition, Robert, that you stay out of it. You have enough trouble with the law. You're facing two trials, a libel suit and two contempt summonses. If you say one more word in public, they will surely put your hide in a penal colony and throw away the key!

—I'll keep quiet if you and Peter bring a suit against her keeper for kidnapping, contraband and unlawful duress.

—Whoa, Robert. First, let's get the facts in the case. We should take Thomas's and Peter's advice on this. After all, it will be up to them as civil barristers to put together a suit.

Like me, Zachary Macauley had been at the forefront of the battle that had abolished the slave trade in England in 1807. He had been a cofounder of the African Association and the Missionary Society. He had served as governor in Sierra Leone, where he had helped establish a colony for liberated slaves taken at sea by the Royal Navy slave patrol. He had even made the infamous Middle Passage voyage on a slave ship bound for the West Indies so that the slave experience would not just be an intellectual exercise for him. Macauley was also the editor of the *Christian Observer*, whose offices were nearby. He had seen the advertisements and wondered how or why his friend Lord Calledon, the governor of the Cape Colony, would have allowed the expatriation of a Hottentot even if she were a Venus.

As we walked arm in arm into the library of the African Institution, I stopped, as I always did, to admire the handsome room which was built like an oval amphitheater. The floors were covered with Persian carpets, the law and history books bound in fine leather. Maps of the world and globes were scattered amongst the long tables and armchairs. Light poured through large arched windows framed in blue silk draperies. The luxurious decoration of the African Association reflected its aristocratic origins. The town house that housed it was situated on Regent's Crescent, one of the most fashionable addresses in London, for the landlord was none other than the Duke of Westminster. There were three or four visitors in the library, and at the end of the room sat the barrister Peter Van Wageninge, secretary of the association.

Peter Van Wageninge was a Dutchman of means who was a passionate abolitionist. Tall, slim and soft-spoken with short wavy blond hair and cornflower-blue eyes, he was also considered one of the most eligible bachelors in London. Somewhat of a dandy, he was famous for his all-black frock coats, narrow trousers and snowy white linen that he sent back to Amsterdam to be washed and ironed. He claimed that he hadn't found an English laundress worthy of the name. Unlike Macauley, he had never been to Africa. He had never even been at sea except for the Channel. His travels in Europe had all been overland. There were rumors that he had caught the eye of one of the Grenville girls and moved in the highest political and social circles. He was popular and charming and had put his fortune, as the London *Times* had put it, where his mouth was.

Van Wageninge looked up, unsurprised, as we approached him.

—Peter, Robert here has something important to dis . . .

—The Hottentot Venus, said Van Wageninge dryly.

—How d'you know?

—I've been assembling a file on her. Why? Because I knew Robert was going to come to her rescue . . . Look at this pile of newspaper clippings, advertisements, posters. Letters have also been coming into the association about her . . .

He pushed a large folder towards us.

—The first editorial letter arrived at the *Morning Chronicle* on October twelfth—that's on the top with the keeper's reply. His name is Hendrick Caesar and he's a South African Boer. The other man involved is a certain physician, named Alexander William Dunlop, a Scot. The Venus has been making headlines for weeks and provoking an avalanche of letters to the editor. The first protest came in a letter from John Kemble, the actor . . . He was alarmed that she might die during the winter from cold and illness and fall into the hands of the anatomists, *knowing*, as he said, *the adventurous hardihood of science.* Zachary and I sat down to read the file in the overstuffed armchairs next to Van Wageninge's desk.

A PROTEST
Morning Chronicle,
FRIDAY, OCTOBER 12, 1810

Sir, you will perhaps anticipate the cause I am now pleading, and to which I wish to call public attention. I allude to that wretched object advertised and publicly shewn for money—the "Hottentot Venus." This, Sir, is a wretched creature—an inhabitant of the interior of Africa, who has been brought here as a subject for the curiosity of this country, for 2s. a head. This poor female is made to walk, to dance, to shew herself, not for her own advantage, but for the profit of her master, who, when she appeared tired, held up a stick to her, like the wild beast keepers, to intimidate her into obedience. I am sure you will easily discriminate between those beings who are sufficiently degraded to shew themselves for their own immediate profit, and where they act from their own free will: and this poor slave, who is obliged to shew herself, to dance, to be the object of the lowest ribaldry, by which her keeper is the only gainer. I am no advocate of these sights; on the contrary, I think it base in the extreme, that any human beings should be thus exposed. It is contrary to every principle of morality and good order, but this exhibition connects the same offence to public decency, with that most horrid of all situations, Slavery.

Your obedient servant,
AN ENGLISHMAN

A REPLY
Morning Chronicle,
MONDAY, OCTOBER 22, 1810

Sir, having observed in your paper of this day, a letter signed "An Englishman," containing a malicious attack on my conduct in exhibiting a Hottentot woman, accusing me of cruelty and ill treatment exercised towards her, I feel myself compelled, as a stranger, to refute this aspersion, for the vindication of my own character, and the satisfaction of the pub-

lic. In the first place, he betrays the greatest ignorance in regard to the Hottentot, who is as free as the English. This woman was my servant at the Cape, and not my slave, much less can she be so in England, where all breathe the air of freedom; she is brought here with her own free will and consent, to be exhibited for the joint benefit of both our families. That there may be no misapprehension on the part of the public, any person who can make himself understood to her is at perfect liberty to examine her, and know from herself whether she has not been always treated, not only with humanity, but the greatest kindness and tenderness.

... Since the English last took possession of the colony, I have been constantly solicited to bring her to this country, as a subject well worth the attention of the Virtuoso, and the curious in general. This has been fully proved by the approbation of some of the first Rank and chief Literati in the kingdom, who saw her previous to her being publicly exhibited. And pray, Mr. Editor, has she not as good a right to exhibit herself as an Irish Giant or a Dwarf etc. etc. However, as my mode of proceeding at the place of public exhibition seems to have given offence to the public, I have given the sole direction of it to an Englishman, who now attends.

Hendrick Caesar

A LETTER TO THE EDITOR
Morning Chronicle,
TUESDAY, OCTOBER 30, 1810

Yes, she has a right to exhibit herself, but there is no right in her being exhibited. The Irish Giant, Mr. Lambert, and the Polish Dwarf, were all masters and directors of their own movements; and they, moreover, enjoyed the profits of their own exhibition: the first two were men of sound understanding, and were able to tell when they were plundered and defrauded of those profits, and to insist on the appropriation of exhibition profits to themselves: the money derived from personal misfortune was their own: it comforted them in the active moments of their existence, or supplied them with enjoyment when laid aside. Do the public believe that one shilling, nay a single farthing, of the profits arising from her exhibition will ever go into the hands of the Female Hottentot, or of her relatives or friends? Who audits the accounts? Who looks after the balance between expense and income? The avaricious speculator, or *the unfeeling gaoler who have brought her here, who receive the money, and—who will keep it. No; after having run the gauntlet through the three capitals of England, Scotland and Ireland, and traversed their provincial towns, dragged through them with greater barbarity than Achilles dragged the body of Hector at the foot of his chariot round Troy's walls, this miserable female will be taken back to the Cape; not enriched by European curiosity, but rendered poorer if possible than when she left her native soil.*

Humanitas

I slammed the file shut without reading any further.

—Damn Boer scoundrel.

—I think these letters are going to incense a mob of abolitionists to take things into their own hands . . . We'd better get over there, said Van Wageninge.

—Oh, the public loves it, cheap thrills, pornography . . . it beats a two-headed gorilla or an albino rhinoceros any day! This kind of exploitation has a sleazy life of its own, borne upwards by the ignorance and intolerance of the English. It will be an uphill fight to wrest her from her keepers, who are making a fortune off her, I replied.

—We must help her, said Macauley.

—Well, the first thing to deal with is the conscience of Dunlop and Caesar, if they possess such an appendage . . .

The next day, Macauley, Van Wageninge and I paid our two shillings and walked into the marketplace of freaks that was at number 225 Piccadilly. It was a Thursday and the stalls and walkways were calm. Thus, we managed to get very close to the stage. We waited for a break and then approached the barker Hendrick Caesar. He acted as if he expected us. We introduced ourselves.

—We're from the African Association.

—Yes, I know of you, said Caesar.

—This is Mr. Zachary Macauley and Mr. Peter Van Wageninge, I am the Reverend Robert Wedderburn. We would like to ask you how you came to manage the person of . . . Saartjie Baartman.

Caesar eyed me with contempt. It was clear he wasn't going to answer to any black man no matter how elegant. He turned away from me to the white men.

—She's my servant.

—Servant or slave, sir?

—I *said* servant.

—In South Africa?

—Well, she's here now, isn't she?

—That's just the point. Our association is a benevolent organization to protect, educate and civilize Africans.

—Well, the Venus is under my protection and she's pretty civilized.

—May I ask how you got her out of South Africa? Travel by Cape Hottentots is prohibited. Did she procure a passport?

—She has a passport issued by the governor of the colony, Lord Calledon, if it's any of your damned business . . . interjected the second man, Alexander Dunlop.

—May I see his signature? He is well known to me.

—By God! No, you can't, said Dunlop. Mind your own business. No reason why I should carry it around with me and no reason why I should show it to you . . .

—I imagine she speaks Dutch.

—Yes.

—Well, this gentleman speaks Dutch, may he speak with her?

—She doesn't fraternize with male members of the audience . . . police ordinance, you know . . .

I eyed the man who had interjected himself into the argument. He was a fine figure of a man, tall and athletic, who could be thirty as easily as he could be forty or twenty. His eyebrows and his thick wavy hair were jet black. His complexion was pale under the artificial brown of seafaring and his eyes were sea green. His features were classical and most agreeable, straight aquiline nose, fleshy lips, angular chin with a deep cleft, small well-shaped ears and a largish skull sitting on a thick column of neck and shoulders. When he smiled, his eyes crinkled up and he displayed a mouth full of large, even white teeth with upper canines that extended lower than the rest but were square rather than pointed. He could surely swim, I thought, certainly sword-fight and shoot, probably ride excellently, and he was definitely not interested in boys like so many English adventurers. He had Scottish blood, like me, but no accent. He was obviously well educated, but perhaps not a gentleman. He was expensively dressed in crimson and blue, but I wagered he was penniless. There was a sort of man who couldn't hold on to money, even if his life depended upon it, even if he came into a fortune. And he was of that race. It was obvious it was simply in his nature; a fatal flaw of character or upbringing or simply fate. He would always be relieved of it in some bizarre manner: war, theft, gambling, women, but he would go on, making even more and losing it, because people could not resist him. That's it, I thought. This man was irresistible. It was more than charm, it was a kind of fatality, a magnetic attraction for both men and women—which was perfectly immoral, and impossible for ordinary people with ordinary brains not to succumb to.

—Miss Baartman, said Van Wageninge in Dutch, are you here under your own free will?

The Venus nodded but said nothing.

—Do you have any family at the Cape?

Silence. Dunlop glared. Of the two men, I thought, Dunlop was the most dangerous. Could I take him? I could feel my Scot's blood rising along with his. Our respective Scot's blood rising with our respective Scot's brogue.

—Brothers, sisters, parents?

—All dead, she said in English.

Dunlop whispered something in her ear. But she waved him away.

—Are you happy here?

We continued on for another ten minutes asking question after question. Finally, in frustration, I asked the Venus directly:

—Would you like to go home? Would you like us to send you home? To pay for your passage? But the Venus remained mute.

The request was repeated in Dutch by Van Wageninge.

—We have organized a defense committee on your behalf and you will be able to explain to a civil court whether you feel you would be better off relieved of the presence of Mr. Dunlop and Mr. Caesar and put under the protection of the African Association, I said.

—Thank you, the Venus suddenly said softly, shaking her head as she contemplated the miracle of a black man denouncing a white one.

We bowed, turned on our heels and left, with the Venus staring helplessly after us. Our three top hats bobbed and weaved in and out of the crowd. I could feel the Venus's eyes upon us even at a great distance. It was only later that we discovered that Dunlop had been absent for several months and had reappeared only several days ago, walking in the door, out of nowhere. News of the controversy around *his* exhibition of the Venus had reached him and he had returned to London to defend himself.

When we got outside, I turned to Macauley.

—Lord Ellenborough will never take her from the custody of Caesar and Dunlop without proof that this exhibition is against her will. And we cannot free her only to send her back into the world without a home to go to. We must argue that if she is taken from her impresarios, we will assume her safety under our own protection. She will not find herself without friends.

In the weeks that followed our visit, the Venus made headlines in the yellow tabloids and the penny press . . .

—The journalistic world is most enamored of Miss Baartman, commented Peter Van Wageninge. Look at this. It's called "Prospects of Prosperity, or Good Bottoms Going into Business" and it has just been published by Walter & Company of Cornhill. It shows Lord Grenville and the Hottentot Venus advancing towards each other with outstretched arms. Behind Venus is a well-dressed man, the showman Alexander Dunlop himself. In Grenville's pocket is a list of the new administration. Behind him are the current ministers looking on unhappily. Grenville is saying, *My dear Saartjie, I come to congratulate you. You are trading in on your own bottom, I see. I expect soon to be in the same situation myself.* She answers: *Me only got half my bottom belong to me. No do much good wid dat.*

—Huh, she's got dozens of songs and rhymes and cartoons about her circulating in London and all of England and Ireland, complained Peter Van Wageninge, laughing in spite of himself.

—We have to get to Sarah Baartman, I concluded. We have all the evidence we need: witnesses, letters to the editors, newspaper articles and advertisements and our own two eyes. I insist we take Caesar and Dunlop to court for keeping the Hottentot Venus in involuntary servitude.

—Robert always comes up with the most radical and violent solution to any problem, interjected Van Wageninge.

It's in my blood, I thought, contemplating the pale whiteness of Van Wageninge. I am a mulatto street boy, the bastard of a Scottish nobleman who sold his mother when she was five months pregnant with him. I came to be a Christian late in life. I am both radical and violent. I was brought up by my grandmother, a poor black slave on the island of Ja-

maica, and witnessed her brutal flogging by orders of her master, my own
father, a white man and a Christian, when I was eight years old. My
grandmother was accused of witchcraft. The terror visited upon my
mother and grandmother marked me, I thought, for the rest of my life,
which began in 1761. At seventeen, I joined the Royal Navy during the
American Revolution. I took part in the Gordon Riots of 1780, led by
the American Negroes Benjamin Bowsey and John Glover. I am a self-
taught historian, a self-taught theologian, a self-taught preacher and orator, who has tried to synthesize radical Christianity and the republicanism
of Thomas Paine. I continue in spite of persecution and blacklisting and
prison to preach proletarian abolitionism. By force of obstruction, persecution and censorship, the Crown hopes to crush me, and prevent me
from preaching freely, but it has only turned me into an author, dragging
me from obscurity to fame. My writings have turned me into a brilliant
and dangerous intellectual. Something I had not been until now. My ser-
mons attract a multitude of listeners in my little church, my *Horrors of
Slavery* has sold thirty thousand copies. My aristocratic father never did
anything for me. The closest I ever came to receiving help from my Scottish family was a cracked sixpence and some beer given me by a servant
at a time when I and my pregnant wife were close to starvation. That at
a time when my father's estates, Mint, Paradise, Retreat, Endeavor, In-
verness, Spring Garden, Moreland and Mount Edgecombe were worth
precisely thirty million pounds . . .

—Robert, said Macauley to Van Wageninge, has done time in Cold
Bath Fields penitentiary, Dorchester prison and Gillspur jail for everything from theft (guilty) to keeping a bawdy house (not proven). He is at
this moment under indictment for using blasphemous, profane, scur-
rilous, gross and violent discourse against the Church of England. That is
why he must stay out of this Venus case and out of the courtroom. If he
even opens his mouth in front of a judge, we are done for.

—In other words, a damn good man.

—My half brother James is the solicitor general for Scotland. Needless
to say, my activities are very embarrassing to him and the family, I said
dryly, amused at Van Wageninge's shocked face.

We spent the next weeks in the library of the institution planning our
suit. Macauley, a redoubtable barrister, felt we had a strong case, but I
knew we would have to produce a writ of habeas corpus in order to get

the Venus away from Dunlop and Caesar. That meant we had to convince
Baartman to bear witness and sign an affidavit against her keepers.

I knew I couldn't stay away from the King's Court. Zachary Macauley
proposed a compromise. I could attend the hearing but I was prohibited
from all speech, on pain of being ejected from the proceedings by my own
lawyers. I was not to sit at their table, but in the public gallery on the upper floor. I agreed to everything, I was so anxious to witness the King versus Alexander Dunlop and his demise as the Venus's keeper.

I knew I had to get over my obsession with the Venus. But her face and
figure haunted me. Flashes of the sufferings of my mother and grandmother assaulted me. I had only to set eyes on Sarah Baartman and she,
and she alone, could evoke the hole dug in the dirt floor to accommodate
my mother's womb swollen with myself while she was being flogged by
my father. There was the vicious torture of my grandmother, Talkee Amy,
accused of witchcraft and burned to death. I had never been to Africa like
Macauley, but I knew the horrors of slavery: the plantation, the floggings,
the neck-collaring, the padlocking, the chains, the ship holes, rape,
sodomy, forced feedings, cauterizing, branding, executions. I had experienced firsthand the slave system of the West Indies thanks to my own father. The Venus had not suffered these things. No, she was more like a
dark-skinned Eve who had wandered out of her African Garden of Eden
into the Inferno of the ignorant, prejudiced, immoral and self-satisfied
British Empire; bloodsuckers feeding on the cadaver of its brown colonials, its greedy industries, the docility of its proletarian class. Sarah's exploitation was, I thought, commercial, spiritual, hypocritical, lascivious
and pornographic. It was the murder of the human spirit that Thomas
Paine so adored. The Venus might *think* she was a *free* agent, but I knew
better. She was being used and misused as a freakish other, a subhuman
symbol of sex and degradation. Venus was only a dirty limerick, a filthy
eye-rolling voyeuristic joke. She was unimportant to the abolitionist
movement, to civil rights and to human rights. She was nothing political. Despite the fact that I had triumphed over the British Empire
and the King, I could not convince one lone peasant girl to give up her
delusions . . . and reclaim her dignity. Why then couldn't I get this
simpleminded shepherdess out of my mind? Why was it impossible
to forget her?

I reviewed my stormy interviews with her. Every time I had taken her small perfect hand, always clothed in red leather or silk, and gazed into her eyes, she had become as immaterial as a ghost. Her eyes had become restless globes. Her high cheekbones had glowed, her forehead had wrinkled, her face had gone all hollow and fleshless, all the sweetness gone. She had been terrified of me—me, a black man.

—Just because I consent to this life doesn't mean I *choose* it, she had said in Dutch.

—I beg your pardon?

—Just because I *consent* to this life doesn't mean I *choose* it, she had repeated in her broken English.

The eternal pout of her lips had taken on an impertinent mournfulness. The Venus had been trying to figure out the meaning of a black man who was white, a black man who was free, a black man who spoke to books. I had frightened her, sitting there, glowering and motionless, bullying her, willing her to understand, amazed to see my deformity in any creature other than myself.

10

The Caucasian race, to which we ourselves belong, is
chiefly distinguished by the beautiful form of the
head . . . Second comes the Mongolian, and then the
poor last: the Negro race is confined to the south of
Mount Atlas. Its characteristics are black complexion,
woolly hair, compressed cranium and flattish nose. In
the prominence of the lower part of the face and the
thickness of the lips, it manifestly approaches the monkey tribe.

—Baron Georges Léopold Cuvier,
Thirty Lessons in Comparative Anatomy

*E*land's moon, the English month of November 1810. A month later,
Reverend Wedderburn sued Master Hendrick for sequestration and kidnapping, dealing in contraband, affront to public decency, and assault and
battery, in the King's Court of Chancery according to my master's curses
and swearing. Master Dunlop was also cited for the same crimes. His
Majesty's prosecutors came to my rooms in St. James's Square with the
King's warrant to question me. What else could I have done? It was
the King's command. I begged that Master Dunlop be present but the solicitor general, a man called James Temple, would not allow it. Only the
solicitor general, the coroner, Master Dunlop's lawyer and the African

Association lawyers were allowed present. All the time they were there, my thoughts were only of Master Dunlop, listening to his every command. It was habit since his sudden and unexpected return, only days before the trial was to begin.

—Why did you come back? I blurted out.

—Because I *said* I was coming back. Because I promised.

—I believed you were gone forever, that you were never coming back!

—How could you think that, Sarah! When I was working my head off settling my affairs to get back to you.

—You are married.

—Not anymore. I'm divorced now.

—Why didn't you tell me?

—And have you throw me out? I had no choice! Would you have left the Cape with me? I'm sorry I deceived you. I'm sorry.

—You could have told me in your letters.

—Letters?

—The letters you wrote to me while you were away.

—I wrote to you? Huh. Yes. Well . . . Of course I couldn't tell you by post! I had to wait until I could speak to you face-to-face! Let me see . . . these letters, will you?

I handed over the three sheets and the three envelopes with my name written on them. Master Dunlop unfolded the sheets and frowned at them for a very long time.

—Who read you these letters? You can't read.

—Master Hendrick.

Master Dunlop's hand was shaking as he handed back the sheets of paper.

—Here're your letters, Sarah.

—What's wrong? I asked.

—Nothing. Nothing, he replied turning away, cursing. I told you everything. Hendrick didn't read everything. He . . . left out parts. He didn't read you everything I wrote . . .

—Why would he do that? I asked.

—How would I know, you stupid cow? How would I know? Because he hates me . . . because he hates you—because you're nothing but money to him.

—And to you?

—Now what made you ask me that?

He had disappeared for six months and was now back as if he had just gone for a stroll around St. James's Park, reclaiming my dowry and once more promising marriage.

—When?

—As soon as we're rid of the abolitionists, he repeated, especially that bastard Wedderburn.

—And why should you be in charge of anything, grumbled Master Hendrick, you sold your shares of Saartjie to that actor Henry Taylor!

—Only *half* of my shares! I know the English well enough to know that a foreigner like you hasn't a chance in an English court of law! A colonial to boot! English xenophobia would work against any foreigner, but especially against a just-conquered colonial importing slavery, which the motherland only abolished three years ago . . . the Crown will listen to English radicals like Wedderburn, that reverend bastard—and Macauley, that effete aristocrat . . .

—They've presented a complaint, whined Master Hendrick.

—You've nothing to worry about, Hendrick, now that I'm back—I'm a Scot in my own country, and a surgeon in His Majesty's navy.

—They claim I'm free, I interjected meekly.

—And so you are, Sarah—who's talking about *slavery* except them? You are perfectly free—free to become a ward of the state! Free to be put in the workhouse, the poorhouse, the whorehouse, the jailhouse or the damned fuckin' crazy house! Is *that* what you want, Miss Baartman? Which do you prefer? Ha—none of them? Well, this country, this lovely England, has lots of them for the likes of you—and they *love* to stick people, including your precious Mr. Wedderburn, *in* them!

Dunlop paced up and down, pointing first at Hendrick and then at me.

—I'd just like to see you, Sarah, when your African Institution friends, after gaining as much publicity as they can off of you for their radical causes, put you in a charity ward! Then you'll be all alone in England, without me, with no friends, no protection, no money, no husband . . . Without me! Do you hear?

I collapsed at Master Dunlop's warnings. Whom could I trust? These strange white men? The white black man? Or Master Dunlop, who had returned? Was he my only chance? I loved him. I would stick with what I knew. I had no other choice.

The lawyer that my masters had hired for the trial was as smooth as ivory, hard as a diamond barrister named Sir Stephen Geelesee. We were to reply in the King's Court to the accusations of Master Macauley and Master Robert Wedderburn. Master Alexander and Master Hendrick would have to produce proof that they had not brought me into England without my consent or as contraband.

—The allegations are, said the lawyer, that you smuggled the Venus out of the Cape without the knowledge of the governor, Lord Calledon, and that she was kept under duress and publicly exhibited against her will. You must prove she gave her consent before leaving Cape Town. Can you produce a contract between you and her, in which there is remuneration and a share of the profits, concerning the exhibition?

—Of course not. Saartjie can't even read, let alone have the slightest idea of what a contract is.

—When did you leave the Cape?

—In May.

—And when did you arrive in England?

—In September.

—I'll have a notary public draw you up a contract in Dutch, dated October twenty-ninth, 1810, between you and the Venus certifying your relationship as one of employer-domestic servant. We'll have to have someone read it to her in Dutch and swear she understands it, and then, have her sign it with her mark. It would run from March 1810, *before* you sailed from the Cape, for six years, to March 1816.

—Will you sign it? sighed Dunlop. You've been so strange lately . . .

—What is a contract?

—Exactly like a Hottentot marriage contract: a solemn promise to abide by your word of honor.

—This is the marriage contract according to the English? I asked.

—*Like* a marriage contract . . . not . . . His voice trailed off.

—Well, we will have to make it worth her while. What did you promise her in the marriage contract, Mr. Dunlop?

—Fortune and fame, replied my master, leaving out "marriage."

—A little more concrete than that.

—Well, that Sarah would exhibit herself just as she was. That we would conquer London and share the box office receipts in two equal parts.

—I will not wash anybody's feet, I said. And no housework, I said importantly.

The lawyer and Master Dunlop looked at each other, smiling.

—You will even receive a salary, Saartjie.

—How much?

—Twelve guineas a year . . . for six years, that's seventy-two guineas in all . . .

I thought it over.

—That's more than ten pounds, isn't it?

—Indeed.

The notary public, whose name was Arend Jacob Guitard of Sweeting's Alley, read the contract aloud in Dutch, asked me if I understood it, then I had to sign another affidavit swearing that I understood what he had read to me. This would be the defense of my keepers before the King.

—Twelve guineas per year, for domestic duties, repeated Master Guitard, the Dutch interpreter. You will also allow yourself to be viewed by the public of England and Ireland *just as you are*. All your expenses including room and board are to be paid by Mr. Dunlop. He accepts responsibility for your transportation from and to South Africa, in case of illness he will pay all medicines, doctor's fees. If you want to return to South Africa, Mr. Dunlop will defray the cost of repatriating you.

I was astonished. This was more than he had promised at the Cape.

—And the receipts, I said.

—He will hold your share of the profits until the end of the contract, which runs from March tenth, 1810, to March tenth, 1816. When you return to the Cape, you will be not only famous but rich.

—What are you going to do about the men from the institution? I finally asked him. I knew these men were coming back.

—Nothing. We're covered by the contract . . . our contract . . . Let them rant and rave. They can do nothing. We have a valid contract unless you repudiate it.

—What she does beyond that is no one's affair, insisted Master Dunlop to the African Institution men. This show is a private arrangement between our maid, myself and Colonel Caesar which is perfectly legal. Our private arrangements are not subject to any interference from you or from English law. As I have repeated, this woman, a member of the Khoekhoe tribe, also known as a Hottentot, is under the direct protection of Lord Calledon, the governor of Cape Colony. I received permission from him to remove Saartjie from the colony and have a passport signed by his lordship.

—And are you prepared to produce these documents?

—In court. Not to you, sir, and not to a bunch of lawyers, abolitionists and radicals who think nothing of depriving this poor female of her livelihood under the pretense of indecency and morality and Mr. Wilberforce!

—You will certainly have to answer in court to our allegations, as we have no intention of retracting them, warned the Dutchman.

—And leaving this woman a beggar on the streets of London by your actions or obliging her to accept transport back to Africa, like a convict, is, I suppose, *only your right!*

—We are a beneficent association for the civilization of Africans . . .

—And you want Sarah here to become dependent on the charity of a beneficent association for slaves, paupers and morons, shouted Master Dunlop. Is that what you want, Sarah? he said, turning to me.

—I don't want no charity. I don't want be shut up in a refuge for ex-slaves. I don't want be shipped back to Jamaica or Sierra Leone! (All this had been carefully explained to me.) What did these men want with me I thought? Was I not unhappy enough as it was? True, my master had returned. But all I had in the world was my contract with him.

—We consider Baartman here your prisoner.

—You, said Master Hendrick, are the ones who want to make Miss Baartman a prisoner . . . for your own political ends . . . and those of your Liberal friends in Parliament. Miss Baartman and Lord Grenville are a little too popular these days . . . and have gotten a little too much publicity . . .

This time, there were even more men. Some were those who'd been present before: an older, stout man from the African Institution, the solicitor general, the Dutch gentleman, who had spoken to me in Dutch; but with them was a mob big enough to hang me. There were King's men, the African Association men, Dutch men who translated for me and wrote down everything I said. The black man who was white had returned but did not speak. It was the Dutch gentleman, Master Van Wageninge who asked me most of the questions. But the white black man kept whispering in his ear, his eyes never leaving mine.

The tall Dutchman with wavy blond hair had swallow-colored eyes enlarged by his thick spectacles, which he kept taking off, and chewing the ends of, and putting back on. He spoke very fast and in High Dutch that I hardly understood. Then, all at once, he switched to Low Dutch and smiled beneath his thick blond mustache. I smiled back and told him his linen was so white, so starched and so well ironed I bet he sent his shirts back to Holland to be washed. At this he laughed and admitted that, indeed, he did send his laundry to Amsterdam.

—We are all members of the African Association and the African Institution, he continued in Low Dutch, this is Mr. Macauley, and this is Mr. Robert Wedderburn. You remember the Reverend Wedderburn and me from Piccadilly?

So the white black man's name was English too.

—As we said then, we are the association to protect and defend Africans and other persons of color. We were in the forefront of the fight to abolish slavery on British soil, and now that this is achieved, we make sure all former slaves and slaves that enter Great Britain, as you have, are assured of their status as free persons. Do you understand?

—I am not a slave, I insisted, I am a free woman.

—I understand that, but there seem to be constraints on your movements and your bodily freedom.

I remained silent. Was I to admit I had been lured by Master Dunlop to England under false premises? My future husband? They would send me back and I didn't want to go back. I would die if I went back.

—I understand you have already sworn your affidavit before the Crown, but here, now, with only a translator, said Master Van Wageninge, you have the chance to revindicate your freedom if you are being misused.

Misused, I thought. My fortune was gone, my bride's dowry spent by my master without marriage, my only means of earning a living the subject of a trial. And here were a posse of white men ready to make a fool of me, Sarah . . . I shook my head.

—I don't have no complaints, I said in Dutch.

Without showing any dissatisfaction at my response, Master Van Wageninge, calm and collected, insisted.

—It is not that we wish you to prosecute your employers; we wish only that, after such a long struggle, the law as applied to chattel slavery is upheld and respected in the British Isles and that people of color on British soil have the safety and protection of the law.

—We are quite prepared, interjected the stout white man, to finance your passage back to Africa with no strings attached, if you so desire. You could rejoin your friends and family . . . We have done this for many colored.

I listened in silence to his speech, stirred in spite of myself, marveling at the fact that all this could be going on in the world without anybody in the Cape, white folks or black, ever knowing anything about it. I wondered just how much power these white men (including Master Wedderburn) had. Could they really protect me? Was there no other way to remain in England? Would I end up, as my masters had said, in the workhouse, the jailhouse, the crazy house or the whorehouse if I left them? Was there anyplace for me on earth at all? Wasn't one cage as good as another? I didn't dare ask. The white black man spoke into my silence, looking me directly in the eye, willing me to understand.

—Sarah, he began, we all have seen the exhibition at number 225. We were appalled and shocked at the violence of the gestures of Mr. Caesar, his threatening attitude vis-à-vis your person. I understand he is *not* a member of your family, a father or brother who would have a legal or moral right over your person. Therefore, if you *are* a free person, you have the right to demand reparations for such treatment and that such treatment in word and deed cease. We are here in the name of decency to make sure no physical harm comes to you as a result of your economic dependence on your . . . employer or guardian. I understand you are not yet twenty-one years old.

—Master Caesar is not my employer nor my guardian. I have a contract with Master Dunlop, this gentleman. Soon I will have my twenty-second birthday. I am not a slave . . . not a slave. I am free.

—These men, I believe, mistreat you and misrepresent themselves.

—And you would do better? A missionary? I remembered the reverend and my ten pounds.

—We are not missionaries, we have no religious affiliations, we are a civil rights organization.

—Then why are you called Reverend, I asked the Reverend Wedderburn.

—Because I have a license to preach, he answered.

—You are not like the Reverend Freehouseland.

—Who is the Reverend Freehouseland?

—I was his slave as a child. He's buried here in England. In Manchester, I added. I've come to visit his grave. I won't go back until I see it . . .

—But once you've done that, wouldn't it be best to return to your family and friends?

—All dead. All murdered, I lied.

—But not against your will, he answered, shocked at my reply. We can't leave you to your own devices in a strange country, that would be most inhuman.

—What is inhuman?

—Inhuman is what is happening to you, Sarah. You are the unwitting collaborator of your own exploitation, agent of your own dehumanization! You are no more a *real,* genuine Hottentot than I am. You are a fake, a myth, a joke, a misrepresentation, a victim used to promote a freakish mythology . . . a false blackness . . . a grotesque caricature of so-called savagery. Look at the penny pictures of you! Think, Sarah. Think for yourself. No one else. Neither chains nor dungeons nor the terrors of being burnt alive can prevent us from thinking freely, neither can they prevent us from moving, speaking, writing or reading books freely.

—Books?

—Yes, books.

—Books for white people. Books don't talk to black people.

—Oh yes they do. Otherwise teaching slaves to read wouldn't be a crime . . . would it . . . Can't you read, Sarah?

—No.

—No?

—I wouldn't when I was little. I won't now.

—There's one book, the Good Book, that every human being should read.

—The Bible. That's what the Reverend Freehouseland said.

—And did the Reverend Freehouseland care for you?

—I don't know.

—Did you love him?

—Yes. The only good missionary I ever knew.

—And where is he now?

—I already told you. Dead. In Manchester.

—England?

—Yes, master. Dead and buried like I said.

—Don't call me master!

The reverend turned away slowly, disgusted, I suppose, by the pig-headedness of a simpleminded herdswoman, a shepherdess, who couldn't read. For I knew in my bones that he was a parody, a stumbling mouthpiece for truths that couldn't save me. If I courted destruction, then let it be on my own terms.

—Remember, he said sadly, the words of Marcus Aurelius: Man loses no other life than the one he's lived and he lives no other life than the one he loses . . .

—Just because I consent to this life doesn't mean I chose it, I repeated in Dutch.

—You haven't understood a word I've said, have you?

Yes, I wanted to say, I understand you. I understand that your ideas about me are more important than me myself. You see me as yours, as much yours as Master Dunlop sees me as *his*. You see me as a means to your goal of revolution, and rebellion, against the English. You are so angry you don't really see me at all—only as an object in the eye of the storm. I don't trust you, white black man, I thought. You don't like me because I'm not your ideal. You want to be *like* them. I don't. That is the big difference, I thought, between you and me.

—I don't care to understand you, I said.

But I thought this: Your ideas are the only important thing to you. Not me myself. For example, you do not even speak my language, so who are you to talk of *my* history, *my* ideals, *my* representatives, *my* duty to allow you to save me. Not only don't we have a common language between us, we must speak the white man's language even to understand each other . . .

—I'm not a slave . . . I'm a free woman.

—Oh God, Sarah, flee, unhappy Hottentot, flee, as the philosopher Diderot said, as I plead with you to do—hide yourself in your forest! The wild animals that live there are less dangerous than the monsters under the empire of which you will fall. The tiger will perhaps tear you to pieces, but he will not steal your life. The other beast will ravish your innocence and rape your freedom. Have the courage to take up your hatchet, your bow and poisoned arrows, and rain them down on these foreigners so that there survives not one to bring news of their disaster . . . It's the only way, Sarah. Sarah?

—Either you succumb to their crazy opinions or you massacre them without pity—because, because, Sarah, they believe that if you don't think like them, you are unfit to live . . . unfit to inhabit this world . . . that your existence has no justification . . .

—I am a simple woman who herds sheep, you know?

—When I was a little girl, I continued, things were different for the Khoekhoe. We had water and grazing land. Now, we have nothing except the rusted iron and tarnished beads we exchanged for our cattle . . .

—The earth belongs to God, Sarah, who gave it to the children of men, allowing no difference for color or character, just or unjust. Then, the encloser and the engrosser turned the land into *private property* and created slavery. The weak, then, had to solicit the villain to become the villain's slave . . .

The Reverend Wedderburn bit his fingertip, trying to find the words of a sermon that would convince me. He had long bitten his nails down to the quick, until they were sunk into little pads of flesh at their tips. He began again.

—I have Scottish blood, he said, that goes back to 633, but my African blood goes back to the beginning of time . . . I am free. Being free, I am free to revolt! Slaves and unfortunate men cultivate the earth, adorn it with buildings, fill it with riches. And those riches are stolen by the ruling class, who set the slaves to work in the first place! Pray, was there ever a solitary savage who was rich? Are you rich? I say, don't acknowledge them. Acknowledge no king, no priest, no father, no master. Only direct action is valid. It is degrading to human nature to petition your oppressors . . .

—God is no respecter of persons. The revolution moves on without Him. The English working class, the Scottish peasantry, the black Haitian, the African slave, the Irish bond servant, the American Indian are all one and the same. All await the jubilee: Isaiah 1:20, I bring good tidings to the afflicted: to bind up the brokenhearted, to proclaim liberty to the captives, to open the prison doors of those who are bound, like you, Sarah, you in your cage—you must believe me!

—Are you married, Master Wedderburn?

—I no longer have a wife, and don't call me master. I'm your brother, not your master.

He sat down and wiped his brow. I just sat there like a dumb animal, not reacting to anything, as if I didn't understand anything.

—Don't, for God's sake, call me master!

—To me, you are like the rest, only darker.

—Oh, Sarah, Sarah, he said, hurt to the quick, how can you say that to me?

—You, white black man I'm lookin' at . . .

—No, Sarah, you are not looking at a "white" black man. You are looking at a free and liberated black man. I'm the first free black man you've ever set eyes upon . . . And you don't even know it! You are still afraid to look white people in the eye—Look up, Sarah! Open your eyes . . . You can be as free as I . . .

He took my hand in his two great ones.

—I am a low, vulgar man, incapable of delivering my sentiments in an elegant and polished manner, but when I saw you, naked, the object of ridicule, humiliated as my mother and grandmother were, your soul shrunken and besmirched by those bigoted, ignorant, smug, cruel, lewd, corrupt villains. Because of their own cowardice and prejudice, they give in to the most obscene and low impulses of human nature: to ridicule what they don't understand. I truly despair of my fellow man. I despair of my own vocation to defend the cause of truth, of religious liberty, of the universal right to freedom of conscience . . .

—You don't believe me, do you?

I couldn't answer. My mouth seemed filled with the sweet mush they fed me as a girl to fatten my hips.

—You can't believe that I am smarter, better, more powerful than your knuckle-headed, hairy ape Afrikaner bosses . . . can you?

I flinched at the tone of his voice. I was on trial . . .

—You angry, I said.

—No, Sarah. I want you to live, that's all. I *need* you to live.

—Live?

—Only I can save your life. Only the law and I. I consider this a matter of life and death. Why won't you believe me? What stops you from trusting me? My color?

Trust no one, especially those who sleep on your bosom.

The white black man stumbled on, staring into my eyes with a kind of desperation. I willed myself not to understand. Not to understand one word he was saying. It was weakness to try to understand him. I saw what whites saw, a crazy nigger in Englishman's clothes, hiding . . . waiting to pounce upon them with his poisoned spear.

—I beg leave . . . Sarah . . . humbly to save you.

—No.

—To help you testify against your keepers.

—No.

—You must change your affidavit.

—No.

I understood only one thing: I had to hold on to Master Alexander, now that he had returned, with all my might. To cross him was destruction. He was my savior, not the Reverend Wedderburn. He was my only chance. I must not let him go.

11

MONSIEUR,

Simple comparative anatomy has practically become a
game: it requires just a glance to detect the variations, the
successive degradations of each organ; and if the effects
each organ produces have not yet been explained, it is
because there is, in the living body, something more than
those fibers and tissues that we see—that is only the me-
chanical part of the organism, or, so to speak, the passive
instrument of vitality, and between that first disturbance
of imperceptible elements and the sensitive movement
that is the end result, there occurs a multitude of intermediary evolutions of which we have no idea.

—BARON GEORGES LÉOPOLD CUVIER,
Letter to J. C. Mertrud on
Thirty Lessons in Comparative Anatomy

*E*land's moon, the English month of November, 1810. When I
appeared at the King's Court with my two Dutch interpreters, I was
surrounded by a mob of spectators, reporters and police. Crowds of
abolitionists were loudly demonstrating and mounted police had to open
a path for me through the screaming, shouting mob to the courthouse
door. The courtroom itself was still almost empty.

I passed the sweepers and there lingered one lone cleaning lady with a
duster. I glanced about me. The wide arched windows, two stories high,
looked out onto the Thames. They were framed with heavy black and
gold velvet drapes embroidered with the arms of King George. The en-

tire chamber was paneled in dark oak trimmed with gilt, ebony and bronze fittings. A huge crystal chandelier hung down from the center of the ceiling, flanked by two smaller ones at each end of the oval room. The leather-upholstered benches yawned into the silence of the hall and vapors of paper, ink, old documents and mortal fear rose and mixed with the faint smell of tobacco, damp wool, soap and brass polish. But there was still another odor that permeated and overpowered the rest, the odor of sanctity: white law, white God and imperfect, fragile white men's justice.

At the end of the hall rose the magistrates' boxes, majestically framed by the King's colors, the Crown's colors, the colors of the British Empire, on which, I was told, the sun never set. Behind the magistrates' chairs were words I didn't understand, on a gold background, but I could read: IN GOD WE TRUST. I sat down, gloved, hatted and swathed in cashmere shawls which completely hid my shape and my person. I pulled down my veil and watched the players enter through its haze.

Master Wedderburn entered first and sat down in the front row. He nodded but did not greet me. I tried to guess who would walk through the padded doors next. It was Eland's moon, the mating month. Where was that faint scent of African violets coming from? I wondered. Then I turned my head and followed the ponderous footsteps of Sir Stephen Geelesee, our lawyer, walking up the aisle to take his place at the defense's table, in his black and scarlet robes, white cravat and curly white wig. Master Wedderburn pretended to study some papers he had taken out of his briefcase. He was so concentrated on this little bit of playacting that he failed to notice the Dutchman Peter Van Wageninge enter until he was at his side, whispering in his ear.

The courtroom began to fill up. Outside, the large crowd continued to form. Proof of my notoriety. The morning's newspapers were filled with headlines, articles and cartoons about the trial. A satirical engraving was being sold on the sidewalk, just outside the courthouse. It was entitled "The Hottentot Venus." It depicted an ugly, gross engraving of me naked except for some beads, standing back to back with Lord Grenville, who was dressed in old-fashioned court dress and who looked at me over his shoulder. Half kneeling between us, using a pair of compasses to measure our *pair of broad bottoms* was a famous playwright named Richard Sheridan, who was also a member of Parliament. Even though I couldn't read the caption, I knew what it said because the mob outside were all shouting the words. *Well, I never expected broad bottoms from Africa! But such a spanker beats your lordship's hollow!*

Master Macauley entered the courtroom and, moving quickly, slipped his considerable bulk into the seat beside the Reverend Wedderburn, but Master Wedderburn merely sighed deeply and remained silent. We all rose as the presiding judge, Lord Ellenborough entered the room.

—Aye, aye, all rise for his lordship, the Honorable Earl of Ellenborough, the crier shouted.

Lord Ellenborough entered followed by the attending magistrates. The judge's long, flowing ermine-trimmed red robes gave him a theatrical air. His high white court wig added six inches to his rather small person, and despite a long narrow chinless face and famous Christmas-tree eyebrows, he seemed to me to radiate authority, temperance and dignity. The first thing he said was that he tolerated no nonsense in his courtroom and was determined to keep the cartoons, circus atmosphere and penny posters out of the proceedings. Lord Ellenborough, it seemed, was related to Lord Grenville. The solicitor general then rose and addressed the magistrates with his opening argument.

—I am applying to your lordship on behalf of an unfortunate female who is at present exhibited to the view of the public in a manner offensive to decency and disgraceful to the country. I apply to you on behalf of a helpless and ignorant foreigner brought to this country and exhibited against her consent by those in whose keeping she is. I am aware that the Court cannot grant the rule for which I am applying unless they be convinced that she is under restraint and that this exhibition is against her will. However, I see no reason why a writ of habeas corpus should not be issued to bring her before the coroner and attorney of the Court in the presence of proper persons.

—I am somewhat at a loss, your lordship, as to how to frame this motion—whether it should be for a writ of habeas corpus or whether it should be for a rule. I will proceed to read the affidavits upon which my application is founded and then take direction from the Court as to the manner of shaping the motion. I submit the affidavit of William Bullock, owner of Egyptian Hall, and call him to the stand.

In the King's Bench

—Will you please state your name and profession to the Court.

140

—William Bullock of Piccadilly in the county of Middlesex, proprietor of the Liverpool Museum.

—Will you please tell the Court what you know of the Venus and her keeper Mr. Dunlop.

—Sometime in or about the month of August, I recall, I was applied to by Mr. Alexander Dunlop, who I believe either is or was an army surgeon and who stated that he had then lately arrived from the Cape of Good Hope to purchase of me a camelopard skin of great beauty and considerable value, but the price being greater than I chose to give, no bargain was then made, although I afterwards had a subsequent interview with Alexander Dunlop and purchased the skin.

—Is this the only thing Alexander Dunlop offered you?

—Alexander Dunlop in the course of conversation with me informed me that he was in possession of a Hottentot woman who he had brought from the Cape of Good Hope.

—And did you consider that proposition? Why do you think Mr. Dunlop and company entered onto this project?

Master Bullock eyed the prosecuter.

—Why were *they* doing this? he answered. Money certainly.

—And of course this went against your ethics and morality.

—Yes.

Master Bullock was adamant.

—I could not, he repeated, in good conscience exhibit a live human being in an animal museum no matter how . . . extraordinary. But I did purchase the giraffe skin from Mr. Dunlop and it is now exhibited in the Great Hall as part of my collection.

—How much did you pay for it?

—For the skin I paid one hundred guineas.

—And how much did Dunlop ask for the Venus?

—I don't care to answer that.

—Please answer the question.

—Five hundred pounds, at the same time informing me that he was under the engagement to return her to the Cape of Good Hope in two years. Mr. Dunlop expressed to me previous to the time I purchased the camelopard skin that he would rather dispose of the whole concern together, meaning, as I understood and verily believe, the skin *and* the Hottentot woman, but when I purchased the skin, Mr. Dunlop remarked that, as he had disposed of the other part of the concern (meaning thereby, as I understood and believe, the Hottentot woman) to advantage, if I would make him a handsome offer for the skin I should have her as a bargain. Mr. Dunlop at the time I was in treaty for the skin described the extraordinary shape and make of the woman and that she was an object of great curiosity and would make the fortune of any person exhibiting her to the public. I felt that such an exhibition would not meet the countenance of the public and I declined acceding to Mr. Dunlop's proposal and only purchased the skin.

—And did you imagine how she would look stuffed and naturalized and placed amongst your specimens?

Master Bullock flinched as if he had been burned.

—I am a collector, not a taxidermist! Of course I imagined how she would look naturalized, stuffed and placed amongst my skylit African flora and fauna, along with my other animals. My museum of natural history is designed not only to display the natural world as it is, but also to influence the minds and behavior of the people who visit my museum to contemplate their own higher, rationalized human behavior and establish the distance between human and animal nature. But when I met Sarah Baartman, I was amazed that she spoke our language—English. But if she possessed a language, the King's English, rudimentary as it was, I believed that meant she possessed the *humanity* of the King as well! No! I could not exhibit another human being no matter how spectacular!

—Did you ever consider denouncing Mr. Dunlop to the authorities as Mr. Macauley has done?

—Well, I began to eye the two men, one a colonial and the other an officer and a so-called gentleman, with suspicion. One was insisting it was my patriotic duty and the other that it was my scientific duty, but why were *they* doing this? As I said, money certainly. But I thought Miss Baartman must be the mistress of one of these men as well. Which one? And if so, wasn't he her pimp as they say? I felt uncomfortable. I realized I was contemplating a commercial venture based on this poor creature that might even be illegal and get me in trouble with the police. The Hottentot was the living, breathing personification of crime: sex, deformity and slavery.

For by now I was sure she was a slave, illegally imported into England. I felt cramped as I faced Miss Baartman in her carriage that day. An explorer had once said to me that nothing more uncannily focused the projection of guilt for the slave trade, for the empire, for one's own savage and immoral impulses, than those moments when one white man confronts another white man in the depths of the jungle. And for me, Miss Baartman was the jungle! I even said so out loud. I said, *This is the jungle!* I jumped out of the carriage, no longer able to stand the sight of Miss Baartman. I refused any more dealing with Mr. Dunlop, except for the giraffe skin . . .

I was surprised Master Bullock didn't tell the Court how he had sat in my carriage and pinched me and joked about my backside and haggled over my price. Or how he had sung my birthday song by naming me Venus, or how he had been so frightened at what he was doing, he had had to escape from my sight once he had decided I was human, because it had turned his stomach.

—And do you believe she was smuggled into England as contraband?

—I know Alexander Dunlop and the Hottentot female and Hendrick Caesar, who now exhibits the female, all came to England from the Cape of Good Hope in the same ship. Alexander Dunlop, Hendrick Caesar and the female now live together in the same house in York Street, Piccadilly. I have since been informed by Mr. Alexander Dunlop that he has been so unfortunate as to have sold and disposed of his interest in the exhibiting of the Hottentot woman and that he has now next to nothing to do with her.

—Could you specify who you mean?

—I mean the Hottentot woman—

—Her real name, please.

—Sarah Baartman, sir.

—Could you point out to the Court her person?

—She's sitting over there. *(He pointed at me)*

—And you refused to exhibit her?

—How could I in good conscience exhibit a live human being in an animal museum, no matter how . . . extraordinary.

—Thank you, Mr. Bullock. You are dismissed.

—So your lordship may perceive that this unfortunate creature was offered to William Bullock for sale, which is sufficient proof that she is a slave and not a free agent, continued the solicitor general, his white wig bobbing as he paced.

—I now introduce, he continued, the affidavits of Mr. Babington, Mr. Macauley and Mr. Van Wageninge, all illustrious members of the African Institution, a society the object of which was to abolish slavery in Great Britain and, now that that great cause is accomplished, is to meliorate the conditions of the Africans. Upon learning of the disgraceful exhibition of this female, these gentlemen went to see her and found her exhibited in such a disgraceful and disgusting manner, I will forbear going into the particulars . . . I now read to the Court their sworn affidavits, and call to the stand Mr. Macauley.

SWORN AFFIDAVITS

Zachary Macauley of Birchin Lane London Merchant, Thomas Gisborne Babington of the same place Merchant, and Peter Van Wageninge of Water Lane Thames Street London Gentleman. Severally make oath and say first this Deponent Zachary Macauley for himself saith that he is Secretary to an Institution called the African Institution the object of which is the civilization of Africa and the said Zachary Macauley having understood from different public advertisements and otherwise that a native of South Africa denominated the Hottentot Venus of a most extraordinary or unnatural shape was publicly exhibited for Money in Piccadilly . . . And these Deponents Peter Van Wageninge and Thomas Gisborne Babington say that the said female is called by the Exhibitor towards the persons standing round the stage and they are invited to feel her posterior parts to satisfy themselves that no art is practiced—And these Deponents Peter Van Wageninge and Thomas Gisborne Babington do verily believe from the dejected appearance of the said female and from the obedience which she pays to the commands of her Exhibitor that she is completely under restraint and control and is deprived of her liberty. And these Deponents further severally say that during the time they were present the said female at one time appeared very morose and sullen and retired into the little recess off the stage and appeared unwilling to come out again when called by the Exhibitor and the Exhibitor felt it necessary on that occasion to let down a curtain which when drawn separates the stage and little recess from the other part of the room. And this Deponent Thomas Gisborne Babington saith that the Exhibitor after the curtain was let down looked behind it and held up and shook his hand at her but without speaking and he soon afterward drew up the Curtain and again called her out to public view and she came forward again upon the stage. And these Deponents severally say they are informed and believe that the said female's name is Saartjie and that the name of the person who has the possession of her is Hendrick Caesar—

[signed] Zachary Macauley
Thos. Gisborne Babington
P. Van Wageninge

—May it please the Court, I call to the stand Mr. Zachary Macauley. Master Macauley took the stand, and while he was testifying to what he had seen at 225, I watched the face of the Reverend Wedderburn, who followed the testimony as if he himself were on the stand, squirming and muttering and repeating phrases and wringing his hands and rolling his eyes in disgust. I wondered why it was not he on the witness stand, defending me . . . rather than Master Macauley.

—And would you say, Mr. Macauley, that the woman in question was under duress and in physical danger . . .

—I definitely do believe she was under duress and threatened . . .

—Could you specify she . . .

—The Hottentot Venus . . .

—Her real name please.

—Sarah Baartman.

—Could you point her out to the Court.

—She's sitting there. *(He pointed at me)*

—Thank you, Mr. Macauley. You are dismissed.

—May it please the Court, I now read the affidavit established on November twenty-seventh, 1810, at the residence of Sarah Baartman in Duke Street, St. James's Square, in the presence of Sir James Temple, Esquire, coroner of the Court, and the solicitors of each party without the presence of Mr. Dunlop and Mr. Caesar. And I call Sarah Baartman to the stand.

The Result of the Examination of
the Hottentot Venus—
Nov. 27, 1810

She does not know when she left her native place she being very young
when she came to the Cape: the Brother of her late Master, Peter Caesar, brought her to the Cape: she came with her own consent with Peter
Caesar and was taken into the service of Hendrick Caesar as his nursery
maid; she came by her own consent to England and was promised half
of the money for exhibiting her person—She agreed to come to England for a period of six years; She went personally to the Government in
Company with Hendrick Caesar to ask permission to go to England:
Mr. Dunlop promised to send her back after that period at his own expense [*sic*] and to send the money belonging to her with her—She is
kindly treated and has everything she wants; Has no complaints to make
against her master or those that exhibit her: is perfectly happy in her
present situation: has no desire whatever of returning to her own country not even for the purpose of seeing her two brothers and four sisters:
wishes to stay here because she likes the Country and has money given
her by her Master of a Sunday when she rides about in a Coach for a
couple of hours—Her father was in the habit of going with Cattle from
the interior to the Cape and was killed in one of those Journeys by the
"Bosmen." Her mother died twenty years ago—she has a Child by a
drummer at the Cape with whom she lived for about four years yet being always in the employ of Hendrick Caesar; the child is since dead—
She is to receive one half of the money received for exhibiting herself
and Mr. Dunlop the other half—She is not desirous of changing her
present situation—no personal violence or threats have been used by any
individual against her; She has two Black Boys to wait upon her: One of
the men assists her in the morning when she is nearly completely attired
for the purpose of fastening the Ribbon round her waist—her dress is
too cold and she has complained of this to Hendrick Caesar who promised her warmer clothes; Her Age she says to be twenty-one and that her
stay at the Cape was three years—To the various questions we put to her
whether if she chose at any time to discontinue her person being exhibited, she might do so, we could not draw a satisfactory answer from
her—She understands very little of the Agreement made with her by

Mr. Dunlop on the twenty-ninth October 1810—and which agreement she produced to us—The time of Examination lasted for about three hours—and the questions put to her were put in such a language as to be understood by her—and these Deponents say they were informed by the said female that she could neither read or write.

[signed] S. Solly
Jn. Geo. Moojen

For the first time, Lord Ellenborough intervened:
Question: What is your name, age, and occupation?
—My name is Sarah Baartman. I am twenty-one years old, having left my homeland at the age of nine years old to come to the Cape as a slave to the Reverend Cecil Freehouseland. I returned home at age fourteen and married. When my husband was killed, I returned to the Cape when I was seventeen years old and I went to work as a children's nurse for Mr. Peter Caesar, brother of one of my present employers. His brother, Mr. Hendrick Caesar, and Mr. Dunlop brought me to London with my own consent as his partner.
Question: Your occupation, then, is nursery maid?
—Yes, before I was taken into service by Mr. Dunlop.
Question: How did you arrive in England and how do you make your living here?
—I came by my own consent to England and was promised half of the money received for exhibiting my person just as I am . . .
Question: For what length of employment?
—Six years, sir.
Question: Did you receive permission from the governor of Cape Colony to leave the colony as a protected person under the guardianship of the governor?
—I went myself to the governor's house in Cape Town to ask permission to go to England with Master Dunlop.
Question: For how long was this arrangement to be for?
—Master Dunlop promised to send me back after six years at his own expense and to send at the same time all the money belonging to me.
Question: Do you have any complaints against Mr. Dunlop and Mr. Caesar for harsh or inhuman or unfair treatment?
—I have no complaints to make against Master Caesar or Master Dunlop, sir.

Question: Would you characterize your situation as a happy one?

—I am happy in my present situation, sir.

Question: Would you like to go home? Return to your own country?

—I have no desire whatsoever to return to my own country, sir.

Question: You do have family? Two brothers and one sister, isn't that so? Wouldn't you like to return to them?

—No, my two brothers are dead. I have not seen my sister since I was eight years old. She may be dead too.

Question: Why do you wish to remain in England?

—Because there is no slavery on English soil.

—Any other reason?

—I like the British Isles and wish to remain here in liberty and freedom with money given to me by my master to spend as I please.

Question: And what do you do with this money?

—I ride in coaches on Sundays. I shop on Bond Street and Oxford Street. I buy gloves.

Question: Tell me a bit about your background. Where do you come from?

—My father was a herdsman who was killed on Khoekhoe lands, where he had assembled his herd to go to the Xhoa market. He was killed by Boer raiders. My mother died almost eighteen years ago when I was an infant. I was married to a drummer, called Kx'au, with whom I lived for four years. I had one child, !Kung, who died a babe just after the murder of my husband.

Question: How much of the money do you receive for exhibiting yourself?

—I receive one half, and Master Dunlop and Master Caesar the other half.

Question: Are you desirous of changing your present situation?

—No, I am not.

Question: Have any threats or personal violence been used by Mr. Dunlop or any individual against you?

—No violence has been used against me. At least, not by them . . .

Question: You are happy then? he repeated. *You have no complaints to make to the Court?*

—I have no complaints. I have two servants to wait on me. They help me dress, I lied. However, my clothes are not those of my climate. I would like heavier, warmer clothes, but I have complained about this to Master Caesar and he has promised me warmer clothes.

Question: How long were you employed by Hendrick Caesar before you came to England?

—Almost four years, at the Cape.

Question: Can you, if you choose, discontinue exhibiting yourself at any time?

—I . . . have a sacred contract with Mr. Dunlop, to whom I have promised myself and certain things . . . as well as certain years of my life.

Question: Yes, but if you choose, can you refuse to continue with the exhibition of your person, without fear of reprisals?

—I don't understand the question.

Question: (repeated)

—I have a contract.

Question: Do you understand the terms of your contract?

—Yes, I do.

Question: Have you read the terms of your contract?

—I can't read or write.

Question: Then how can you say you understand the terms of your contract?

—It was read to me out loud in Dutch, which I understand, by the notary public, Master Guitard.

Question: When was the agreement drawn up?

—I don't know.

Question: When was it read to you?

—I don't remember, ah, it was read to me . . . yesterday.

Question: Only yesterday, November twenty-seventh, 1810?

—If you say so . . .

Question: But the agreement is dated October twenty-ninth, 1810. How do you explain that?

—I don't know. I can't read. The contract was read to me. I believe Master Dunlop's word that the contract will be honored . . . that this contract is sacred.

Question: Did any other person except Mr. Dunlop's notary read or read to you this . . . contract?

—I don't believe so, but I don't remember . . . I have no recollection.

Question: You understand we are here to help you. To ascertain the truth. Is there anything you wish to add to your affidavit?

I wanted to say that for three hours you have bothered me with your questions and inquiries as if I were a criminal or a slave. I am a free woman! I am not a criminal. I am not a slave. I am not a prostitute or an immoral person. My only crime is that I cannot read or write and that I am a Hottentot. I am only seeking asylum from my enemies, from people who kill Hottentots. Instead, I bowed my head and said nothing. Still that question came.

Question: You are in danger of your life if you return to the Cape, is that what you are saying?

—I am saying that I will die like all Khoekhoe if I return. I'm saying that I have a contract! A contract! A contract!

The prosecutor for the King representing Zachary Macauley and the Reverend Wedderburn paused. He hadn't been able to get any kind of accusation out of me. Sir Stephen was jubilant. Sarah Baartman had not cracked. She had held her ground. Her keepers had nothing to fear.

The solicitor general and the judge both made a last effort to persuade me.

Question: Are you under any restraint at all, moral, physical or mental?
(Silence)

Question: Wouldn't you like to return to the bosom of your tribe? To stop being exhibited as a freak?
(Silence)

Question: What have you been promised for your silence?
(Silence)

—I would like to be rid of you all! I said out loud.

I was shouting now, but so were the men from the African Institution. And the judge was hammering for silence. Everyone was determined to set me free, even if it killed me. I refused to answer any more questions. My affidavit, as they called it, had been read. I had told them all I knew. I was not an outlaw nor contraband. I was not a prostitute. What more did they want? I trusted none of these white men. The Reverend Freehouseland would have known whom to believe. The rainmaker would have known whom to believe. But I didn't know whom to believe. Was I to end up in the hands of charity, of a beneficient society for slaves, paupers, morons and the like, to be shut up again in a shelter, a refuge, to see the world once more through a keyhole or a coffin? The only alliance I had now, I thought, was to the other things-that-should-never-have-been-born.

—Miss Baartman, said the judge, you may step down please . . . and watch your step.

It was now Sir Stephen's turn.

—I introduce to the Court the affidavit of Mr. Alexander Dunlop and Mr. Hendrick Caesar.

—Does your affidavit state that the Venus speaks Dutch? asked Lord Ellenborogh.

—Yes, my lord, her keeper spoke in Dutch to her. The persons who interviewed her spoke in Dutch. She answered without interpreters, her keeper or any other person under whose control she has ever been, not being present.

—Mr. Macauley has stated that she is exposed in an indecent manner and that she appears to act against her inclination.

—She is dressed, my lord, in a thin dress, assimilated to her person, that does exhibit all the shape and frame of her body as if naked.

The questioning continued with another magistrate, Justice Le Blanc.

Lord Justice Le Blanc: What is your rule, Mr. Doty?

Solicitor general: My lord, I apply for a rule to show cause why a writ of habeas corpus should not be granted to bring up the body of this female.

Lord Ellenborough: Does anyone understand her language?

Solicitor general: Not the Hottentot language; but it is stated in my affidavit that her keeper and the representatives of the Court state that she understands and speaks Low Dutch, imperfectly.

Lord Justice Le Blanc: Well, if she is brought forth, she must go where she pleases. The Court can't take her out of one person's control to place her in another.

Lord Ellenborough: Indeed, it is she who must make an election: that she wishes to go back to her own country—the rule to show was granted. Her affidavit in the absence of her keeper is part of the record, no person accustomed to exercise any sort of control over her was present, there being only present, on behalf of the keeper, a person who also understands the language. You yourself have heard her testimony. I'll now hear from the defense, Mr. Geelesee.

Sir Stephen Geelesee: Your lordship, the district attorney has not shown cause for granting a habeas corpus to bring up the body of the female African Sarah Baartman, who is exhibiting in London under the title of the Hottentot Venus. She has already been examined, apart from her keeper, by the master and coroner of the court in my presence. It seems to me, your lordship, that the motion for granting a habeas corpus has two aspects, first, that she was exhibited in an indecent manner, and secondly that she was under restraint. With respect to the first, I consider that the present application is not the way to remedy it, if it is true. But in fact, the Venus was not only clothed in a silk dress, but had a cotton one under it. Moreover, I must inform the Court that the only circumstance in the affidavit that indicates for the motion—namely, that she is under restraint—has been removed. It was said that the keeper used a menacing attitude with his hand, which Sarah Baartman seemed to obey in fear . . .

Sir Stephen paused for effect.

—That person has been removed and another substituted. And yesterday, the master of the Crown Office himself attended and examined Sarah Baartman with two Dutch interpreters, one on behalf of her keeper and one for himself. The result of that examination is evident in the text of the entire affidavit.

Lord Ellenborough: Before we can remove her from her present situation, we must be satisfied that she is an object capable of making an election: that she feels pain from constraint in which she is at present held and that she is desirous of being put under the care of persons who will restore her to her own country.

Sir Stephen Geelesee: Nothing, your lordship, in this affidavit or her testimony indicates that Sarah Baartman has any desire to be removed from England or from her present situation. On the contrary, I submit the supplementary affidavit by Mr. Arend Jacob Guitard, a notary public, stating that he has translated the agreement between Mr. Dunlop and Miss Baartman from English into Dutch and has read it twice plainly and distinctly to Saartjie, alias Sarah, Baartman and that it appeared to him that she understood the contents thereof and was therewith satisfied—if the African Institution wishes to protect the financial interests of the Venus, my clients would be pleased if they would appoint a trustee to take care of her share of the profits of the exhibition. But since it is evident from her own sworn testimony that she is under no restraint, the case against Mr. Dunlop and Mr. Caesar should be dismissed.

Lord Ellenborough: Does the district attorney still sustain his motion for a habeas corpus?

Solicitor general: The district attorney does not. The attorney general concedes that the motion cannot be sustained, but I wish to add that regardless of the outcome of this procedure, anyone hearing of this action must certainly feel that it is very much to the credit of this country that even a Hottentot can find friends to protect her interests. I trust that henceforth the Venus will be properly taken care of and those gentlemen who have so honorably taken the trouble of looking into her situation will continue to see that her interests are protected.

Lord Ellenborough: This case is dismissed. But not before I issue a strong warning that if any immodest or indecent exposure of this female foreigner should take place, those who have the care of her must know that the law will direct its arm with uplifted resentment against the offending parties . . .

Lord Ellenborough rose. The court was adjourned. The men of the African Institution remained immobile. The Reverend Wedderburn held his head in his hands.

Sir Stephen rushed me from the courtroom, jammed between my two interpreters. Neither Master Hendrick nor Master Alexander had appeared in court.

Lord Ellenborough believed I was being handsomely paid and protected; Sir Geelesee had trumped them by offering to turn over my finances to the institution or give me up altogether. The notary public Arend Jacob Guitard, who had read me my rights in Dutch, had all fallen into Master Dunlop's trap. I heard the Reverend Wedderburn say to the abolitionists:

—God hath chosen the foolish things of the world to confound the wise; and God hath chosen the weak things of the world to confound the things which are mighty . . .

But on the streets, they were clapping, singing and chanting my song.

> *Oh have you been in London towne,*
> *Its rareities to see:*
> *There is, 'mongst ladies of renowne,*
> *A most renowned she.*
> *In Piccadilly Street so faire*
> *A mansion she has got,*
> *In golden letters written there,*
> *"THE VENUS HOTTENTOT."*
>
> *But you may ask, and well, I ween,*
> *For why she tarries there;*

And what, in her is to be seen,
Than other folks more rare.
A rump she has (though strange it be),
Large as a cauldron pot,
And this is why men go to see
This lovely Hottentot.

Now this was shown for many a day,
And ere for many a night;
Till sober folks began to say,
That all could not be right,
Some said, this was with her goodwill:
Some said, that it was not,
And asked why they did use so ill
This ladie HOTTENTOT.

At last a doughty knight stood forth,
Sir Vikar was his name;
A knight of singular good worth,
Of fair and courtly fame.
With him the laws of chivalrie
Were not so much forgot;
But he would try most gallantly
To serve the HOTTENTOT.

He would not fight, but plead the cause
Of this most injured she;
And so, appealed to all the laws,
To set the ladie free.
A mighty "habeas corpus"
He hoped to have got,
Including rump and all, and thus
Release the HOTTENTOT.

When speaking free from all alarm,
The whole she does deride:
And says she thinks there is no great harm

In showing her b——ksides.
Thus ended this sad tale of woe,
Which raised well, I wot,
The fame, and the revenues too,
Of SAARTJIE HOTTENTOT.

And now good people all may go
To see this wondrous sight;
Both highborn men, and also low,
And eke the good Sir Knight.
Not only this her state to mind,
Most anxious what she got;
But looking to her latter end,
Delights the HOTTENTOT.

I was so famous, the English started to name things after me. Not only were there the newspaper articles and editorials and letters. There were the penny posters, the handbills, the cartoons and caricatures. There was Hottentot Venus soap, Hottentot Venus bleach, Hottentot Venus chocolates, a Hottentot Venus pastry made of whipped cream, chocolate, honey and almonds. There was Hottentot Venus coffee and Hottentot Venus tea. Hottentot Venus rouge and Hottentot Venus corsets. Hottentot Venus cigars were sold on Bond Street as well as Hottentot Venus gunpowder. Hottentot was the name for anything crude, ugly, inferior, savage or simple-minded as well. And on Sloane Street, at Christmas, a glove manufacturer opened a new shop and called it the Hottentot Venus . . .

12

Isolated bones, thrown pell-mell, almost always broken and turned into fragments, here is all our relationships give us and the only resource of naturalists.

—Baron Georges Léopold Cuvier,
*Discourse on the Revolutionary
Upheavals on the Surface of the Globe*

*A*pril 1811.

Sloane Street, Thursday, April 18, 1811

My dear Cassandra,
I have so many little matters to tell you of that I cannot wait any longer before I begin to put them down. I spent Tuesday in Bentinct Street. The Cookes called here and took me back, and it was quite a Cooke day, for Miss Rolles paid a visit while I was there, and Sam Arnold dropped in to tea.

The badness of the weather disconcerted an excellent plan of mine—
that of calling on Miss Beckford again; but from the middle of the day, it
rained incessantly. Mary and I went to the Liverpool Museum and I had
some amusement though my preference for men and women always in-
clines me to attend more to the company than the sight. But I willingly
gaped at a thirty-foot-long boa constrictor, which made the story of the
Laokoon very believable, and a sixteen-foot-high giraffe, the museum's
latest acquisition, which I found very pretty, its head like a horse and a
mild innocent look at the top of an immensely long yet graceful crane neck.
The stuffed bear in the same case looked quite small by comparison.

After gazing at Mister Bullock's creatures, we crossed Piccadilly Square
to 225 to gawk, it is the only word that expresses it, at a creature of another kind; a freak that John Kemble, at dinner the other night, at the
D'Entraiques, told me about; the Hottentot Venus, a woman from the
Chamboos in Austral Africa, who is on display just as the giraffe in Mister Bullock's Liverpool Museum. She has gone through a sensational trial,
brought by the African Institution against her managers, who were finally cleared of all charges.

Mister Kemble had been most affected by this spectacle and I must say,
I was happy to be only in the company of one of my own sex. For I was
shamed by the pudeur and forbearance this poor woman displayed in the
face of the brutish, pornographic voyeurism of my countrymen (and
women). They plucked and prodded this small creature and called her
names and verily acted like a bunch of baboons. The comedy of manners
being exhibited by the masters of the world towards its colonized slave
population was more like a morality play of oppression and rejection on
one hand, versus a kind of defiance of all white English morality and
opinion on the other. It was not an amusement. It was an erasure of time
and distance between our civilization and its antithesis, this African
Venus, the irony of whose name was not lost on me or the audience, and
even played its part in this charade. For the Venus was a parody of white
English beauty and womanhood, as far from our pretensions of gentility
as one could possibly imagine. Yet, there, in a cage . . . in the most dire,
primordial circumstances, the Venus had a dignity and a humanness that
was totally lacking in her spectators and put them to shame. I shed a tear.
Mary did too—at her vulnerability, a feminine vulnerability we all are
burdened with in the face of a masculine society. I was revolted. I tried as

did several other ladies in the audience to make eye contact with the Venus, to communicate the sympathy I truly felt. But there was no communication except insults and threats, neither between the public and the Hottentot nor between the Hottentot and the white females in the audience. To be sure she is ugly, she has an enormous, astounding posterior, but her face is actually not unpleasant and she is very young. She is now a household word in England, a synonym for brute ugliness and a celebrity in Londonian Society and the popular press, who use her as a plaything and a satiric political tool against the Grenville party. Not a day goes by that there is not another wicked, obscene cartoon or caricature in the daily press, even the Times . . .

The politics of her, the obscenity of her, as well as her servitude are a scandal and a blot on English Society. But even the worst of scandals become romantic and even respectable in two thousand years; witness Cleopatra, Caesar, Mark Anthony and other gentlemen. The most virtuous read of Cleopatra with sympathy, even in boarding schools, and were she, by some miracle, blotted out of the book of history, the loss would be enormous. The same applies to Helen, Phryne and other bad lots. In fact, now that one thinks of it, most of the attractive personages in history, male or female, especially the latter, were bad lots. And the true Venus? Haven't the most scandalous acts in history been done in her name? In the name of passionate, unbridled and uncompromising love? Shouldn't we love anything called Venus, I asked myself, gazing at that strange, humiliated, black creature . . . if you are a woman? There is nothing that makes our sex more aware of our own oppression than witnessing the horrendous, blatant oppression of the black and brown races. Or a black or brown member of our own sex. I shudder to think I actually paid to see this!

I bless my stars that I have done with Tuesday. But alas! Wednesday was likewise a day of great doings . . .

Love to all.
Yours affectionately,
JANE

Miss Austen, Edward Austen's Esq.
Godmersham Park, Faversham, Kent

I lifted my pen from the paper and thought about what John Kemble had said about our prejudices and our belief in our own superiority and our ravishment of the world because of it, of which this poor dislocated creature was a symbol. What had I really felt, standing there in the crowd with Mary, witnessing this cruel humiliation of one of my sex, but a secret, sniveling joy at my own safety and invulnerability . . . wasn't that why I loved freak shows? She, the Venus, was the Other, I was me, Jane, safe within the confines of my privileged provincial white world. I could never be she. As long as I did nothing to trespass it.

And that was the rub. Cowardness. The four feathers. My options, I thought wryly, were limited to this suspended pen I held in my hand whose ink bled onto the middle finger of my right hand. And no, I was not going to use this pen to denounce her suffering or what I had seen. Or to write about her or recognize her plight in any other way than in this letter to Cassandra . . . Forgive us, I thought, our trespasses, Lord, and deliver us, or at least, quarantine us, from evil . . .

13

But the empire of man alters this order. It develops all the variations to which the type of each species is susceptible and derives from them products that the species, left to themselves, would never have produced. Here the degree of variation is still proportional to the intensity of its cause, which is slavery.

—BARON GEORGES LÉOPOLD CUVIER,
Discourse on the Revolutionary Upheavals
on the Surface of the Globe

*C*rooked Fire, the English month of April, 1811. The trial had made me even more famous, having heightened the public's curiosity about me. Long lines of people still formed outside number 225 to gawk at the Venus. Even Lord Grenville showed up to thank me for having given him so much publicity. His party had won the elections by what the scandal sheets called a *split bottom*. My notoriety was now nationwide. Even in the provinces, newspapers reported on the London trial.

The bawdy song was on everyone's lips just as my shape and color was in everyone's eye, and on everything a merchant could sell. I was recognized in the street if I ever dared venture outside Duke Street, and sometimes pursued. Master Hendrick and Master Dunlop were now richer than ever. They moved my exhibit into a separate exhibition hall at 53 Piccadilly Street. During his disappearance, Master Dunlop had sold half his quarter share of me to another Englishman from the north of the British Isles, Henry Taylor, the roving Shakespearean actor who had accompanied Master Kimble to my dressing room more than a year ago. He said he planned a tour of the rest of England and Ireland for us. This was to be our farewell tour.

I clung to my clan of things-that-should-never-have-been-born, who lived in the jungle of 225 Piccadilly. At times it was as if I had fallen back into the wild forest of home and my childhood and all these creatures that roamed around me were only Magahâs's magic. Not real at all. I gave them all names so I could recognize them—lion, flamingo, giraffe, elephant, zebra, jackal—but I learned they all had real names like mine: Caroline Camancini, the thirty-inch fairy, Anna Swann, the albino, John Randian, the human torso, Lorenzo Dunnett, the man with the revolving head, Sigmund Sully, the skeleton man, Paul Desmule, the armless man who hurled knives at human targets, Grace McDaniels, the mule-faced woman, Dolly Dimples, the fat lady, Joseph/Josephine Herring, the double-sexed man. They had all added noble or military titles to their names: Caroline was princess, Adolph was captain, Paul was marquis, Sigmund was lord, the dwarfs were all generals. There was Baron Little Fingers, Prince Ludwig, Duchess Leona, Baroness Anna. Everyone had three names: a Khoekhoe name, an English name and a fake title. Just like me . . .

We freaks gathered every day after our performances to talk and drink, eat and laugh, play cards, try on costumes, converse about all the things ordinary people spoke of: what we ate or drank, how we slept, whom we loved. We spoke of what we despised, what the weather would be the next day, the latest fashion, what we had bought in the shops on Bond Street—hats, gloves, jewelry, sweets, beer, gin, chocolates; we spoke of famous people, the theater, music, even future dreams, like weddings or children. We gathered in taverns and inns. We would crowd into these dark spaces and talk all night. By necessity, we were night people. At dusk, we scurried like mice out into the half-light and blue-dyed shadows with torches, oil lamps and candles, avoiding the eyes of normal people. Like ghosts, we escaped our stage sets, the huts, cabins, tombs, shacks, platforms, happy to be free of the oppression of unwanted attention. A passerby might start, but we managed to avoid at night what we sought by day—the public.

Of all of the extraordinary people, I had come to love the thirty-inch fairy, Caroline, best. She was a perfect miniature person, who had entered the world of the circus as a small child and was still only twelve years old. She had been stolen, given away or sold by her family. Others like Caroline, JoJo, the dog-faced boy, Percilla, the monkey-girl, Emmett, the alligator-skinned boy, John, the elephant-boy, had all been abandoned by their parents or were orphans. They had all lost their dead or living mothers. We were all exiles: blacks in the kingdom of whites.

I saw in Caroline the child I had lost. I was black in a world full of white people. She was thirty inches tall in a world of people who were five and three quarters feet high. Many times I would pick her up and carry her into places built too high for her and sometimes she would lead me into places colored persons were not allowed to on their own. And so we became a couple. More than friends. A mother-daughter mutual assistance society. One day, Caroline asked me:

—Is that your real name, Hottentot Venus?

—No. It's a make-believe name.

—What's your real name?

—Sarah . . .

—And what does Hottentot Venus mean?

—Well, you know what Venus means.

—She's a goddess, said Caroline. And a planet.

—Well, Hottentot is a Dutch word, which means "to stutter." It is an insult given to my people by the Dutch, who couldn't learn our language. It's an ugly word. My tribe is called Khoekhoe.

—Say something in your own language.

—*Ssehura ke ti !naetseetsana/onsa.*

—Which means . . .

—The name Ssehura is my birthday name.

—Caroline Camancini's not my real name either.

—Oh no?

—Well, Caroline is. But I'm not Sicilian. I'm from Dublin. Princess Camancini is my stage name.

—What's a stage name?

—Well, like Venus or Princess. It makes you more mysterious, more real to the audience. Would you read me a story?

—I don't know how to read.

—Why don't you? Everybody knows how to read!

—Because books don't talk to black people, only to white people like you.

—You're wrong, Sarah. Books speak to everyone regardless of what color you are. That's the whole *idea* of a book. A book is a whole country. A book gets you out of the prison of your mind. And to read is to write. And to write is to own yourself . . .

—Can you write too?

—Of course. I keep a diary . . .

I studied Caroline. If my son had lived, I thought, he would be five years old and twice the size of Caroline. Caroline was sitting on my lap, cuddled against my breast. I hadn't held a child in my arms since Cape Town, now almost a year gone.

—Then I'll read *you* a story.

She jumped down.

—I'll get my book. It's called *Grimm's Fairy Tales*. You know, the Irish really believe in fairies. My mother believes in fairies, my papa too. The book is all about fairies . . .

—You are not an orphan?

—No, my parents are alive . . .

—I had a little child, but he's dead . . . My voice trailed off.

—Once upon a time . . .

—The book is almost as big as you are!

The story she read was about a toad and a prince and a princess, a witch and a forest.

—We have almost the same story.

—You should learn to read, Sarah, I can teach you.

—Then could I learn to write . . . letters?

—Reading and writing go together, you can't do one without doing the other . . .

—Would you read some writing for me? Writing that came in a letter?

—A letter sent to you?

—Yes. Some time ago.

I pulled out the letters I had received from Dunlop while he was gone, which Master Hendrick had read to me, and set them on Caroline's miniature lap. She unfolded them slowly and studied them carefully.

—Why, this isn't real writing at all, these are only pages of X's, XXXXXXX, it means nothing. It is just scribbling . . .

—There are no words that say "Dear Sarah"?

—No.

—There are no words that speak of a voyage, and a ship, and returning to London?

—None.

—What?

—No, none of that. It is as if the pages were blank with no writing at all because there are no words . . . Only these crosses.

—No words?

—No, there are no real words, just a lot of X's, it's gibberish—like Hottentot, smiled Caroline.

—And there's no name . . . Nowhere where it says Alexander Dunlop?

—Someone's played a joke on you, Sarah.

There was nothing to do except face up to my master.

—There was nothing on those sheets of paper Master Hendricks read to me except X's . . .

—Who told you that?

—A fairy.

—I don't know what you're talking about, Sarah.

—You tricked me!

He paused for a moment.

—It was Hendrick, not me.

I hated him more at that moment than the white men who had killed my father.

—You never wrote to me!

—Don't be stupid.

—I'm not stupid! I shouted.

—No, said my master slowly, just stupid enough to believe a fairy freak . . . all those so-called X's—why that's your own language, Sarah. I wrote to you in Khoe. Hendrick can read Khoe. You can't.

—Khoekhoe don't write.

—How do you know, woman?

I was taken aback, but I held my ground.

—Khoekhoe write only in the sand, I replied.

—That's because you are too stupid to invent paper! How could I send you a message in sand?

I fingered my lores, uncertain. Could the curse of !Naeheta Magahâs, the-thing-that-should-never-have-been-born, be written? A dull confusion settled over me and everything around me. It pounded in my temples, going round and round in my head. Was this another of their tricks? Was my master lying to me? Was everyone in the entire world lying to me? Or was it just my own Hottentot stupidity? My head throbbed and my vision blurred. I could hardly see at all. To stop the pain, I began to drink in the afternoons or indulge in pipes of *dagga* or morphine. I began to take sips of brandy or gin at night to sleep. But the more I drank and smoked, the more lonely and disgusted with myself I became.

I began to prefer English gin to brandy or the *dappa* of home. Only the cut-glass decanter of colorless firewater produced in me that level of inebriation that erased the humiliation, ridicule and insults heaped upon me every day. To be, as the English called it, in my cups, or, as the Dutch said, *enn borreltje,* was to ever tap my head against the iris-blue sky—I could fly, I could dance, laugh, sing, something gin made you do, not *dappa.* One evening in a restaurant in Bond Street after a bottle of gin, I danced on the table to the music of the twelve-piece orchestra. The next day, there was a cartoon in the London *Times.*

I could never understand how people saw me not as I was but as what they, in their mind, imagined me to be. For example, I was only four feet seven inches tall and my skin was yellow. Yet the English caricaturists always painted me as huge as a whale, weighing a ton and black. I was pictured as being as tall as a white man like Lord Grenville, who was five feet eleven, or Thomas Pelham, who was six feet tall. My bottom, as the English called my buttocks, was equal to the prime minister's bottom although I was half his size, and to that of the foreign secretary, who was three times my size. How to explain it? My masters tripled the advertisements and printed five hundred more engravings.

I wondered if gin was the medicine the rainmaker said she didn't have. This magic that allowed me to survive? I began to crave the contents of my crystal flagons more than anything else. At night, in my room, I would quietly drink myself to sleep either from the amber bottle (brandy) or the colorless bottle (gin); somehow I preferred the colorless bottle, but it depended on my mood. If I was mad, it was gin. If I was sad, it was brandy. I began imbibing my precious tumblers earlier and earlier in the day, until I approached the five o'clock teatime. Alone in my dressing room, between shows, I drank to forget Master Dunlop. I drank to forget Master Caesar. I drank to forget the massacres. I drank to forget what the rainmaker had said. I drank to forget the trial. I drank to while away the time. I drank because I was ashamed; I drank because I needed to drink. I thought no one noticed, but Caroline did.

When I wasn't working at number 53, I visited her at number 225. Late in the evening, I would trudge down Piccadilly Street, which was really a roundabout, to see her. Caroline seemed to me more frail than ever, her eyes larger than her tiny hands, her skin white and clammy. She received more than two hundred visitors a day and was kept on exhibit twelve or thirteen hours each day.

—Sarah, you have got to stop. You are drinking much too much gin.
I grinned.
—Not too much, Caroline, just enough, just enough.
—Bad for you.
—It helps me sleep.
—Then why do you drink at five?
—I never drink at five. I have tea at five. I love tea . . .
—Dr. Gilligan says . . .
—Little children yes. But I am a full-grown woman.

I needed *vaderlantje,* needed it in my bones, my sinews, my soul. I was in terrible anguish if I found myself out of sight of my bottle of brandy or my carafe of gin. Then, there came that time when I realized I could not live without drinking. This was the winter of 1811.

And when the snow and rains came and the chill of the dull sooty English winter was at its worst, tiny Caroline fell ill. Her doctors bled, cupped, purged the miniature body to no avail. The fairy princess died in my arms of pleurisy.

The death of Caroline brought back sharp memories of the day I had burned the body of !Kung on the beach. I kept the Sicilian fairy's book of Grimm's fairy tales as a memento, although I still couldn't read it by myself. I also found a pair of her tiny doeskin gloves and added them to my extravagant collection. The Sicilian fairy's keeper, a certain Dr. Gilligan, along with his wife and brother-in-law, an actor, had stolen her body away from their lodgings on Duke Street, St. James's, in the dead of night. They had disappeared owing the landlord twenty-five pounds. Left behind were the fairy's tiny cast-iron bed and all her costumes. But even worse, Dr. Gilligan had sold Caroline for five hundred pounds. She was bought to be dissected and used as an anatomy lesson for the Royal College of Surgeons. The other circus freaks claimed her death was never reported to the police and that another anatomist had offered Dr. Gilligan even more for her body. When Caroline's father arrived from Dublin to claim her remains, her skeleton was already on display at the Royal College. Caroline's tragic end frightened me into drinking even more. For I also realized that a fickle public was getting tired of the Hottentot Venus.

Master Dunlop and Master Caesar began to have fewer receipts. The price of viewing went up to four shillings. My room was locked at night and the key hung around my master's neck. I no longer cared. I was sick at heart. Master Dunlop decided that a tour of England would revive my spirits, and our popularity in London. They would miss us while we were gone. He made still another promise that at the end of the tour, we would go home to the Cape.

—The working class and the country gentry deserve the shows of London. They are as curious to see the wonders of the world as the Londonians are . . .

—Am I to exhibit myself once more, to prove that I am free? I asked.

—You will recover your notoriety as well as add to the cashbox, replied my master. We have been in London more than two years and tens of thousands of people have seen you. It is time to move on.

We soon had bookings for Bath, Maidstone, Dublin, Leicester, Birmingham, Liverpool, Nottingham and Manchester. To me, they were simply more English names to learn, points on a map. Except for Manchester. There, my beloved Reverend Freehouseland waited for me. I could at least stand and weep over his grave. My only solace now were the cut-glass tumblers of Booth's gin I had lately acquired a craving for. The spirit shops on Bond Street all knew me now by name. I knew what to do in order not to be afraid anymore—not to feel the English contempt, their black laughter, their black looks, my black silence. I would drink.

We left London towards the middle of June for Leicester. London had begun to stink as piles of refuse accumulated all over the city and rats and stray dogs and cats roamed the streets. I was glad to be leaving the city. In

167

spite of myself I felt a dull expectation. Scores of white-clad ladies and gentlemen who had not yet fled nonchalantly picked their way across the rotting garbage on the streets to take tea. The carriage and the supply wagon rumbled down the cobbled avenue leading from St. James's Square at great speed. It was the season of cholera, typhus and diphtheria in London. Since I had had none of these diseases, it was just as well to remove ourselves from the city and its filth, which putrefied under the June sun. Who knew but that I would find peace in the countryside? After all, I had Master Dunlop's word that he was now divorced and that I would be married before the autumn was over. By dawn we had reached the outskirts of the mill town of Leicester. From a distance, Leicester resembled a shimmering storm of dust, soot and cotton lint. A cloud swirled around the entire city like a fog and rose up over it, blotting out the sun. From the haze and heat, a rainbow appeared for a brief moment in the gray sky. As we approached, the stench of dyes, caustics and ammonia assaulted our noses, and entering the city, we heard the thump of heavy machinery and the vibrating looms shaking the ground like drums.

—You can be sure, said my master, that this town has never seen anything like you.

The heavily laden covered wagons in which we also slept and that carried all we possessed—our luggage, the tents, the sets for the exhibit, even the plants and painted posters—rumbled into town. We would stay only a week or so in each town, and searching for new lodgings in each city would waste too much time. Only in the large towns like Manchester, where we were to meet Master Taylor, would we seek out separate lodgings. I was used to traveling from place to place, I had spent my childhood in a tent that could be pitched in less than an hour by a woman as we moved from grazing land to grazing land, following the seasons, living off the land. Now I had returned to that life as we moved through the English countryside.

It was filled with greenery and majestic woods. Every acre was cultivated and sculpted by man's hand, not like the wild and savage landscapes of the Cape. Here all was neatly trimmed, walled in, planned and tended. Nothing was left to chance, to the winds and rains, to the devices of Mother Nature.

Leicester was a mill town of thirty thousand, where fifteen thousand workers were employed to print calico. It was a neat solid town, and every day, new inventions doubled the output of weavers even as they learned to use the flying shuttle and the power loom. Women and children worked beside men just as they did in the coal mines, the brick kilns, the porcelain kilns and the salt quarries. As our carriage entered the city, a whistle blew, signaling the end of the working day, and factory workers aged from five to sixty swarmed out of the crowded sheds and brick and wooden buildings and onto the narrow winding streets heading towards their low, thatch-roofed cottages. They looked as poor as Hottentots, I thought, as if poverty knew no frontier and no race. It was said that the world could not subsist without the poor, for if all were rich, none would submit to the demands of another. It was, then, God's own will, that some were rich and most poor.

We raised the tent just outside of town, in a field of clover. The next day, I stood on its stage in my cage and my silk sheath, glaring down at the pallid, dirty, red-eyed audience, who silently gazed back at me in awe. I was indeed a female the likes of which they had never seen. I wore and did the same things I had done in London, but I felt in less danger with these country folk even though their faces and their jokes were just as cruel. They brought their animals, dogs, goats, chickens, and their children, who either stared amazed or burst into tears. Many women came, their hands bright blue from the indigo dyes. We had hired a sword-swallower and a fire-eater, Mr. Henry and Mr. Lockwood, to open the show. They performed their act to polite applause. Then, I appeared. To one side stood the gentry and the mill owners, to the other stood the mill workers, the farmworkers and scattered policemen to make sure there was no disorder. The best part was the fireworks we set off in the meadow.

We made our way from town to town with our penny playbills and makeshift tent. From the looms of Birmingham to the chalk quarries of Liverpool to the steelworks of Leeds, the potteries of north Staffordshire, the foundries of Sheffield, the mines around Newcastle, the glassworks and distilleries of Bristol, the naval dockyards at Chatham and silk looms of Spitalfields. Everywhere there were poor, everywhere there were people willing to spend a shilling (for our price had gone down) for a lottery, a pint of beer or a ticket to see the Hottentot Venus. Despite our dismal living conditions, we kept going where there were tickets to be sold. Once, in Bensham, hundreds of men with red eyes and green hair came from the brass works and frightened me more than I amazed them. The men arrived at work at five o'clock in the morning and left it at eight o'clock at night, so we gave our performance at ten.

All over the Midlands, we encountered riots, strikes and lockouts because of the Luddites and the trade unions, who were trying to organize the guilds and mill workers. More than once, we were barred from a town because of police curfews, or an ordinance against any assembly of more than three people. Towards the end of September, we approached Manchester to meet up with Henry Taylor's Touring Shakespeare Company. He would, Master Dunlop assured me, take over our itinerary, which he had organized and paid for in advance. I was curious to see to whom I had been sold.

Manchester was a town of red brick or brick that would have been red if the smoke from the kilns, the brass works, the pottery works, the steelworks had allowed it to be. As it was, it was a red town painted black in strange and ominous designs, like Magahâs's face. There were tall chimneys out of which serpents of smoke trailed on forever and ever, coiling and uncoiling into a snake pit of dark clouds. It had a canal with black water and a river that was purple. There was rattling and trembling from the ironworks and foundries which sounded like the screams of mad elephants. There were several large streets and numerous small alleys and courts around which the laborers' hovels and common latrines were built. Thousands of cottages were built back to back with privies in front and open ashpits in the streets, with a cellar for coal and food and one small room in which to do all the cooking, washing, eating and another in which to sleep. Heaps of refuse and dirt spilled out onto the lanes and alleys. Dark faces peeped out from creaked doors and open windows, watching the circus wagon make its way towards the town square by way of the quay. We gradually moved away from the wretched hovels to a more affluent area, with tall, imposing public buildings: the town hall, the prison, the hospital, the government offices, warehouses, hotels and theaters. Even more than in London, prisons looked like castles, banks like Roman temples, theaters like Egyptian tombs.

—Manchester, said Master Dunlop, is a textile town, Sarah, and don't ever forget it. As a surgeon, I can say without exaggeration that there is more filth, worse physical suffering and moral disorder in the basement population of Manchester than in the worst prisons in Europe. Almost half of all children born into the working class in Manchester die before they reach five years of age.

Was this, I thought, the heavenly Manchester of the Reverend Free-houseland? Was this where all his sweetness and kindness had been born and was buried?

We had almost reached our destination when a filthy woman in rags, whose age you could not tell, suddenly appeared beside the coach, running as fast as the horses, grasping the door handle of the carriage:

—You, you people the circus? she panted. You need a freak boy? Seven years old. Born with a humpback and a curved spine. I'm selling him cheap for a good home. He sings sweetly and doesn't eat much. My little brother . . .

She raced along beside us, crying out to us without running out of breath for about two hundred paces, and then she dropped back, unable to keep up with our horses. We left her standing in the middle of the lane, one hand on her hip, the other on her head, holding her head rag in place and trying to catch her breath. As I looked back, I had the sense that I had already lived this scene long, long ago; the frozen body of the woman, with the sun behind her casting a long navy shadow, was so familiar to me—it seemed like a lost melody.

—Wait, I said, clutching Master Dunlop. I know that woman, slow down.

—The hell you know her, Sarah, that's impossible. You've never been in Manchester before; how could you know some Manchester working girl?

—But the boy, the humpback.

—We don't need any more freaks or any more mouths to feed. He'd probably die on us anyway.

—But you're a doctor . . .

—*Was* a doctor—not anymore. Look, we've arrived.

By the time we had unloaded our luggage and given the horses to the stableboy, the woman had caught up with us again. She kept her distance, simply squatting in her filthy skirts, pleading with her eyes. Despite the restraining hand of my master, I went over to her. She started with surprise when she saw my face, but quickly recovered.

—Who are you? I said, as if in a dream.

—M'name's Alice Unicorn . . . ma'am, at your service.

—We can't help your little brother, but I need someone to help me undress . . .

Before I could get the words out, she had sprung at my trunk, picking it up and curtsying at the same time, a mean trick.

—Come, I said, we'll get you something to eat. You look like you're starving to death.

—Ain't ate in four days, ma'am. Lost my job at the mill, couldn't feed my brother.

—Come on, Sarah, my master called from the steps. And don't pick up that beggar!

—She's not begging, I said, it is I who am asking. I nodded and Alice Unicorn followed me into the inn. Henry Taylor was nowhere to be seen, so I sent Alice to the kitchen to be fed and climbed the stairs to my room.

Suddenly I knew what the forlorn, ragged girl reminded me of. Running alongside the carriage with her elbows flapping, her neck outstretched and despair in her eyes, she made me think of my mother trying to escape the guns of the Boer patrols. Except for the dirt and grime which made her as black as I was, she looked like a female Reverend Freehouseland—same heavy, dark eyebrows, same-color eyes, same straight nose, same mouth. She could have been his daughter.

By the time the roving actor's troupe arrived the next day with its owner, Henry Taylor, Alice had already unpacked my clothes, prepared my bath, washed my linen and taken Caroline's little dog out.

—You saved my life, ma'am. I was going to drown myself and Victor in the river last night.

She said it so matter-of-factly that I knew she was telling the truth, that last night she would have died if it hadn't been for me. Alice firmly believed this and I believed her. It became a kind of emblem between us. Her life was mine because I had rescued it.

—Shabby as we are, said Master Taylor, his bright eyes blinking, we contrive to make a good show when we enter a town. There are handbills and drums and maybe a piper. We lodge in inns or the houses of tradesmen, use barns to store our properties and put on our costumes. We raise a tent with banners in a meadow or a marketplace if there is no theater or town hall. Or we have even taken a large room in an inn and turned it into a players' house by suspending green draperies from the ceiling (the color of players' curtains must be green). Hard as this life is, I'd have no other . . . If I have money, he laughed, I lend it. If I have none, I do without. We players are a set of merry undone dogs, he laughed again, and though we often want the means of life, we are seldom without the means of mirth. We play the country fairs and the houses of country squires alongside the acrobats, freaks, musicians and singers, ropedancers, fortune-tellers and keepers of strange animals such as bears and Hottentots . . .

14

Why would the actual races not be modifications of those
ancient races that are found amongst fossils, modifications which would have been shown by local circumstances and the change of climate, and explained by the
long succession of years?

—BARON GEORGES LÉOPOLD CUVIER,
*Discourse on the Revolutionary Upheavals
on the Surface of the Globe*

*C*rooked Fire, the English month of April, 1812. So this was the man
who now owned one fourth of me, I thought. He was short and stocky
without being fat, although he had a potbelly and his legs were bowed.
But his face was the handsomest I had ever seen, even more beautiful than
John Kemble's, and his eyes were an unearthly green, as green as African
orchids. His eyes as well as his mouth never stopped laughing, and despite
myself, I was caught up in his mirth and could not resist his good humor.
He was also, as we all would find out, a softhearted crook, ready with any
scheme to fleece the public or cheat at cards, for which he had an uncon-
trollable passion. Except when he was in costume, he always wore a green

scarf wrapped around his neck, a gold earring and, on his left little finger, a signet ring bearing a coat of arms he claimed was his. He was, he told us one night, the illegitimate son of the Earl of Carnarvon and had been born at Highclere—then he changed it to the Earl of Moira of Donington Park in Leicestershire. No one believed him, but we all loved listening to his extravagant lies.

After Alice became my temporary servant, she and Master Taylor would try to outdo one another with outrageous tales of their hardships and childhood. This is how I learned that Alice was only a few years older than me, although she looked twenty years more. She was perhaps five feet five and had sloping shoulders, wide hips and ample breasts that she bound in linen. A year before, her father had died a violent death, crushed under an avalanche of tons of clay slush that had gushed from the brick factory kiln near Bridestone, where he worked. Her younger sister, who had worked in the Wedgwood porcelain factory, had died of lead poisoning and her older brothers and sisters all worked in the kilns or coal mines of Manchester. Alice had been taken out of the nail factory, where she had been put to work at seven years old, and allowed to attend school until she was twelve. She had learned to read and write and count in the hope that she might enter the convent of St. Jeremy just outside of the town as a servant girl and perhaps even a novice. But, she explained, her religious education had taken a bad turn because her natural skepticism and rebellious nature were not the clay to make a nun. She had resisted religion in her nunnery just as I had resisted reading in my orphanage. Yet we both agreed the nunnery and the orphanage had been the only safety we had ever known in life. When it was decided she was not fit for a nunnery, Alice was sent into service in the manor house of the Duke of Chester. There she began her life of service as a weeder in the vast Italian-style gardens of the park, then she worked as a scullery maid, a kitchen maid, a laundry maid and finally as a dairy maid. The duke employed forty-six servants, sixteen of whom were upper servants divided into many grades and ranks. Thus she had learned the workings of a great house from top to bottom, just as I had learned to keep Mistress Alya's mansion.

—There were special china cloths and dusters for housemaids, she explained, glass cloths for the butler, pocket cloths for the footman, lamp cloths for the porter, horn cloths for the servants' hall boy. The dustpans were all numbered; each housemaid had her own and had to learn how to hold it together with a candle in one hand so that she could use the brush with the other. Alice also had to learn to polish the metal fittings on furniture with fine sand, how to polish paintwork with cream dressing, how to sweep carpets with damp tea leaves, how to remove old polish with vinegar, mix new beeswax with turpentine; how to wash high ceilings with soda and water while standing on a stepladder nine feet high; how to dust brocaded walls and rub them down with tissue paper and silk dusters; how to unstring and scrub venetian blinds; how to take up and beat carpets; how to whiten corridors with pipe clay and spread French chalk on hardwood floors before a ball; how to make a bed, how to lay a tea table, remember at what time sunlight came into the various rooms so that the blinds could be drawn to protect the furniture or that windows could be opened to air the room . . .

—I could tell you a thing or two about cleaning a house . . . Ever have to tie up a heifer's tail to keep her rump clean?

—You're joking, laughed Alice.

—*My brush is my sword; my broom, my weapon/Sleep I know not, nor any repose . . .*

—And for that I earned five pounds a year as an under-housemaid, laughed Alice. But I was on my way to being an upstairs maid when one of the duke's sons caught me under the stairs, raped me and got me with child. I was dismissed as soon as the steward found out about my pregnancy and thrown out without a reference. Without a reference there was no hope of finding another job in service. After the baby came, I found work as a wet nurse and had to leave my child in the care of my mother. I named him Eric. When he was eighteen months old, he died during the week of Lent. I couldn't get home to give him a proper funeral for a month because my mistress had guests. I never went back. I got a job in a textile factory working the loom, quite a step down from service in a great house. I found a hovel to rent and moved out of my mother's shack in the brickfields where she worked. My mother had given birth to twelve children, five of which survived until adulthood. Just after my father died, she told me she was pregnant again and could no longer keep my little brother Victor at home. What was I to do? I told her I would take him in. But I lost my job at the mill after an accident damaged my loom. The superintendent fired me without pay and once again without a reference. I was out on the street. I'd been looking for work for months. I'd put Victor out to beg, that's when I saw your circus caravan arriving.

Alice had had a life more wretched than a Hottentot's. She had lost her baby. She too was an orphan. She was my sister under the skin. I vowed to keep her close to me and find a solution for Victor.

—But if you come with us, what will happen to Victor?

—But he can come too! He doesn't eat much and he can be a freak! He has a *big* hump and spindly legs, we can make him into something. He can sleep under my bed. I will take care of him, I promise.

Master Taylor had the answer.

—Well, he said, there are three types of freaks: a natural-born freak, a made freak and a fake freak. Our little Victor here would fall into the category of a "made" freak, if he's willing to learn the trade and endure a little pain. People need thrills, they need to wonder about somethin', including the marvels of nature. This is what I call show business. Show business is the art of catering to the slenderly learned and common sort. It is the same as accounts of murders, executions, witchcraft and other prodigies. The English are a nation of starers and they have a taste for monsters that cuts across all classes. Strange sights and monstermongers have never been more popular and all kinds of deformation bring fame and fortune. Now our little prodigy here is going to have a fine, monstrous birth. I am going to stick a giant turtleshell, which I know *exactly* where to find, on his *natural* hump and produce a wondrous little turtle-boy whose head peeks in and out of his body as if by magic and his skinny legs curl up inside his shell jus' like a real turtle when he crawls . . . With a shell, Victor will be a sensation, he's small and scrawny enough with his spindly legs to convince anybody he was born a turtle! Let's see your face now. Yes. A little coal dust around the eyes, a fake beak for a nose, a scaly neck and you'll be perfect! I agree to take him along if he's willing to become a player! He must never let his guard down in public or allow himself to be seen as anything else than Victor the turtle-boy . . . When I finish with him, they'll all be singing:

> *Come neere, good Christians all,*
> *Behold a monster rare,*
> *Whose monstrous shape no doubt foretells*
> *God's wrath we should beware . . .*

Alice jumped for joy. It was a wonderful idea.

—But he's got to be funny, see? The people want to laugh at terror, not run from it! The people need to laugh at him, continued Victor's new manager.

And, I thought to myself, Yes, Victor, you must survive their laughter. And that was the hardest. Without my daily pint of gin, I could never have survived.

Now that I was in Manchester, I determined to find my beloved Reverend Freehouseland. Alice and I eventually found his grave in the quiet, frozen, treeless cemetery behind the gray stone bell tower of Christ's Church in the parish of Littleburn. Large flakes of snow began to fall and I drew my long red cape around me. As we stood, our heads bowed, a new reverend, who resembled him, approached us.

—You are strangers here, he said. Are you new workers at the mill?

—No, Reverend, we are circus people on tour. We will be here only a few weeks. But this woman, Sarah, was a slave to the Reverend Freehouseland at the Cape Colony. She was freed by him before he died. She came today to find his grave and pay her respects.

—An African? A member of Cecil's mission? At the Cape?

—Yes, from the Cape of Good Hope. A lady from the Cape of Good Hope, repeated Alice.

—Well, this is where he lies in peace. He pointed to the gravestone:

CECIL JAMES FREEHOUSELAND
Beloved son, servant of God
African missionary to the Heathen.
Savior of Their Souls
1756—1796
Psalm XV

—So you are a Christian? the priest said, turning to me.

—No, Reverend, I was never baptized.

—It is never too late, he said. Allow me to instruct you while you sojourn here, as a tribute to my old friend Cecil.

—You knew him?

—We were in the seminary together. We are both from Manchester, native sons, so to speak, who traveled to far-off places, I to China, Cecil to Africa . . .

—I wouldn't read the Book, I confessed. It wouldn't talk to me.

—What book?

—The Bible.

—Well, he paused, perhaps you had your reasons.

—Yes, I couldn't read.

At this, he laughed, the sound swishing out of him like the wind.

—Who are you?

—Well, let's say, Reverend, interrupted Alice, Sarah has traveled far and wide because of her extraordinary body. People in England had never seen anyone like her before, neither her color nor her shape. Most have never seen a black person.

—People pay to see her because her skin is black?

—That partly. And for other things as well. She is famous in London. She is known as the Hottentot Venus.

—And you travel the countryside like this, alone?

—No, Reverend, I answered. We travel with my two masters, a dog, a troupe of actors, a few musicians . . .

—And you are a slave to these men?

—Not a slave. Yet they own me. I have made a sacred marriage contract with one of them. The others are his partners.

But the reverend didn't understand.

—You understand, child, that living with a man who is not your husband is a sin.

—A sin?

—But, Reverend, she is chaste, protested Alice.

—Nevertheless. It is unseemly. I don't think Father Cecil would approve.

—Then save her, Reverend, said Alice.

—I intend to, Miss . . .

—Alice Unicorn.

—It is the least I can do for Cecil. Why, I couldn't walk past his grave if I didn't at least try.

—He left me ten pounds in his will but it was never paid to me by his family.

—And you came all this way here to claim it?

—I came to escape from the Cape. To be free, to earn money to save my clan.

—The Freehouselands are all good Christians.

179

—Perhaps, but also thieves.

—You were but a child then.

—All the more shame.

—Come with me, child. The reverend turned and started towards the church. I was glad Alice was with me. She knew the ways of the English. I would have been frightened all by myself. Inside the church, the ceiling rose high above my head and curved even higher in stone arches of great beauty. The aisles flickered with lit candles, the polished wooden benches reflected in the gloom. At the end of the long hall was a simple altar draped in white linen and a high wooden pulpit on which hung a gold crucifix.

—Can you read at all, Sarah?

—A little. A fairy taught me. And now, Alice is teaching me.

—Well, if you can read and understand the prayer book I'm going to give you, and answer a few simple questions, I can baptize you and welcome you into the flock of Jesus Christ as a Christian and an Episcopalian. Would you like that? It means that you can no longer live in sin with those men without an act of holy matrimony.

—But I'm their servant.

—And I'm her chaperone, Alice lied.

—Nevertheless, said the priest sternly, the Church of England would not approve.

I said nothing. Perhaps this was what Magahâs meant. Eternal wandering amongst whites without ever reaching a destination. I had walked from home to Cape Town on a road that had no turnoffs, no crossroads; it simply had gone on, mile after mile, in a straight line. I would never see the Cape again, I thought. I would never retrieve my ten pounds. I would never ever hear another Cape lion roar. The Reverend Freehouseland had guided me to this end-of-the-world.

—The Lord be praised, said Father Joshua, for bringing me one of his lost sheep.

—Lost sheep? I am a shepherdess.

—The Lord is our shepherd, child, but it certainly doesn't hurt that you are one too. I'm expecting your visit soon, Sarah.

I nodded and took Alice's arm. It seemed to me that my salvation was a huge and ominous undertaking. It was more, I thought, than just a ritual passage from childhood to adulthood. It was a passage from Africa to England.

—I have my own way of illustrating truths, the reverend began on my first visit. I preach the love of Christ, the need of regeneration and the judgment to come. I regard a Christian as a fully developed man or woman and as a creature that has not only civil, domestic and social duties but a body, a brain and a soul to be cared for. You understand?

Slowly, he led me through simple passages he called the word of God. He would hold forth on a subject passionately, then pause and say, "Let's hear what the Savior says," and seek a passage in the New Testament. Then, he would make a bold, striking comment. Sometimes funny, sometimes referring to my own life or to the circus, although he had never come to see the spectacle. The idea that God was speaking directly to me began to take root in my thoughts. I never for a moment doubted that he, the preacher, believed he was reading the words of God. Many times the word "shepherd" would appear in the text—*The Lord is my shepherd*—and he would laugh and point to me and speak of my father's flocks. And a long, pent-up sigh or a smile or a tear would escape me, I could never predict which. I was completely in his hands.

He was a better actor than Master Taylor. He could imitate a drunken man before a judge, an angel announcing the end of the world, a glass-blower making a vase or a carpenter building a house. He would imitate a man cutting down a tree, pulling in a fishing net, a swallow rising on its wings, a turkey strutting, a dog barking, a wolf howling at the moon. He had a particular shrug of his shoulders, and if he spoke of hypocrites, he would draw his face down and make himself so funny, so pompous, that I had to laugh. I was never bored or afraid. He kept me breathless and awake with his parables, as he called them, from his life, from his journeys, his cold nights, his warm seasons, his travels in China, his struggles with sin and the lightninglike power of evil.

—Some men like their bread cold, some like it hot. I like mine hot, he would say.

He gave me a prayer book and said that when I could read aloud the passages he chose, he would baptize me. To do so, Father Joshua had to ask permission from the Bishop of Chester, a formidable man who lived in Wedgewood. After that, we met in the Sunday school room, full of pictures and flowers, an organ and a melodeon. It smelled of beeswax and chalk, of wild ferns and the good odor of children. It made me think of painted caves, rough mountains, calm sea and !Kung. I learned from Father Joshua that Father Freehouseland had suffered greatly in Africa from a host of disappointments, illnesses and solitude. He had missed his wife after she had returned to England.

—I do believe he bought you to free you, Father Joshua said one day. I can't believe he was a slave owner.

—Oh, he bought only children, I said, or very young people, and always in the name of the Lord. He bought us to save us . . .

On the day Father Joshua announced to me that I was ready for baptism, he already had the bishop's permission. I was overjoyed. It took place the following evening at vespers. The church was almost full. The sound of people finding the hymn was like the rustling of peacock feathers. They all stood, all sang, all welcomed me into their Kingdom. Alice stood as my godmother and Victor as my godfather. All my Christian masters were there: Master Taylor, the saint; Master Dunlop, the knight; and Master Caesar, the patriarch.

As the chalice of water trickled over my head, I closed my eyes and the image of the one-legged purple heron came to me, just as if I were standing alone, deep in the African forest.

December 1, Register of the Collegiate and Sarah Baartman, a female Hottentot from the Colony of the Cape of Good Hope, born in the borders of Caffravia, baptized this day by permission of the Lord Bishop of Chester sent by letter from his Lordship to Jos. Brooks, Chaplain.

Witness, Joshua Brooks

We all gathered around the headstone of Cecil James Freehouseland. I wore a new hooded cloak, made of the finest double-milled wool and of such an intense scarlet that it threw a glimmer whenever it moved. It was long and full with large folds like the closed wings of a flamingo. The white men had won in the end. I was a Christian. I had a Christian name, Sarah, and I had a Christian country, the Kingdom of God. I was safe from damnation as a heathen.

—Can I be married in a church now that I am baptized?

—I have a better idea, replied Master Dunlop like a bolt of lightning.

—Why don't we return to the church with Father Joshua this very moment so that he can marry us tonight? We can use this, he said. He took a brass ring off his little finger.

And so, that same evening, Alice and Victor were again witnesses. My master was now my husband, my keeper was also my bridegroom. The Reverend Brooks was happy to forgo the publication of the marriage banns. I had time only to lay my bride's bouquet of mistletoe on the grave of my late master before the circus left for Bath. I whispered my news to him, thinking it would please him to know I had finally come into his Kingdom of Christ.

—If he wanted to keep you from ever running away from him, the best way to do so was to have married you, complained Alice. If you ran away as a slave, you could go for help to the African Institution and the Reverend Wedderburn. If you run away from Dunlop now, as his wife, he can send the constables after you to bring you back as his property and no one will lift a finger. No one will help you because you are legally his. He can shut you up in his house and throw away the key. He can starve you or beat you or rape you and no policeman or magistrate can touch him. He can shut you up in an asylum forever and no doctor will contradict him. As your husband, he now possesses *all* your money. Your dowry, your earnings, your capital are his to do with as he pleases. He's recovered three-quarters of you without spending a shilling!

> *That which the husband hath is his own.*
> *That which the wife hath is the husband's.*

—He at least had to pay you as his servant, and as his slave you could claim your freedom on English soil. As his wife, you are nothing except his property. He doesn't have to pay a wife. He has only to feed you and clothe you and provide a roof over your head. As your legal husband, all your money is now his. So is your body. That's the law. You have given up liberty, estate and authority to a man. And on top of that, Sarah, would you ever dishonor yourself by running away from your husband in the eyes of God? No! Well, I think it's all Hendrick Caesar's idea. This way he can return to the Cape of Good Hope with his money and his conscience clear. And now Dunlop has you back even though he sold you to Henry Taylor. You're his property again. Just as before. This time he's gotten you back without paying . . . Don't you see?

But I didn't see.

15

Understand that the word "species" means the individuals who descend from one another or from common parents and those who resemble them as much as they resemble each other. Thus, we call varieties of a species only those races more or less different which can arise from it by reproduction. Our observations on the differences amongst the ancestors and the descendants are therefore for us the only reasonable rule, because all others would take us back to hypotheses without proofs.

—Baron Georges Léopold Cuvier,
*Discourse on the Revolutionary Upheavals
on the Surface of the Globe*

*B*lack moon, the English month of May, 1812. Despite all of my husband's promises to return to Africa, our life of touring England lasted for two more years. Master Hendrick did indeed decide he wanted to return to the Cape with his share of the profits. With him went the last of my past, the last of my Africa. I would not miss him. I didn't love him, and as a master, he had been neither kind nor honorable. As a matter of fact, I probably hated him, although this sentiment never came to the surface of my thoughts. In all, I was happy to be rid of him. The idea of never seeing him again filled me with joy. I never saw or heard from him again. His face faded into forgetfulness and became only a blur in the long procession of men to whom I had belonged. He would return to his family with my riches. Some other servant would wash his feet while he discussed the triumph of his Hottentot Venus in faraway London. He left at the end of 1812 on the same ship on which we had all arrived, the *Exeter*. Master Dunlop took the rest of the money as my dowry and the last expenses left our cashbox empty. The tour of England and Ireland became a necessity instead of a choice. During those years of 1812 and 1813, we crisscrossed the Midlands, the northern counties of Lancaster, Cumberland and Yorkshire, and Northern Ireland. We traveled by caravan, covered wagon and coach. Our painted canvas posters advertising the Hottentot Venus were always hung on the sides of our carriage along with the advertisements for Henry Taylor's theater. Along the way, actors, clowns, freaks, animal trainers, musicians and magicians joined or left our little troupe, falling off or climbing on at will, in the backwater villages, country fairs and itinerant markets selling everything from cattle to cotton. Many of the vagabond performers disappeared as quickly as they came, leaving nothing behind, not even a memory. Like Master Caesar. I was now divided between my husband, Master Dunlop, and the actor Master Taylor. Just as I forgot Master Caesar, I forgot the countless cities and towns, castles and manor houses, villages and fairs in which we performed.

My attachment to Alice Unicorn grew. When we could, we would close ourselves up in the caravan and read the Collects, the Bible, the *Times Almanac* and *Reading Made Easy*. Master Taylor had lent us his copy of *The Complete Works of William Shakespeare*. Victor as the turtle-boy was a sensation and grew into a popular attraction. Our "made" freak earned money both for himself and for his sister.

—Since men's minds are haunted by the desire to change nature's smallest quirk into truth based on their own fantasies, then let us oblige them with our turtle-boy, Master Taylor would say as he stuffed Victor's head down into his papier-mâché neck.

Victor's "neck" was a cardboard collar covered with snakeskin, wide enough to poke his head in and out of. Strapped to the hump on his back was a giant turtleshell that Master Taylor had bought from another circus man in Liverpool. The transformation was amazing and terrifying. Each day Victor the turtle-boy was born out of snakeskin and a lie. His rebirth into a thing-that-should-never-have-been-born was only so that

Englishmen could marvel at the wonders of nature and cross themselves that there but for the grace of God went they. They cheered and clapped and whistled and laughed as if the very meaning of their lives depended upon his deformity and his sorrow.

Whenever we appeared in a new town, our masters would go off to find some game of chance where they might win something to supplement our meager earnings and fill our purse until the next town: craps, poker, *trente-et-un*, anything that might keep us until the box office opened. We left a string of bad debts behind us: unpaid hotel rooms and angry gamblers we had fleeced. Even though he was my husband, my master rarely slept in the same room with me, and when he did, it was usually to sleep off the effects of a night of drinking and gambling. I was grateful for his neglect. Although I had been happy with Kx'au, I had never understood the fascination connected with the performance of sex. I had never been transported by the ecstasy that was supposed to accompany it.

We appeared in the large cities of Northampton, Nottingham, Wakefield and Leeds. We had become true vagabonds by now. There was little pretense of an acting troupe. We were a circus and freak show of chattering monkeys, a turtle-boy, some acrobats, a giant named Captain Battery and a Hottentot called Venus. We traveled in our ragtag caravan while the poor—the workers, the herders, the shepherds and peasants—for whom threepence was too high a price to pay for amusements, rebelled against their rich landlords and owners, for which they were named the Luddites. Like the Khoekhoe, once they rose they were quickly put down by the police and constables hired by the factory owners.

The revolt spread and seemed to follow our route, arriving just after we had left, or just before we reached, a new city. Workers convicted of machine breaking were sentenced to death under the Frame Breaking Act of Parliament. After one attack in Yorkshire which left a mill owner dead, over one hundred workers were rounded up, seventeen of whom were hanged. Alice almost left the circus to return home to join the rebels when a mill in Manchester was set on fire and thirty-seven weavers were charged with sedition. When we did return, eight men had been sentenced to death and thirteen transported to Australia. We didn't stay long. We were suspected not only of harboring criminals but also, because of Alice, of spreading sedition.

We traveled further north to Ireland. The revolts lasted for two more years. Several times we hid Luddites and escaping clothworkers. For a short while, we believed the Luddites might start what Alice called a revolution. But eventually most of them were caught, and the last of their heroes, James Towle, executed.

Time passed, and whatever else I did in those years of roaming through the countryside, I saw into the very heart of the mighty. How many Englishmen had stood before my body in awe, mirth or contempt? Alice guessed a thousand days of a thousand people. A million souls. Could this have been possible? I could not conceive of such a number until she said:

—All the migrating birds of the Camboos River in the sky at the same time.

In Pale moon, the English month of June, 1814, everything changed. We arrived in Bath, where Master Taylor's players were to perform for the Earl of Bath and his friend and guest the Earl of Bedford. Bath was a spa built around warm springs, a tawdry place where gentlemen came to dance in top boots, wore swords and smoked in the presence of ladies. Soldiers, adventurers, rogues and gamblers abounded. Lodgings were so expensive we lived in the covered wagons of the caravan. Sedan-chair men were rude and quarrelsome and duels were as common as drunkenness. The whole city was taken up with having a good time. In the morning ladies were fetched in a closed palankeen and transported to the baths, already dressed in their bathing clothes. While music played, white women's bodies were tended and flattered. A little wooden dish floating in the pool held their handkerchief or nosegay or snuffbox. Men were on one side, ladies on the other, but often the sexes mixed, conversed, made vows or appointments for later and sometimes made love. Then they would all return to their lodgings for an evening of theater and amusement.

It was in Bath that a Frenchman named Réaux, who owned a dancing bear, joined the players. I took him for the devil. First he had appeared out of nowhere. Then, there was his dancing bear, Adolph, a huge red-eyed beast hung with rattling brass chains that followed him everywhere. Alice told me he was a Breton and played the French bagpipe, to which his bear danced. But it was his appearance that struck me, for he resembled his bear. His face was covered with a thick black beard and mustache, so that his mouth was invisible. His nose resembled a snout with its large wide nostrils. He had the small yellow eyes of a bear and from sideburns to eyebrows his oversized head was covered with thick bristly hair, which stood up in tufts as if raised by the wind whether there was any wind or not. To press it down, he wore a wide black felt hat with a deep brim. The hat seemed to be part of his head. He also had the paws of a bear, huge, hairy wide hands with short fingers and long nails. His body was bearlike with thick rounded shoulders and a wide, muscly, hairy chest. It seemed he was the closest to an ape a man could be without being one. Yet he was a polite, practical man, a renegade noble turned republican on the run since the Revolution, in which he had lost everything. We exchanged few words and tried to avoid each other. I could not imagine what I could have to say to Master Réaux. Sometimes he danced all alone with his bear, the two of them locked in a strange war dance of stamping and turns that was both mysterious and ridiculous. The lone Réaux would dance, oblivious of everything and everyone, and the bear would circle him, imitating each movement, while the morose strains of bagpipes surrounded the two animals with sound. But he was a white man, I thought, and so his strange looks were deemed acceptable if ugly. But to me he was a monster.

For their performance before the Earl of Bath, Master Taylor chose a comedy by William Shakespeare called *A Midsummer Night's Dream*. It was my favorite play because it began in a wood in a faraway land that could have been the Cape. And it was about things-that-should-never-have-been-born, animals that I knew by name, and fairies that reminded me of my beloved Caroline. They had names that I recognized: Peaseblossom, Cobweb, Moth and Mustardseed. And there was an African lion that roared. Alice also loved this play, and she read it over and over to me, because in it there was a weaver, Bottom, and a clothworker, Starveling, and there was a love story between Lysander and Hermia. There were songs about spotted snakes, thorny hedgehogs, bears with bristled hair, and spells and charms that Magahâs might have possessed. Then, at the end, when the lion roars and the couples mate and the things-that-should-never-have-been-born promise that *the blots of Nature's hand/Shall not in their issue stand;/Never mole, hare-lip, nor scar,/Nor mark prodigious, such as are/Despised in nativity,* we freaks cheered and I cried as the fairies blessed us with sweet peace and safety and rest. I clung to Alice and wept in longing for that same sweet safety and rest. I was twenty-five years old and as tired as a field slave of sixty. I had learned to drink and I had learned to read, and I had learned to curse my keepers in their own language.

—Now, now, Sarah, said Master Taylor, I know it's a beautiful play and it reminds you of home, but if you boo-hoo like that much longer, we'll all start to cry. Look, he said, tears rolling down his face, I'm crying already.

—You cry on cue, Master Taylor.

—Not always, Sarah, not always. Life as I've known it is a crying matter . . . a crying game . . . Roulette perhaps or strip poker, I can't figure out which—

—You are like Puck. You can fly away.

—And you cannot?

—My contract, Master Taylor. Have you forgotten?

—I might own you, Sarah, but you don't belong to me—there's a difference. I, for example, belong to the theater. I belong to the characters I play—rather badly.

—Like Mr. Kemble, the actor?

—Well, hardly. I'm just a poor journeyman. He's a true genius.

—I met him once. He came to see me. He cried. He wrote a letter to the African Institution about me, which is why we had to go through the trial.

Master Taylor was silent. Perhaps he was speechless for the first time in his life. Or merely searching for something, some role, some quotation. Then, he said:

—John Kemble's tears were probably genuine . . . Sarah.

—And yours?

—Mine, he said coolly, are those of a professional . . . mourner. People like you and me are born to mourn and weep . . .

Halifax was the next town. Its blazoned wooden signpost will always remain in my mind's eye for it was the turning point in our wanderings in England and it marked my life forever. It was Chewing Wood moon, July, 1814, the wars of Napoleon were over, and what was left of the circus limped into Halifax, where we were to perform for five days. My master planned to stay for the rest of the summer. The pretty city was built around a marketplace, which opened at seven twice a week. As soon as the bell rang, hundreds of merchants, factors and buyers appeared, walking down row after row, inspecting each specialty: wool, worsted, cotton, silk.

Some of them would have their order books, with which they matched colors, holding them up to compare with the cloth. When they saw something that suited them, they reached over to the clothier and in a moment a deal was made or not. In little more than an hour, all the business was done, and in the half hour that followed, the cloths would all disappear as if by magic, carried off to the merchant's house, to a warehouse or to a ship anchored on the river.

Tens of thousands of pounds had changed hands in less than an hour. The boards were taken down, the trestles were gone, the market was empty, its cobblestone square as clean as a whistle. This happened, we learned, twice a week. There were no beggars in Halifax, no idle people, only fresh healthy air, prosperous good people, all employed. This was how I had imagined England to be when I left Cape Town. What I thought I would find in the Reverend Freehouseland's Manchester. Alice Unicorn was also fascinated by Halifax.

—The clothiers live in splendid, neat houses, surrounded by grazing land for their cattle, Alice told me. Every clothier has a horse to fetch wool and provisions, to carry yarn to the spinners and his goods to the market. The workers and their families live in cottages on their own land, all spinning, carding, dying cloths . . . It brings tears to my eyes, she concluded, this is how the world should be . . .

Halifax was only a few miles from the sea and connected to it by canals, which brought the great ships almost into the city. Breezes opened my nostrils to the salt air. A strange calm settled over us and the circus. Master Dunlop spent a great deal of time gazing at the schooners in the harbor, traveling the thirty miles to the sea to inspect them. It was a good place for theater. The multicolored canvas tent we now performed in was full every night. Halifax had a handsome temple and next to it a public square where the tent could be set up. It also had a rich population. We sent an unshelled Victor out with the handbills. We didn't stay in the caravans but in a comfortable inn in the center of the town. Master Taylor ordered new clothes for everyone. I ordered new dresses for myself and Alice. The receipts in such a city would be good. I could demand anything of my husband and master, I reasoned.

The large sums of money that circulated in Halifax attracted adventurers and gamblers. There was a gaming house, a casino and a private club where cards were played. And so it was that Master Taylor was happy to settle in peaceful, prosperous Halifax as well. Even little Victor was happy. I was lulled into a state of peace that could almost be described as contentment. We now had enough money to return to the Cape. I hoped Alice would come with me.

When neither Master Taylor nor my husband came back to the inn one night, I thought nothing of it. They often stayed out all night gambling with their cronies and drinking at the pubs which lined the quays of the canal. It was not until the afternoon of the second day that I heard loud male voices singing "The Ballad of the Hottentot Venus for the Ladies of Bath" as their heavy footsteps slowly climbed the creaking wooden stairs.

> *Fair Ladies, I've sail'd, in obedience to you,*
> *From BATH, since the last Masquerade, to PERU:*
> *There, to guard 'gainst all possible scandal to night,*
> *I turn'd Priest, and have conjur'd my Black-a-moor white.*
>
> *A strange Metamorphosis!—Who that had seen us*
> *T'other night, would take this for the* Hottentot Venus;
> *Or me for poor Jack?—Now I'm priest of the Sun,*
> *And She, a quere kind of Peruvian Nun:*
>
> *Though in this our Novitiate, we* preach *but so, so,*
> *You'll grant that at least we* appear *comme il faut.*
> *In pure Virgin robes, full of fears and alarms,*
> *How demurely she veils her protuberant charms!*
>
> *Thus oft', to atone for absurdities past,*
> *Tom Fool turns a Methodist Preacher at last,*
> *Yet the Critics, not we, were to blame—For 'od rot 'em,*
> *There was nothing but innocent fun* at the bottom!

Finally Master Taylor opened the door and staggered in. His unshaven beard and red eyes meant he had come straight from the whorehouse of the night before without washing. But he was curiously sober all of a sudden. My master was nowhere in sight, but as it was his custom to go to the public baths after a night on the town, I thought nothing of it.

—Sarah, I've got a letter for you from Alex. Before I give it to you, let me say that he shouldn't be judged too harshly. It was my fault as well as his . . . We . . . We've lost you . . . at cards last night. I'm sorry. I took the envelope from his dirty hand. It was not sealed.

July 30, the SS Hudson

Sarah,

Read this letter carefully because you can read now. The news I have for you will not make you happy. Your new owner is Réaux, the Frenchman. I wagered your contract as part of a sum I bet playing trente-et-quarante *and lost. Then, Taylor tried to win you back by wagering his own part and he lost as well. I have decided to disappear from your life at the same time. I have signed on as ship's surgeon on the SS* Hudson, *leaving Halifax or rather Hull this night for South Carolina. I know I swore I would never go to sea again and especially on a slaver, but I have no choice. You are no longer mine. I cannot clothe or feed you. I cannot pay Henry what we owe him or any of my other creditors from Bath or Halifax. As some of them are local criminals, the most prudent thing to do is to disappear.*

In losing all our profits and capital, my shame is such I cannot face you. Sieur Réaux owns you for the remaining two years of your contract. He has agreed to pay you the twelve guineas a year we agreed upon in your contract plus he will pay your servant Alice another five guineas. There are no profits to share with you. Your jewelry, food, clothes, lodgings, transport, doctor's bills, tobacco and gin have consumed your share.

Think of me as dead. For I will surely be very soon. And do not forgive me, rather forget me.

Adieu.
Alexander W. Dunlop, Esq.

P.S.: As for our marriage, we are not married, Sarah. I was never divorced. Or rather we are married and I am a bigamist. If you don't know what that means, ask Henry.

It was hard for me to read the letter because it was written in a trembling hand and my hands shook, but the message was clear. My husband was gone forever. Alice took the letter from me.

—Give me that, she said.

She had guessed from my face what I had read. Indeed, I stood there, cursing in Khoekhoe, in English and in Dutch, barefoot in the middle of the stifling room, almost naked in my thin sheath, yet shivering as if I was freezing to death. A great snarl escaped me, half scream, half war cry. Not my master! Not him! But it was him. He had sold me! He had lost me at cards. And he had thrown me to the dogs. My whole life passed before my eyes. Sobbing and screeching, I threw myself at Master Taylor, who stepped sideways, and I found myself in the arms of Master Réaux, his big chained brown bear just inches away. I smelled the beast.

—Unless you accept the rest of your contract, he announced, it's either the workhouse, the poorhouse, the jailhouse or the whorehouse, Venus . . .

The following week, I received another blow. Alice decided to stay in Halifax with Victor.

—I 'ave found work in the mills, Alice confessed. I can earn enough to rent a small cottage and take care of Victor. He's too frail for this life.

—You too? I cried. But I knew Alice was right. Why should she roam this island with a bunch of things-that-should-never-have-been-born for my sake?

But my heart broke.

—I will never forget what you did for me and Victor. You saved m' life. But I'll only cost you money you don't 'ave anymore. 'Ere I can earn my own keep and not be a burden to you. I will never forget you. I am your servant and your friend, your witness and your godmother. We are one. And if Dunlop comes back to Halifax, I want to be here to castrate him . . .

The next day, Alice and her brother left the circus for good. Shortly after that the burgesses of Halifax shut down the theater and the freak show on grounds of indecency and endangering public safety. A constable came and nailed a notice on the tent pillars. But what the town fathers were really afraid of were large gatherings of mill workers in one place. The ghost of the Luddite riots still roamed the cobblestone streets of Halifax. Without Master Dunlop's protection as a doctor and army officer, true or not, we were no more than a collection of paupers, vagabonds and strays to the police. We were forced on the road again, but this time it was different.

—We're planning to take you to the Continent, said Master Réaux. Your real worth is in the big cities like Paris and Amsterdam, where the gentry and the literati can get a look at you, not these backwater country squires and workers bent on insurrection. Napoleon's wars are over. He has abdicated and is exiled to Elba. King Louis is restored to the throne, I can go home.

Alice had already told me the rumors about the mysterious Sieur Réaux, who had so changed our lives. He was an aristocrat, a younger son of a family destroyed by the French Revolution who had barely escaped the guillotine. He had fled to England, where he had some family, but they had cast him out as a traitor to his class and a renegade. He had quit his social class and begun the life of a reprobate, a gambler and a duelist. He had killed several men. His career as an animal trainer had started when he jumped into a bear cage and wrestled the animal down on a dare. He had traveled to Russia, to Crimea, to India, to Africa. He had joined Napoleon and had served at Borodino. But he had deserted the army and was a wanted man with a price on his head, which was why he had been hiding in England. No one knew his Christian name. He never spoke of his family or his origins. His accent was that of a gentleman and he spoke the King's English and the provincial's French. There were also rumors that he had been dismissed from the army because of homosexual behavior, that he liked boys, hated women, was a morphine addict. Had he been a spy for Napoleon? For Louis XVI? For Louis XVIII? Did he work for the British secret service? Was he really French? Sieur Réaux raised all kinds of questions and provided not one answer. Alice had heard him say he would kiss the ground of France if ever he had the luck to return. Perhaps, I thought, he's only homesick, like me.

On September 9, Shit moon, 1814, we set sail for Le Havre from Southampton on the mailship the HMS *Beagle*. Sieur Réaux did not say a word during the crossing. His silver-blue eyes under his sealskin top hat, his black mustache under his pug nose, his wide shoulders draped in his short black cape, his immense height, and long legs encased in brown and black riding boots, all seemed like separate visions to me, never coming together as one. The person of Sieur Réaux loomed huge against the sails and ropes of the mailboat. I was terrified of him. Alice and I had even sent a letter to Robert Wedderburn in London, explaining our plight and begging him to rescue us, but our plea went unanswered. Perhaps he felt I had spurned his help once, why should he offer it again? Nevertheless, under my skirts, my feet were hobbled by a thick chain. I was Sieur Réaux's prisoner, yet to a passerby, with his arm around my shoulders enfolding me tenderly, he seemed like an attractive husband or guardian steadying me against the movement of the ship and the slippery wetness of the deck.

The hard years in the provinces of England had sapped any will I had to escape. I was empty inside, or rather too empty inside to resist. At twenty-five, I was an old woman who wanted only her *dagga,* her gin, her tobacco, whose body had been used up by the thousands of eyes that had devoured it. It had been battered by so much curiosity and ridicule, it disgusted even me. I refused even to look into a full-length mirror anymore. I had only one wish, to survive, to hide enough money to buy my passage home, to escape Sieur Réaux and stay out of the workhouse, the jailhouse, the crazy house or the whorehouse. I had once been rich, now I was penniless. Once again, ten pounds was a fortune. Under my red riding hood, I was in rags. Would the French police help me? How could I prove who and what I was? I glanced sideways at my master, who was absently lighting a small cheroot and gazing out upon the gray, troubled waters with satisfaction. Adolph was chained in the hold of the ship, along with several other animals. Adolph came from the Caucasus Mountains of Russia and was very old for a bear. He weighed six hundred pounds, his pelt was as stiff and prickly as a hedgehog and he smelled really awful. We were both Master Réaux's creatures. The only difference was that I couldn't dance and Adolph was not baptized.

—I have a surprise for you.

—Yeah . . .

—No, really. I'm not such a bad man, Sarah. I'm going to go see if Adolph is all right. I'll be back, he said as he left me standing on deck.

Alone and heartbroken, I recalled the beginning of my voyage now four years past. I tasted the salt of tears, nausea and the sea wind. Memories of the crimes committed against me welled up inside me like a nest of vipers: the search for the Reverend Freehouseland, Master Hendrick's return to South Africa, my husband Dunlop's betrayal, the lonely years of wandering with Master Taylor, and finally the loss of Alice and Victor.

It was a warm day and the sea was so calm a light breeze was strong enough to move the boat forward. It skimmed the surface, its sails humming, seagulls shrieking overhead. Small white-capped waves skipped across the dark blue depths to the horizon. The sun shimmering on these waters is the African sun, I thought suddenly. This sky could at any moment turn pink with the flight of a flock of flamingos. I could be dead from all the alcohol I drink. I vowed to make the world pay the price of my humiliations. I had a name, in the eyes of Christ: Sarah, Sarah Baartman. I had a country, which was his Kingdom, and I had a final destination, Africa. I was the ward of no one, the property of no one, the whore of no one, the freak of no one, the slave of no one, the beloved of no one. I leaned too far out over the shimmering waves, my hands slid off the railings, I closed my eyes thinking that this sea was the only freedom I was destined for.

—You won' quit this earth as long as I'm o' it, a voice close to my ear whispered. There was only one voice like that one—Alice's.

—You came! I cried.

—You saved my miserable life. I owe you mine. Victor is safe with a good family. I a'ways wan'ed to see Paris.

We fell into each other's arms, laughing and crying.

—Oh Lord, murmured Alice, more to herself than me, wha's to 'appen to us now?

Part III

All the women you ever met
Ask for them, every one!
I am not a woman but a world
My clothes need only fall away
For you to discover in my person
One continuous mystery.

—GUSTAVE FLAUBERT,
"Quidquid Volueris"

16

All the parts of a living body are connected: they cannot function unless they function together; to wish to separate one from its mass is to remove it into the classification of dead substances and to entirely adulterate its essence.

BARON GEORGES LÉOPOLD CUVIER,
Thirty Lessons in Comparative Anatomy

*S*eptember 1814.

To Baron Georges Léopold Cuvier, director, King's Museum of Natural History, King's Botanical Gardens, St. Bernard-sur-Seine

September 13, 1814

Monsieur,
The original of the enclosed portrait (engraved), who comes from the banks of the Chamboos River in South Africa, is at this moment in Paris,

about to be presented to the scrutiny of the general public. The naturalist will find in the exceptional configuration of the Hottentot tribe a fascinating phenomenon. Before opening the exhibit to the public, I propose to hold a private exhibition and would be most flattered by the honor of your presence on this occasion, Tuesday the Twenty-seventh, rue Neuve-des-Petits-Champs no. 15, between noon and six o'clock. I have the honor to be, Monsieur, your devoted servant.

Sieur Réaux

I gazed out the window at Notre-Dame, as I thought about the letter I had written Baron Cuvier. The carriage carried me along the quay of the Right Bank towards the Palais Royal. It stopped before the staircase of honor of the palace and the lackeys rushed to unfold the steps of the landau, I stepped out into the September sunshine. Almost on cue, the vast fountains of the Palais Royal sprang up from their basins in a panoply of gushing water and spiraling jets spectacularly enhanced by the bright broad daylight, which danced on their surfaces and fragmented the reflections into droplets of gold and silver. I watched the play of water for a long moment, counting how many minutes out of my life I could now spare for this beautiful spectacle. When I felt I had wasted enough time, I strode up the steps and into the stone building. I was home, I thought. In Paris where I belonged.

The fountains were fed by the huge waterworks located between the Palais Royal galleries and the rue St. Honoré. The ducts, sluices, locks and valves that controlled the fountains' movements lay within view of number 7 Cour des Fontaines, where I, Sarah, Alice and Adolph had set up housekeeping.

The quarter of Les Fontaines had been in the past and still was my absolute domain. It was almost as if the Revolution had never happened, I thought. It was a district that had survived the Terror intact. The narrow cobbled streets remained as they had been in the Middle Ages. The places of pleasure and sin had reopened in the wake of Robespierre's demise and never looked back. The quarter had catered to the fastidious tastes of the Napoleonic aristocracy and now was the playground of the Restoration courtesans, gamblers, sea captains, sailors, army officers and actresses. There was a tavern for every theater, a bar for every hotel, a hotel for every prostitute. There had been a time, I recalled, when I had rolled up to the

Thousand Columns café in my own handsome, coral-red, liveried landau. It had had green leather upholstery and my blazon painted on its doors. I had stepped out of this marvelous vehicle with a different beauty on my arm every evening. I blinked. This was a different world now, just as I was a different man. I would not be happy if people guessed who I had been in the past. So diminished was my person that I even kept my Christian name a secret. With a name so distinctive and so formerly famous, someone might guess who I truly was. It seemed to me that this small dangerous parcel of Paris was the only thing that hadn't changed in the fifteen years I had been gone.

It was almost dawn and around the roulette tables were about fifty or sixty people, most of them, including myself, mere spectators. My time to gamble had not yet come, I thought, but soon it would, as soon as I had presented my Hottentot to the scientific world and set up my exhibition hall, right here next to the casino. But just breathing the air gave me wings. I had gambled and won the Hottentot by a stroke of luck. I didn't intend to waste it. Every species of gambler was concentrated around me; the addicted but unlucky doctor, the courtesan, the professional gambler, the adventurer, the Russian countess, the furloughed lieutenant, the arrogant duchess, her ladyship from London, the Oriental potentate. Here was the ultimate human equality as the chips were thrown onto the table, the faces intent, eyes on the small round roulette ball, which turned and churned, all united in greed and vice, I thought. No one could claim he was better than the other. All classes mixed pell-mell together as in the days when my inferiors had had the nerve to call me "Citizen" instead of Marquis. There were people of all nationalities: Italians, English, Greeks, Moroccans, Spanish, Dutch, Belgian, Swiss, Polish. The representatives of a Europe that was only now emerging from wars that had torn the fabric of European civilization into shreds. All ages were represented too, I mused, young, middle-aged, in the prime of life, decrepit and already dead. Yet there was a uniformity of expression that was the hallmark of gamblers: veneration and innocence. They could all have been sitting in pews in Notre-Dame, so intently religious were their expressions. So nothing had changed at all.

A lackey passed by carrying a tray of fluted glasses filled with champagne. The croupier swept the hundreds of glistening napoleons into his basket as he repeated the hypnotic *Faites vos jeux, Rien ne va plus.* I clenched my fists. My fingers ached to fling out a napoleon or two. But, I reasoned, that would come soon enough.

I was illegally dressed in a French officer's uniform. It suited me best and its military elegance had seduced many women. It gave me a kind of regimental neatness that my ravaged soul did not possess. It gave me the appearance of belonging to society and its rules in a way that I had never practiced. Moreover, it gave me physical comfort as few things did: the heavy gold epaulets weighing on my shoulders, the fine worsted of my pantaloons, the slight acid odor of my polished brass buttons, the starched cleanness of my linen and collar band. Several beautiful women had glanced my way. I smoothed my mustaches and moved closer to the handsomest one, the one wearing the most expensive *parure*. Actually, everything except my luck at cards was turning out as I planned. In desperation I threw a napoleon onto the table: black. Nine. The wheel turned. Nine won. Happily I scooped up my winnings. It was enough to open a barrack along the rue St. Honoré for the Venus. I took a carriage back to the courtyard of Les Fontaines, not trusting the dangerous streets with the stake we had to live on for the next few weeks. I had considered getting rid of Alice, but I realized I could not take care of the Venus on my own. Alice gave me the necessary freedom to exploit Sarah. Alice was in fact my accomplice and as such invaluable, just as I had threatened Sarah, I had threatened her as well with the jailhouse, the workhouse or the whorehouse, and since she was just as terrorized of all three, as Sarah was, she complied.

My ground-floor apartment at number 15 Neuve-des-Petits-Champs looked out onto an interior courtyard in which a single tree grew and around which a representative section of the quarter's population was housed. Within lived freaks and prostitutes, gamblers, con men, actresses, musicians, magicians, high-wire acrobats, dancers, clowns, racketeers, usurers, professional gangsters. Only steps from the notorious Palais Royal galleries and a world apart from the sumptuous apartments of the King around the corner. There I lived with Sarah and her maid.

When we had stepped off the *Beagle* mailboat onto French soil, my eyes had filled with tears and I had fallen to my knees and kissed the ground.

—This is the first time I've been home since 1791, I said, rubbing my eyes like a child. From this moment it will be different, I had decided. My luck had changed, I had won the Hottentot Venus!

I looked up at the sky. Caesar and Taylor and Dunlop were all in the past now. There was only me and Venus. Adolph, sitting in his iron cage, yawned and let out a loud sneeze. He shook himself, fluffing out his pelt, and let out a large fart. Alice and Sarah laughed but I was so happy I didn't even smell my bear's antics.

The bright sunlight touched the rolling flat lands of Le Havre village, a sleepy harbor west of Paris. The mail and passenger coaches waited to be loaded and to receive passengers. Other voyagers were hurrying to and fro, admonishing the porters to unload their trunks and crates. A few of the passengers cast curious looks at our outrageous entourage. Sarah had pulled her veil down. Alice picked up a satchel and looked at me expectantly.

—We'll stay here at the inn overnight, I said. If we start out for Paris now, we won't be there before nightfall and I don't want to enter the city at night. I want to return in broad daylight so our carriage can take us through the city, along the Quai de Branly past the Ile de la Cité to rue St. Honoré and my old quarter. I want to savor every moment of our arrival.

I had intended to go straight to the vaudeville theater with my idea of a play about the Venus. Sarah and Alice stood close by, dazed by the sunlight and dizzy because the ground under their feet, they complained, still seemed to move with the motion of the ship. The countryside was beautiful. Everything looked clean, serene and prosperous. I called a porter with a cart. I pointed to the baggage and told him to take it to the inn, and then to Adolph, to be moved to the inn's stables. Adolph was sitting quietly, licking his paws. The porter's eyes widened and we had a furious discussion about his transport. Finally a cart pulled by a bullock was found to move Adolph and we three humans walked to the village square, on foot, Indian file, following the porter with the luggage. Alice and Sarah spoke together as they walked, thinking I could not overhear them.

—If we try to get away now, where will we go and what will we do for money?

—Whore, said Alice without hesitation.

—You've never done that in your whole life, Alice Unicorn, and neither have I.

—Just because I've never done it doesn't mean I don't know how to do it!

—Then why didn't you in Manchester? When you and Victor were starving?

—Perhaps we should have stayed in England, where at least we can speak the language . . .

—Never mind about the language. Adolph can't speak French either. He has learned only to dance . . .

At this, I interrupted their whispered conversation.

—Bears don't learn to dance, I said. They are tortured into dancing. The trainer smashes their teeth in with hammers to destroy their most important means of defense. Then their noses or lips are pierced with a metal ring and attached to an iron chain. Then they are cast onto burning coals or hot metal grilles while the music of drums and tambourines play. Soon, the bear is rearing on its hind legs, hopping from one foot to the other to escape the flames and the fire. From then on, whenever the bear hears music, he repeats the same movements whether there is fire or not, even when there are no flames . . . only tambourines. He remembers the pain. That's how you teach bears to dance . . .

My eyes never left those of Sarah.

I knew that Sarah was still grieving over Dunlop's abandonment. She kept looking over her shoulder as if she expected him to jump out from behind one of the hedges. But now her eyes fastened on Adolph's cage in despair.

—He's gone, Sarah, I admonished her. By now he's in the middle of the Atlantic Ocean. I moved ahead of them still listening.

—Perhaps we should go to America, whispered Sarah to Alice.

—Perhaps. But there's slavery in America. And at the moment, we're in France. We can think about the United States of America tomorrow. But it's not for Africans, Sarah . . . Resign yourself. Dunlop has deserted you, and for the second time.

—If we run, who's going to hire us, not speaking any French?

—You don't have to speak the language to do what we're going to do.

—Just dance on hot coals like his bears . . .

—We need Réaux. We are lost without him. He has shelter and money. We don't. He has the cashbox.

—Four years in England and what do we have to show for it? Sarah said.

—But, whispered Alice, we are humans, not dancing bears. We can run . . .

I laughed to myself at their ignorance and naïveté. Nobody ran away from me.

The next day, in the late afternoon, the Paris stagecoach left the flat rolling plains of Normandy and made its way into the city. It was sunny and brilliant, just as I had predicted, and our entrance through the gates occurred just as the bells of Notre-Dame tolled. I directed the stage to rue St. Honoré, my old quarter, and by nightfall we were installed in a rented flat. Adolph still waited at the stables in Le Havre. Within a week, Sarah was once again the Hottentot Venus. I advertised her in the *Journal de Paris:*

Just arrived from the Chamboos River in the Cape. The most
extraordinary specimen of primitive humanity ever to be shown
in Paris. Open to the public at 188 rue St. Honoré from eleven in the
morning to nine in the evening. Admission: 3 francs per person.

Sarah's Venus was an immediate commercial success, much to my delight. She was the talk of Paris. Newspaper articles, posters and engravings began to appear. Queues formed outside 188 rue St. Honoré. High society began to frequent my small barrack either to amuse themselves or reserve an appearance of the Venus at their next soirée. Eventually, I thought, the Venus's fame would reach the literary and scientific worlds, but by now I didn't even need their guarantees. My letter to the great naturalist and scientist Baron Cuvier remained unanswered, but the public had taken to the Hottentot, and Sarah, though often drunk or sick, did fulfill her contract to entertain and amaze them. Alice was a perfect governess to keep her in shape to perform and provide her with companionship. My only worry was Dunlop. I was afraid he might show up again out of the blue and claim Sarah's gains as her husband. This was what Sarah dreamed of, I knew, but I didn't waste a lot of time worrying about it. I guessed he was probably in America . . . or dead, either of which suited me fine. I did have my problems with Alice, who was so protective and solicitous of Sarah that I had had to make several concessions as to how long I could exhibit her by day, her private doctor's bills, her bottles of gin, her extravagant purchases of expensive gloves, hats and rhinestones. To be sure, I thought, Alice asked nothing for herself except her salary and she saved me great expense by doing the shopping and the cooking if we ate at home, which was rare since I spent most of my time gambling, whoring or simply passing the time with other show-men. But Alice was not the only one who felt protective or had affection for the Venus. There was Madame Romain, known as the "la Belle Limonadière," who ruled (and owned) the sumptuous Palais Royal café called the Thousand Columns.

La Belle was almost as fat as the circus freak who lived in our building, but she had the face of an angel. She was the daughter of a prostitute and at twelve her mother had sold her virginity for a fortune. She had begun to work in a house of prostitution and was noticed by a very rich gentleman who took her as his mistress and set her up in a small hotel in Passy. She remained his mistress for almost twenty years, leading a bourgeois life of ease and leisure. She had had one son, by her lover the Baron de S, and she had blackmailed him into adopting the boy. When he reached the age of sixteen, he was sent to Napoleon's Ecole Polytechnique, and he was now a young officer unaware of his origins. Belle intended to keep it that way, al-though she was proud and enamored of him. When her patron died, leav-ing her son part of his fortune, Belle sold the hotel and bought the Thousand Columns with enough left over to turn it into the most deca-dent and fashionable of the Palais Royal cafés. Here, she ruled night and day, having returned to her old life without a qualm or a regret, sitting be-hind the cashbox on a high stool that looked like a throne, from which she surveyed everything and everyone like a sea captain, bejeweled and re-spected, a diamond tiara perched on her blond wig, which flowed in happy ringlets down her back. She controlled a platoon of pimps, gamblers and bodyguards and was well protected, thanks to the baron, by the Paris po-lice, who not only left her and her girls alone but often asked her for help in solving the nightly crimes of the quarter. She also ran a gang of small boys whose only function was to protect her important clients from expo-sure by running warnings, like carrier pigeons, from one brothel to the other. Belle's salons were always open to high officials who wanted meet-ings with the underground and the Corsican mafia or to strike deals be-tween important criminals and the police. As long as you were on the right side of her, she was a loyal, protective friend, full of French common sense.

Amongst the inmates of number 188 was a dwarf named William, better known as William the Cock, William the Prick, William the Dick or William the Will, who had a normal-sized head and a larger-than-normal-sized penis, which was as long as his short legs. The dwarf's great specialty was to walk between the legs of women or climb up their limbs like a monkey hidden by their skirts. He was courted and adored by the quarter's prostitutes. Hardened courtesans who had not had an orgasm in years used the small man as a living, inventive dildo. William the Cock always obliged, having become a master of the art of cunnilingus. He wore a padded codpiece that hung almost to the ground and made dirty bawdy jokes about it that never failed to excite the most obscene hilarity in his audiences. Cheerful and boisterous, he was the mascot of the Cour des Fontaines and a star attraction at the vaudeville theater. It was perhaps his elegies of the Venus that led to the preparation of a play based on her persona and popularity. The Venus's success was tremendous. She needed neither publicity nor endorsements. Parisians flocked to see her. In only a few weeks she was a citywide celebrity and a subject of conversation in the salons of the rich and wellborn. The gazettes sang her praises. In the quarter of St. Germain a glove shop reopened its doors under the new sign "The Hottentot Venus." And on October 24, only five weeks after our arrival from England, a new play, *The Hottentot Venus* by Théaulon de Lambert, opened in vaudeville. It was a new record for the production of a play composed and written around a news item. Its subtitle was *Hate to the French*. Sarah and Alice and William the Cock and I were in the first row of the opening performance. Only I and the dwarf really understood the play's humor. Sarah and Alice couldn't understand why the Venus never made a real appearance. For me, it only made my Sarah more valuable. I decided to raise the admission price by fifty centimes. But Alice had her hands full with Sarah's drinking.

—Sarah, she begged, you've got to stop drinking . . . The doctor says . . .

—I don't care what the doctor says.

—Well, at least take your medicine . . .

—No medicine . . . except my *dagga*.

—Morphine . . .

—No.

—Oh, Sarah, Sarah. Alice would say when she thought she was out of my hearing, Let's run away before it's too late . . . You're sick. You need to rest. We could go back to England. I can take care of you . . .

I worried, but Sarah's attitude had a morbid rigidity, a dull stubbornness that was possibly the stupidity of her race, a dense, angry, dreamy resistance to changing anything until her so-called inheritance, which she equated with her dignity, was restored. She never spoke to me about the dowry she had paid out to Dunlop, but several times I heard her speaking of it with Alice.

—But you've made thousands of pounds, protested Alice. You've made ten hundred times ten pounds. You think Dunlop is coming back for you, but I tell you, Sarah, he's not! He's gone. Forget him.

—He's my husband.

—He's a bigamist.

—I've forgotten what that means . . .

—It means, Sarah, that he has two wives and one of them is white. He's a traitor, a thief and a liar, Sarah, and a cruel deceiver of women . . .

—Leave me be, Alice, leave me be . . . she would say. And Alice would do just that. Or go out and buy her a bottle of gin.

—The vaudeville play *The Hottentot Venus* tells the story of a young man who decides to marry a savage instead of his well-brought-up cousin Amélie, said William the Cock, trying to explain the comedy to Sarah.

—Then, Amélie says, it is certainly strange to see a Hottentot lady.

—The Chevalier responds: A lady! She's a Venus, Madame. A Venus who has arrived from England and who at this moment is admired by every connoisseur in Paris!

—*Amélie:* She's beautiful then?

—*The Chevalier:* Oh! A horrifying beauty!

—Then continued William, he sings:

> *Already tout Paris sings*
> *Of this amazing woman,*
> *First, she speaks little*
> *Her song seems barbarous*
> *Her dance is quick and burlesque*
> *Her size a handsome handful*
> *It is said her hymen's been engaged,*

But this Venus I bet
Never makes love.

William began to recite all the parts, first of Amélie, then of the Chevalier.

—*Amélie:* One surely speaks much of her.

—*The Chevalier:* It isn't just a question of her, ahem . . . She has her little Hottentot songs that are so gay that all the ladies have already ordered their dresses and *douillettes* à la Hottentot this winter.

—Then, said William the Cock, in the final scene, the Chevalier unrolls the portrait of the Hottentot Venus that he shows to all the cast of characters *and* the audience. Everyone screams in horror and says in unison:

What a peculiar adventure!
What looks until now unheard of!
With such a shape!
She can't be a Venus!

—And finally, continued the dwarf, the Chevalier sees the error of his ways and marries his cousin and lives happily ever after. There was even an American in the audience the other night who shouted out in the middle of the play that this marriage was mis . . . miscegenation. When I asked him what that was, he said marriage or fornication between a black person and a white person . . . Imagine, that's a crime in America, punished by fine and prison.

—Prison?

—In America, of course. In France we abolished slavery under the Revolution. We produced the Constitution and proclaimed the freedom of our black brothers in the Bill of Rights. Under the Directory, this act stood. Then Bonaparte came along and reestablished slavery again in the islands of the West Indies. The prisoner of Elba, intoned William the Cock, has had the last word . . .

All that winter, the Venus's fame grew. She began to make appearances at aristocrats' private soirées, to mingle with the bourgeois of St. Germain and the courtesans of the Tuileries and the Palais Royal. She was happiest with the petit bourgeois of the faubourg: the butcher, the baker, the lace maker, the cobbler, the confectioner, the milliner and the dressmaker. To them, she was Madame, a prodigy, a celebrity, who was also a client who paid well and promptly. I received many demands for an appearance of the Hottentot Venus at the various grand receptions of the winter season. I refused many, but from time to time I accepted and Sarah obliged me by donning her transparent dress and mask and allowing gentlemen and ladies whom she would never see again to gaze at her person with pity and horror. This was usually manifested by nervous laughter and coarse commentary. Didn't they ever get tired? I thought. Weary of making themselves laugh at something which was not funny? Why was this laughter always so forced, and unnatural? I'm sure Sarah would rather have heard the rough, pure laugh of a hyena.

In late February, the Venus was to appear at a reception of Madame de C, held each month in the luxurious salons of her Paris hotel. The cream of Parisian society attended: painters, writers, politicians, actors, opera singers, scientists and intellectuals of all sorts. Sarah was happy to appear because there would be music she could listen to while allowing herself to be stared at, whispered about behind her back and talked to as if she were blind, deaf and dumb. Madame de C ruled her salons with an iron hand, dispensing invitations, excluding this person or that, depending on her whim or the latest newspaper or court gossip. Sarah was to be the surprise of the soirée.

I accompanied her that night. She stood for a moment on the steps of the Hôtel de C on the rue du Bac in the heart of St. Germain, facing the long line of rectangular windows interspersed with lit torches, all blazing. She stood, immobile for a moment, her red cloak around her shoulders, in the frame of one of the French doors, the light from which threw her shadow, long and black, onto the shiny cobblestones. The windows shone with the world of the rich and powerful, being served, holding conversations, exchanging in the most human way banalities, secrets, gossip, arguing, postulating, cajoling, lying, out of pride or ambition or maliciousness or faith, honor, strategy, simple greed or simple amusement. Male figures, or rather figurines, glided by in rich military uniforms, or black evening clothes. The ladies on their arms wore satin and lace, mousseline and crêpe de chine. Sarah tied a black lace mask across her eyes. I had told her once: *If people cannot see your face, their imagination will invent a face more terrifying than even yours could be* . . . The majordomo said nothing as we entered the salon. He knew who she was. The odor of human flesh, cut flowers, perfume and the chalk spread on the hardwood floors of the ball-room rose to my nostrils.

The gathering combined Madame de C's society friends with the luminaries of Paris and Europe. There were the writers Stendhal and Chateaubriand. The sculptor David d'Angers. Napoleon's personal physician, Corvisart, the scientists Cuvier, Gay-Lussac, Arago, Etienne Geoffroy Saint-Hilaire. There was the actor Talma, Madame Destutt de Tracy, the senators Monge and Laplace. All were discussing the latest book of the exiled Madame de Staël and the existence of ideal beauty in Lessing's *Laokoon*. Like a box of sweets, everyone was filled with the cream of knowledge and the cherry of himself.

—Madame, my Venus Hottentot, said a tall man softly suddenly at her side. I have a picture of you sent to me a long time ago, I recognize you . . . You do understand me? Aren't you the Hottentot Venus?

I turned quickly and saw it was the Baron Cuvier, his pale avid eyes devouring Sarah.

Baron Georges Léopold Chrétien Frédéric Dagobert Cuvier, director of the Museum of Natural History, surgeon general to Emperor Napoleon, peer of France, director of dissident cults, president of the Institute of France, inspector general of public education, member of the Council of State, lifetime consultant of the University, member of the Academy of Sciences and of the French Academy, grand officer of the Legion of Honor was known as "the Napoleon of Intelligence." He was famous for his prodigious energy, output and extraordinary burden of responsibility. His fame also rested on his sanguinity, his brilliant political tactics and his penchant for changing sides at the right moment. That was how the suave and famous naturalist had survived the Revolution, the reign of Napoleon under which he had so prospered, and the Restoration of Louis XVIII, who had, despite Cuvier's long and intimate ties with the ex-Emperor, appointed him to his Council of State. The doctor had suffered no political consequences at all because of his deep loyalty to Napoleon Bonaparte. On the contrary, his scientific reputation begun under the Emperor's patronage had catapulted him to the highest echelons of prestige and power.

—If the princess is amazed at your deformity, he said, Science, I must say, is confounded.

There was cruelty and irony in his voice but nevertheless I allowed

Sarah to follow him towards a group of people. I vowed to ask him later about my unanswered letter of months ago. The orchestra struck up, and for a moment, the Venus thought everyone in the world loved her. Cuvier escorted the Venus to her hosts, the prince and princess. I could not believe my luck! Now he could claim he had unearthed the body of the Hottentot, like one of his fossils, quite by accident.

—Here is, Madame, my Venus Hottentot, he repeated dozens of times as he greeted his friends in the crowd as if it were one of his famous "Cuvier Saturdays." Sarah I could see, was happy. I had complained to her about the scientist who had refused to examine her before her exhibition opened in Paris and whom I had never heard from since. I wondered vaguely what would be the outcome of this unexpected encounter.

But Cuvier escorted her from one group of people to another, from famous writers to fellow scientists to a bouquet of magnificently dressed matrons busily fanning themselves.

—The portraits of Sarah Baartman, said Stendhal, who was standing next to Etienne Geoffroy Saint-Hilaire, have invaded all of France. They have an exactitude, which is an antidote to the exaggerations of the English caricatures.

—I have seen the vaudeville play *The Hottentot Venus*, which is quite amusing.

—What can we do now that the English have taken all our African colonies?

—Allow me, Madame, to draw your portrait, requested Léon de Wailly, a painter for the court.

—Is there a difference between a Hottentot and a Bushman, Chevalier Geoffroy Saint-Hilaire? asked the Vicomte François René de Chateaubriand. You with your studies of monsters? Which is the most savage?

—Etienne's been searching for the missing link. Is this it, Etienne?

Several ladies, themselves in transparent dresses, approached the Venus and struck her with their fans. Others peered through the gossamer dress, their eager eyes searching.

—I have long had a passion for teratology, said Geoffroy Saint-Hilaire to Stendhal, that is, the study of monsters. I have actually induced the birth of abnormal chicks by manipulating the embryos in the shell . . . Notice that the Venus has the beginnings of a snout that's larger than that of the red orangutan that inhabits Madagascar . . . Notice the prodigious size of her hips and buttocks, protrusions that inspire comparison to the female species of the maimon and mandrill monkeys. This pathological condition is called steatopygia, a term I derived from the Latin roots for fat and buttocks but not in use outside of scientific circles . . .

A small group of ladies gathered around Sarah, begging her to remove her mask.

—Oh no, dear, said one, you're pregnant. Do you want to give birth to a Hottentot baby?!

—Oh, she must be too ugly to look upon in her entirety.

—You haven't seen the vaudeville play about her?

—But you don't actually *see* her, injected a voice.

Sarah turned, startled that her reflection, with its feathers, pearls and glass beads, repeated itself in the cut-glass mirrors a thousand times. The banqueting black curves of her buttocks reflected over and over and over again into infinity. The conglomeration of dark-skinned Venuses invaded the pristine gilt-and-white-framed glass as if they had shattered them with cannon, dissolving the image into a regiment of effigies.

—What is it? screamed Madame Destutt de Tracy.

Suddenly, as if an alarm had been sounded, a whole group of ladies stampeded to the back of the salon where the orchestra played, pushing and shoving each other and hiding themselves behind the salon drapes. Sarah looked startled, caught unawares. The violence of the women's reaction surprised her. Their panic induced a reverie that made her seem to sink downwards before my very eyes. Her head fell onto her breast, her arms hung slackly, her eyes filled with tears. It was as if she had been knocked unconscious by the blow of this final humiliation.

—Now, now, ladies, cooed the princess, Madame de C. She is only a prodigy and a freak, not a spotted leopard! She can't hurt you, can she, Baron?

—Absolutely not! She's to entertain us with a recitation . . .

Madame Destutt de Tracy and her friends opened a path for the Venus as she made her way to where the orchestra sat.

—*Je suis ici pour chanter pour vous,* began poor Sarah.

She began to sing in English "The Ballad of Dame Hottentot." Her voice quivered but the notes were high and clear.

Have you gone to London
And seen the sights of the City?
One can see the most famous of women
In Piccadilly she lives
In a splendid mansion
On which you can read these words
Written in letters of gold
"The Hottentot Venus."
If you ask her why she lives there
And what makes her famous,
They will tell you she has a bottom
As large as a stove
That's why the Gentlemen
Push and shove to see
The admirable Hottentot.

—How grotesque! How extraordinary. How disgusting. How quaint. How interesting. How pathetic. How clever of the princess. How ridiculous of the princess. How filthy. How stupid. A freak of nature. A savage. A gorilla. I don't understand English. It's English? No. African? No. Hottentot! Impossible, Hottentots don't have a language!

Sarah's plaintive wail pierced the frivolous babble of the ballroom and shocked it into silence. Tears streamed down Sarah's face under the lace mask as if they had spouted from some unseen fountain far away. Finally, there was scattered applause. It came from Stendhal, Cuvier and Arago. The baron, I noticed, was mesmerized by the Venus. It seemed to me his fascination went beyond simple scientific curiosity; a mere desire to possess the means of solving a mysterious equation: Was she real? And if so, was she human? Did she have a soul? And if so, where did she stand in the great Chain of Being? I could see the baron doing the calculations in his head, almost fainting with desire. What, I thought, did this babbling stupid assembly know about real phenomena? About the deep dark revolution of catastrophes? Here was a true scientific gold mine and people laughed or fled. Sarah's eyes behind the mask and the baron's held one another's gaze for a moment in mutual incomprehension. Cuvier seemed at a loss for words. Did he think it was cruel what he had witnessed? Or, as

I suspected, had there grown in him a kind of primordial fascination beyond the social or the theatrical for the Venus? This man who classified and catalogued all living things . . . I was beginning to wonder how this encounter was going to turn out when one of the many journalists reporting on the party approached the baron. I overheard his conversation with the man I knew only as Pierre.

—Imagine, said the reporter, that this Hottentot we're laughing at is a French girl, a young white female who, having gone to the Midi for the sea air, has been kidnapped by a band of Berber pirates and taken to a stronghold somewhere in Africa. From there, she passes through the hands of an Arab who transports her over Mount Atlas and conducts her to Timbuktu, where he exhibits her to the natives as the Parisian Venus . . . She sobs, she cries, she calls in vain to return to her beloved country. And she'll die far from the object of all her affections . . . This is the Hottentot Venus's fate, sir . . .

—Baron Cuvier.

—I know who you are, Doctor. Pierre Songe, reporter for the *Journal des Dames et des Modes.* I was reporting only on the princess's ball, but now I have another story to write. The Venus's story. Care to comment, Baron? Personally I am appalled and moved by this pitiful spectacle. What about you? Like freak shows?

The baron studied the journalist in complete puzzlement. What, he asked, did white females, kidnapped or not, have to do with the Hottentot Venus? What did the white race have to do with Africans? They were two separate and distinct species.

—My problem is to establish the scientific relationship between them, not to contemplate white girls . . .

The baron turned away. I was sure he didn't want to talk to the newspapers. He didn't want to express an opinion. He just wanted to retire to his laboratory to digest what he had just witnessed: the wondrous discovery of the Hottentot Venus. I came up behind the snubbed reporter.

—I know who you are too, said the man. You are this creature's keeper, Sieur Réaux. Where did you find her? How long have you had her? How old is she? What does she eat? Is she really a genuine Hottentot?

—Would you like to talk to her? Alone?

—Are you serious?

—I will allow you to escort her home in a hired cab where you can ask her anything you like if you promise an article in tomorrow's *Journal des Dames et des Modes.*

—Tomorrow? Give me a day to write it.

—You can stay up all night and write it.

—Agreed.

The journalist escorted Sarah home in his carriage, and in doing so got his exclusive story. He published it the next day in an article everyone in the Cour des Fontaines would read. The Venus, in learning to read and to write, had also learned to lie. The life story she told the sympathetic reporter had little to do with what had truly happened to the real Sarah Baartman. Nevertheless, Sarah's life had made the morning newspapers on page two. She was truly a celebrity. It changed the way the Venus was perceived by the Cour des Fontaines. La Belle Limonadière took Sarah under her wing, William the Will, Cock and Penis offered her love and affection. Mickey Foucault offered her a loan to go back to Africa. The vaudeville theater sent her free tickets to their play. The chocolatier sent her a huge box of chocolates named after her. The florist delivered a bouquet of African orchids named after her. The patrons of the Thousand Columns all rose as she entered, and gave her a round of applause. Several clients bought her gin. A committee of acrobats, clowns and dwarfs petitioned me to reduce her hours of work so she could get more sleep. Alice vowed to wean Sarah from the bottle and from her unreasonable fear of me and her unreasonable fear of leaving me. She knew if she was to save Sarah's life, she might have to kill me or have me killed. I contemplated that thought calmly. And certainly the thought gave neither me nor, I wager, her any sleepless nights. But I noticed that Sarah was never the same after that. Her melancholy took on a morbid cast and her drinking increased even more. But all in all, her appearance at Madame de C's ball had the consequences I had been hoping for.

The Baron Cuvier finally answered my letter of six months before. He respectfully requested my permission to examine and sketch the Hottentot Venus for a period of three days at the end of March at the Museum of Natural History. The baron then wrote an accompanying letter to Inspector Boncheseiche, chief of the first section of the Paris police, and sent a copy to me.

We would like to profit from the circumstances that the presence in Paris of a Hottentot female offers us in order to convey with more precision than was possible up to now the distinctive characteristics of this curious race. We will have her drawn and engraved. We have for this reason contacted the master of this woman presented to the public under the name of the Hottentot Venus. He has pointed out certain constraints to our wishes due to obligations contracted with your administration, in that Sieur Réaux needs your authorization in order to conduct his Hottentot across the Seine to the King's Botanical Gardens. We ask you to have the goodness to bestow it.

Your obedient Servant,
Baron Georges Cuvier

—I don't want to go, said Sarah, I'm afraid. I don't want to pose naked.

—You will go, I order you to, I said. I was jubilant.

—I don't have to obey you. I'm a free woman.

—Oh really?

—Yes. And I won't take off my clothes.

—You stupid cow. The contract I won from Dunlop was for six years. There is still a year and three months to go.

—It doesn't matter. Alice and me, we're leaving.

I eyed Sarah, my nostrils flaring. I had had all that I could stand of Miss Baartman.

—I could sell your contract to a number of people, Sarah, several impresarios are anxious to exploit you: circuses, vaudeville, the anatomists . . . Madame de C's salon was good publicity, so was Songe's article. The scientific world is not so bad—and it's certainly better than the crazy house, the jailhouse, the poorhouse or the whorehouse, I repeated. Except these doctors and scientists and so-called intelligentsia are worse cannibals than circus owners or impresarios. True, we do it for money; but they talk only about contributing to knowledge, scientific progress. Those cheap bastards only want their theories, their experiments, their decorations and academies, their trophies and stipends and publications. Yet we are more honest. The entire world is a voyeur, and that includes our "Napoleon of Intelligence!"

—We're still leaving this time, pouted Sarah stubbornly.

—You *think* you're leaving, Sarah, but you aren't going nowhere. Not only did I win Dunlop's contract, but I bought *you* as his wife. In England, a man can do that, didn't you know? In Halifax, a man can sell his wife if he has a good reason—like bankruptcy or debt. It's perfectly legal, an ancient English custom known as wife sale.

—What! exploded Alice.

—Wife sale is illegal and a crime, she shouted from the doorway. You could never make it stick! Besides, Dunlop is a bloody bigamist.

—Try me, I said. And you'll both end up in a whorehouse. This contract gives me, as her husband, complete control of all her worldly goods . . . *That which the husband hath is his own. That which the wife hath is the husband's.* She belongs to me as wife and I am her husband. Only incidentally does Sarah have a contract with me as impresario. In court Sarah is nothing but my appendage. I am tutor, guardian, owner, treasurer and head of household, protector and moral authority. Until death, girl.

—You son of a bitch, screamed Alice.

On March 20, Napoleon escaped from his prison on Elba and returned triumphant to a Paris Louis XVIII had fled just hours before. He restored himself as Emperor of France. One of his first proclamations was to abolish slavery and the slave trade that he himself had reimposed after the Revolution five years before. For the third time Baron Cuvier changed camps, and rebaptized himself a Bonapartist, and I got out my old Grand Army uniform. Who would remember now that I had deserted?

17

There are no missing links . . . What law is there which would force the Creator to form unnecessarily useless organisms simply to fill the gaps in a scale?

—BARON GEORGES LÉOPOLD CUVIER,
Thirty Lessons in Comparative Anatomy

Twisted Ears, the English month of March, 1815. The sharp light was almost blinding and it cut everything into different shapes of color: triangles, squares, circles, outlined by milk-white stone. The King's Botanical Gardens were the most beautiful I had ever seen. Magnificent and precise, laid out with a ruler and a compass, the gardens were very different from the English gardens and parks I had known up until now.

Master Réaux held my arm tightly as he walked me through the gates, emphasizing what an important day this was and how I was to comport myself. He went on to explain why it had been necessary to have this exhibition at all. I put one foot in front of the other, listening not to him but to the sound of my leather boots scraping against the pink and gray pebbles underfoot. Alice had dressed me in the most conventional clothes I possessed. Somehow I felt my most important garment should be my own dignity. After all, I was not at number 188. I was not to meet a mob of carnivalgoers but the cream of Parisian intelligentsia; scientists, writers, artists, doctors and professors had all gathered here to behold my person. This was hardly our "public." These were the masters of the world. Of one thing I was sure, I would never allow these white men to examine my sex. I would cover myself with the white handkerchief I carried in the pocket of my dress. My apron was my own business.

—Baron Cuvier has agreed to certify your scientific importance in *La Quotidienne* next Saturday.

I didn't answer. Master Réaux had not received permission for us to cross the Seine to the Museum of Natural History in the King's Botanical Gardens until the end of March. During that time the exiled Napoleon had returned from Elba, invaded the Gulf of Juan, rallied the army sent to stop him and incited a general rebellion which had borne him triumphantly to the gates of Paris. Bonaparte had entered Paris on the shoulders of the army on March 1 as Emperor once again—and on the coattails of King Louis, who had fled the same day. Even now, Paris was still caught up in the jubilation of Napoleon's return.

We made our way towards the tall white château situated at the end of the gardens.

—This is fantastic publicity for you, repeated Master Réaux. The baron is famous as "the Napoleon of Intelligence" and he's Napoleon's surgeon general—his favorite scientist! It's a miracle of good luck! I asked him if he wanted me to introduce you but he just looked at me very strangely and declined, saying he had his own introduction ... So, don't open your mouth unless someone asks you a direct question. You are not here to talk. You are here to be seen. Great painters will draw you as well and the professor baron will allow me to reproduce one of the illustrations for our own publicity ... besides the certificate! Imagine the most famous, most brilliant mind in Paris ... in the realm ... the Emperor's surgeon general ...

I wasn't listening to Master Réaux. I hadn't listened to him since we stumbled off the mailboat from Southampton and he had kissed the ground of his native France. He had even shed a tear, but was smart enough to keep me from the money I had earned since then. Alice found out that he had been a deserter from Napoleon's army before he had been an animal trainer. And that before that, he had been the black sheep of a respectable French family. I was busy thinking of all this when his voice interrupted my thoughts.

—Are you listening to me, stupid? Didn't I tell you to wear your circus dress?

—I wanted the great masters to see me *as I am,* not with a *costume* on . . . That's for the crowds at number 188 . . . It seemed to me . . .

—It seemed to you? Since when do things *seem to you?* How would you know what they want or wish to see? Have you ever been to the Museum of Natural History in the King's Botanical Gardens before? Have you ever seen a scientific laboratory before? Or the greatest collection of specimens, animals, fossils and skeletons on the Continent? Do you know Cuvier himself has a private collection of 11,486 items? You give me any more lip and I'll smash you one . . .

He drew me closer to him and pinched my arm. He rubbed his jaw.

—Look how beautiful these grounds are . . . I wonder who's invited to the lecture . . .

The day was warm and the light clear and calm as after a storm. It was spring light and spring weather and at the end of the perspective stretching perhaps half a mile stood the Museum of Natural History between two avenues of chestnut trees. Halfway up the avenues was a large pool with a shining, spouting fountain of stone animals. From the fountain radiated triangular flower beds and sculpted boxwood shrubbery. The pool reflected the sky. The château of white stone had two sets of steps leading to twin entrances. The slate roof with its glass dome gleamed, and above the dome flew the Emperor's flag. On either side of the gardens were somber woods where tropical plants from Africa and India grew in glasshouses. These were called hothouses and plants for the garden were grown in them all year round. This was why the gardens were called Le Jardin des Plantes.

In the distance I spied a large blue-and-green-striped tent from which the most beautiful music came. I turned my head from left to right, not having time as we walked to take everything in: the gardens which descended to the banks of the Seine, the tall trees, the caged animals, the dark-frocked men strolling amongst the clipped hedges. I saw two elegantly dressed white men hurrying towards us. One was dressed in black with a black shirt and black cravat and black trousers. Only his shiny golden decorations flashed in the sunlight. He was hatless and his bright wavy red hair stood up in the breeze. The other man was slightly smaller, dressed like a peacock in bottle green and lavender. He too was covered with decorations and was hatless. His receding blond hair plastered down across his bald pate was worn long and pulled back in a ponytail. As they approached, my master adjusted his stiff white cravat nervously.

—Here they come, he croaked. Remember to curtsy. Let me do the talking. Just greet them with a nod. Don't smile. Don't speak unless you are spoken to. I'll . . . I'll take care of this. Remember your French?

—*Bonjour, messieurs.*

—And you curtsy like you would in South Africa.

—And I curtsy . . . I repeated.

I regretted not having insisted that Alice come with me. My heart was racing. I was about to encounter science thanks to the man who was approaching slowly with a stately stiff-legged walk.

—Bitch, stand up straight . . .

—Yes, Master.

We came face-to-face with the two men.

—Good morning, Sieur Réaux, may I introduce the Chevalier Etienne Geoffroy Saint-Hilaire, professor of zoology at the University of Paris . . .

—Good morning, sirs, chirped Master Réaux.

—*Bonjours, maîtres,* I murmured.

As I curtsied a cold chill went up my spine. There was no recognition in the baron's eyes. As if this were the first time we had met. Didn't he remember the ball? His introductions? The unblinking gaze of the doctor was as cold as ice and inspected me as if I had just arrived in a crate. How could he pretend he had never beheld me before? It was the cold stare of a cobra, paralyzing with fear before striking. I felt my chest being squeezed tighter and tighter as if in a fatal embrace, one in which I recognized my own fate in helpless horror. Oh Lord, this man's a murderer, I thought. I kept my eyes lowered, my lower lip trembled, my hands were wet and clammy in their gloves. I had what Caroline called stage fright. This was not the Parisian mob but God himself.

—So here is my Hottentot Venus!

—So it is, Baron. Here she is. Your missing link . . .

—There is no missing link, Monsieur, the Creator wouldn't be so . . . silly.

Master Cuvier turned on his heel and started walking towards the imposing white palace at the end of the gardens. He spoke over his shoulder.

—Welcome to our new museum. This is my home. I used to live on rue de Varenne, but when I was named director here, I moved into a part of the museum. It seemed so much more efficient. I rise early, at five, and by seven I am in my laboratory. I moved my own private collection of skeletons and fossils here with me, some eleven thousand. You've never been here before? This path to the right leads to our zoological gardens, which you, Monsieur Réaux, as an animal trainer will be very interested in seeing. We have myriad specimens of birds, reptiles, even an elephant. All bounty from the voyages of the *Geography* and the *Naturalist* under the command of the explorers Levaillant and Nicolas Baudin.

I walked several paces behind them, my head down, my heart racing as if I were on my way to the guillotine.

—Look! I suddenly exclaimed.

There was a great purple heron standing on one leg, staring at me. Suddenly she opened her wings as if in an embrace, hopping pitifully.

—We allow peacocks and herons to roam the gardens at liberty. It delights the visitors to come upon them. Their legs are fettered with brass weights so that they cannot fly away, said the baron.

Master Geoffroy Saint-Hilaire trailed behind me, taking up the rear, his eyes boring into my back. I wore a dress of thin white silk, cut straight and caught by a girdle just under the bosom, held by a green sash. Over it I wore a large cashmere shawl and a wide-brimmed bonnet of green and blue grosgrain decorated with cock feathers. I carried a parasol against the sun like white women did.

—Your Venus, Monsieur Réaux, doesn't look like she's African. I expected her attire to be much more ferocious.

—It is in deference to the occasion and your excellencies. The Venus didn't think her circus costume appropriate for such a momentous occasion.

—Well, remarked Master Geoffroy Saint-Hilaire, who wore sunglasses against the light, it's her *shape* we are interested in, not her taste in clothes . . .

I walked, my back straight, embarrassed. These men, these great scientists who so honored me, sounded no different from my circus public. I bit my lip, trembling. A hot flash, then a cold chill, drew up my spine, filling in the holes that Master Geoffroy Saint-Hilaire's eyes had made.

We passed the blue and green tent from which the music came. Instinctively I turned towards it.

—This temporary tent is for the guests who have come to the lecture. We will visit it shortly as my guests are eagerly waiting to see you. But first I would like to show you some of the museum's specimens, many brought back by our Emperor's Egyptian expedition.

—Venus, Master Réaux shouted as my footsteps wandered towards the tent and the music.

—Stay away from the violins . . .

I had discovered white music at the Cape in the music room of Mistress Alya, and then again in London, where Caroline had taken me once to Covent Garden to see an opera. I learned that music was more than just pleasure. There was hidden meaning to it, more than simply a marriage or a war, but meaning within the sound of its soul. It was something I had never thought of before, but music expressed sadness and happiness, landscapes and the sea. Music said that there was a right way for things to be ordered so that life had a shape and was not brute noise or brute events. Things didn't just happen, said the music, they occurred within something called destiny. Music made you glad you had been born.

Reluctantly I turned away from the beautiful sounds and mounted the steps of the museum. At the top, still another gentleman joined us.

—May I introduce Count Henri de Blainville, said the baron, my collaborator and illustrious author of *Prodrome of a New Distribution of the Animal Kingdom* . . .

From the very first, I didn't care much for Master de Blainville. He was a man without color: skin color, hair color, eye color, all blended into a dirty, nasty gray fog that hovered over him like the shadow of a flock of migrating birds. He was more bird than man anyway, I thought. There was something owlish about him and he had a way of hovering over people, his elbows slightly cocked, as if he were about to take flight. His feet spread in a Y like a duck's. He spoke in a chirping high voice, his little tongue moving in and out of his beak in a sparrow's twitter. He followed me around like a pelican, lining up behind me and goose-stepping to my back. As much as Baron Cuvier affected somber black on black, Master de Blainville dressed like a peacock in yellow, lavender and bright greens as if to attach streamers of color to his colorless person. This only made him look more like a bird than ever—a parrot perhaps, with its endless incessant chattering. For Master de Blainville never shut up. He was round, with a round (and as I said) owl-like face with round eyes behind round spectacles, round shoulders, round hands, round knees, round stomach and a round rear end. Just as Baron Cuvier was all straight lines and angles, Master de Blainville was all crookedness and curves.

I was surprised when I found myself in the main gallery of the museum, which rose like a church to a glass skylight surrounded by large rectangular windows. I had never visited Master Bullock's museum in Piccadilly, although I had begged to be taken there many times. I cried out in delight and amazement at being surrounded by all the animals of the savanna; still as statues and dead as wood, yet so lifelike. My heart beat faster: giraffes, elephants, a hippopotamus with all its teeth, buffalo and zebras. But what was more amazing were the skeletons standing amongst them, as if an invisible hand had reached into them and pulled the bones from their forms, throwing them into the air where they had assembled into their original shapes before descending to earth. An orangutan, a forest ape and a dozen other four-legged beasts stood beside their skeletons. In the center was a giant tortoiseshell taken from one of the creatures I had seen on St. Helena. In death, they all stood stiffly, at attention like soldiers, beside their own bodies, nude ghosts, pale, white and luminous; the jaw of a whale, the ribs of a shark, the spine of a crocodile, all warning me to run for my life. Then I spied the trophy heads: severed heads of Chinamen, of Bushmen, of Indians, of Khoekhoe staring back at me from their glass boxes.

As their eerie voices reached me, I bolted for the door with a cry.

—Poor creature, said Master Réaux to the others, she thinks they are real and are going to eat her.

The white men stood in a circle like hyenas, laughing at me. I tried desperately to control myself, repeating to myself that these exhibits were only skinned and stuffed animals, not real souls . . . but what of the human severed heads? In the next gallery, all reason abandoned me. This was the bird room. It was decorated to resemble a forest except that every bird in it was dead. The vaulted stone ceiling and stone walls, the high stained-glass windows gave the space the appearance of a stone cage or a crypt in a mountain. Thousands and thousands of birds sat silent in glass cases, singing no more, taking wing no more, carefully stuffed and mounted as if a whole forest had been emptied. I shrieked with horror and ran from the hall, the silence of the birds still in my ears. Behind me, I heard the laughter of the men. But I didn't care. Outside the building, I tried to breathe, yet breath would not come.

Around me the landscape emerged like a dawn and I realized there were other real animals imprisoned here as well. The woods were strewn with small pavilions of stone and imprisoned within them were wild animals. There were an elephant couple with their calf in one pavilion. There were orangutans, monkeys and baboons in another pavilion. A great ape, tall and lonely, gazed back at me from a cage made of iron and wire.

—There is nothing here except cages and prisons, I said to the men, who had followed me. Suddenly, they all seemed to understand my distress, for they looked at me with a kind of amused pity as if to say, Well, what did you expect? These animals are dead. This is a zoo. We are their keepers because we have the power to keep them, silly girl.

—*Tout est mort ici.*

—Perhaps, said Master Geoffroy Saint-Hilaire, clearing his throat, we should retire to the reception tent for a glass of champagne before our lecture begins in the pavilion of comparative anatomy . . .

But I couldn't face the men in the striped tent. My eyes caught those of Master Cuvier, who had been studying my reactions as if I were one of his stuffed birds.

—No, I said, shaking my head.

—Count, would you be so kind as to escort Mademoiselle Baartman directly to the pavilion of comparative anatomy? I want her appearance to be a complete surprise. Perhaps her . . . keeper Sieur Réaux can accompany you. I will be there directly.

The pavilion, set in the park, was round, two stories high, with a dome which sparkled in the sun. Over the portal, shaped like a temple, was written in gold letters PAVILION OF COMPARATIVE ANATOMY. Inside, it was an amphitheater with benches climbing up to the high windows and painted ceiling. It was decorated with stuffed animals and birds perched on high pillars. A large reptile was nailed to one wall. Another wall was covered with shelves crowded with jars of liquid containing things for which I had no names. Below the shelves stood a large gray slate rectangle framed in wood—a *tableau noir,* it was called. A long table of violet granite was placed before it. Near this was a revolving platform similar to the ones we used at the circus. There was a small stepladder nearby, a chair, a speaker's lectern, and in the corner was a tall blue and white Dutch stove. The theater was empty. A solid ray of light from the windows struck the central enclosure, which was surrounded by a wooden balustrade separating the audience from the lecturer. From that point, the empty benches rose in circles, yawning back at me. The room smelled of blood and some other scent I did not recognize, except it might have been my own fear. I stared up at the empty seats and coughed, choking a bit on my own saliva.

—Try to pull yourself together, Sarah, I'm going back with the count to the reception. You be a good girl. We'll be back in an hour. Try to rest—there's a little dressing room behind that green door there . . . There's nothing to be afraid of and there's nothing to be nervous about, after all you've done this hundreds of times . . . Meanwhile, get yourself undressed.

—Undressed! I cried.

—Madame, said Master de Blainville as they left. I didn't answer either of them. I was about to throw a wicked tantrum. I was about to scream that I would not pose naked—that I would not show them my apron. That I was not a stupid beast. I would not play their game of . . . of zoo as they had planned.

Noisily the men filed into the theater. They spoke loudly and jovially, I suppose because of the champagne they had just consumed. Others spoke in serious, hushed tones, all of which blended into an incomprehensible babble that could have been Khoekhoe. Through the opening I could see an audience of about sixty men in afternoon dress and top hats. Within the circle of the balustrade stood the masters de Blainville, Geoffroy Saint-Hilaire and the baron.

At the back of the room stood four men not dressed as the others, but in loose-fitting indigo smocks and large felt hats. Artists. They were setting up their easels and were preparing, I imagined, to paint my portrait.

My image had been reproduced in London so many times that I had no doubt as to what they were doing.

There was one young man about my age who was not like the rest and who reminded me of the never-forgotten Master Kemble. He stood like a hawk, a mysterious half smile on his face, listening to the other men converse. He had neither pencil nor paper nor easel. His hands were covered in red clay and before him stood a small wire figure on a pedestal to which he was applying small bits from his fingers. He would do this throughout the lecture until he had stolen my shape completely.

The noise abated when Master de Blainville rose to announce that the session was open. He nodded to Baron Cuvier, who raised his notebook in the air. Master de Blainville cleared his throat and then began.

—Gentlemen, everyone here has heard of the Hottentot Venus, a Bushwoman who has been exhibited for the past year as a circus attraction at 188 rue St. Honoré in Paris. Today, an unusual set of circumstances allows us to examine this extraordinary subject for three days, here at the museum, in the nude, for sessions of up to six hours a day. Discussions of all the implications of her appearance here, her origins, her physical properties, her race and her scientific position in our classifications of the human race of mammals will be the main topics of discussion of our colloquium. I see that colleagues from as far away as London, Brussels, Amsterdam, Brest, Marseille and Lyon are here at the invitation of our esteemed director, Baron Cuvier, commander of the Legion of Honor.

—I would like to remind you, gentlemen, that smoking is not allowed in the laboratories for reasons of safety. There will be several breaks for smoking and refreshments. I will ask you to keep silent during my introduction and the baron's discourse.

—As I said, the Hottentot we are about to examine this afternoon was born on the river Camboos in the Cape of Good Hope, in austral Africa, and is a female of about twenty-six years old, of the Bushman or Hottentot race . . . her color and formation certainly surpass anything of the kind ever seen in Europe or perhaps even produced in the world . . . She is a pure and priceless specimen of the great Chain of Being, and as such is inestimable in value . . .

Applause greeted the end of Master de Blainville's introduction. The baron rose, a long pointed cane in his hand.

I felt a burning in my head, in my womb, in my soul, as if I danced on hot coals like Adolph. Flames licked at my skin and the amphitheater of men seemed to be taking bites of my flesh. I concentrated on the young man, who was stealing my shape as the baron's French incantations reached me and although I understood little of what he said, his words ignited a furor in me, leaving me breathless and gasping. His voice seemed to fill the universe with revolutions and more revolutions as time passed.

He beckoned me towards him with his forefinger. I stepped forward timidly. I was holding my handkerchief in front of me to hide my private parts, but otherwise I was completely naked.

18

A true historian must have the power of reshaping the universally known into what has never been heard and to announce what is universal so simply and deeply that people overlook the simplicity in the profundity and the profundity in the simplicity. An eminently learned man and a great numskull, those go together very easily under a single hat.

—BARON GEORGES LÉOPOLD CUVIER,
Correspondence

*M*arch 1815. I could feel the Venus's gaze upon me like a kind of enchantment. She would not take her eyes from me, and as I felt a rush of blood that ended in a blush, I wondered if she was trying to send me some kind of message. I believed in fate. After all, I had not been invited by name as the other artists had. I was here only as a substitute for my illustrious patron, Jacques-Louis David, the most famous painter in France.

—Nicolas, he had said, I don't want to insult the baron by ignoring his invitation.

Ever since Bonaparte's return, my boss, old political animal that he was, had been lying low until the Emperor consolidated his power. At the moment, the Emperor was still at war.

I was sure that my employer resented Cuvier's miraculous ability to survive intact three political regimes not only without a hint of a prison cell, exile or death but, on the contrary, with an avalanche of important positions, honors, decorations and powerful responsibilities. Louis David's life, on the other hand, had hung in the balance in 1793 when he had been arrested as a supporter of Robespierre and released only as a result of his wife's intervention. He had been at that time an ardent republican, a member of the National Convention and a signatory of the death warrant of Louis XVI. After the Revolution, he had changed his allegiance to Napoleon and had painted his coronation. He was, I thought cautiously, fence-sitting between the deposed Louis and the restored Napoleon, waiting to see which way the wind blew. As were many of the celebrities, I thought, whom I had seen milling around the green-and-blue-striped guest tent in the garden. Now, at exactly four o'clock, everyone was jammed into the pavilion of comparative anatomy to behold what the baron doctor called "my" Hottentot Venus, who, he claimed, would prove his theories about the great Chain of Being . . .

No one in Paris, I thought, refused an invitation from Georges Léopold Chrétien Frédéric Dagobert Cuvier, peer and baron of France, weighed down with so much power spanning the Revolution, the Empire and now the Restoration.

How did he do it, I wondered. No man in history had elevated the art of organization of time and the cultivation of each moment. With Cuvier, each hour was dedicated to a certain task, each task had its own laboratory or bureau, and each bureau was perfectly equipped for each task. My boss, who had had dealings with Cuvier while he had been painting his portrait, said that the great man moved from bureau to bureau, functioning without a second of distraction, like a machine.

—You like him, don't you? I said.

—I admire him, my patron had said. Why, he even insisted on posing with a book so he could read while he sat for me, so as not to lose any time . . .

I had studied that famous painting, while it had been in the studio. The masterful portrait had been that of a melancholy, cold and fastidious aristocrat with bright red hair, pale skin and military bearing. The eyes held a compelling and consuming intelligence just as the mouth held an over-whelming arrogance and avariciousness. It was so beautifully painted, I thought, that it wouldn't have mattered if the subject had been a mur-derer. And that, the baron certainly was not. After the Emperor, he was simply the most brilliant man in France.

I was twenty-six years old and had been David's assistant since the age of twenty. Before that, I had served as apprentice to Charles-Philibert du Saillant, in whose atelier I had learned not only the art of watercolor and engraving but also lithography. But now, I specialized in the sculpting and portraiture of animals, and as an animalist, I spent a great deal of time at the King's Botanical Gardens and the Museum of Natural History.

I came from a modest family of grain merchants. I knew I was lucky to be admitted into the company of this elite group of men. I had a healthy respect both for my elders and for my betters and rumor had it that even Bonaparte might show up at his old friend's museum today.

I knew the three other artists present: Nicolas Huet, Léon de Wailly and Jean-Baptiste Berré. I made a beeline to their side. They were all hud-dled together in the back of the auditorium, as intimidated by the forces gathering in the amphitheater as I was.

—I'm not going to do anything today, said de Wailly, I'm just going to see what this creature looks like.

—Well, then you'll be a day behind getting your watercolors printed and published, because *La Quotidienne* and the *Reporter* are both here to see what Cuvier has up his sleeve.

—What about you, Nicolas? Sculpting today or just looking?

—I don't know, I replied honestly, I'm going to play it by ear.

—It seems she's some kind of hermaphrodite with the genitals of both a man and a woman.

—Supposedly all Hottentots are.

—No, they're supposed to be the missing link between Negroes and the orangutan.

—You've never been to see her show down near the Palais Royal?

—You doing sanguine or watercolor? Surely not gouache.

—I haven't decided yet. I've brought everything. I'm thinking to do some charcoal today.

But that morning, even the most successful painters felt apprehensive before the challenge of illustrating one of the great Baron Cuvier's scientific specimens.

—She'll be absolutely in the nude for these drawings.

—You know, this may be all Geoffroy Saint-Hilaire's idea, not Cuvier's; after all, Geoffroy Saint-Hilaire is the expert in teratology.

—Freaks, not monsters.

—He experiments on the embryos of chickens to produce abnormal manifestations or deformation.

—Well, that may be Geoffroy Saint-Hilaire's obsession, but the baron is interested in the classification of the races . . .

—Everyone smells adventure, joked Berré, confrontation with the unknown, the unexplored, the odor not just of Africa but of the primordial, the monstrous, the real Eve . . . She's the real Eve . . .

—Shush . . . Here comes de Blainville.

I took the time to arrange my sculpting tools and armature on the pottery wheel which I had already set up while de Blainville was making his introduction. The amphitheater was full as medical students filed in to fill up the spaces left empty by the guests and professors.

There was an excited buzz in the room when the Venus stepped out of the side room, timidly, holding a handkerchief before her, but otherwise in the nude. I caught my breath. I had never seen a female body quite like the Hottentot's, and I brushed my hair out of my eyes and began to sculpt furiously as Cuvier began his lecture. That was when the Venus had focused her mysterious chestnut gaze on me. The baron approached the lectern and began to speak. I concentrated on sculpting her, raising my eyes only to register the forms, curves, shadows, lines . . . I lost myself in my work, thinking only of somehow reproducing this extraordinary mortal—this African Eve . . .

—There are two things that I would like to demonstrate, began the baron. One, a detailed comparison of this woman with the lowest race of the human species, the Negro race, and the highest race of primates, or the orangutan. Secondly, to explain in the greatest detail possible the abnormalities of her organs of generation. I will commence by presenting to you, also in as much detail as possible, the background of this woman as has been extracted in Dutch and English from the subject herself.

—Sarah Baartman, better known under the name of Saartjie in England or the Vénus Hottentote in France, was born around twenty-six years ago to Bushman parents in the European part of the Cape Colony near Algoa Bay, now known as Zwarts Korps Bay, in the Graaf Reinet district, about five hundred miles from the Cape. Kidnapped at the age of nine, she remained in the hands of the Dutch and the English, whose language she therefore speaks. Everyone in Paris has had a chance to see her during her eighteen-month stay in our capital and verify for themselves the enormous protuberance of her buttocks and the brutality of her face.

—You will notice that her movements also have something brusque and capricious that resembles that of the orangutan. However, her memory is good, exceptional even. As I have said, she speaks Dutch, which she learned at the Cape, and English passably well, and has begun to say a few words in French. She has a good ear and sings and dances while playing her guitarlike instrument. Her height is a bit over one meter thirty-nine, or four feet seven inches, which, in comparison to that of her compatriots, is fairly tall.

—Her trunk seems extremely short, because of the extraordinary swelling of her backside and accompanying parts; nevertheless, the center of the length of her body is still the pubis, and one can say in general that the proportions of these parts resemble closely those that one finds in the Caucasian race. Only the arms are a little bit shorter.

—The head is remarkable for its general form and for certain details of its components. Considered in its ensemble, it is evident that she does not have exactly the aspects of a Negro head and that there is more of a rapprochement to that of an orangutan: an observation already noted by Dr. Barrow. Generally small, the head seems to be composed of two parts, one the cerebral cavity or cranium, and two, the face or snout, which does not join the profile in a manner to form a straight line, where the inclination determines the facial angle, but unites one to the other at the base of the nose almost at a right angle, in the manner one sees most markedly in the orangutan; so that the forehead is straight—almost vertical—and the rest of the profile is concave like that of the primate or the monkey species. The symphysis of the chin is not very elevated, and instead of bending forward in order to make what we call a chin, it flees perceptibly backwards; all these characteristics are found, but in a way, indeed, a lot more marked, in the orangutan.

—The teeth are beautiful, very white, close-set and big, especially the upper incisors, which seem to be proportionally even larger than in the

Negro race; the canines are not sharp at all. The oblique layout of the incisors in the two jaws gives the aspect of pincers.

—The lips are quite thick and sharp, though perceptibly less than in the Negro race; they are badly formed, that is to say, the upper one doesn't have a median point corresponding to the lower one, the corners are lowered; the half canal of the upper lip is hardly marked; both are pale pink.

—The mammaries are very big, hanging quite near to the hemispheric median line towards their lower part. They go down to the line the crook of the arm makes, two or three inches above the navel. The nipple is very thick. Its color is dark brown, the areola, of the same color, is extraordinarily large.

—Concerning the organs of generation, in the ordinary position, that is to say in the vertical position, we can see no trace of a kind of pedicle which would be formed by the large lips, as can be seen in the figures of M. M. Perron and Le Sueur.

The Venus must have heard certain words, I thought, repeated again and again that were similar to the English . . . race, orangutan, monkey, Negro race, Caucasian race, Tatar race . . . Hottentot . . . *extraordinaire . . . remarquable . . . surprenante* . . . very big, very small. Her name, Sarah . . . She must understand some of this, I thought.

But the Venus seemed determined that not one doctor or scientist would view her apron.

—The upper limbs, continued the baron, are quite thin, short in general, though well built; the shoulders, quite narrow from their base, the forearm is short and well shaped, the hand is very small, with delicate fingers, very remarkable and charming.

—The pelvis, in general, is very narrow, but it seems even narrower because of the tremendous swelling of the lower and posterior parts of the trunk; it is indeed what, at first sight, is most striking when looking at this Hottentot. Her buttocks are really enormous, they are at least twenty inches high, jutting out six to seven inches from the dorsal line, their width being at least of the same dimensions. Their shape is quite singular; instead of starting from the end of the loins, they spread horizontally, in an upward curve to their summit, to form a kind of flat saddle. It is said that Hottentot children literally ride on this saddle. We easily establish that the majority of this mass is cellulofat, which trembles and quivers when this woman walks, and when she sits down flattens and spreads out.

—Her formation is extraordinary, first because of the enormous width of her hips, which exceeds eighteen inches, and secondly because of the curve of her buttocks, which protrude out more than six inches. For the rest, she is normal in her proportions, both body and limbs. Her shoulders, her back, the height of her bosom have grace. The curve of her stomach is not excessive.

—To conclude, said Cuvier, raising his pointer, among us, the Caucasian forehead is pushed forward, the mouth is pulled back as if we were destined to *think* rather than *eat;* the Hottentot has a shortened forehead and a mouth that is pushed forward as if he were destined to *eat* instead of *think.*

—What is most striking about the physiognomy of the Hottentots? The face resembles in part the Negro in the curve of the jaw, the obliqueness of the incisors, the thickness of the lips, the shortness and regression of the chin, and in part the Mongol in the enormous height of the cheekbones, the flatness of the base of the nose and the forehead and the eyebrows and especially the horizontal slits of the eyes.

—Her hair is black and woolly like that of Negroes, the eyelid horizontal and not oblique like that of Mongols; her eyes are light brown rather than dark, her complexion is a brownish yellow . . .

—On the contrary, the white race to which the civilized people of Europe belong, with its oval face, straight hair and nose, appears to us the most beautiful of all. It is superior to others *also* by its genius, courage and activity. There seems to me to be a cruel law which has condemned to an eternal inferiority the races of depressed and compressed skulls . . . as we see in the Hottentot—and experience seems to confirm the theory that there is a relationship between the perfection of the spirit and the beauty of the face.

—Therefore, the Hottentots are the most appallingly barbarous of men, sharing this honor with the polar people. According to Linnaeus, there is a serious question about their human status.

—The Hottentots have no language to speak of, no social organization, they believe in no religion, do not cultivate the land, have no money or manner of official barter, have no government, no fixed residences, no concept of property, no cuisine, no hierarchy of nobles and leaders or even a priestly class. They are the most degraded of human races, whose form approaches that of the beast and whose intelligence is nowhere near great enough to arrive at a regular government. They are at present wards of the English government in the Cape for reason of their imbecility.

—In other words, interrupted a voice from the audience, your purpose is to provide a detailed comparison of this woman with the lowest race of humans, the Negro, and the highest specimen of apes, the orangutan . . .

—Correct. And number two, continued Cuvier, to provide the most complete description of the abnormalities of her genitalia . . . which I will now attempt to do.

—Moreover, said another voice, we can thus use the premise of phrenology to identify individuals or races that stand out at both poles of society: those with a propensity for making important social contributions and those with a greater than normal tendency towards evil. The former are to be encouraged, nurtured and developed in order to maximize their potential for good. The latter need to be curbed and segregated to protect society from their predisposition to crime.

—May I just add here, interjected a second phrenologist, that according to my studies, the African skull is overdeveloped in the organs of philo-progenitiveness and concentrativeness, accounting respectively for the African's alleged love of children and proclivity for sedentary occupations. Thus he is underdeveloped in conscientiousness, cautiousness, identity and reflection.

—The shape of their heads binds them more than us to the animals, said an anthropologist. The animal world, as you all know, is divided into four branches; the invertebrates, the amphibians, the mollusks and the protozoans. This division depends on the brain and the nervous system—the brain of the Hottentot being by nature the smallest and weakest of the species . . .

—As a physician and a proponent of polygenism, I would say it is obvious from your lecture today and the specimen standing before us that the black race is an entirely different species and does not originate from the common stock with the white race. As for cranium size, which marks the difference between the two, I estimate the brain size of different races by filling the cranial cavity with sifted white mustard seed. I then pour the seed back into a graduated cylinder and read the skull's volume in cubic inches . . .

—I think it's fair to say that in competition with the white race, the African that you see before you represents the missing link between ape and Caucasian . . .

—May I quote Enlightenment philosopher Voltaire, who wrote, The more I reflect on the color of these peoples, on the gobbling that they use to make themselves understood instead of an articulated language, on their countenance, on the apron of their ladies, the more I am convinced that this race cannot have the same origin as we do . . . I ask you, is this a separate race gentlemen, which we are dealing with here, independent of both the Negro and the Caucasian? Or, a sub-race of the Mongolian race? Or a hybrid? Or is this a mythic creature!

—Race, added a Scottish naturalist, rising from his seat, is everything. Literature, science, art—in a word, civilization.

The baron now made a motion to preclude comments and return to his exposition.

There was some commotion as an English physician rose to contradict Cuvier.

—Whatever Negroes lack in intelligence, they make up for in instinct and feeling. They have excellent heart and above all the possibility of all virtue, he concluded.

—Hear! Hear! repeated a Belgian naturalist. The Negro has the same possibilities as a European child. It remains a matter of education. We, as anthropologists, as men of science, can only record, measure, examine, observe scientifically, not make qualitative judgments . . . That is for *political* science to make . . .

—Monsieur, added an American anthropologist, I have personally studied more than a thousand skulls in my laboratory in Boston. So many in fact that my students call me Golgotha!

At this, the entire audience laughed in unison.

—I have determined, the American continued, that the scientific hierarchy of intelligence is as follows: the Germans, the English, white Americans, on one end of the scale, the Hottentots and the aborigines of Australia at the other end.

—Speaking of white Americans, added an anatomist from Lyon, Thomas Jefferson, the naturalist and former President, has stated in his *Notes on the State of Virginia,* so excellently translated by our colleague, the Marquis de Condorcet, that blacks, whether originally a distinct race or made distinct by time and circumstances, are inferior to the white in the endowments of both body and mind . . . The first difference that strikes us, he wrote, is that of color. Whether the black of the Negro resides in the reticular membrane between the skin and scarfskin or in the scarfskin itself, whether it proceeds from the color of the blood, the color of the bile, or from that of some other secretion, the difference is fixed by nature.

—I too, added another naturalist, excitedly, have studied hundreds of skulls exhumed from three cemeteries in Paris and have compared them with those of other races. As comparisons I choose skulls where the inequality of intellect is evident: African Negroes, American Indians, Hottentots, oceanic Negroes and Indians.

—What about the comparison of male skulls with female skulls? May I point out that the relative smallness of a woman's skull depends on both her physical inferiority and her intellectual inferiority . . .

—The Hottentot should not be classified as *Homo sapiens* but as *Homo monstrosis monorchidei.*

—It is the notion of the great Chain of Being which has cemented the Hottentots into their place in the world!

—Hottentots are the very reverse of humankind . . . So that if there's any medium between a rational animal and a beast, the Hottentot lays the fairest claim to that species, according to Ovington's writings. Who better to be the connecting link between the human species and brute creation?

—Such is the dependence amongst all the orders of creatures; that the apprehension of one of them is a good step towards the understanding of the rest. And this is the highest pitch of humane reason: follow all the links of this chain, till their secrets are open to our minds; this is truly to command the world; to rank all the varieties and degrees of things so orderly upon one another; that standing on top of them, we may perfectly behold all that is below and make them all serviceable to the quiet, peace and plenty of Man's life.

—I am a monogenist, but if we admit the supposition that humankind consists of distinct families, surely there is none that presents a stronger claim to be regarded as a race of separate origin than the Hottentots, distinguished as they are by many moral and physical peculiarities.

—Hottentots are Negroes even though their hyper-negroidness puts them at the bottom of this category and therefore at the absolute bottom of the Chain of Being, with the exception of idiots, lunatics and mixed bloods . . .

—The Hottentots are the most degraded of human races except for the Bushman, whose form resembles that of a beast and whose intelligence is never great enough to arrive at regular government. They were born slaves.

—Probably in no former period of the world has the destruction of any race of animals whatever been affected over such wide areas and with such startling rapidity as in the case of the savage man . . .

—One can roughly divide the nations of the world into the living and the dying—the living nations will fraudulently encroach on the territory of the dying.

—Like jackals.

—Or cannibals, I thought to say out loud. The fervor of dogma mounted in the stifling room.

—What is the function of steatopygia? Does it function like the tail of the fat-tailed sheep or the hump of a dromedary?

—A change in the environment, said another voice, causes changes in the needs of organisms living in that environment, which in turn causes changes in their behavior. Altered behavior leads to greater or lesser use of a given structure or organ: use could cause the organ to increase in size over several generations, disuse would cause it to disappear. Wouldn't this be the case with the Hottentot apron? The natural degree of lasciviousness and voluptuousness of the Hottentot has evolved into the perfect organ!

—Hear! Hear!

—That is brilliant.

Cuvier nodded, trying to get to the crux of his lecture, but the anatomists were enthusiastically debating this riveting question, tripping over one another in the stampede to assert their opinions.

—The average standard of the Negro race is two grades below our own based on my intelligence chart. The Lowland Scot and the English North Countryman is a grade superior to the ordinary English. The ancient Greeks were very nearly two grades higher than our own, that is about as much as our white race is superior to the African Negro.

—There is a vast difference, a British naturalist insisted, between the prognathous and the orthognathous people of Britain. The Irish, Welsh and lower classes are prognathous whereas all men of genius are orthognathous. It is part of my theory of Nigressence, which links the Irish to Cro-Magnon man and the Africanoid races . . .

—Look at the Hottentot. Is he shaped like any white person? Is the anatomy of his frame, his muscles, or organs like ours? Does he walk like us, think like us, act like us? What an innate hatred the Saxon has for him!

—A death sentence is justified against those unavowed by God, those who have defrauded natural reason and those who are neither nations in right nor nations in name!

—The decisive events of history are determined by the iron law of race, asserted another French anthropologist. Human destiny is decreed by nature and expressed in race.

Cuvier allowed this to resound throughout the hall as a rallying call and a litany before he reined in his apostles.

—Let us now, continued the baron, come to the crux of our examination: our Hottentot's *sinus pudoris*, or curtain of shame, better known as the Hottentot apron.

A sudden hush came over the room. I had been busily sculpting the Venus and had hardly followed Cuvier's lecture and the discussion that had taken place. But when I looked up, I saw that the Venus's light brown eyes were still upon me after all these hours. Sarah Baartman and de Blainville were at present having a tugging match as she tried to retain the white handkerchief that covered her pubis and de Blainville tried to snatch it away. Each time, Sarah won and de Blainville, angry and frustrated, glanced at Cuvier in despair while the Venus stared at me, defying the ogling scientists by hiding through careful compression of her thighs the very object of their desire. I had to laugh. She stood as frozen as my perfect sculpture, which in the tumult seemed to take on a life of its own.

—It was Péron, continued the baron, in the second volume of *The Voyage to the Austral Lands,* who approached the subject in a different way, stating that the apron didn't exist in Hottentots, but in Bushwomen, who also have excessively developed buttocks, and that this apron was not the development of any other part of the female anatomy but a special organ added on by nature.

—Linnaeus reported that it was the primitive vestige of the Hottentot's animal origin. He also reported finding it in the female *Homo troglodytes,* his second and lowest species of humans. John Ovington wrote in his *Voyage to Saratt* in 1689 that women who had these aprons were hermaphrodites. Voltaire argued that these women must belong to a separate race. Levaillant called the *sinus pudoris* a product of depraved taste and insisted that these aprons were merely caprices of fashion and coquetry.

—Peter Kolb suggested that it served as a natural fig leaf. Sir John Barrow added that it guarded Hottentot women against rape since it was impossible to penetrate an aproned woman without her consent. He believed that it was a hypertrophy of the labia and nymphae caused by manipulation of the genitalia and considered beautiful by Hottentots and Bushmen as well as tribes in Dahomey and Basutoland.

—For us today, the most important question concerning what is variously known as the female *tablier,* the *tablier égyptien,* Hottentot apron, *joyau,* longinympha, macronympha or, as Linnaeus called it, the *sinus pudoris,* or curtain of shame, is: Is it a product of nature or human manipulation? Or is it like mermaids, sirens and centaurs, an illusion that is entirely imaginary and chimerical? All this speculation must give way to scientific facts.

—The Hottentot apron exists. We have before us a living specimen, a genuine Hottentot of the race described by Jensen, Barrow and Levaillant; one everyone here has been able to view during her eighteen-month stay in our capital . . . Sarah Baartman's genitalia and buttocks summarize her essence. The remarkable development of her labia minora or nymphae which is so general a characteristic of the Hottentot and Bushman race, is sufficiently well marked as to distinguish these parts at once from any of the ordinary varieties occurring in the human species. I contend that the apron is a morbid development of the inner vaginal lips divided like two wrinkled, fleshy petals which, if raised, form the figure of a heart. These two rounded appendages are different lengths in different subjects, some not more than a half inch, in others three or four inches. Although I am a dedicated monogenist, this may be one of the anatomical marks of the nonunity of the races . . . which . . .

The baron turned to watch de Blainville silently struggle with Sarah Baartman.

—Nothing proves the primitive character of our Hottentot like her exaggerated sexual organs. Advanced humans are sexually restrained. Animals are overtly and actively sexual. Sarah's exaggerated sexual organs are proof of her inferiority and animality. Which we will explore in tomorrow's session since Miss Baartman seems unwilling to cooperate with Monsieur de Blainville today. I conclude on this note.

—May I contest that? I interloped, suddenly exacerbated, almost crying with rage. Humans are the *most* sexually active primates and humans have the largest sexual organs. Thus a human with larger than average endowments is in proportion, if anything, *more* human—not to mention the connection between human sexuality, the brain and conscious imagination . . .

—Mr. . . . Tiedeman, the animalist, I believe. We will have to take this up tomorrow. We have run out of time and any willingness on the part of Madame Baartman to accommodate us, said the baron. I therefore bring this session to a close and reconvene the conference, here, tomorrow at eleven o'clock.

The regiment of scientists filed out of the auditorium as if they were an expedition of explorers trekking through the wilds of Africa. They traversed the elegant gardens Indian file, staying close together for safety, each following behind the other across the immaculate paths to the reception tent.

The quartet's music wafted across the neatly tended diamonds, squares, circles and crescents of the pink-pebbled walks, the blossoming sumac, fleabane, goldenrod, geraniums and multiflora roses. It flooded the low hedges trimmed to perfection, the decorative sculptures, the medicinal plants, flowering bushes. I adjusted my sunglasses as I emerged from the auditorium and surveyed the expanse of garden. I spied Sarah in the distance, a wide hat hiding her face, her white skirts wrapped closely around her in the slight breeze. She was more than alone. She seemed the most solitary figure I had ever seen: a mysterious doomed character out of a romantic novel, the eternal Other . . . She stood close to the aviary, outlined by its wire mesh and ironwork. I wondered if she was contemplating freeing all those birds. That, I thought, would enrage the baron all right, perfect French bureaucrat that he was, for the birds belonged to the state, which owned the museum. I wondered if I should walk over to her instead of joining the others. I had known many artists' models, had seen many women's bodies, had drawn, engraved and sculpted them. I was not shy or embarrassed that I had created her form in clay from life. I was anxious only because from afar, Sarah Baartman seemed so uniquely remote, and unapproachable; it was as if she were indeed a whole race unto herself . . . But I didn't dare approach her.

But then, she spied me in my artist's smock, felt hat, long wavy hair and wide black bow and beckoned to me. Later that afternoon she told me that I was the only man in the entire room of physicians whose eyes hadn't made her feel naked.

19

Thus, if the viscera of an animal are so organized as only to be fitted for the digestion of recent flesh, it is also required that the jaws should be constructed as to fit them for devouring their prey; the claws must be constructed for seizing and tearing it to pieces; the teeth for cutting and dividing the flesh; the entire system of limbs or organs of motion for pursuing and overtaking it; the organs of sense for discovering it at a distance.

—BARON GEORGES LÉOPOLD CUVIER,
*Discourse on the Revolutionary Upheavals
on the Surface of the Globe*

Twisted Ears, the English month of March, 1815. At first, I didn't mind. The slow, beelike droning of Master Cuvier's soft voice in my ear lulled me into a trance. I stood; I walked, I jumped, I bent over, I turned around; I raised my arm, I lifted my foot, I held out my hand; I turned my head from side to side as in a dream. And as in a dream, the world was turned upside down. I kept my eye on the artist who was producing the effigy of me out of red clay. Not as red as his flaming red hair which fell in long waves to his shoulders, which were broad and sloping. His eyes were the color of the ocean under thick straight red eyebrows, and his face was painted with tiny red dots. After studying so many white faces, I judged his not only handsome but good. He wore a loose dress gathered at the neck in a bow. He had beautiful large hands which squeezed and molded the clay. I kept my eye on him because his eye on me was attentive, respectful, almost tender. The scientists were brusque, frightening and contemptuous. They interrupted each other, raising their voices or talked over each other, each tripping over the other's words and finally ending in shouts. Their voices ranged from low and dignified to rowdy, from cool politeness to utter rage; their mouths worked, spittle flew, hands waved, elbows gesticulated, arms swayed, feet tapped. It was like a slow-motion dance, with each man calling on his rainmaker for rain, in supplication or as a command. Words in a language I didn't understand flew about; sometimes like a gnat I would catch one or two: *Hottentote, tablier, Africaine, Cap de Bonne Espérance, belle, bête, sauvage* . . . I was indifferent to all that. I had been commanded to appear and I had done so against my will. For three days now, Master de Blainville had been trying to get me to drop the white handkerchief I held in front of my sex so that the baron could examine my apron. I refused. He pleaded. I resisted. My eyes appealed directly to the baron, whose long sharp stick tapped me gently from time to time as his discourse got more and more animated. Master de Blainville tugged at my handkerchief and I tugged back. I was determined that my apron would remain what it had always been to these men: a mystery.

By the third day, I was exhausted and numb with shame. I began to understand the contempt these men had for my body, for my color, for my humanity. I could have been a dog, a Siamese twin, a two-headed turtle. It was all the same to them. They were only interested in my monstrosity, *Homo monstrosis*, they called me, a new species of mankind. Like Hottentots baying for war, they farted and belched, coughed, stamped their feet, rolled their eyes, bared their teeth, spat, hawked, scratched their balls, slapped themselves, played with their ears, pulled at their hair, arranged their clothing as if I could not observe them—as if I could not return their rude gazes and bold scrutiny. As if they were in their water closets; as if they, not I, were naked. Their voices, their argumentative tones, their questions and answers flew past me like a hail of poisoned arrows, each one finding its mark, wounding my flesh so viciously I sometimes wondered whether they were only words. I experienced waves of nausea. It didn't matter that I couldn't understand what they were saying since I *felt* it in my flesh, as I had with the vaudeville play. They were out to prove that I, Sarah Baartman, was not human.

On the last day, Master de Blainville offered me a gold napoleon to lower my handkerchief and show them my apron. He held it in his outstretched hand exactly as Master Dunlop had done years ago. He stood there, in his peacock clothes, his plastered-down hair, his chirping, smirking arrogance, and disrespected me for the last time.

—I know you love money, he said. This is no different from your circus performances. I've paid my money, now I want my show!

It was as if I had seen a ghost or worse, as if !Naeheta Magahâs herself, the horrible dwarf, the fantastical witch, the thing-that-should-never-have-been-born, had risen up before me, shaking her braids and, in the supreme insult of a Khoekhoe, showing her ass. I screamed back at her in Khoe, pleading and bowing, cajoling and begging forgiveness. Then, as the rainmaker lunged towards me, I jumped back and struck out, hitting, of course, not Magahâs but Master de Blainville, almost knocking him off his feet. He in turn began to curse at me, consigning me to hell and purgatory as a heathen. Our shouting match went on for minutes, as I leapt around from one foot to the other like a monkey, my movements jerky, frenetic and hardly human, before the baron intervened, seizing me and holding me against his chest.

Out of the corner of my eye, I saw the sculptor leave the room in disgust, throwing down his tools and covering my image with a cloth. He didn't return for the final session. The other artists remained until the final moment, desperately working to finish their paintings. At last, I stepped down from my pedestal. I had won the war with Master de Blainville and he slumped, dejected, on the steps of the podium.

That night, my last appearance as Venus over, I was half asleep in my tent. Alice, who had come to fetch me, snored on the camp bed beside mine. Suddenly, the flap of the tent lifted and two dark figures loomed in the moonlight. Alarmed, I let out a little screech, which woke Alice. I knew it couldn't be Sieur Réaux. Alice leapt to her feet, grabbing a heavy stool as a weapon, croaking,

—Who's there?"

By that time, I was on my feet as well, a sheet pulled across my body, leaving, I remember, one breast exposed. My eyes were red and my lips trembled. I had been dreaming of the massacre.

—Don't be alarmed, came the silky voice of Master Cuvier out of the darkness. It is only I . . . with your Emperor. His Majesty wants to inspect you.

Master Cuvier's face appeared first, lit by a twelve-armed candelabra which shook a little, making the light flicker and giving his familiar face a sinister glow. Just behind him appeared the face of the Emperor. I knew him by sight even though he was wearing neither his three-cornered hat nor his crown. He was bareheaded, his thin brown hair combed forward and pasted to his forehead in fringes. His bright round eyes shone in the candlelight. The shadows of the tent hardened the contours of his face, yet it was a young face, I thought in surprise. My mouth had fallen open, my left hand clutched the sheet in front of me. I remained upright, frozen, while Alice dropped to her knees in a curtsy.

—Sire . . .

I almost laughed out loud, and to stop myself, I too curtsied low. The Emperor, I thought, in the King's Botanical Gardens. To visit a freak show in the middle of the night. Would my tormentor take His Majesty to visit the baboons after he left here? I wondered. Or would it be the king-size giraffe? I was trembling with rage and with cold.

The two men stood there like their effigies in Madame Tussaud's wax museum. Master Cuvier had on evening clothes and the Emperor was in a white uniform covered with medallions and decorations. They stared at us, two naked or practically naked women, one white and one black, as if they were visiting a lunatic asylum. *The whorehouse, the crazy house, the workhouse, the poorhouse,* ran through my brain. These men had the power of life and death over us. Alice had called Napoleon "the Butcher of Europe" for having killed a million of his own soldiers in the name of his ambitions to conquer Europe.

Without a word, the men circled us. With his sword, the Emperor plucked away the sheet, leaving me naked. He tapped me with his stick and made the clucking sound a coachman makes to urge his horses on. Then, thinking I did not understand French, he said:

—True, the Venus does resemble a baboon. In ancient Egypt, she would be worshiped as a goddess. Certainly her arse is amazing; as for her resemblance to a hermaphrodite, it is an interesting idea and would explain her organs of generation . . . or is it a fusion of several organs?

—I have examined her thoroughly and have deduced that it is not, sire.

—You must make her part of your new report to me on the state of science in France.

—The next report will be the state of science in Europe, sire.

—All barbarians are more or less ugly people. Beauty is the inseparable companion of the most civilized nations. Of course the Negro is ugly. How could it be otherwise? There is nothing more contemptible than a Negro except a Jew. Let us forget Africa, never to return to it, for Africa is not part of the historical globe, it is outside history . . .

The Emperor walked around me one last time. He stooped low because of my smallness to have a better look at my face and to peer into my eyes. His were the eyes of a jackal. He made snorting, clucking noises like a naked ape. After he had finished his inspection and was satisfied with his conclusions, the two men departed as abruptly as they had arrived, leaving us speechless.

—The Negro presence in the world of the present, echoed Bonaparte's voice as it receded into the distance, is there to prove how far mankind has come in establishing control over himself and his world. Otherwise, they are expendable. They represent only regression into the dark past. Like three quarters of the world's population, they do not deserve the right to exist.

The Emperor spoke as if it were his last word on the subject. Silence closed in around us as we sat there, dressed now in our underwear, shivering.

—That little imperial penis! cursed Alice. I hop' someone assassinates him for good! Who wan's him back? I'll take poor Louis any day!

I remembered that someone had once said Napoleon had only one testicle . . . like the Hottentots . . . I lay down and drifted off into a terrible dream. I was eating my leather leggings crouched on a vast frozen plain, empty of everything. My feet and hands were frozen and I had a deep wound to my skull that was surely fatal. I bled onto the crystals of snow, which stretched desertlike, treeless, to the horizon. Suddenly, I was blown away by a cannon shot, my body parts scattered in all directions, arms, legs, head, torso flew off, each portion sliced into neat quarters as an entire army marched over me, stomping my body into the ground; horses, cannon and men rolled on, trampling what was left of me under their feet until I was a tiny speck on a wide plain of white crystals, blinded and unable to breathe. I woke up coughing, my teeth chattering and my eyes full of tears. Like melted snow, they ran down my cheeks.

Alice was still asleep. In the gardens beyond, the caged animals began to awaken. Bird noises, then the scream of an orangutan, followed by the yawn of an ape, then the sneeze of an elephant. I felt sick. I felt stiff and sore, as if I really had been run down by an army. At least, I thought, the examination was finished. Never to be repeated. I would never have to see the baron again.

I dressed without waking Alice and slipped outside. In the hazy blue light of almost-morning, I walked to the monkey pavilion. I stared at the sleeping families through the high wire cage. I looked for a trapdoor that I could pry open to free them. But I found nothing. One of the free peacocks hooted behind me, and as I turned, the purple heron appeared, a fringe of foliage surrounding her. She ruffled her feathers, then, dragging her ball and chain, limped away. The air still had a cold edge, but I was covered by my shawl and my shame.

I wandered through the Jardin des Plantes until I came to the aviary with its hundreds of imprisoned birds. Indigo filtered through the mesh screening, which crisscrossed the fading Twisted Ears moon. I found the entrance. I began to pick the lock with my buttonhook as the dwarf William had taught me. I swung open the gates.

I hoped the birds would save themselves but they sat there, sleeping under their wings, until I burst into the cage myself, flapping my arms and screaming in Khoe, emitting a piercing ululation into the still air that startled them all out of their reverie. Awake now, they gathered above my head in a wedge of beating wings. They scraped against the wire mesh, searching for a way out, then understanding, at last, the wedge took flight, fleeing the prison as I never could, striking a wingbeat as they rose as one, circling higher and higher, swooping into a trajectory due east.

When I returned to the tent, Alice was frantic.

—Where were you? A servant came to say the carriage to take us home is waiting at the gate.

—And the baron?

—He sent word by the same servant that he thanked you for your contribution to science . . . And that a purse has been sent to your keeper Sieur Réaux.

As the light rose over the King's Botanical Gardens and the first streaks of gold pierced the darkness like the first day, its occupants began to fill the silence with sound. But there were no caged birds to be heard. The silent aviary was deserted. Today, the newspapers would write about the Hottentot Venus's three days at the Jardin des Plantes and of the mysterious disappearance of hundreds of birds. And my master would be happy because receipts would rise with the publicity and the cashbox would once again be full. My contract had only a year to go. Then I could return home and begin again. I began to hope. I was young. I had years and years to live, I thought.

Alice and I walked down the long, wide avenue lined with chestnut trees that led to the bank of the Seine and the waiting carriage. It took the Pont de Sully bridge back across the river to the Tuileries, the Louvre and number 7 Cour des Fontaines and all who lived there—that rout of prostitutes, gamblers, circus freaks and beggars who shared our anthill of wretchedness. We returned to la Belle Limonadière, the dancing bear Adolph, the dwarf William, the alligator-boy Emmett, the giant Prince Ludwig and Joseph/Josephine the hermaphrodite. All still asleep under their ragged wings. I had believed myself to be free. But some claimed I wasn't even worth my own existence.

I discovered a dark side of Alice one night when a drunken ship captain invaded the ghetto of our family of freaks at the Thousand Columns. I couldn't take my eyes off the fair-bearded American, who looked so much like Hendrick Caesar I wasn't sure it wasn't he.

—What're you looking at, nigger?

—Me?

—Yes, you bitch.

—Nothing, Master, I said, turning away towards William the Cock.

—Well, keep ya' eyes to ya'self, gal. Don't like no Negroes giving me the evil eye . . . What you doin' in here anyway? Hey, he shouted. This place for Negroes too? I buy and sell niggers where I come from—Nobody drink with niggers in Gates, North Carolina. We string 'em up. Suddenly, he rose and walked over to where I sat with Alice, William, General Tripe, and Joseph/Josephine. The American stood glowering down at me as I cowered, not daring to meet his eye.

—What all you freaks need is a good buggering—for all you pains-in-the-ass . . . Whores, niggers, sodomites . . .

He pulled me up by my hair. The little people scattered, only Alice stood her ground, silently, like a lioness.

—Oh, you her girlfriend?

—I'm her servant.

—Her servant! Since when niggers got servants? Her lover, more like it, you fucking lesbian bitch.

—I 'ouldn't press m' luck if I were you.

—First, bitch, I'll take care of Venus here, and then I'll take care of you . . . Nothing I like better than to teach a lesbian slut a lesson 'bout who's boss!

As quick as lightning, Alice was upon him, her elbow struck him in the throat, knocking the wind out of him as she twirled on the balls of her feet and caught his wrist as her left knee smashed into his testicles. With a vicious butt to his forehead, she smashed his head down on the oak table, twisting his arm painfully behind him, bringing the entire weight of her body upon him as if they were making love, pinning his head and chest to the table. As quick as a magician, she pulled a weaver's shearing knife from under her skirts and pressed the point just below the man's ear. In the blink of an eye, Alice swiped it across his neck, just under his chin, drawing a thin trail of blood. The man, seeing his own blood on the table, screamed.

—You touch her again and this knife will cut your balls off and I will serve them to you for dinner, you bastard . . .

The American struggled, feeling the droplets of blood trickling down his neck. By now the whole tavern, not understanding the English spoken, had fallen silent, fascinated by the more than understandable body language.

—You, you let me go, you damned lesbian bitch! You cunt sucker—woman fucker! Freak!!

—I neither love women nor hate men, said Alice, I simply detest strangers.

She released the man, who lurched away, cursing, only to be dragged away by two of La Belle's bodyguards to the exit as excited French broke out amongst the onlookers.

It was true Alice didn't like strangers. She had been raped by a vagabond on the road to her factory as a young girl. It was also true that Alice couldn't stand to be touched except by Victor and me. I never asked Alice about her former life, although from time to time we exchanged

252

stories about the past. I didn't know if my governess dreamed of a man, a love, a family of her own . . .

—You and Victor are my family now, she would say, now that Ma and Pa are dead.

After those days at the King's Jardin des Plantes, we often slept in the same bed as sisters would, or babes. The nights when Alice did crawl into my bed and curled up beside me were the only nights I didn't dream of the massacres. Alice understood the whores and the prostitutes and they in turn loved and respected her just as all the freaks did. Although Master Réaux might beat her occasionally, Alice held her own and even he never dared to go too far. After that night, I often wondered if Alice had ever murdered anyone, since she carried such a weapon on her person. A weaver's knife was deadly. It was hooked and razor sharp on both sides, its steel could cut the warp of velvet clean with one swipe. There was always an air of quiet violence about her that was ten times more frightening than the French bluster of Master Réaux or the vulgar harangue of the American. Alice, I was sure, was capable of killing in cold blood. Someone had showed her how.

Three months after his late-night visit with the baron, Napoleon Bonaparte ceased to exist. On June 18, 1815, he lost everything on the battlefield of Waterloo. He had no clothes, no empire, no army. The Emperor was as naked as I. He abdicated and the victorious English sent him to the Cape of Storms, the windswept, storm-swept wilderness of St. Helena, so near home. He would share his island with the giant tortoises and the Hottentots. Perhaps, I thought, he might send a specimen to his friend the baron. The Emperor's final reign had lasted exactly one hundred days.

Paris had thrown off the last traces of Bonaparte like a discarded glove. When I asked Alice why the English kept the Emperor alive on his desolate, windy and wretched island, she said it was because the English were determined not to make a martyr of him by killing him.

—He is more dangerous dead than alive, repeated Alice. The only result of all his wars, except for his murdered Grand Army, is that the French are now dressing like the English and the English like the French and every man in Paris is imitating Lord Brummell by dressing all in black . . .

—It is as if, said Alice, the Emperor, like a species of insect, had suddenly become extinct.

Ever since the Jardin des Plantes, Master Réaux had become more and more suspicious of Alice and more violent than I had ever seen him. He now locked me up at night, ordering Alice to keep all doors locked and windows sealed because of my fragile health. The punishment for disobeying him was being thrown onto the streets with a denunciation to the police for prostitution.

—The workhouse, the poorhouse, the crazy house or the whorehouse, Alice, just like Venus, he threatened. He would raise his hand to me. Sometimes it would simply hang there, quivering in midair, but sometimes it would descend, on a wall or a piece of furniture, or on Alice's neck, nose or stomach. He never beat me because I had to appear unmarked in my cage the next day. So his wrath fell on Alice, who took the beatings for both of us. He had, in fact, knocked out two of her front teeth. That was the reason why Alice did not accompany me to the duke's ball.

In the middle of August, Broad Green moon, another hundred days after the return of King Louis, I was commanded to appear at a ball given by the Duc de Berry for the restored aristocrats of the new reign of Louis XVIII, who had once again entered Paris, in the wake of the departed Emperor. He was back on his throne.

The duke had insisted that I come as he had seen me at number 188. And so, I donned my flesh-colored skin-fitting silk sheath, my kaross of fox fur, my beads, my leggings. I painted my face and braided my hair. And I drank a whole quart of dry gin, washed down with my daily draft of morphine.

The ball took place at the Berry Hotel in St.-Germain-en-Laye, where aristocrats, monarchists and former Bonapartists all mingled together and raised their glasses to the King. Those left in the officer corps of the Grand Army, now restored to the Crown, were there, shimmering in new uniforms. Not all Bonapartists betrayed their leader. Many had gone into exile like Prince Bonaparte and the imperial family. Many of the English officers quartered in St.-Germain-en-Laye, their former enemies, were invited as well.

It was true that the guests at the ball looked different to me from a year ago. It was not fashion. It was because I now saw white people not as white people wished but as they really were. The hundreds of ex-

Bonapartists, ex-revolutionaries and new Bourbonists swarmed through the gold and white rooms like a troop of baboons. There was something brusque in their movements, something dog-sick in their faces, as they chattered and chewed and moved from room to room like rodents scavenging in garbage. How was it, I wondered, that they had become the species and I the audience?

Under the blazing chandeliers, they sweated and exuded their feral smell, disguised by sweet-smelling, heavy perfume that up until now I had found so seductive. The lavish colors of the rooms, the feathers and plumes, the loud dresses (for white was no longer in fashion) contrasted with the men's black penguinlike frock coats. The garish military uniforms in red, white, blue and gold dissolved into the shawls of cashmere and silk and reflected multicolored in the surrounding mirrors. The thump of dancing feet in the crowded ballroom echoed hollowly against *boiserie* and hardwood, making as much clatter as a rampaging troop of elephants. And like a troop of elephants, the occupants lifted their trunks and brayed, and that braying resounded in my ears and in my head, it seemed, all the way back to Table Mountain. Their laughter was an affront to me. Their joy made my skin crawl. My repugnance at their color, shape and smell assaulted me.

As the musicians gathered to accompany my performance, I asked myself who these people were to decide who was human and who was not; who was normal and who was a freak; who deserved to live and who was not worthy of existence? Who were they to proclaim the People of the People fit only for extinction? Weren't we, the People of the People, the humanity of humanity, the humans of humans, more than expendable?

Revolt engaged my heart. I was here to amuse a public who didn't deserve the effort it took for me to remain upright, to keep my heart beating, to keep myself from shattering into a thousand pieces. The mirrors no longer held the terror they once did as my surrounded image repeated itself over and over and over. The mirrors simply told the truth; just as my world had been annihilated from the face of the globe, theirs was thus doomed.

There was an air of anticipation and gaiety in the room. The masters of the world were ready to listen, to smile, to laugh, to play, to baptize, to bless, to condone, to nullify. They were ready even to forgive me for my shape, for my color, for my small brain and my curious ways. They were ready to indulge me with charm and pennies, laughter and affection, condescension and hilarity and then *forget me!* Forget me, ignore me or even dispose of me. I could be killed because I deserved only oblivion. Their indifference to what I had done before tonight or what I would do after tonight, or whether I would even exist after tonight, withered my soul.

The Duke announced my arrival. Hundreds of eyes turned towards me, waiting. Hundreds of lips murmured puns and comments. Hundreds of heads were pitched to my next move. I held my breath. Out of the corner of my eye, I saw the baron. Since the Jardin des Plantes he was everywhere I was. He stalked me like a police inspector stalking a murderer. Sometimes I spied him in the audience at number 188. Sometimes I recognized his carriage outside the Cour des Fontaines. He had begun to frequent the Pied de Porc and from time to time the Thousand Columns. Our eyes met, but instead of his smooth and composed voice, I heard the snarl of Robert Wedderburn's plea: *Flee, unhappy Hottentot . . . flee. Hide yourself in your forest. Wild animals that live there are less dangerous than the monsters under the empire of which you will fall!*

—Let's hear the animal sing, opted a voice from the crowd.

—Yes, what are you waiting for, Hottentot? Sing!

I held out my hand, my hand, a simple human paw of bone and flesh, and brought it to my chest, pounding again and again.

—I am not an animal. My name is Sarah Baartman. I am a woman! I am not an animal. My name is Sarah Baartman. I am a woman!

I squeezed my eyes shut until they ached from the pressure. I tried to distinguish what was real and what I was dreaming. Which surfaces were solid and which were only reflections of themselves. After a moment, who knows how long, I jumped onto the banquet table laid with silver and crystal candelabras, flowers and all manner of edibles: cantaloupes, radishes, butter, anchovies, olives, tuna fish, shrimp bisque, veal consommé, salmon hollandaise, York ham, filet Richelieu, queen's mouthfuls, pigeon salami with truffles, fillets of sole, ducklings, roasts of pork, pheasant, oysters, wild boar, cranberry rum and kirsch sorbet, fried figs, chestnuts and sixteen desserts, upon which I trod, like a heifer, with my bare feet.

—*Je ne suis pas un animal,* I repeated in French. *Mon nom est Sarah Baartman! Je suis une femme!*

—My God! She talks!

—This is marvelous!

—She speaks French!

—I thought she was a Hottentot!

—This is quite a show!

—Better than the vaudeville play!

—Is this part of its act?

My heart broke. The audience believed I was acting. I climbed the pink marble pillar as if it was a tree and hung there, swinging, while people cheered from below. The room filled with clocks and turned into the King's Court amphitheater. The baron, who had hidden himself behind a column, was horrified. But then he disappeared. I looked around for him, but he was nowhere in sight. He must be here, I thought, but he was not. Three lackeys arrived to pull me down, but first they would have to catch me. The crowd roared. The clocks moved. Time passed. I lost track of it as people began to panic and run and overturn their chairs. Someone screamed; a wild woman! Flying clocks were everywhere now, speeding past me. Even with my eyes shut, they were there. I was higher than I had ever been; I looked down on the upturned faces. How had I gotten here? I was beginning to enjoy looking at things this way; from a bird's-eye view—the birds I had freed or stolen. I closed my eyes to make things come into focus. Now I could see not only my hand but also my left foot, my knee and right elbow, my head, my backside. The marble pillars, the gilt mirrors, the yellow silk draperies, the chandeliers from which I hung, all took wing like the birds in the aviary. If I could only get away, I thought, into my own private darkness, branded on the back of my eyelids, all would be well. From there, I could find my way back to Table Mountain, where I could search for the glowing rock crystal, which was like looking at the sun because it contained all colors: purple, scarlet, coral and violet. I opened my eyes to survey the multitudes below. Their shrill voices spiraled upwards to knot in my hair and my gaze was drawn into the orbit of my own befuddlement.

—Disgusting!

—She's drunk!

There were whistles and shouts.

—Call the police.

—She's out of control!

—Get this chattering baboon off the chandelier!

—Back to the zoo!

—Look! She's weeping . . .

—Poor creature . . .

—Pitiful child . . .

—Outrageous bitch!

—Scandalous whore!

—Foolish coon . . .

My mask fell off. Out of the corner of my drunken eye, I spied again the black-clad police-inspector-doctor Baron Cuvier, who watched me from the corner of the room, an ugly dark pillar wedged between two mirrors. He had returned, still stealthily stalking me like a hunter, intent on his prey and without mercy, when all I craved from him was mercy. Mercy. I was one colored woman against a thousand dead white men.

How come I here? How come I here? I asked myself. Wherever I looked, I was not there. Could the baron see me when I couldn't see myself? The whites below swarmed in circles, which broke into colored patterns and then arranged themselves into still other shapes. I was tired. Perhaps I could come down. I looked straight up into the precious crystal teardrops and flickering points of light of the chandelier poised above me, coming closer and closer, crashing down. Of course. The sky was falling in chunks of glass and light, piece by piece. My head wobbled. I loosened my grip and fell, my backside smashed onto the banquet table. The dark pillar was there to break my fall, his gray eyes turgid like troubled water. I shook him off, annoyed, and attempted to rise, afraid I would cry. He took my hand and helped me down. He covered my nakedness with his frock coat and told the duke to look the other way. He told the audience to circulate, that there was nothing more to see. The show was over.

—May I sit down? I asked.

—In the cloakroom, he said.

In the cloakroom, which was small and dark and hot with only torches burning, the baron-doctor-inspector was vague and uncertain, as if he were a simpleton who couldn't read or write. He was still in his shirtsleeves.

—You were the one who stole my birds!

—I didn't steal them, I freed them.

—To free property is theft.

—Property is theft.

—Not the property of the state.

—Birds don't belong to the state, birds are free . . .

—I love you, Sarah.

—Then leave me alone, I whispered, astounded.

—Men don't leave what they love alone.

—Honorable men do.

—I . . . have the medal of the Legion of Honor, see? I am a grand officer!

—Yes, I see, you're wearing it on a ribbon around your neck.

—Sarah . . .

—And what hope is there that your *honor* will make a difference?

—None for your race, Venus.

—*That*, I believe.

—You bloody better believe it!

In three strides, he was upon me. In one blink, the angry, hungry will of a long frustration—not sex but the tyranny of disgust, incomprehension, mystery and lies, all collided in a moment's incandescent ejaculation.

—Sarah!

I stared at the baron's erection, defenseless, and knew I was going to die here in this lion's den as the Baron crouched there, his eyes gleaming, his wild red mane rising, ready to rape. A savage beast poised to pounce on me, his lamb. I wouldn't have been surprised to see him flip his tail like a panther or grow horns like a rhinoceros. This was the jungle.

Fear made me finger !Naeheta Magahâs's lores, which always hung around my neck. For the first time I repeated the rainmaker's curse, softly at first, then louder and louder in Khoe, adding the clicks and inhalations, the expulsions and the sound of a cork popping, ending in a whistle of pure terror as the power of the incantation escaped my lips.

If you advance towards me with malice or violence as my enemy, your eyes shall go blind, your penis shrivel and your testicles fall off. Plague, flood, famine and exile will befall your children and their children to the last generation and their final extermination.

The baron stopped dead in his tracks as if a bridle held him back. He reared like a stallion being reined in and crashed down hard on his high-heeled red shoes. He discovered he was speechless, paralyzed and unable to move. He broke out in a cold sweat, his forehead shone, his bright pale eyes popped out of their sockets as he clutched first his heart, then his erection. It was gone. I slipped by him and fled. *Flee, Hottentot.*

Outside, the waiting carriage loomed, shiny and dark. Sieur Réaux opened the door and unfolded the steps. Safely inside, I cowered against the cushions as the baron raced to the carriage. Breathless and panting, he pulled the door of the landau open.

—These exhibitions should never be repeated, Réaux. She's become quite dangerous. Possibly demented. Watch her carefully. You'll have to be vigilant from now on . . . of this unhappy monsteress . . .

—It will be in all the papers tomorrow, said Master Réaux.

—She won't remember anything.

—It's bad for business, he said, handing the baron back his coat.

—And for the Museum of Natural History as well . . .

The baron reached inside the carriage and grasped my hand and kissed it. Then he lowered his forehead against it a moment and disappeared.

—It seems, said Alice, waving the *Journal des Dames et des Modes,* that you reverted to your savage state last night. You jumped on the duke's banquet table, stomped on the food, beat your naked chest with your fists and hooted in your vile language. You climbed the marble pillars of the duke's dining room and hung by the chandelier . . . It was only the superior intelligence and sangfroid of the illustrious naturalist Baron Cuvier that saved the day, taming you like a lion trainer without the aid of baton, whip or net. Not to mention firearms. His august presence not only calmed the wild woman, who recognized in him a superior will, and who, taking his hand, followed him meekly out of the hôtel, but reassured the duke's numerous guests that they were in no danger from the savage.

—I don't remember anything, I lied.

—Of course you don't. You were drunk, that's why.

—All I remember is that all at once nothing resembled what it should have. The duke's ballroom looked like a jungle of wild animals. I smelled them. And the world was either upside down or backwards.

—Oh, Sarah! You've got to stop drinking. You've got to stop the morphine. It's killing you.

—All I remember is a horde of screaming white monkeys dressed like white people who tried to attack me. I was only trying to escape . . . to explain who I was! What did I do?

—Read it for yourself, Sarah! Alice threw the newspaper towards me.

You can read, she said sharply. And while you're at it, read a few pages from the Good Book as well! It will do you no harm! She slammed down the Bible on the table next to my bed.

—And think about it! Remember what you told me in Manchester: that you had gained a name—Sarah Baartman. And that you had gained a country—Christendom.

—You're angry.

—I'm not angry, I want you to behave yourself.

—I'm incapable of behaving myself because of the *natural imbecility* of Hottentots!

—Save me your wit.

—What else do I have to believe in?

—Believe in Jesus Christ our Lord. He was a simple shepherd like you, it's so sad . . .

—He was a white man, I said in a voice that was sadder by far.

—Réaux wants you locked up at night. He's afraid you want to escape. He's given me all these keys to lock every door behind you.

—I'm too sick and too weak to flee.

—You can get well, Sarah. And once you're well, you *can* escape—back to England. You have friends who could help you—the Reverend Wedderburn . . .

—I'm not a slave. I'm not charity.

—You are if you don't leave Réaux.

—What about the contract, the promise? Master Dunlop's contract?

—Your contract is with the devil. Your contract is a lie and a farce! Dunlop is a lie and a farce. How can you still love him? He deserted you. He's a liar. He's a bigamist. Why do you still honor him? Why do you honor the contract? The contract he *lost* to Réaux says that you are a freak, an animal to be bought and sold! They *rent* you out, Sarah, like Adolph— like a dancing bear or a two-headed gorilla. And Dunlop, *your* Dunlop, is responsible for everything! For all your unhappiness. He's a thief, a liar, a confidence man and a racketeer. You were never anything more to him than an indentured servant!

—No! It's not true! Never. I'm free. Free! Leave me alone!

—I won't leave you alone. I've left you alone too long as it is. For two years I've left you alone!

—You won't leave me.

—No, Sarah. Never. You saved my life and now I must save yours—or die trying.

—I'm so lonely.

—I know.

—It's like the fog that came over me the other night, I screamed. I couldn't see through it, yet I kept walking and walking as if I were walking back to the Cape, walking back to Africa, but blindly, without my eyes, without a map, without knowing whether I'd ever get there . . . and there were no birds, no cattle, not a living soul . . .

—Here, drink this.

—This isn't gin, it's the medicine the doctor prescribed!

—Yes, and now you'll have your bath and I'll go out and try to find some food for both of us—something you can swallow.

Alice kissed me. Obediently I drank the medicine. I allowed her to undress me and to fill the tub to the brim. She lit all the candles. The monsters all emerged from the shadows. The freak show monsters. The Cour des Fontaines monsters. The Jardin des Plantes monsters. The Duc de Berry's ball monsters.

I was never the same after that. The episode at the duke's ball was written into vaudeville, a new caricature circulated in the gazettes and newspapers, memorializing that night as well as a pornographic chanson of a dozen stanzas. I was so famous, Master Réaux claimed he was afraid I'd be stolen or kidnapped. But I knew the true reason. He began to lock me in. Sometimes he handcuffed me. But all through the Paris autumn I got sicker and sicker. I was determined to stay well enough to work. I continued to play the Hottentot Venus in her cage, rain or shine, six days a week. The cold November rain seeped into my bones. Receipts began to fall, but I was sure that by the following spring, when Dunlop's contract had finally expired, I would have enough for Alice and me to return home.

Melancholy often overtook me as winter deepened. I bought Alice two new front teeth. I spent the rest of my allowance on gin, into which I dissolved morphine, opium or laudanum and sometimes all three. I wore a mask to hide the circles under my eyes and gloves to protect my delicate hands. It did my lungs no good that the winter of 1815 was the coldest in memory. Alice spent all her time tending the scorching hot stove that burned day and night without ever keeping me completely warm. Alice repeated over and over again that I would die if I didn't stop drinking. But Alice also knew that I would die if I *did* stop drinking.

Nothing like the duke's ball ever happened again, although my hideous visions of the world upside down never ceased and seemed to come more and more frequently. Often I would be taken back to Magahâs's cave in dreams and nightmares. Often when the same painted bulls stampeded across my bedroom floor, I simply turned over or pulled the covers up over my head. This made me afraid to sleep lying down, so I slept sitting up, a decanter by my side. French food began to make me violently ill. There was nothing I could digest anymore and I began to nourish myself with flower bulbs, roots, milk and honey. This sent Alice scurrying around Les Halles to find me berries, dried apples and fruits. For amusement, I chewed tobacco, played dominoes and mah-jongg with Saw, the Chinese dwarf, and fucked men for money. When Master Réaux found out I received men willing to pay to touch the Hottentot Venus, he was furious. Then he did an about-face and began to bring the men himself, pocketing the money they gave me. I was too sick to protest. Too drugged even to care. I had my plan. It was just a matter of putting it into practice.

Only the things-that-should-never-have-been-born remained steadfastly loyal and human. The freaks rallied around, cheering me up, insisting that they had all gone through periods of melancholy and survived. It would pass, they said, and pass it did. In the dead of December, I rose from my bed and ventured outside. I walked along the Seine, past the Louvre, clinging to Alice, who seemed to grow stronger as I grew weaker.

—If you stay in Paris in this weather, Sarah, you will die. I know the doctors say you have pleurisy, but you've got TB, girl, tuberculosis, she said, I've seen it dozens of times in the clay pits . . .

—I feel better. I feel light.

—You must leave Paris. You must return to Africa, like the doctors say . . .

—My contract . . .

—Bugger your contract! This is your life you are playing with! Run.

—Will you come with me?

—What would I do in Africa?

—Make a new life. White women are scarce there.

—What's a new life?

—No whoring around.

—And you?

—Me too.

—It's money, Alice continued. We are prisoners because we are poor.

—I know where the cashbox is, I said.

—You won't break your contract because of a promise, but you'd steal the cashbox!

—It's money that's owed me. It's my money.

—And would you kill Réaux if he caught you?

—If he tried to send me to prison.

—Wouldn't you kill him anyway?

—What are you up to, Alice?

—Well, would you?

—I'd kill the baron. I'd kill Baron Cuvier . . .

—Why do you hate him so?

—Because he has no respect for living things. He prefers everything dead.

—In a few weeks it will be your birthday. Why don't we plan it for then?

—The robbery or the murder?

—Both, said Alice Louise Unicorn as we walked along the Quai des Orfèvres, past the Préfecture de Police.

Baron Cuvier continued following me. He had recommenced after the ball and he now followed me everywhere. His pale face had plagued me now since August. When I went to the Marché Neuf for flowers or Les Halles for food, he was there, perhaps just having come from the Paris morgue or the Hôpital de la Pitié. I pretended not to notice him and he would do the same if I surprised him, yet the same afternoon, I would spy him in the crowd at the circus, staring, staring and waiting. His tall, solitary figure haunted me. He never said a word. But he always returned. He was within my perimeter even now, I thought. He was watching me. I stopped short as his figure flickered behind me in the doorway of the Church of St. Germain l'Auxerrois. He followed us to the Place des Deux-Ecus. Then he disappeared. It took all my strength to climb the stairs at 7 Cour des Fontaines. I, who used to run down a bull, trot alongside a yearling, trek twenty miles, did not have enough breath to climb three flights of stairs.

264

Today, there was no freak show because it was New Year's Day and it was my birthday. I had been feeling poorly for several days now, enough to alarm Alice into sending for the doctor. He explained once more that I had to return home or I would die. I knew this. I had already planned our escape for tomorrow even as Alice had left the door unlocked. I had stolen the cashbox but I hadn't told her yet. I wanted to be sure that I had the strength to flee. By this time tomorrow, I thought, we would be on the mail sloop of His Majesty's navy on our way to London.

I slid down further in my bath. I lifted my pipe to my lips, preparing to float away on a cloud of *dagga*. I wanted to forget the filthy walls, the things-that-should-never-have-been-born, the specter of Baron Cuvier's pale face, my illness, my lost dreams. But before I could draw the smoke into my sick lungs, I was seized by a spasm of coughing that triggered a pain in my chest which grew like a cactus, raking my chest until it burst into a terrible gurgling sound. A thick warm liquid filled my throat. It took me a moment to taste blood and realize it was not the small spots I sometimes saw on my handkerchief, but a full-scale hemorrhage. Disbelief more than fright roused me from the rose-tinted water. I rose from the bath, shedding bloodied water which flowed downwards in rivulets over my thighs. Speechless, I hid my apron with my right hand, surprised that I had no thoughts about leaving. How could I imagine that death would not end my life? That I, monster that I was, had procured for myself a posthumous life that would last for centuries? A life far more monstrous than this one.

Outside, the ice on the Seine slid back and forth, snow fell on the dancing skaters and drifted against the houses like ocean foam, a carriage passed by, its wheels muffled by the cold white sheet that lay everywhere and on my soul. The hooves of the snorting, smoking horses pocked the virgin snow as their heads stretched downwards against their harnesses.

I heard my mother singing my birthday song, punctuated with her soft clicks and coos. My name song. Ssehura. With a flick of her tongue, my mother posed a riddle. Reaching out blindly for her, I cried for help in Khoe. I knew only that I was twenty-seven years old and I wanted to live.

20

SIRE

The brain is at the same time the last station of sensible
impression and the receptacle of images that memory
and imagination submit to the spirit. It is, within that relationship, the objective instrument of the soul.

—Baron Georges Léopold Cuvier,
Letter to the Emperor Napoleon
on the progress of science before 1789

*J*anuary 1816. When I returned to the Cour des Fontaines, I found the
door I had left unlocked slightly ajar, not exactly as I had left it. Something was wrong that I couldn't put my finger on. Slowly I pushed the
door further open and stepped inside. As my foot touched the threshold,
I realized what it was. There was an absence within. Sarah was gone.
Surely, after all our plans, she hadn't left without me? Would there be a
note telling me where to find her? Would there be a rendezvous at an inn,
a stable, the mail coach?

Fear coiled itself around my knees like Sieur Réaux's boa constrictor.
My knees buckled. This was not right. It was too hot, almost suffocating,

and there was a smell I couldn't place, like wet clay. The door to Sarah's room was closed. Had I closed it upon leaving? Light flickered through the crack beneath the door. My hand went to my throat.

—Sarah?

—Sarah? I repeated.

—Sarah, I whispered again before I flung open the door.

Even before kneeling beside the inert body, I knew she was dead.

—Lord 'ave mercy, I moaned as I crossed myself.

She had left, I thought selfishly, without saying goodbye. She's left me alone in this God-forsaken place. I looked around and then up at the ceiling as if I expected to see Sarah's spirit hovering there.

The Venus, or what remained of her, had fallen over the side of her bed, her head and upper torso stretched across it. Her head was turned to one side, and clutched in her left hand was the Bible she had so adamantly refused to read for so long. There was a note sticking out. I lifted the cover of the book to retrieve it. It was addressed to me in Sarah's childish scrawl. I didn't read it. I couldn't through my tears. Hurriedly, I slipped it into my coat pocket. I was sobbing now, my whole face pulled down in inestimable grief, open, raw and limitless. I lifted the Venus's hind parts and laid her on the bed, straightening out the limbs and arms so that she lay straight and neatly placed in the center. Then I lit as many candles as I could find and placed them at the head and foot of the bed. I washed and clothed the naked body, tugged at the bloodstained sheets to change them, cursing and sweating. When I was finished, I took off my coat and hat and sat down in a chair. I dragged it up to the side of the bed with my heels so that I could study Sarah's face. I slipped my hands into Sarah's red kid gloves. She possessed dozens of pairs, leather, silk and satin, always in red. It was as if I had slipped on her skin. I decided to wait for Réaux to come home. I would not leave Sarah alone, I thought. I would wait here until her keeper came back from his whoring before going to look for a priest. Snow still swirled outside. It was almost dawn, and in the small circle of light made by the candles, I bowed my head, sobbing.

I understood suffering and I was moved by pity. There is no kindness of the heart without a measure of imagination and I had imagined Sarah better than Sarah had imagined herself. My heart, like the rest of me, was made of steel. My short life (I was only thirty years old although I looked fifty) had witnessed every species of death: from disease and starvation, heat exhaustion in the brick fields, black lung in the mines, white lung in the mills, suffocation in the dye factories, lead poisoning in the lime pits, crushing, mangling, hemorrhaging, tuberculosis, cholera, typhus, small-pox, the plague, infanticide, hanging and firing squad. But never, I thought, had I seen a more lonely or pathetic death than Sarah's.

I stood perfectly motionless, lost in myself, listening for Réaux's foot-steps; only the hem of my skirt stirred in the draft: The rays of the rising sun broke over my disheveled hair. The sudden flood of light enhanced the opulence of my form and the vigor of my real age. We had been to-gether not only servant and mistress but godmother and godchild, which meant neither would abandon the other. Out of mutual loneliness and de-spair, we had become sisters under the skin and all that that meant. We had framed a hard yet orderly pattern in our relation to Réaux, our mu-tual enemy yet our master. I had been Sarah's servant but also her jailer. I had taken Réaux's money and locked Sarah's door every night, turning the keys over to him. We had lived together in the same house, yet each had kept her own private rituals, utensils, rhythms, sins and vices, each one had recited her own private litany of pain, independent of the other. We had submitted to this ugly, brutal woman-beater to escape the whore-house, the crazy house, the workhouse or the jailhouse. But never again, I vowed, would fear rule my life. I lifted my bowed head and swore I would avenge my friend Sarah if I never did another thing in life.

And again, I heard Sarah's voice, feebly but with a penetrating effect in the quiet of the room. The enormous discord of her sobs, as if sent from some faraway and remote spot, beyond the reaches of human suffering, crushed every bone in my body. Sarah was gone and I, Alice, was to blame. I had stood and watched, played the dunce, the joker, the errand runner, the governess, serving as a shield for Réaux and as a shield for Sarah's descent into hell. A passive white woman who, even though a ser-vant, had more prerogatives than her colored mistress. Sarah had saved my life and I had repaid her by failing to save hers.

When Réaux returned in the early hours of the morning, drunk and happy, he let out a wail and a string of curses that sent a chill down my spine. He could have been Othello lamenting his murder of Desdemona.

—Saartjie! My own Venus! Sarah! he howled, waking up those who were still sleeping and bringing a curious crowd to the door.

—Murderer, I screamed to his face and for all to hear.

But Réaux no longer saw or heard me. He had sunk into the quicksand of his own torment. He struggled for several moments and then, as if I had dealt him a blow to the head, sank to his knees; his arms stretched downwards, his hands clasped. The other inhabitants of the Cour des Fontaines, the sleepy freaks, the wide-awake whores, the sailors and soldiers of vanquished disbanded armies, the circus managers, the beggars, the thieves, the waiters from the Pied de Porc, all gathered in the doorway of the small room for a last look at the Hottentot Venus. Their faces, deformed by disease, alcohol, accident, smallpox, imbecility, insanity or simply God, glowed in the light like a religious painting. I fought my way through the gathering crowd and the babbling cries. I must, I thought, get to the parish priest. Sarah was a Christian. I felt a hand on my sleeve, it was William.

—Father Lawrence is at la Belle Limonadière's place. I'll go to fetch him.

I nodded mutely, making my way past William and down the crowded staircase. People were arriving from everywhere, blocking the winding staircase and flowing out into the courtyard. The Venus is dead, they whispered. The news of Sarah's death traveled by word of mouth up and down the corridors, the streets, the alleys, the impasses of the quarter. Slowly, all the things-that-should-never-have-been-born filed by the supine Venus, openly weeping or stony-faced with grief, their horrendous faces and deformities half lit by the flickering candles, which cast their black forms against the wall as in a shadow play.

—The Hottentot Venus is dead.

—The Hottentot Venus is dead.

By the time I had returned with the priest, the crowd had dispersed and in its place were the police prefect and Baron Cuvier. Réaux had composed himself and the corpse was already wrapped, mummylike, on a stretcher, ready to be transferred to the waiting cart below. As Sarah had died without witnesses, explained the inspector, the police would carry out an inquiry before she could be released to her nearest kin, if there were any kin. Helplessly Father Lawrence and I watched Sarah's body being taken away. Two men carried the canvas-wrapped body down the stairs and past the still-lingering crowds. Snowflakes fell on the corpse as it was hauled into the two-wheeled *charrette*. The *croque-morts* asked no questions when the illustrious Professor Cuvier ordered them to go to the morgue instead of the Hôpital de la Pitié nearby. It was, after all, none of their business. The *charrette* struggled over the rutted ice and garbage.

I snatched Sarah's red cloak from its hook. Sarah and I were both familiar with the Paris morgue. I hurried towards it. The morgue dated from 1804. Built on the Quai du Marché Neuf, not far from Notre-Dame, it received the bodies of the unidentified dead, fallen on the pavements of Paris or drowned in the Seine. The dark, cavernous stone building built on the foundation of medieval ruins also received the murdered, the hanged, the guillotined, the aborted and the indigent from the Hôpital de la Pitié. Newborns, children, adults, victims of smallpox, executed criminals, all lay in neat rows, waiting to be identified. The dead were separated from the living by a wall of cut glass, through which not only people searching for a family member peered but the general public on any given day, out on an excursion or a Sunday afternoon walk. Whole families stood on the balconies overlooking the pens, fascinated by this exhibition of death. Sarah and I used to come here on occasion for that very reason.

The mortal remains of these nameless strangers were exhibited for three days in hopes of identification. Adjoining the morgue was the clerk's office, the autopsy room and the coroner's cabinet. At the end of the exhibition period, the body could be buried and a signed death certificate, made out as "person unknown," issued. The morgue also served the nearby Préfecture de Police, which deposited body parts and merchandise recovered from grave robbers and body snatchers. For the morgue was also a place of traffic for the anatomists, phrenologists and physicians who searched for cadavers to dissect. The bodies, skeletons and fetuses were the coveted objects of the medical schools and laboratories and universities.

So it was not surprising, I thought, that Réaux had notified Baron Cuvier of the sudden death of Sarah and that less than an hour later they were both in the morgue bartering over the price of her body while Geoffroy Saint-Hilaire arranged the paperwork with the clerk on duty. The baron had even brought one of the artists from the Jardin des Plantes, Nicolas Tiedeman, to make a death mask of the body. He was the one who told me Sarah had been sold to the baron for five thousand francs. The young handsome sculptor had brought his modeling kit. I watched as he stuffed a bit of beeswax in each nostril to avoid fainting from the stench of rotting bodies and began to make Sarah's death mask. I willed myself not to think about the consequences of the episode at the Jardin des Plantes where they had met. Sarah had been ill even then, I thought, yet an amphitheater full of doctors had failed to observe this simple, poignant fact. She had been dying before their very eyes and not one had bothered to live up to his Hippocratic oath. They had seen not a human being, but a specimen for their delectation and nothing more. Her anemia, her fever, the yellowed whites of her eyes, the labored breathing, the tremors of advanced alcohol poisoning, the general physical weakness I had observed so minutely, had gone unnoticed and untreated by sixty great Parisian physicians. And a girl had died, as Nicolas Tiedeman pointed out, because their prognosis had had to do not with her humanity but with her distance from it. I was no longer surprised by the nausea and revolt I felt not only against the physicians but myself. I watched as Tiedeman squeezed the soft wax tightly, ruining the work he had just accomplished. Finally he simply sat there in the dim and wretched pit, motionless, letting unbidden tears roll down his cheeks.

—They want me to make a death mask . . . but I cannot, he said sobbing. I walked over to him and put my hand on his shoulder. We remained so, both helpless. The oil lamps and torches cast grotesque black shadows over the entire assembly of anatomists, physicians, functionaries, hospital workers, gravediggers and *croque-morts*. There was no sound except the silence of the dead.

Tiedeman wiped away his tears and resumed sculpting. I watched the death mold take shape under his swift movements. He vowed to me he would never sculpt a human figure or face again. He would remain an animalist who sculpted beasts of the forest, the sea creatures, domesticated animals: bulls, dogs, cats, geese and those inhabitants of the jungle one called savage . . . the lion, the lynx, the leopard, the panther. They were all species that didn't recognize and didn't anticipate death. That innocence, he said, he would try to capture for the rest of what was left of his life. There had been a human being in mortal danger and he had stood by, a passive murderer, he repeated over and over. And without a particle of pity, he blamed himself. I was too mortified to confess that I too had done the same thing. Tiedeman began packing up his supplies. His hands shook. He earned his living with his hands, he said. If they shook, what would become of him?

—I am not a great sculptor, he continued. Not even a competent one. I was lucky to have been accepted in David's atelier. I helped him finish portraits of great men.

Tiedeman, his sculpting kit on his back, took my hand as we traversed the shadows and chiaroscuro of the morgue. He cast the same freakish silhouette of a hunchback as Victor's turtle-boy. An indifferent guard waved us out, not bothering to ask us to sign the register since he assumed Tiedeman was one of Cuvier's men. We passed poor, ill-clad, desperate people looking for a lost relative, a missing wife, a husband who had disappeared, a stolen child, all the dramas and tragedies of the human comedy. I had been too late to claim Sarah Baartman. She had been claimed by her enemies. We were both almost running now, our legs pumping, our capes flapping, desperate to escape from the purgatorial shadows of the morgue. In our rush, Tiedeman bumped into Sieur Réaux, whose broad shoulder knocked the animalist's thin frame against the filthy wall. I stepped back into the shadows. I didn't want to meet Réaux here. I had another meeting place in mind. And another plan. Réaux begged his pardon.

The room was bare when I returned in the early hours. Sarah's long red cape swept the bare hardwood floor as I inspected her vandalized room. What Réaux hadn't packed up or sold had been taken by thieves and souvenir hunters. The posters were stripped off the walls. The furniture was gone. Sarah's clothes were gone. Réaux had taken the jewelry that was left. I had only the opal ring I had slipped off Sarah's finger as I had dressed her. The pamphlets, newspapers, clippings and receipts had all disappeared. All that I salvaged from the sack of Sarah's room was her Bible, the red cloak I was wearing, the opal ring and several pairs of the red silk gloves she so adored.

I opened the shutters and the low January sunlight streamed in. Sarah's bathtub stood in the middle of the empty room. No one had been able to lift it down the winding staircase.

I had no more tears left. I had failed to rescue Sarah's corpse and arrange for the Christian burial Father Lawrence had promised her.

Réaux had sold Sarah's body to the anatomists—to Cuvier, the Hottentot-lover. By tonight I would be gone. I dipped into the pocket of Sarah's cloak and pulled out Sarah's letter—her last words:

THE LORD IS MY SHEPHERD
I SHALL NOT WANT
HE MAKETH ME TO LYE DOWN
IN GREEN PASTURES
HE RESTORISH MY SOUL
TO AFFRIKA

I was so dumb with grief, I thought I might never speak again, might remain in mute horror for the rest of my life. My eyes sought escape from the bare room. Through the window, I could see the top of the lone leafless tree swaying to and fro as in a nightmare. I thought I might wake and find Sarah there trying on a new pair of gloves. I settled into that state of partial wakefulness that is the worst part of not sleeping. I remembered how Sarah and I spent the afternoon off that Réaux had begrudgingly given her shopping, buying gloves, eating ice cream or chocolates or both. How we had strutted down Bond Street under new black umbrellas. How I had held Sarah's morphine-crazed body in my arms, listening to her tales of Africa. How I had cradled Sarah's head over a washbasin while she vomited the leftover poison of a night of drinking and brawling. How we had read together the Collects, *Reading Made Easy*, the *Times Almanac* and the Bible until Sarah could read them by herself.

I saw Sarah's hand reaching out to me that first night in Manchester when I had been sure I would not see another dawn. I still remembered the feel of the cold cobblestones scraping my knees through the dirty rags I had been wearing. There should have been a sign, some warning, a black crow, a bat overhead, Sarah's purple heron—something that should have warned me, I thought. I should never have left Sarah alone New Year's night. And now my heart beat and beat and beat and wouldn't stop like Sarah's and wouldn't let me sleep or eat. I clutched the tiny slip of paper, Sarah's last will and testament, and vowed to avenge her death and all that she had endured. It was the only way I could think of to assuage my own terrible guilt. I had let Sarah die. I had to make sure she was buried.

I went through the newspapers looking for clues as to where they had taken Sarah's body. Some of the papers already carried the death notice of the legendary Venus: *Le Mercure de France, Le Journal de Paris, La Quotidienne, Les Annales Politiques, La Gazette de Paris.* Finally I found what I was looking for in *Le Journal Général de France.*

Taking place at this moment, on the premises of the Museum of Natural History, is the molding of the body of the Hottentot Venus, who died yesterday of an illness that lasted only three days. Her body offers no visible trace of her sickness if not a few reddish brown spots around the mouth, on her thighs and hips. Her stoutness and her enormous protuberances have not diminished and her extremely kinky hair has not straightened out as it ordinarily does with Negroes who are ill or after their death. The dissection of this woman will supply Mr. Cuvier with an extremely curious chapter in the history of the variations of the human race . . .

I stifled a cry. I could never recover Sarah's body now. The Venus was in the hands of politicians, scientists, masters of the world.

OBITUARY

WEDNESDAY, JANUARY 3

THE ANNALS OF POLITICS, MORALS AND LITERATURE

The Hottentot Venus was the subject of several plays and various caricatures; she will no longer be of interest to anyone except the scalpel of a naturalist and then a few material parts of this divinity will occupy no other Olympus than a jar . . .

The light died and the lone tree in the Cour des Fontaines shivered under its hoar. I continued to smooth the folds of Sarah's red riding hood mechanically, like Mr. Taylor's mad Lady Macbeth trying to wash murder away. The cloak was warm and glistening to the touch, the double-worsted wool soft and thick under the fingers of my Manchester weaver's hands. In the sad bare room, the incandescent scarlet cape cast its red glow like a lamp. I kept reading the obituaries, letting each sheet that I read fall to the floor, where they surrounded me like sea froth, their curled edges raking my skirt. I rocked back and forth on my heels as I read. I knew all the facts, the dates, the names that were not written, the stories that would never be told and the lies that always followed death. I was surprised Sarah was so famous. There were announcements in the London papers and as far away as Brussels and Amsterdam. But there would be none, I thought, from the Cape of Good Hope. Dunlop would never read Sarah's obituary in America.

I thought of the Reverend Wedderburn. I imagined him standing in the middle of Piccadilly Square, this day in the miserable January drizzle, his overcoat whipping around him, reading Sarah's obituary in the *Morning Post* or the London *Times*, his lips moving, tears making it impossible to continue to the end. *Paris has now to deplore . . .* it would begin. Years ago, we had written a desperate letter to him from Halifax but we never received any reply; if it had arrived, we might already have been on our way to Paris, disappearing from the face of the earth without a trace. What if he had come? I wondered. What if he had come?

In the dirty gray light illuminating the sordid room, I lined up all the men through whose hands Sarah had passed. I lined them up as one would for a firing squad: the two brothers Peter and Hendrick Caesar, the doctor Alexander Dunlop, the Reverend Freehouseland, the collector William Bullock, the abolitionist Robert Wedderburn, the judge Lord Ellenborough, the actor Henry Taylor, the preacher Joshua Brooks, the animal trainer Sieur Réaux and finally the naturalist Georges Cuvier.

I tied their hands behind their backs, blindfolded them and shot them dead, walking amongst the prone bodies, executing each with a coup de grâce at the base of their skulls with a long-barreled, ivory-handled Smith & Wesson pistol. As I buried in my imagination each body in the cemetery of St. Clément, I whispered to Sarah's ghost, This grave is yours. This grave is yours.

Oh Lord, I thought, had I been her soul's murderer too? The twelfth apostle? And had I, Alice, like Judas, held her down, pinned her under my own body for twelve pieces of silver, to keep myself and Victor alive? I felt the shadows gathering around me like crouching beasts, slowly turning as the sun turned, as the courtyard darkened with the passing time, as the fog rolled in, blocking the view from inside.

One day, Sarah had asked me how white women could ignore the slavery of their black servants, their rape and concubinage, the illegitimate and pale children that were regularly born. Were they blind? Or did they think that their servants' humanity counted for nothing or that their husbands' and brothers' and fathers' honor counted for nothing because a black woman was not worthy of jealousy? I had not known what to answer for I had seen this blindness in others, but had not recognized it in myself. Yet it had affected my sight as well, no matter how much I had loved Sarah. And God knows I had loved Sarah! I hated what men had done to her, all of them, with their locks and their contracts, their penises and their pretensions, their dicks and their diplomacy, their codpieces full of hot air, their wars and their science, their factories and their industries, their progress and their enlightenment, their establishment and their dreams of glory.

I noticed another piece of news on the front page of the same *Quotidienne* I held in my hands. It probably would have made the rainmaker, Magahâs, smile. Or at least the purple heron.

FOREIGN NEWS

LONDON, JANUARY 1, 1816

Yesterday, Bonaparte's famous carriage captured by Prince Blücher's troops at the Battle of Waterloo was removed to the museum of Mr. William Bullock in Piccadilly Circus, London, where it will be exhibited shortly to the public.

21

MONSIEUR THE PREFECT,

A South African woman exhibited by Mr. Réaux under the name of Vénus Hottentote has just died, Cour des Fontaines. This occasion to acquire new information about this singular race of humankind obliges me to ask permission that the cadaver of this woman be transported to the anatomy laboratories of the Museum of Natural History. Our colleague Professor Cuvier, who instructs in comparative anatomy, assures me that he guarantees all matters of decency, appropriate to the circumstances, will be exactly observed in the interest of the general public.

—ETIENNE GEOFFROY SAINT-HILAIRE,
Letter to the prefecture of Paris, January 2, 1816

Great Eland, the English month of January, 1816. As always, the white man won. The baron looked down his long hawk nose at my prone body, scalpel in hand, as I lay on the marble slab of the dissecting table under the skylight of the amphitheater of the pavilion of comparative anatomy in the King's Botanical Gardens. It was hard for me to believe that my war with white men was lost. Just like that of the Khoekhoe. But the baron smiled. His eyes held only tender greed as he surveyed the uncharted landscape of this, his utmost desire: my map of Africa. I couldn't weep because there are no tears in a cadaver.

He hunched over me, devouring every detail as if I were his most treasured possession, the most precious of his thoughts, the most honorable of his decorations, the most brilliant of his discoveries. The great scientist, who had presented me to Napoleon during his hundred days, was now nothing more in my eyes than a hankering canine, an expert in rapine who had snatched my body from the Paris morgue in hopes of stealing my soul.

—We will now proceed with the dissection of the female baptized Sarah Baartman, known as the Hottentot Venus, who some of you examined during her appearance here in this very amphitheater on March fifteenth, 1815. The subject before you succumbed to pleurisy aggravated by tuberculosis and alcoholism. She was also found to have had congenital heart disease. Her death occurred on January first, 1816. The subject was twenty-seven years old. The cadaver is fresh and in a perfect state of conservation.

An African light invaded the amphitheater. Through the skylight it delineated every crease, every cravat, vest, top hat, cloak, frock coat. It molded each beaver hat, shirtsleeve, grain of wood. It invaded my sightless eye, making me blink, caught every coil of my sprung hair, every pore of my grayed skin. It flooded the strange fierce face of the baron, making a halo around his wild red hair. It flowed over the wooden benches that climbed up the walls, filled with a hundred surgeons, anatomists, naturalists, phrenologists, medical doctors and members of the general public. No one was less than eight yards away from my body. The light produced an exactness that illuminated everything, including the terrible will of one man. The baron stood in the center of this sunlight and pretended to explain me to a world that detested me. He was determined to possess me in death as he had never been able to do in life. For despite those few seconds of war at the duke's ball, I had had a will that matched his. I had been in charge of the heifer's milk. Without my permission he could not drink.

The baron was dressed for work in a voluminous smock, fur cap and a large scarf rolled around his neck. He had on unpolished riding boots. I waited. Once again the Khoekhoe's herd rode across the circle of the domed sky, dancing, running, stampeding through time, sometimes in quick step, sometimes in slow motion, just like the herds in Magahâs's cave raced as if trying to escape some catastrophe—a flood, a fire, an earthquake or calamity unknown to its race until now.

The baron raised his scalpel. It flashed like a bolt of lightning, as if his hand were the hand of God himself. He stood alone in the circle of light; his assistants with their towels and basins stood nearby in the shadows, as if not to mar the perfect aura of godliness.

As the knife slit me from collarbone to anus, the baron's voice, light in timbre, kindly and serene, declaimed:

—There is nothing more famous in natural history than the Hottentot apron, and at the same time, there is nothing that has been the object of so much argument. For a long time many denied its existence; others pretended it was the result of artifice and caprice; and amongst those who regard it as a natural conformation, there are as many opinions as there are authors about the female organs of generation that produce it. This organ is variously known as the female *tablier*, the *tablier égyptien*, the Hottentot apron, longinympha, macronympha or, as Linnaeus has named it, the *sinus pudoris*, the "curtain of shame."

—Nicolas de Graaf made the earliest reference to the Hottentot apron in 1640 as "an ornament the women have in certain places consisting of short thongs cut from the body, which hang down." The phenomenon was then described by William Rhye in 1686 as *Feminae hottentice* and by Johann Friedrich Blumenbach, who insisted on the impossibility of the apron and its mythical origins in *Hottentotarium Fictitium.*

—Gentlemen, Sarah Baartman's apron is not fiction. I have the honor of being the first to dissect and describe in anatomical detail the appearance and function of this celebrated protuberance.

—At the end of this dissection, gentlemen, I intend to show you exactly and definitively just what it is and what function the external generative organs of this woman are, and their place in the great Chain of Being. Meanwhile, I will describe the anatomical makeup of a species of humanity at the very bottom of the chain of evolution. Somewhere between the human species and the subhuman orangutan . . .

—Sarah, the specimen before you, measures 1 meter, 39 centimeters or 55 inches. She weighs seventy-five pounds eleven ounces. Her color is yellowish light brown. The nose is small and flat and the face in general is heart-shaped, measures 10 centimeters in length, with high Oriental cheekbones, pointed chin, pulpous lips and a wide interocular space between the eyes, which, characteristic of the Mongol race, are horizontal, and light brown with bluish iris. The high projections of the cheekbones, also typically Mongolian, and the abnormally small ears are her most striking characteristics. The shape of the cranium is dolichocephalic, measuring 16.5 centimeters by 12.5 centimeters.

The violet granite was cold under my back. The scalpel slid around the circumference of my skull. I screamed but no one in the hall could hear me. Master Cuvier's countenance had the bright sheen of anticipation as he lifted my brain from its cavity and weighed it on the spot. I realized the soul was not located in the brain for I felt nothing as he dropped it into the bell jar held by his assistant, where it floated in the liquid like coral.

—The weight of the fresh brain, continued the baron, is 28 ounces and the inner cranial capacity is 15.5 by 11.5 by 11 centimeters. The proportion of the weight of the brain to that of the body equals 1:43.25.

—As for the Venus's steatopygia, the height of the fatty cushion (the distance from the vertebral column and the furthest point of the buttock) is 16.5 centimeters. At its thickest part, the steatopygia measures 4.5 centimeters. The fatty mass overlies the regio glutea and sacrococcygea and continues over the regio coxalis. The arrangement of connective laminae tissue presents three superimposed strata which diminish in height as they approach the skin. This structure alone makes possible the fact that the fatty cushion retains its greatest arch upwards despite gravity. The steatopygia therefore consists of fibrous laminae ligamenta suspensoria . . . In other words, I can therefore verify that the protuberance of our Hottentot's buttocks has nothing muscular or skeletal about it but arises from a fatty mass of a trembling and elastic consistency situated immediately under her skin and which vibrated with all the movements that the woman made.

—As I have noted earlier, Sarah's conformation is striking because of the enormous width of her hips, which extend 18 inches, or 45.7 centimeters, and by the predominance of her buttocks, which protrude more than 6 inches, or 15.2 centimeters, the rest of the subject is perfectly normal in the proportions of her body and limbs. Her shoulders, her back, the height of her bosom have grace. The curve of her stomach has nothing excessive about it. Her arms are well made and her hands . . . charming.

I felt no pain either in my excised brain, my excised sex or my excised fibrous laminae. As the baron cut out my heart, I wondered where, then, resided that soul that could weep for what had come to pass?

—Gentlemen, I am now going to take up the question of the external genitalia, or the organs of generation, of our Hottentot Venus. I reserve subsequent studies on other aspects of their first inspection here at the King's Botanical Gardens. Last March, nothing could be ascertained out of the ordinary in relation to their organization. The Venus kept her apron carefully hidden either between her thighs or even more profoundly inside her body. It is only now, after her death, that we can satisfy ourselves as to what she possessed. Our first objective is to study this extraordinary appendix that nature has made, a special attribute of her race . . .

The baron had arrived at last at the place in Africa he wanted to be, most wanted to possess. Not the Congo nor Ethiopia, not Sierra Leone or Sudan or even Egypt, but Cape Table. I listened to him murmuring like the litany *Liberty, equality, fraternity,* the litany *Prepuce, pubes, pudendum,* lavishing the skill of a sculptor and the heart of a butcher to excise the mysterious apron he was now free to explore without my consent. Over my dead body. His mind seemed to race ahead of his words. His hands probed deep into my uncharted cadaver while uttering the sighs of a man in the throes of overwhelming passion. The long nose held a drop of perspiration; the azure-blue eyes either burned with intensity or closed in ecstasy as he continued his meticulous ravishment. My cadaver became the unexplored Africa, the Dark Continent, dissected, violated, probed, raped by dead white men since Roman times.

The scarlet rays of the setting sun stole over my yellow-gray skin. They leapt from wall to benches to return to the circle where the baron fucked the Venus, inventing the dogma that would rumble through History as Truth. This time, my audience was not the braying, giggling, merry mob of Piccadilly. This was the intelligentsia born of the Age of Enlightenment: medical doctors, anatomists, paleontologists, alienists, naturalists, evolutionists, who sat around the baron's podium as around a campfire, their haunches cramped on hard wooden benches, their pens raised in the sign of benediction, the Christian cross. God was on their side and the iron-fettered weight of all civilization.

The baron's scalpel completed the extraction of my sex and anus and held it high like a flag.

—Prepuce, pubes, pudendum, he exhorted as he put the organs in another jar. The audience rose as one, applauding wildly.

—Gentlemen, I have the honor to present to the Academy the genital organs of this, my Venus Hottentot, prepared in a way that leaves no doubt about the nature of her apron . . .

—Ahhh, a strangled cry like that of an excited baboon erupted from the baron's thin lips.

—The great Chain of Being. The great Chain of Being! The great Chain of Being, he cried out as he ejaculated, his hand deep in my entrails. He was stuttering like a Hottentot. M-m-my pri-pri-primary research, he babbled, has as its subject this extraordinary appendix which nature has made, I can verify, a special attribute of Sarah's race. We soon ascertain that it is exactly as the naturalist Péron drew it. Although it is *not* possible to adopt his theory. Effectively, the apron is *not,* as he maintained, an organ of particularly extreme size. It is the development of the nymphae, the inner lips of the vulva, to a length of about four inches.

—The labia majora presents a semicylindrical protuberance, about four inches long, of which the lowest extremity gets wider, branches off to form two thick wrinkled petals, two and a half inches long by one inch wide, each rounded at the end, their bases widening along the internal edge of the labia majora and turning into a fleshy crest which ends up at the lowest angle of the lip.

—If we raise these two appendices, they form together a heart shape, the center of which would be the place of the opening of the vulva.

—Gentlemen, what you have before you is a fantasy creature without language or culture, without memory or consciousness, who has entered our consciousness as the epitome of sexual power: a Venus. Before you lies Sarah Baartman, a Hottentot, who arrived in London in 1810 and Paris in 1814 to extraordinary success with the public in circuses and exhibition halls, almost a mythological figure like a mermaid. What does she mean to science—a connection to the lower species of humankind, a reminder of our civilized progress towards rationality and away from animalosity. Before you lies the Hottentot, notorious as early as the fifteenth century as the ultimate savage. The first explorers came upon this species even earlier, fascinated with its language, whose impossibility to comprehend has contributed to the Hottentot legend.

—In the great Chain of Being that credits the Hottentot as being the missing link between animal and human realms, Sarah Baartman is the true transitional figure between man and ape.

—The chimpanzee corresponds closely to the lowest degree of man . . . from this lowest degree, emits the brutal Hottentot, and from her Reason and Science advance . . . The great Chain of Being . . . The great Chain of Being . . . repeated the baron reverently.

So, I thought, the soul is not located in the sex, for I feel nothing now that it is gone, floating in a jar, labeled Hottentot Venus, that circulates amongst the savants.

As my girl's soul searched for an exit, I contemplated each organ as it emerged from my body, dissecting my own anatomy as the baron went on to read me. I marveled at the beauty I found in these glistening, vibrant, multicolored, invisible inhabitants of my body—full of tiny stones and veins, threads and filigree of diamonds of surpassing wonder within which human life lay balanced between fragility and resistance. It was all there, before my very eyes. Greatness. Goodness. Godliness.

The anatomists passed the bell jar containing my sex from hand to hand. The glass container shimmered. The reverent hands fondled the pristine preparation like a relic. Indeed, it traveled from fingertip to fingertip, all eyes upon it like a Holy Grail, each glance devouring a small bit of the tissue within . . .

—In conclusion, gentlemen, said the baron over the excited murmur of the audience, I would like to reaffirm, in answer to certain arguments put forth lately, that no Africans, nor Bushmen, nor Hottentots, nor any race of Negroes could have given birth to the celebrated Egyptians, who built the civilization from which we can say the entire world has inherited its principles of law, of science and perhaps even religion! How could the pharaohs, our sublime ancestors, be Africans? he asked, holding high the bell jar with my brain so that all in the amphitheater could see. Then he picked up the head of an Egyptian mummy that lay on the instrument table and held it aloft in the other hand.

—Look at this head, which I present to you so that as Academicians you can compare it with that of Europeans, Negroes, Hottentots. Bruce yet imagines that the ancient Egyptians were Cushites or woolly-headed Negroes related to the Shangalla of Abyssinia . . . Now that we can distinguish races by their skeletons and skulls and we possess so many ancient Egyptian mummies, it is easy to assert that whatever the color of their skin, they belonged to the same race of men as us; that they had a skull and a brain as voluminous; that, in one word, they made no exception to that cruel law which condemns to eternal inferiority the races whose craniums are depressed and compressed. I have examined more than fifty heads of Egyptian mummies and I can assure you that their heads are of Caucasian origin and not one displays the characteristics of Negroes or Hottentots . . .

The good doctor had actually raised his hand in emphasis, and again heartfelt, enthusiastic applause followed. He then turned quite suddenly to one of his assistants, who held out a basin of clean water in which he slowly washed his hands.

When he had cut my heart out, I had realized that the soul was not located in the heart either. For I felt no loss, no pain, no amputation as the baron threw it into the tin bucket where my liver, kidneys and intestines lay. The slop pail holding my internal organs including my heart would be thrown to the pigs.

The baron now bowed to the crowd, clicking his heels.

—I now turn our Hottentot and this assembly over to the honorable Etienne Geoffroy Saint-Hilaire, who will complete the maceration of the specimen and excise the Hottentot skeleton, which, once assembled, will be on exhibit here at the museum until further notice.

The baron turned as the awed audience applauded his back, and walked his stiff-legged stately walk out of the amphitheater, pulling on his black frock coat as he went, drying his hands on the famous initialed towel he always wore attached to his watch pocket.

I never saw him again.

At that moment, a cloud darkened the skylight, canceling the ember-red circle in which I lay on a table of stone, surrounded by dark-suited, top-hatted assistants and my own entrails. For a fleeting moment, the amphitheater was plunged into darkness, then the gas-fired chandeliers blazed and a mob of young males rushed down the steps to the wooden balustrades surrounding the dissection table. Like a herd of South African red-legged zebras, they stampeded for a last look at the Venus. As I lay in state, they filed by one by one, peering first at me, then at my pickled brain in its tall bell jar, then my macerated sex. This was the closest I ever got to a Christian funeral, for I would never be buried. My hide would go back to London and into a Scottish lord's cabinet of curiosities. My genitals and the contents of my head would remain on a shelf in this very museum. My homeless soul was puzzled. Was I free? Or was I still a bondswoman? Was my contract fulfilled at last?

How come I here? How come I here?

Night was falling. Oh, cry, cry into the barrel of my glistening intestines, sweep away my shit, raise the anchor of my gallbladder. Oh, lift my breeze and return me to the salt lands. Shame my jailers, curse my masters, lift my skirts, match my pride. Oh, great purple heron, wade in the Seine, transport my soul, leave the shepherdess not at their mercy! Throw this herdswoman onto the back of a raging bull, stampede me to deliverance, rescue me from the slaughterhouse of science. Oh, shame, shame, shame on you, masters of the universe. Shame on Dapper and Barrow, Levaillant and Diderot, Voltaire, Jefferson, Kolbe, Rousseau, Buffon, and fuck you, sirs! You are no gentlemen. This is no freak show. I am on display without compensation or compassion, in the name of all mankind and the great Chain of Being. The Hottentot Venus, archetype of inferior humanity. The very last layer of the human pie. Undo all this, sirs. Undo all this. Undo me.

The mob streamed by me like a serpent, closer and closer, demanding the Holy Communion of my mismeasure, a gang following the baron's rape. The silence of Holy Communion persisted as the scientists filed from the auditorium. Amongst them was my artist, Master Tiedeman. His eyes were clay red from weeping. He watched as they lifted my mortal remains and wrapped them in a winding cloth, ready for the potash and lye, which would remove the flesh from my skeleton and reveal it, naked, to the world. Only the granite table on which I had lain remained to be washed. A charwomen began to scrub the violet stone with pork bristles until it was spotless. I pronounced my curse once more drawn on my map: Until my ashes float upon the Orange River, until my bones bleach on the shores of Africa, until my soul roams Table Mountain, I vow on the head of my dead infant, no one will have peace, neither Africa nor Europe, neither victor nor victim, neither science nor faith, and no white man, neither dead nor alive. So help me God.

22

Isn't there some glory for man to know that he has broken through the limits of time and recorded by means of various observations the history of the world and the succession of evils that proceeded the burst of humanity?

—BARON GEORGES LÉOPOLD CUVIER,
The Animal Kingdom Distributed According to Its Organization

December 1819. I had chosen red glove leather for the binding of this first edition of *The Natural History of Mammals* that Geoffroy Saint-Hilaire and I had written and just published. In the soft candlelight of my library, I ran my hands over the smooth exquisite kidskin chased in gold leaf and black. The subscriptions had been tremendous. We had received orders from the four corners of the globe. More than a thousand volumes had already been subscribed. I suppose one would find it ironic that after destroying the Venus, I should guarantee her a place in history by engraving her image in the pages of *The Natural History of Mammals* for all time . . . I had heard that Venus's hide had been naturalized and sold to a Scottish lord for his cabinet of curiosities, but I had nothing to do with that and don't know for a fact if this is true. I do know that, to my knowledge, the Venus was never buried in the cemetery of St. Clément as decreed by law. There was an 1813 police ordinance for the burial of autopsied cadavers: the debris of human remains resulting from medical autopsies was to be buried in the cemetery of St. Clément, Paris. I now exhibit her skeleton, her brain and her sex in the King's Museum of Natural History, where, along with her wax death mold, she stands in case number 33. She has become since her death a scientific icon and, as this book of animals illustrates, proof of the moral, intellectual and physical inferiority of her race and those races that resemble her; that is, the missing link between animal and human species—the lowest rung on the scale of human existence . . . The great Chain of Being. I stared at the oversized printed velum. The five-volume set was almost two feet square, containing original illustrations illuminated and drawn from living animals, including Mlle. Baartman.

My eyes caressed the frontispiece. Paris 1819. Printed by the King's lithographic presses and His Royal Highness the Duc d'Angoulême, 58 rue du Bac . . .

I turned to Venus's page. She was preceded by the white polar bear and followed by the spotted leopard. As she stared out at me from the page, the night previous to the dissection came flooding back to me. Etienne Geoffroy Saint-Hilaire and I were sprawled exhausted on the stiff furniture, drunk not on the brandy we held in our hands, but on the exploits of the previous night at the morgue. We were being served coffee in this same library by my sad-eyed wife, Clémentine.

—What luck, said Geoffroy Saint-Hilaire, to have the cadaver so fresh and in such good condition.

—It was your intervention with the prefecture of police that made it possible, my friend, thank you.

—Réaux's price was abominable.

—The Venus is priceless. I would have paid double if Réaux had only guessed it.

—What a scoundrel . . .

—Well, he's no gentleman, that's certain. He's only an animal trainer after all.

—It's a pity, just a few months ago, the Venus was alive and well, a living, breathing organism full of vitality.

—She was sick, Etienne. It was obvious during those days here. She was suffering from alcohol poisoning and tuberculosis amongst other things.

—Well, we were not there as doctors there to make her well, but to observe her as a monstrosity.

—Any animal's death, continued Geoffroy Saint-Hilaire, is a sad one, even if one believes that in their ignorance they don't recognize death and have no consciousness of it, so cannot prepare for it.

—Do you think that man is any more capable of preparing for death just because he sees it coming, Etienne? Really?

—We all go blindly into the unknown, you mean?

—I mean we are all blind. We don't even know what death is. Is it merely the absence of life? And if so, where in the body does the spark of life reside? The heart? The brain?

—And do all categories of men go to the same place?

—We are all God's children.

—Poor wretched creature. How I pity her.

—Pity ourselves, dear Etienne, for she has gone perhaps to a better place, and we are stuck here in this desperate metaphysical struggle for survival.

—You would change places with her?

—Well, it would answer all our questions about religion and the hereafter, wouldn't it? The chaos of the Revolution has only reinforced my great desire for order. All my life I've studied in fossils, the results of annihilating catastrophes. It is for that reason that I seek calm and stability . . . it is my nature to prefer destruction to transformation. It is metamorphosis that scares me.

—Well, it would also solve my problems of celosomia, cyclocephaly, anencephaly, twin monsters, hermaphrodites *and* answer the question posed by the study of teratology as morally permissible given that God makes monsters. Now wouldn't it?

—There's a difference between physical anomaly and monstrosity.

—Indeed, there is, and I intend to prove it by fabricating embryonic monsters in laboratory bell jars myself.

—I look forward to the consummation of these experiments. It is a decisive line of inquiry.

—Naturalists have a sacred right to consider these questions growing out of men's physical relations as merely scientific questions and to investigate them without reference to either politics or religion or morality.

—I am most anxious about our colonies and French nationhood. The secrets of the indigenous people we have conquered must be explored in order to guard and control them in their environment by minute scientific, objective observation—the standards of resistance in occupied territories is, as the late Emperor has said, a matter of scientific and military intelligence. Know the enemy—hence we must delve beneath the surface, bringing the interior to light—the hidden genitalia of the Hottentot and all like her, and come to certain universal conclusions—if we want to be the rulers of the universe . . .

—These are questions that should be chewed over and ingested slowly, I daresay, from our point of view.

—The pathology of the underdeveloped races must be digested and execrated in a way that places the habeas corpus of the savage squarely on the spit for all to contemplate and profit by.

—We need more and more craniums, more and more skulls to measure the capacities of the skull and determine the hierarchy of intelligences . . . said Geoffroy Saint-Hilaire.

—We are entering a new era, Etienne, that of scientific anthropology, we no longer have to act on our instinctive knowledge of human nature. We now have machines to measure the cranium volume, the facial angle in relation to the ears, the size of the ears, the texture and length of the hair, the color of the skin, the morphology of the pelvis, the length of the arm and the forearm, all these things will define and buttress our conclusions as to the eternal inferiority of the Negro . . . the eternal inferiority of the Negro . . . the eternal inferiority of the Negro . . . I paused.

—Classification should proceed from the most complex structure, the brain, to the simplest, the organs of generation. The primary research, I said as I picked up my gold-rimmed coffee cup and popped a chocolate into my mouth, should have as object the extraordinary appendix that nature has made, so to speak, a special attribute of her race . . . Yes, of course . . . her apron.

Thinking back now, as I reread my text, I notice I failed to describe accurately a certain aura of innocence, of purity about Sarah, as if indeed this child of Africa had come to us straight from Eve's garden. This impression persisted even in her most sordid and degraded situations. It surrounded her like an armor or a grail. I have no scientific or rational explanation for this odor of sanctity except to consider it that part of her that was human. Or perhaps, the part of her that was nature, the link between man and the Creator. Nevertheless, I am surprised by the sudden tears that fall now on her image, for truly and sincerely, I have no regrets.

23

Sire,
The moral sciences start beyond this limit: they demonstrate how a particular idea is born from these repeated
sensations, and from the comparison of these general-
ized ideas, a combination of ideas, judgments; and out
of these, reason and will . . .

—BARON GEORGES LÉOPOLD CUVIER,
Letter to the Emperor Napoleon
on the progress of science since 1789

*L*ittle Eland, the English month of December, 1860. Master Tiedeman made his way across the Jardin des Plantes and entered the stone
façade of the Museum of Natural History. He had done so every month
since my installation as exhibit number 33 nearly forty-five years ago.
Master Tiedeman was still handsome, but his red hair now was bone
white, his hands shook and his step was stiff and faltering. He was an old,
old man. It was a cold winter's day. His long, wet woolen cloak hung in
stiff folds like an Oriental skirt and his walking stick struck the polished
wood floors of Salle number 6 like a drum. He always came late to see me
to avoid the crowds that came to stare at the collection of stuffed wild an-

imals, trophy heads and mummies. As he approached, he frowned on finding himself not alone. There was another tall figure standing in front of exhibition case number 33. He stood shoulder to shoulder beside the stranger who was obviously an English gentleman of means. Master Nicolas removed his hat, as he always did before my skeleton. It hung from a hook like a strange fruit beside the glass cage, which contained my death mold. Then, he recognized the other man.

—Sir, are you Charles Darwin, the evolutionist and author of the newly published *On the Origin of Species*? I would recognize you any-where!

The other man simply smiled that strange English lifting of the upper lip and nodded shyly. For almost fifty years I had observed all the speci-mens in this museum and all its visitors and I had never seen a white man who so resembled an ape. The jut of the jaw, the flat nose, but above all the slanted, protruding brow over the tiny round black eyes gave him that appearance. The gentleman too had removed his hat and his bald pate shone in the overhead light, accentuating the enormous slope of his prominent forehead, which completely overshadowed his fiercely intelli-gent but simian eyes. His thin, chimpanzee-like lips were surrounded by a magnificent white beard of great thickness which ran into his small ears.

This famous book of his had provoked a great war amongst the natu-ralists who frequented the museum and discussed such things in my pres-ence, on which, as a good servant, I eavesdropped. They had over the years, divided themselves into two groups: the monogeneticists and the polygeneticists. The theory that man was not created by God, but evolved from lower animals, had caused a furor in the Reverend Brooks's Church of England. And here was its author, staring at my skeleton as if his life depended on it. For a while, the two white men stood silently in front of my case. After his outburst, Master Tiedeman pretended to read its label, which he already knew by heart and which was as explicit as the old cir-cus posters. I eavesdropped on the following conversation.

—The Hottentot Venus offers certain particularities that are more strongly marked than they are in any other race, but it is well known that these characteristics are not constant, remarked Darwin.

—The great writer Gustave Flaubert comes here often to see her, old Master Nicolas said, quoting the famous writer by heart:

... and his whole soul would swell before nature like a rose blooming under the sun; and he would tremble all over, under the weight of an inner exquisite delight, and his head in his two hands, he would fall into a lethargic melancholy ... his soul would shine through his body, like the beautiful eyes of a woman hidden behind a black veil.

These forms so unattractive and so hideous, this sickly yellow complexion, this shrunk skull, these rachitic limbs, all of these would put him in such an air of delight and enthusiasm, there was so much fire and poetry in these ugly monkey eyes that he would seem then as violently moved by a galvanism of the soul.

Master Tiedeman fell quiet. The silence of the two neighbors lasted a long time as each man was lost in his own thoughts, not thinking of the other man standing beside him, or why one of them had spoken.

—Oh, said Master Darwin, she is superb, varnished, polished, waxed, magnificent. I didn't know the Zoological Department had made such a superb skeleton ...

—I stole her skull in 1817, the very year her skeleton was put on display here. I spirited it away to my atelier and kept it for more than a year, drawing it every day. I drew it more times than I can count, but it was not only for that reason ... I imagined her very lonely in this place. I ... wanted to keep her company. I don't regret it. I'd do it again. No one was the wiser. I returned it because I believed she was haunting me, and I got scared. I come to visit her here once or twice a month, but when there aren't the crowds that are here on Sundays. This is the first time I have ever found someone else at this hour. I don't know why I'm telling you all this, except that I am Nicolas Tiedeman, one of the artists who sculpted her from life and in the nude in 1815 during Napoleon's hundred days. I never turned over my model to Baron Cuvier, or exhibited her death mask, I couldn't bring myself to do it.

—Ah, the late esteemed Dr. Cuvier, replied Master Darwin.

—Sir, Master Nicolas blurted, I must congratulate you on your stupendous *On the Origin of Species* ...

—Well, thank you, although I am fully convinced of the truth of my views, I by no means expect to convince experienced naturalists whose minds are stocked with a multitude of facts all considered, during numerous years, from a viewpoint directly opposite to mine . . . It is so easy to hide our ignorance under such expressions as the "plan of Creation," "unity of Design," "the great Chain of Being" . . . Monsieur Tiedeman . . .

—Small, isn't she?

—Yes, quite.

—I never fail to be surprised by her smallness. Her air of surprise, the yellow color of her skin, her silence, her lack of recrimination . . .

—I personally am revolted to find human remains amongst the stuffed animals.

—I have studied and drawn every line, wrinkle, pimple and muscle of her body, the shape of her ears, the set of her jaw, the layers of fat over bone . . . It took me far into her wildness, her geography, and convinced me that the whole human race was one, said Master Tiedeman.

—Of course, remarked Master Darwin, there is only one race of mankind. One tree with many branches advancing from its origins in the midst of time towards the perfection of the species by natural selection. One day, with instruments and techniques we can only dream of, in one great leap of the imagination which scientists call discovery and artists like yourself call inspiration, but which in both cases is divine intuition, it will become clear and common knowledge.

—What about the ethnographic chart established by Count Gobineau and so eloquently refuted by the Baron Humboldt?

—We think we give an explanation when we only restate a fact. Anyone whose disposition leads him to attach more weight to unexplained difficulties than to a certain number of facts will certainly reject my theory. A few naturalists endowed with some flexibility of mind, like Huxley for example, may be influenced by my volume; but I look with confidence to the future, to young and rising naturalists, who will be able to view both sides of this question with impartiality. Whoever is led to believe that species are mutable will do good service by conscientiously expressing his conviction; for only thus can the load of prejudice by which this subject is overwhelmed be removed. When the views entertained in *On the Origin of Species,* or when analogous views are generally admitted, there will be a considerable revolution in natural history . . .

—A considerable revolution! laughed Master Tiedeman, more like a cataclysm or, as Baron Cuvier would say, a catastrophe . . .

With this, Master Darwin chuckled, a mild, gentlemanly snort. He seemed not sure why he was having this conversation with a man he didn't know. Master Darwin was nothing if not the caricature of a stiff, reserved Victorian gentleman, who didn't speak to strangers. Yet I had brought them together.

—I have a confession to make. I saw the Hottentot Venus when I was a little boy, with my mother. I must have been six or seven. She is as fascinating to me now as she was then . . . to my childish eyes. I recall that my mother was disgusted, for she was an abolitionist, like my wife, Emma. I have rarely seen her so angry. She knew people, like Jane Austen, who had seen the Venus in the flesh when she had been on display in the circus in London . . . then to see her here, in that glass cage . . . stuffed . . . Poor creature . . . Cuvier's brain may have weighed twice as much as hers, but he was also her double or triple in body weight. He was twice as tall and I'm sure his kidneys too were twice as heavy.

—Is it true that the heart is practically the same size and weight in all grown humans whether they be six feet two and weigh six stone or four feet and weigh two?

—It is one of the mysteries of human anatomy, replied Master Darwin.

—Baartman's heart was not preserved.

—Anatomists don't consider it a scientific organ of measure . . .

—I wonder why?

—Perhaps it's not a scientific organ at all, but a metaphysical one . . .

—I don't think scientists, in their own heartlessness, trust that organ . . .

—Perhaps they don't. But one day, a heart will be interchangeable with another . . . a damaged heart will be replaced by another—all organs will be.

—Incredible . . .

Master Tiedeman's eyes returned to my skeleton hanging from the ceiling.

—Strange, seeing her this way always brings tears to my eyes. I will never forget those three days that I sculpted her right here in the museum's amphitheater. Forty-five years ago, March fifteenth, 1815, during Baron Cuvier's famous lecture . . .

—Then you knew the baron personally . . .

—As a young man of twenty-six. I'm seventy-one now.

—Well, sir, I'm fifty-one. Strange . . . but I have the same birth date as Abraham Lincoln.

—Really? The American President?

—Yes, February twelfth, 1809.

—What'll he do now, after Fort Sumter?

—He will abolish slavery, sir, and keep the Southern states in the Union by force of war . . . he has said that he'll free some slaves, all slaves or no slaves, in order to preserve the Union of the United States of America . . .

—The Confederate states think differently.

—The Confederacy is like the dodo bird, it is a doomed species, ready for extinction, because it has not adapted to its environment . . . I have collected many geological and biological specimens, studied many fossils and made observations of the numbers, diversity and living habits of different forms of life. One day I came across a species of ant in which I discovered the *slave-making instinct.* This remarkable instinct is found in the *Formica sanguinea.* This ant is absolutely dependent on its slaves; without their aid, the species would certainly become extinct in a single year. The males and fertile females do no work. The workers or sterile females, though most energetic and courageous in capturing slaves, do no other work. They are incapable of making their own nests, or of feeding their own larvae. When the old nest is no longer suitable and they have to migrate, it is the slaves that determine the migration, and actually carry their masters in their jaws. So utterly helpless are the masters that when I shut up thirty of them without a slave, but with plenty of the food which they like best, and with their larvae and pupae to stimulate them to work, they did nothing; they could not even feed themselves, and many perished of hunger. I then introduced a single slave *(F. fusca),* and she instantly set to work, fed and saved the survivors; made some cells and tended the larvae, and put all to rights. What can be more extraordinary than these well-ascertained facts? If we had not known of any other slave-making ant, it would have been hopeless to speculate how such an instinct could have been perfected. I tried to approach the subject in a skeptical frame of mind, as anyone may well be excused for doubting the truth of so extraordinary and odious an instinct as that of making slaves. Hence I will give you, Mr. Tiedeman, the observations that I have myself made. I opened fourteen nests of *F. sanguinea* and found a few slaves in all. Males and fertile females of the slave species are found only in their own proper communities, and have never been observed in the nests of *F. sanguinea*. The slaves are black and not above half the size of their red masters, so that the contrast in their appearance is very great. When the nest is slightly disturbed, the slaves occasionally come out, and like their masters are much agitated and defend their nest. When the nest is much disturbed and the larvae and pupae are exposed, the slaves work energetically with their masters in carrying them away to a place of safety. Hence, it is clear that the slaves feel quite at home. I never saw the slaves, though present in large numbers in August, either leave or enter the nest. Hence I consider them as strictly household slaves. The masters, on the other hand, may be seen constantly bringing in materials for the nest, and food of all kinds. The slaves habitually work with their masters in making the nest, and they alone open and close the doors in the morning and evening.

—One day I chanced to witness a migration from one nest to another, and it was a most interesting spectacle to behold the masters carefully carrying their slaves in their jaws.

—Another day I noticed about a score of the slave-makers haunting the same spot, and evidently not in search of food, but of new slaves; they approached and were vigorously repulsed by an independent community of the slave species; sometimes as many as three of these ants clinging to the legs of the slave-making *F. sanguinea*. The latter ruthlessly killed their small opponents and carried their dead bodies as food to their nest, but they were prevented from getting any pupae to rear as slaves.

—Now I was curious to ascertain whether *F. sanguinea* could distinguish the pupae of *F. fusca*, which they habitually make into slaves, from those of the little and furious *F. flava*, which they rarely capture, and it was evident that they did at once distinguish them: For we have seen that they eagerly and instantly seized the pupae of *F. fusca*, whereas they were terrified when they came across the pupae of *F. flava* and quickly ran away.

—One evening I visited another community of *F. sanguinea* and found a number of these ants entering their nest carrying the dead bodies of *F. fusca* (showing that it was not a migration) and numerous pupae. I traced the returning file burdened with booty for about forty yards, to a very thick clump of heath, whence I saw the last individual of *F. sanguinea* emerge carrying a pupa; but I was not able to find the desolated nest in the thick heath. The nest, however, must have been close at hand, for two or three individuals of *F. fusca* were rushing about in the greatest agitation, and one was perched motionless with its own pupa in its mouth on the top of a spray of heath over its ravaged home.

—Such are the facts, confirmed personally by me, in regard to the wonderful instinct of making slaves. The *F. sanguinea* does not build its own nest, does not determine its own migrations, does not collect food for itself or its young and cannot even feed itself: it is absolutely dependent on its numerous slaves. The masters determine when and where a new nest shall be formed, and when they migrate, the masters carry the slaves. The slaves seem to have the exclusive care of the larvae, and the masters alone go on slave-making expeditions. In England the masters alone usually leave the nest to collect building materials and food for themselves, their slaves and larvae.

—I will not pretend to conjecture by what steps the instinct of *F. sanguinea* originated. But as those ants that are not slave-makers will, as I have seen, carry off pupae of other species if scattered near their nests, it is possible that pupae originally stored as food might become developed; and the ants thus unintentionally reared would then follow their proper instincts and do what work they could. If their presence proved useful to the species that had seized them and if it were more advantageous to this species to capture workers than to procreate them, the habit of collecting pupae originally for food might by natural selection be strengthened and *rendered permanent for the very different purposes of raising slaves.* Once the instinct is acquired, even if carried out to a lesser extent than in our British *F. sanguinea,* I can see no difficulty in natural selection increasing and modifying the instinct, always supposing each modification to be of use to the species until an ant abjectly dependent on its slaves was formed.

—Is this not an ant-sized explanation of the history of slavery in the Western world? laughed Master Darwin, his close-set, black-button eyes glowing with malicious humor. Of the stupid morbid dependence of white American Southerners on their slaves and the institution of slavery?

—I expect President Lincoln would enjoy the fable . . . said Master Tiedeman. I hear he is a formidable tale-spinner, joke-teller and orator.

—And a most unhappy and unattractive man. We are both, Lincoln and I, very ugly men, laughed Master Darwin, my cranium being the exact replica of the Neanderthal man's, and his being not too far away . . . Just look around you, doesn't it look like I belong here? Master Darwin gestured with his big square hands. I wondered how he dissected such fragile and delicate fossils with such short pudgy fingers.

—But getting back to Lincoln, he continued, a true leader, like a true scientist, must have the power of reshaping the universally known into what is universal so simply and deeply that people overlook the simplicity in the profundity and the profundity in the simplicity. This is Lincoln's genius. This isn't always easy, neither in the battle for survival in war nor in science. An eminently learned man and a great numskull can go together very easily under a single hat.

—Like Cuvier and his great Chain of Being?

—Oh no. The work of Cuvier is primordial, his theory of catastrophe brilliant. Every scientific discovery stands on the shoulders, or rather on the brain, of its predecessor. There are still three questions I intend to address in future volumes: firstly, whether man, like every other species, is descended from some preexisting form; secondly, the manner of his development; and thirdly, the value of the differences between the so-called races of man . . .

—Of all the attempts to account for the differences between the races of man, there remains but one left; namely, sexual selection—which appears to have acted as powerfully on man as on animals . . . I don't expect that sexual selection will account for *all* the differences between the races . . . An unexplained residuum is left, but it would be inexplicable if man had *not* been modified by this agency—which works such powers and is so overwhelmingly potent and present . . .

—Finally, ended Master Darwin, it may not be a logical deduction, but to my imagination, it is far more satisfactory to look at such instincts as the young cuckoo ejecting its foster brothers, ants making slaves, the larvae of ichneumonoidea feeding within the live bodies of caterpillars, not as specially endowed or created instincts, but as small consequences of one general law leading to the advancement of all organic beings—namely . . . let the strongest live and the weakest die.

—Should we have let the Venus live . . . have left her alone?

—She does live . . . for better and for worse—one day the world will catch up.

—Sarah should have a decent burial, blurted Master Tiedeman. She should not be hanging here, a vulgar trophy, swaying in the wind . . .

—She's here in the name of modern science, anthropology, ethnology . . . paleontology . . . zoology . . . anatomy . . .

—You really believe that?

—After all, it is science, civilization, history, progress, truth which are at stake.

—Really?

—Absolutely.

—I love those big words, except you left out the one most important: beauty.

—Yes. That too, beauty . . .

—Ho ho, you dare pronounce the word beauty in front of the Venus . . .

—She *was* beautiful, wasn't she?

—Yes, she was. Beautiful . . .

—Did you communicate with this Hottentot?

—We spoke once.

—You spoke?

—In broken but comprehensible English. Sarah was a simple girl, a shepherdess, a herdswoman full of humor and mother wit, whose life had taken a turn that she found to be incomprehensible. She was gentle, as simple people are, neither a monster nor a prostitute—although she had many friends in those circles. She was solitary, without defense and very lonely. She sang sweetly, she loved music, finery, perfume—a girl like any of our peasant girls. I found her much more temperate than a stage actress or a carnival attraction. She was not that kind of person. After all, we invented her, made her what we wanted and expected her to be—without us, she either wouldn't have even existed or, if she had, wouldn't have been of much interest, as she was an ordinary, banal human being with the same dreams and reactions as any farm girl of her age . . . That she became a cause célèbre and a paragon of Western ethnology, a living legend and an icon of scientific racism, is incredible . . . or at least a fatality . . . and our own fault. *We* created Venus. She belongs where she will never be: Table Top Mountain, South Africa.

—That day, Sarah told me about the Hottentots. She assured me that they were not at all stupid as whites believed. With a few clicks of his tongue, a chief can command an army of warriors, a mother can sing a lullaby, a father can chastise his son. Two people can make love.

—She told me that a measure of equality exists within the Hottentots between men and women, whereby sons take their mother's name and daughters their father's. Equality is implicit in the fact that young people can live together in an unmarried state. Women have control over the allocation and distribution of milk, which is the wealth of a cattle-based society.

—If a man drinks milk without his wife's permission, her family can take the cow or sheep, even if he owns it, and slaughter and eat it. Women have property rights. Women have the power to punish their brothers if they disobey the rules of etiquette by the device of shaming, of ridicule. Marriage requires a bride-price and the bride's consent. The dowry goes to the mother, not the father. Divorce is common and is usually requested by the woman. Women are not seen as beasts of burden, the hut remains the property of the wife and she welcomes whom she likes into it, irrespective of the husband's will or permission. And if anything untoward happens to disturb conjugal harmony, the offended lady can literally pull the house down around his ears by rolling up the woven matting and taking down the poles and branches, leaving home and taking home with her. Women are the equals of men, therefore. They have freedom of speech in domestic disputes. If a notable dies, his wife can succeed him and lead the tribe. The Khoe word for woman is *taras*, which means ruler or mistress. So Sarah had a tradition of independence . . . She forgot that—or we broke that spirit—we ruined it by preaching docility, fatality and godliness and making her think "constant" was reality, not just another concept of ours—that the status quo is the basis of all civilization!

—There is nothing so unnatural as the status quo, said Master Darwin. In this aspect, man resembles those forms naturalists call protean or polymorphic. Man is so indiscriminate, variable and indifferent that he can turn himself into almost anything—having escaped the rules of natural selection.

—Is Cuvier not the greatest poet of the century? He calls forth destruction, death becomes alive; in a kind of retrospective apocalypse, we experience the terrifying resurrection of dead worlds—and the little scrap of life vouchsafed us in the nameless eternity of time, can no longer inspire anything but compassion, as another writer, Balzac, has said . . .

—Certainly no fact is so startling in the long history of the world as the wide and repeated extermination of its inhabitants, sir.

—It is incredible how those men of the Enlightenment tended to denounce the fables of their predecessors, continued Master Darwin. Philosophy accepts only what it has fabricated itself.

—The philosopher only accepts it as long as it gives him, in turn, an argument to plead the noble savage's cause: innocent victim in revolt against monsters from Europe. Truth prevails, in the end, only as a variation on the fable of dark, unfathomable Africa.

—So science is a fable for believers? Like religion?

—I didn't say that.

—Didn't Voltaire say that history was only fictions of various degrees of probability? continued Master Nicolas.

—Isn't science the same? What do we really know about man that God hasn't already shown us?

—I know that man, all men, evolved from One—within that One is God or evolution or godly evolution . . . replied Master Darwin.

—You've never said that . . .

—Perhaps, but I believe it. There are prudences to observe because of the ferociousness of some of my colleagues on the matter of race and color . . . Did you ever see her after that day?

—I saw her dead. I saw her dissected, her body parts passed around like cotton candy at a county fair . . . *(Softly)* I see her now . . . I see Cuvier washing his hands of her in his silver basin . . .

—I heard Cuvier once arranged for Napoleon to view her privately . . . It is only a legend I suppose, said Master Darwin.

—Why is it, Doctor, continued Master Tiedeman, that white freaks are always exhibited as oddities, the exception that proves the rule, while black freaks, on the contrary, are exhibited as *typical* of their race? With no distinction between them, when they are as different from one another as we are . . .

The doctor didn't answer. He was staring at my skeleton, who was listening to him. For a long time, the sculptor and the doctor stood shoulder to shoulder contemplating my bones, bleached, scraped, polished, assembled and mounted as carefully as a church altar. My skeleton was not covered by glass as my effigy was. I hung loose and free, slightly swaying, comic in my magnificence.

—At some future period not very distant as measured by centuries, Master Darwin continued, the civilized races of man will almost certainly exterminate, and replace, the savage races throughout the world. At the same time, the anthropomorphic apes . . . will no doubt be exterminated. The gap between man and his nearest relations will grow wider, for man will be more civilized. Slow though the process of selection may be, if feeble man can do that much by artificial selection, I can see no limit to the amount of change, to the beauty and complexity of the coadaptations between all organic beings, one with another and with their physical conditions of life, which may have occurred in the long course of time through nature's power of selection, that is by the survival of the fittest . . .

Master Tiedeman was no longer listening. He was contemplating my skull, which he had once stolen, long ago. Then he examined the delicate bones of my left hand. Silent, I turned golden, then red in the reflection of the low sun's sinking. There was a mutable silence as I swayed, and my skeleton invaded the rectangle of winter sunlight coming from the gardens outside.

The glass cases with their inhabitants receded into the deepening shadows, leaving only the luminous outline of Master Darwin's brutish head. The silence overwhelmed us all, the sculptor and the genius and myself, all valedictorian before the legend of the Hottentot Venus. The two men's heads bowed as one to that legend and to that illusion before them. Then, as one, they replaced their top hats. The bells of St. Bernard sounded the hour that tolled six, the closing time of the museum.

They left me as one.

Part IV

CAPE TOWN, SOUTH AFRICA, 2002

To snatch in a moment of courage, from the remorseless rush of time, passing phase of life, is only the beginning of the task. It is to show its vibration, its color, its form; and through its movement, its form, and its color, reveal the substance of its truth—disclose its inspiring secret: the stress and passion within the core of each convincing moment.

—JOSEPH CONRAD,
Preface to *The Nigger of the Narcissus*

Sir,
They want to sculpt my bust. But I do not want them to. My nigger ugliness in all its lifeless immobility would pass into immortality . . .

—ALEXANDER SERGEYEVICH PUSHKIN,
Correspondence

Epilogue

The circumstances in which we put one species or family before another does not entail that we consider it more perfect or superior to others in the system of nature. Only someone who thinks he can arrange all organisms into one long series can entertain such pretensions. The further I have progressed in the study of nature, the more convinced I have become that this is the most untruthful concept ever introduced into natural history.

—BARON GEORGES CUVIER,
Lectures in Comparative Anatomy

*B*road Green, the English month of August, 2002. That was a hundred and forty-two years ago. Master Tiedeman and Master Darwin both lived long lives. Master Darwin lived to be seventy-three. He died rich and famous, elegized by Master Tennyson and buried next to Master Isaac Newton in Westminster Abbey. Master Tiedeman died in 1879 at the age of ninety, poor and forgotten as he had always lived, in the shadow of the great David. Both Master Darwin and Master Tiedeman had fine Christian burials. I, of course, have never been buried. Neither my baptism in Manchester nor my marriage gave me a passport to any sanctified ground. I never ascended to the paradise of my three reverends; neither the fragrant Garden of Eden of the Reverend Freehouseland, nor the green pastures of the Reverend Brooks, nor the great Hall of Justice of the Reverend Wedderburn. I remained imprisoned in my glass cage looking out at the world, as it changed with each dawn, from my transparent window, wiped clear by a cleaning lady into whose unseeing eyes I stared each day, war or peace. At first, I was upset about that, until I realized this oversight gave me the power to haunt the Museum of Natural History, its gardens and laboratories, and to displace myself in time and space as I chose, for eternity or until my soul finally came to rest. This idea of haunting, which the Khoekhoe call "fawn feet," and which I continued to practice at the Museum of Man, more than compensated for never sleeping, never dying and never growing old. In Khoe there is a tree called *kanniedood*, which means "never die"; I became that plant, drawing on its powers invisible to humanity. There were other "fawn feet" in the museum, including Ramses VII's mummy, but that is another story.

The first thing that happened occurred about a year after my dissection. Nicolas Tiedeman stole my skull to measure and create an effigy. I haunted him until, quite spooked, he returned it to my skeleton. So frenzied was he, he almost committed suicide by trying to jump off the Concord bridge. I pulled him back. He did not, after all, deserve death just because of a little thievery. I knew he loved me in his way, and so I *exempted* him. But others I intended to haunt to their deaths or at least accelerate their demises with, if possible, a maximum of torment; the former Masters Caesar, Dunlop, Taylor, Réaux, Geoffroy Saint-Hilaire and of course the eminent Georges Léopold Cuvier, known also as the baron. Alice Unicorn I will come to later.

The baron proved to be the most difficult. He was arrogant, bold, this "Napoleon of Intelligence," but like the Emperor he could be brought down by the weight of his own lust for power. After the Museum of Natural History, he became director of the College of France, then secretary of the Academy of Sciences. Napoleon, who loved him to the end, covered him with honors, including that of grand officer of the Legion of Honor. Louis XVIII had already made him a baron; Louis Philippe named him a peer of France. All this made it easier for me to do my mischief. Such an illustrious and proud personage would never believe he was being haunted by the "fawn foot" of his Vénus Hottentote.

I discovered the Baron's weakness. He lied, he cheated on his research.

He systematically burned, destroyed or ground up fossils and bones that would have falsified or contradicted his findings. I made sure his enemies learned of this and exposed him. I made sure his secret research fell into the hands of his competitors. He had a daughter. I haunted her to death. He had a golden retriever whose severed head he found in his soup one night. I burned down the Academy of Sciences and started another blaze in the nave of the Protestant church he attended. A priest perished. I made sure he died in the cholera epidemic of 1832. All his children died before him. As a species, as he called people like me, he was extinct. His brain was dissected on the same table as mine and preserved in one of his own bell jars. It was, as to weight and size, not that much larger than mine.

Alexander Dunlop, who had sworn he would never go back to sea, accepted a post as ship's doctor on the Dutch pirate slaver the *Brigade*, which sank with all aboard just off the coast of Guinea in 1818 as a result of a slave revolt of a hundred and two of the seven hundred bondsmen.

Hendrick Caesar returned to the Cape and his family in 1814 with the money he had earned by selling me to Henry Taylor. He invested it all in shorthorn cattle. He was soon penniless as drought made his lands worthless for grazing and foot-and-mouth disease destroyed his herds. Yellow fever took his wife and children. For several years he drank and gambled. He lost his preserve in a craps shoot and went to work for his brother Peter. He was massacred in a Zulu uprising in 1827, the same year as the great fire at the Academy of Sciences in Paris.

The Zulu uprising, which destroyed his crops and killed his brother, made Peter Caesar pack his family up, sell his farm and immigrate to the United States. There, en route to Fort Apache, renegades from the same tribe attacked his wagon train of three hundred and fifty-five souls on a wild and lonely plain in the New Mexico territory. His youngest child, Clara, escaped death and was adopted by her Indian captors, who raised her as a squaw. She married a brave, named Elk Heart, who was killed in the Battle of Date Creek in 1832.

Henry Taylor remained in England, returning to Halifax and marrying an Englishwoman named Nellie Bookenshire. Her dowry helped him set up his own theater in which he produced Shakespeare's plays. The theater burned to the ground with them in it in 1833. In his will, he left a thousand pounds to the Orphans Fund for Actors and Musicians.

Sieur Réaux was murdered by persons unknown outside the Pied de

Porc café on the night of January 17, 1816. He was found half devoured in the cage of his dancing bear, Adolph, in the early hours of the morning by his servant, Alice Unicorn, who had gone to feed the animal. Réaux's safe had been emptied and he was buried as a pauper in a common grave at the cemetery of St. Clément without the benefit of rites. It appeared to be an underworld vendetta, as his testicles had been cut off and stuffed into his mouth.

Alice Unicorn returned shortly thereafter to London, where she bought a town house, and brought Victor back home to live. She opened a wool and leather shop in St. James's, which made her a fortune. She married a clergyman in 1819 and had a large family. She never set foot in France again.

William Bullock took one of his most successful spectacles of freaks on tour to the American West. He enjoyed great success for many years. After lucrative runs in Chicago, Minneapolis and Austin, he reached St. Louis, where he was gunned down in a saloon following an argument over one of his actresses. His body, which was to be repatriated to London, was lost when the Confederate ship transporting it was sunk in 1863 by a Union gunship, the *Calledon,* which patroled the Mississippi River.

Etienne Geoffroy Saint-Hilaire, who had survived the Revolution, the reign of terror, Napoleon's defeat at Waterloo, the second restoration and the cholera epidemic that killed the Baron Cuvier, published his *Philosophie Anatomique* in 1818, in which he stated that, philosophically speaking, there was only one species of animal. In 1819, he published his *Natural History of Mammals* with Baron Cuvier, which was a great success and made him famous. In 1830, he and the baron argued their theories in the most famous debate in the history of biology, which went on nonstop for five whole days. Two years later, Baron Cuvier was dead. Geoffroy Saint-Hilaire survived him by twelve years.

The Reverend Wedderburn, whose hand I should have taken, returned to Jamaica after doing time in Cold Bath Fields and Giltspur prisons on trumped-up charges of sedition for his ideas about slavery, abolition and workers' unions. He saw many of his comrades hanged and he himself said he existed for the rest of his life "as though a halter be around my neck." Just like me. He was arrested for running a bawdy house (false) and distributing the first revolutionary tracts to the West Indies (true). For that, he was accused of "blasphemous libel" by the Crown. He defended his own self before the Court and was sentenced to two years' hard labor in Carlisle jail. His final prison terms resulted in his autobiography, *The Horrors of Slavery*, a great success. He died in 1838, after several other brushes with the law, sick, forgotten and penniless in the West Indies, the first advocate of black power.

Napoleon Bonaparte died of arsenic poisoning on the former Khoekhoe island of St. Helena, alone, suffering from a rare illness that slowly changed him into a woman with small breasts and a penis only half an inch long . . . In other words, in the end, he turned into a thing-that-should-never-have-been-born, resembling the Venus he despised.

Abraham Lincoln won the Civil War in America. He defeated the Confederacy, freed the slaves by proclamation and saved the Union. This cost him one dead soldier for every freed slave. But he lost his young son, his wife went crazy and he was assassinated before the end of his presidency. After he signed the Emancipation Proclamation he said, *But for your race among us, there would be no war, although many men engaged on either side do not care for you one way or the other.* He added, *I could conceive of no greater calamity than the assimilation of the Negro into our social and political life as our equal. We can never attain the ideal union our fathers dreamed of with millions of an alien, inferior race among us.*

Other things happened. I found myself included in the Great Paris Centennial of 1889. A great new edifice was built at the Trocadéro and I was moved with great care from the Jardin des Plantes to what was to become known as the Museum of Man. It rose in the shade of the great tower constructed by Gustave Eiffel that year. Paris was illuminated, electrical impulses were sent across the ocean. Surely my glass case deserved a new label. But my label remained the same:

> *Statue in colored plaster*
> *Of the Venus Hottentot, Bushwoman (twenty-seven years)*
> *Deceased in Paris, January 1, 1816*
> *Molded from nature following death*
> *Skeleton of the Venus Hottentot;*
> *Oil painting of the Venus Hottentot;*
> *Brain conserved in bell jar of Sarah Baartman;*
> *The genital organs of the Hottentot Venus;*
> *A wax model of the genital organs of*
> *Sarah Baartman.*

I became a spectator to the twentieth century's dance of death, Europe twice, the Ottoman Empire, Russia, Africa, China, India, Ireland, Korea, Vietnam, Palestine, Israel. From the unexplored, uncharted mystery of Africa, I became the body politic of Africa's intercourse with Europe, which consisted of discovery, exploitation, war, extermination and silence.

At night, I roamed the halls of the museum, playing tricks on the night watchman, opening doors, turning on lights, blasting the radio, rattling locks, cutting off the heat, running water for my bath, stealing doughnuts from the cafeteria, preening in front of the mirror in the ladies' lavatory, banging doors, opening windows, extinguishing lights. Over the years I read every daily paper, book, treaty and report in the museum library. They all spoke to me at last. You get to know a place well when you're on display there ... At night, the trophies raised hell. Hideous ghosts, leathery mummies, severed heads, body parts, Broca's brain, skeletons and fetuses, embryos and elephants, genitals and zebra skins, buffalo bones and jelly-fish, it's hard to describe this purgatory of skulls and bones that danced till dawn. Finally, in 1974, they moved me out of sight downstairs where I was put in the neon-lit, gray-walled, second parking lot, level C. No one passed during the day, except a couple of janitors or a government employee now and again. Then, in 1994, they brought me out again, this time to the Quai d'Orsay Museum. I've spent two hundred years hanging from my steel hook, watching history being made by the masters of the universe; what a freak show, it has been ... Time is no longer measured as it was before; it flows or stands still by new rules and theories. That's why I am not sure of today's date. Which moon is it? Is it a violet day or is it green?

I solved the problem of where the soul lies. It lies neither in the brain nor in the sex, neither in my lost hide nor in my bare skeleton. It resides, I believe, not in the here and now, nor in the future five hundred years from now, but in the past we have lost or forgotten or suppressed, ances-tors whose voices repeat the litany of reincarnation beyond mere time.

Which brings me to this moment. The moment when you have just turned this page and are wondering if such a sad and violent story could have a happy ending. How could it, you think to yourself. So let me tell you what it is. It was fitting that since my life seemed to be ruled by large groups of white men, deliberating my person in vast amphitheaters, their last discussion about me should have occurred in the National Assembly of France, January 29, 2002.

A tall Frenchman, who resembled Nicolas Tiedeman and spoke like the Reverend Wedderburn, and whose name was Nicolas About, rose to his feet in a still greater amphitheater, larger and more elaborate than the King's Court, London, or the Jardin des Plantes' comparative anatomy pavilion, before five hundred and thirty men and several women seated in circular, mounting rungs of dark oak and red velvet of the French Senate, and tried to put all my parts, all my bits and pieces, back together—that is, all my forests and jungles, my rivers and mountains, my deserts and grass-lands, my orchids and *kanniedood* trees, my savage beasts and my migrating birds, my moons and my suns, my lion cubs and penguins, my wheat lands and coffee fields, my diamonds and gold, my Africa—and return them all to the state they were in before. He told this great assembly:

—It is high time that the mortal remains of Sarah Baartman, deprived of sepulture, can know at last the peace of a grave in her motherland of South Africa, freed of apartheid . . .

—The French Republic honors her memory. It is loyal to its convictions and its traditions. Loyal to its Declaration of 1789, which states that ignorance, neglect or disregard for the rights of man is the one and only cause of public wretchedness. Loyal to the Constitution of 1946, in which the French people proclaimed once more that every human being possesses inalienable rights regardless of race, creed or religion. Loyal to the law of 2001, which proclaimed chattel slavery a crime against humanity.

—If Sarah Baartman was the object of outrages, it was without doubt because she was black and a woman and because she was physically different. Attempts were made to make a monster out of her. But on which side is the monstrosity truly found? It has been argued as well that the Venus Hottentot has no legal status and that a law must be passed to remove her from the public domain. Well, just what is she? Are we talking about a simple object in a museum? Or are we talking about a human relic who needs special protection? Does France really own the Venus? Or are we merely her guardian? In no case is the storeroom of a museum a mausoleum worthy of a human being. If the Venus Hottentot has no legal status in France, let it be known that in the world and in South Africa, she is a relic and a symbol. A relic of the past, but a symbol of centuries of suffering under the yoke of apartheid and colonization . . . Sarah Baartman was born in 1789. What a symbol of our Revolution to restore the dignity of this woman two centuries after her death . . .

Oh what pretty words, what pretty words, I murmured.

—I hope that if we vote for the deacquisition of the Venus Hottentot from the collections of the Museum of Natural History, we can offer her a dignified burial in Africa.

(Applause)

—After having endured so many outrages, Sarah Baartman will at last emerge from the night of slavery, colonialism, racism, to recover the dignity of her origins and the soil of her people, to reclaim the justice and peace that has so long been denied her, argued Nicolas About. The French people proclaim once again that every human being, without distinction of race, religion, or creed, possesses sacred and inalienable rights.

(Applause)

—If there is no one else who demands to be heard, said the senator, the discussion is closed.

—We advance to a vote, said the president, standing at his podium, flanked by and gazing at the masters of the universe.

And so they did. Unanimously in my favor. A blinking board much like Master Cuvier's blackboard floated high above the heads of the president and the senators. It held glowing red numbers like a regiment of fireflies.

PRIVATE BILL ADOPTED ON 29 January 2002	No. 52 SENATE ORDINARY SESSION OF 2001–2002
PRIVATE BILL ADOPTED BY THE SENATE *Relative to the restitution by France of the mortal remains of Saartjie Baartman to South Africa*	
The Senate has passed the private bill in its first reading, in which it is said:	
See numbers: Senate: 114 and 177 (2001–2002)	

Unique Article

From the date when the present law comes into effect, the mortal remains of the person known as Saartjie Baartman cease to be part of the collections of the public establishment of the National Museum of Natural History.

The administrative authority has, from the same date, a period of two months to hand them over to the Republic of South Africa.

Conferred in public session, in Paris, on January 29, 2002.

The president,
Christian PONCELET

After that great debate, my bones left my glass cage feet first and were put in a simple pine coffin, covered with the flag of a free black South Africa. The Khoekhoe people had claimed me and demanded my return. The long night of the Dutch, the English and the Afrikaner was over. The sovereign people of South Africa had found their voice and a freed people had returned me to my home. I had become a *raison d'état,* and as such, I had had a whole amphitheater of Frenchmen once again debating my humanity.

And so they did. All my parts and pieces were gathered together pell-mell, my dreams and ambitions, my loves and hates, my sins and goodness, my innocence and guilt, my moon and stars, my biography became one . . .

I was emancipated at last, my brain and my sex placed beside me in a plain pine coffin, I traveled the long dark corridors from the basement parking at level C of the Trocadéro to the Esplanade, where I could see the lead-gray sky beyond the Eiffel Tower. A shiny white hearse sped me away, passing through the places I had lived in Paris: the rue St. Honoré, rue Neuve-des-Petits-Champs, the Cour des Fontaines, the Palais Royal, the Tuileries, the Place des Deux-Ecus, the rue du Pélican, the Impasse des Innocents, the Paris morgue, then north on the autoroute to Roissy and the South African jet that would take me home. The plane lifted, the great black-tipped wings of the purple heron bore me up and out, her long feathers hissing in the wind, her black-tipped beak pointed outwards, her long neck stretching endlessly in a horizontal line above the coast: like the final underline of a signature. The world unfurled below me like a scroll on which Africa was written. The plane descended. The door opened and the African sun burst through, carrying a dulcet scent of blossoms that perfumed my shroud.

Sweet laughter rose in my chest and found a home. What did I really want? Respect. What does a wronged woman want after two hundred years? Recognition. I wanted someone to say they were sorry. I wanted an apology for my orphanhood, my mother's severed head, my husband's missing ears, my father's wounds. I wanted another mother to say she was sorry for the death of my newborn, the extermination of my clan, the epidemics of syphilis, the scourge of smallpox, the famine of men and beasts. Someone care to excuse themselves for the rape of Namibia, the land confiscated, the slaves taken, the cowhide lash on pregnant stomachs, the chains, the death march to the sea, the ships, the traders, the bills of sale? Sorry for the trophy heads, the autopsies, the labels, the measuring, the Chain of Being, the firewater, the salt-eaters, the gold mines, the textile mills, the coalpits, the brick kilns, the clay pits, the baby soldiers, the child workers, the hoots and howls, insults and violence, colonials and conquerors. Isn't it just like a woman to be so unreasonable? So illogical. So emotional. But I am a woman. Would it change history? Would it change the world? Put anyone in prison? Take bread out of their children's mouths? Remove memory? Kill science? No? Then? Just what would it do? Science will never say it's sorry. But science is like truth being in the eye of the beholder. And objective truth is a lie. The baron and I sat alongside each other in separate but equal bell jars for two hundred years in the name of science—the god and goddess of miscegenation, God and his trophy, genius and his shepherdess, Zeus and his Venus, the White man, and the Other . . . I am not an animal. I am a simple woman. I am not an animal. I am a simple member of the human race. I am not an animal. Laughter is my badge of that same humanity. My mirth now sweeps over the multitudes gathered like rain, like dust, like fallout. They hear it.

As my coffin slid from the belly of the machine, amazed, I saw tens of thousands of colored people, more colored people than there was elephant grass on the plain, spread out in all directions as far as my eye could see. They rose as one to greet me.

—Mama Sarah! Mama Sarah, Mama Sarah, they shouted, and their voices richocheted across the plains, an ocean of sound.

I, Sarah Baartman, the dis-human, was now an icon for all humankind. The ten-thousand-voiced chorus of colored women bore my coffin aloft as it slid forward onto that sea of hands and shoulders carrying me to my final and only resting place. I found that my tearless skeleton could only weep.

The new South African police fought to control the crowd, which mutated into walls and bridges, canals and fences, trenches and barricades, trees, forests, rivers, elephant grass, tunnels beneath the lakes, dams, waterfalls, hills, to celebrate my return. My mortal remains were carried to where I could see the green and gold stripes of the Khoekhoe hills where our cattle had once grazed, where the Cape lion had once roared, where the sky had once burned and a thousand seasons had passed.

There in the moon of Broad Green, August 8, 2002, I burned on the beach where I had played with penguins and my mother had sung my birthday song. There I glided like the purple heron, surveying my funeral pyre, which glowed brighter and brighter as it receded into a pinpoint amongst the vast dunes, savannas, lakes, waterfalls, forests, orchards, orange groves, low clouds, deep springs, green pastures of my motherland, upon which the multitudes played, circling my embers like the loose waves of an ocean. My pyre was made of *kanniedood* tree branches, emblem of my immortality, of the People of the People. I was fired back into the embers and clay that had made me. My soul combusted, it soared, it rested, it sang, it was free.

An African breeze lifted my ashes and scattered them like wings upon the sea whose depths drank them. An extinct Cape lion, which was not extinct at all, came and sat beside me. Two penguins wobbled past the water's edge, another heron pranced in the marshes. With a click of my tongue, I commanded a million women to rise up and bear witness to my agony by wearing red gloves in honor of Sarah Baartman. Then all was still.

Acknowledgments

$\mathscr{I}$ would like to thank the following libraries and their staffs: the Bibliothèque Nationale, Paris; the library of the Musée de l'Homme, Paris; the library of the French Senate, Paris; the British Library, London; the Newspaper Library, London; the British Museum, London; the Albert and Victoria Museum, London; the Public Record Office, Chancery Lane, London; the University of Capetown Library, Capetown, South Africa; the New York Public Library, New York City. Thanks also to the following academics: Professor Willy Haacke, the University of Namibia, Windhoek, Namibia; Professor Jouni Maho, Göteborg University, Göteborg, Sweden; amateur French historian Laurent Goblot; and French journalist Gérard Badou. In the writing of this novel, I used many academic and scientific works, but I would especially like to acknowledge two: *L'Invention du Hottentot* by François-Xavier Fauvelle-Aymar (CNRS, Université de Paris I, Sorbonne Publications), and Arthur Lovejoy's *The Great Chain of Being* (the William James lectures at Harvard University, 1933; Harvard University Press, 1942).

In chapter 18, the quotations of the fictive participants are verbatim, unadulterated nineteenth-century scientific writings on race, pell-mell from 1814 to about 1870. These include quotations from Jefferson, Lincoln, Hegel, Darwin, Beddie, Galton, Voltaire, Huxley, Knox, Morton, Drapper, Virey, Mandel, Broca, etc. In chapter 21, the dissection observations combine Cuvier's *Extrait d'observations* with *Anatomical Exami-*

nation of a Bushwoman by Professor H. von Luschka, A. Kock, and E. Görtz (*Anthropological Review*, London, 1870).

I would like to acknowledge Senator Nicolas About's speech before the French Senate, part of which is reproduced here; my admirable agent, Sandra Dijkstra, and my editor, Deborah Futter, whose brilliance and tenacity made this book possible; the support of Elaine Brown; my secretary, Emanuelle Ruffet; my sons, David and Alexis Riboud, and especially my husband, Sergio Tosi, and the memory of my grandmother, Elizabeth Chase Saunders, steatopygia and all. I thank the former South African ambassador to Paris, Barbara Masakela, who read this manuscript, and the Khoekhoe activists and organizations who brought Sarah Baartman home.

As in a never-ending tragedy, the Musée de l'Homme in Paris no longer exists, having been itself dissected and eviscerated of its contents as an institution by government bureaucracy. I close this page with the words of Professor Fauvelle-Aymar: "From then on, the historic processes that rendered them invisible in the eyes of other men (their physical disappearance, ethnic mixing, encroachment of the frontier) are only the final touch that renders them useless in their eyes, less true than fiction . . ." May this fiction make them more than true.

And to conclude: Forgive the African debt, forgive the African debt, forgive the African debt.

About the Author

Barbara Chase-Riboud is a Carl Sandburg Prize–winning poet and the prize-winning author of four acclaimed, widely translated historical novels, the bestselling *Sally Hemings; Valide: A Novel of a Harem; Echo of Lions: A Novel of the* Amistad; and *The President's Daughter* (a prequel to *Sally Hemings*). She is a winner of the Janet Heidinger Kafka Prize for best novel by an American woman, and received a Knighthood in Arts and Letters from the French government in 1996. Ms. Chase-Riboud is a renowned sculptor whose award-winning monuments grace Lower Manhattan. She is the rare living artist honored with a personal exhibition, The Monument Drawings, at the Metropolitan Museum of Art. Born and raised in Philadelphia, of Canadian-American descent, she was educated at Yale University and is the recipient of numerous fellowships and honorary degrees. She divides her time between Paris, Rome, and the United States.